PRAISE FOR TAHOE SILENCE

CHOSEN BY LIBRARY JOURNAL AS ONE OF
THE FIVE BEST MYSTERIES OF 2007

"A HEART-WRENCHING MYSTERY that is also one
of the best novels written about autism."
    STARRED REVIEW - Jo Ann Vicarel, Library Journal

"THIS IS ONE ENGROSSING NOVEL...IT IS SUPERB."
    5-QUILL REVIEW - Gayle Wedgwood, Mystery News

"ANOTHER GREAT READ!!...a view into what it must be
like to be autistic, and it is heartbreaking."
    5-STAR REVIEW - Shelly Glodowski, Midwest Book Review

"McKENNA AND HIS GREAT DANE, SPOT, MAKE A
wonderful investigative duo...Another exciting entry into
this too-little-known series."
    - Mary Frances Wilkens, Booklist

"A REAL PAGE-TURNER...BORG HAS WON
several prizes for his Tahoe series, all richly deserved."
    - Sam Bauman, Nevada Appeal

"TAHOE SILENCE IS A GRIPPING THRILLER with
great characters and a truly fascinating mystery for
Owen to solve."
    - Merry Cutler, Annie's Book Stop, Sharon, Massachusetts

"LOFTY STUFF INDEED... But Borg manages to
make it all go down like a glass of white wine
on a summer afternoon."
    - Heather Gould, Tahoe Mountain News

"GREAT CHARACTERS, LOTS OF ACTION and some clever plot twists...Readers have to figure they are in for a good ride, and Todd Borg does not disappoint."
- John Orr, San Jose Mercury News

"OWEN McKENNA...a forensic-entomologist girl friend and a Great Dane named Spot...a formidable team..."
- Laurie Trimble, Dallas Morning News

"A WELL-WRITTEN STORY about the wonders of nature and the dark corners of some men's minds."
- The Raven, Kate's Mystery Books, Cambridge, MA

"ONCE YOU READ AN OWEN McKENNA NOVEL, YOU'RE HOOKED FOR LIFE!"
- Karen Dini, Addison Public Library, Addison IL

"A CLEVER PLOT, A SPINE-TINGLING CLIMAX."
- Susan DeRyke, Bookshelf Stores, Tahoe City, CA

PRAISE FOR TAHOE KILLSHOT

"A WONDERFUL BOOK containing fascinating characters, hard-hitting action, a fast-paced plot and believable dialogue."
- Gayle Wedgwood, Mystery News

"A GREAT READ!"
- Shelley Glodowski, Midwest Book Review

"BORG BELONGS ON THE BESTSELLER LISTS with Parker, Paretsky and Coben."
- Merry Cutler, Annie's Book Stop, Sharon, Massachusetts

"KEPT ME TURNING PAGE AFTER PAGE. I highly recommend the Owen McKenna mystery series."
- Donna Clark, Librarian, Odessa College Library, Odessa, Texas

"SPOT ROCKS!"
- Nancy Oliver Hayden, Tahoe Daily Tribune

TAHOE AVALANCHE

FOR TERRI)
ENJOY!
TODD BORG

TAHOE
AVALANCHE

by

TODD BORG

THRILLER PRESS

First Thriller Press Edition, August 2008

TAHOE AVALANCHE

Library of Congress Control Number: 2008901410

ISBN: 978-1-931296-16-8

Cover design and map by Keith Carlson.

Manufactured in the United States of America

For Kit

ACKNOWLEDGEMENTS

Many thanks to ski patroller extraordinaire Bob Hoffman for teaching me about avalanches and avalanche control. If I've achieved any verisimilitude about the way snow slides off mountains, either naturally or intentionally, credit goes to him. Bob also gave me many pointers in how avalanche search dogs are trained, and how they are able to perform the miracle of saving people who are buried in avalanches.

Further thanks to Sandy Bryson and her book Search Dog Training. On each subsequent read, it reveals more secrets about how dogs think and act.

Thanks to Liz Johnston, who found and fixed countless mistakes, Eric Berglund, who helped make my sentences work and pointed the way to a better story, and Jenny Ross, whose sharp eye and knowledge of the legal system saved Owen from himself. They are all editing angels sent from the gods of English, and they cleaned up my scratchings into something readable. I can't thank them enough.

Thanks to Keith Carlson for another great cover.

More thanks to Kit. She figured out how to reshape my initial pile of words into something that made sense and helped fine tune the result. Without her help, encouragement, and story judgment, Owen, Spot, Street and the rest of the gang would never have made it to the page and become real to so many readers.

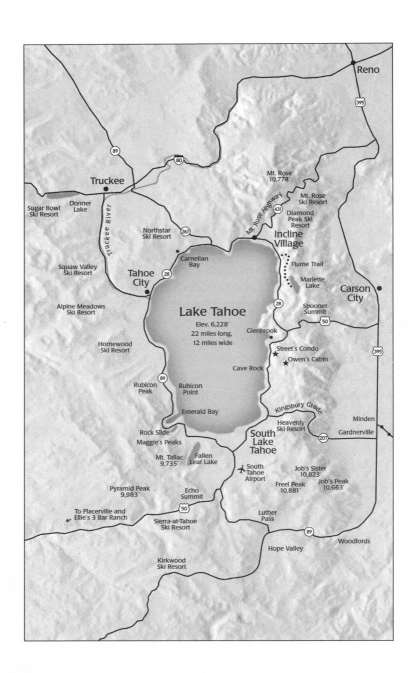

PROLOGUE

March Carrera was twenty yards from his pickup, leaning into the wind of the blizzard, when he heard a deep bass rumble that seemed to come from the earth and sky at once.

The sound grew like rolling thunder, and he suddenly remembered the spring storms that terrorized the tiny trailer town on the bluff where he was raised in Texas.

Two or three times every spring during his childhood, the cry shot through the neighborhoods.

Muerte Cielo!

Death Sky.

It was a phrase the town paper once used after a thunderstorm killed March's friend Peter Dunnel and Peter's dog. When the cry echoed through the village, the residents who weren't at work in the meat packing plant ran to the edge of the bluff and scrambled like ants in a disturbed nest down into the cracks and gulches where the bluff had been eroding for eons toward the plain below. Women clutched their babies and dogs ran with the older children as they filed deep enough into the earth's wrinkles to be safe from the tornadoes, but not so deep that the flash floods would sweep them away.

March Carrera glanced at the sky as he scrambled up the frozen highway toward his truck, shielding his eyes against the driving snow. But there was only swirling gray clouds.

Just minutes before, March had been driving at a crawl, sipping his latte, listening to his favorite rap group as he inched his way north around Emerald Bay. It was 5:00 p.m. on the second Thursday in January and already dark.

The wind and the blinding snow in his headlights let up for a moment. March thought he saw a light just ahead in the blizzard. But then the wind came back, stronger than before, and the light disappeared. He touched his brakes as gently as if an egg were taped to the pedal. Despite his care, the old Toyota truck swerved to the left, wheels skidding on the buildup of freezing slush. He let up on the brakes, corrected to the right, then eased down onto the pedal again as his pickup straightened out and the tires found some purchase on an area of rough ice.

The highway pitched down at a steep angle as it descended toward the head of Emerald Bay. Again it seemed that a light appeared in the driving snow, yellow and dim, and again it vanished. It looked like a vehicle was stuck in the road, its hazard lights caked with snow. The driver would need help.

March worried that he'd have trouble stopping in time as gravity and the weather worked against him. But he managed to slow to a stop. The light didn't reappear, but the blowing snow was so thick, it was impossible to see more than a few yards ahead.

March eased his front wheel into the edge of the snowbank to help prevent a runaway and set his parking brake. He left the engine running so the defrost blower could keep a steady stream of heat on the windshield and got out of his truck.

The storm raged. March pulled his cap down and his hood up and turned his head against a wind that was so filled with ice flakes it would abrade exposed skin. He hurried down the steep road, careful not to slip.

Once more, he thought he saw a light, but the blowing snow blotted it out as a deep rumbling sound seemed to grow from within the earth.

March stopped for a moment and listened. Then came a roar of wind that accelerated to a gale. The wind increased exponentially until it became hard for March to stand up.

He realized in a moment what was happening, and the sudden adrenaline rush made it hard to breathe. March burst into a run. If he could make it back to his truck, he'd have some protection. *Muerte cielo.*

He'd taken only three running steps when the gale seemed to explode. A shockwave of wind as hard as a board swatted March off the highway and into the air. He was blown over the guardrail and out over the drop-off above Emerald Bay. The wind, squeezed before the avalanche and suddenly expanding at 200 miles per hour, blew March's pickup into the guardrail, breaking it off.

The frozen slab pushing the wind was the size of a large office building, and it moved at 80 miles per hour. The avalanche hit the truck, flipped it end over end into the air. The truck slammed into a Ponderosa pine, breaking the top off and leaving the trunk standing, a bare wooden column fifty feet high and three feet in diameter.

March was blown into a red fir, twenty yards out from where the land dropped away from the highway. The wind wrapped his body around the tree trunk like a limp leaf. When the avalanche hit the tree, it snapped the tree off at its base and sent March and the tree through the air toward Emerald Bay.

With a huge whumping thud, the roaring avalanche suddenly stopped. The only sound that remained was the howl of the blizzard and the metallic clinking of a million twigs and branches that came from the sky, shrapnel from trees that were destroyed by the explosive avalanche.

Fifty yards down the highway, safely out of the avalanche path, sat a vehicle. After the avalanche subsided, the driver turned off the emergency flashers, pocketed the small transmitter and drove away.

ONE

I was up Friday at dawn. My morning paper wasn't at my door. My intrepid paper girl, a grizzled, rough-talking, sixty-something mountain woman named Maureen, was reliable enough. But her antique International Harvester four-wheel-drive might not have been up to climbing my neighbors' road with two feet of fresh snow on it.

The latest storm of a record season was just giving up its assault, and only a few light flakes drifted down from the purple morning sky. After coffee and a toasted bagel with cream cheese, Spot and I got in my Jeep and headed down the unplowed river of white. It is a wondrous whooshing sound a vehicle makes floating through deep powder, road noise absent, engine sounds muffled, wheels silent as they make a futile attempt to grab at the road beneath the thick, cottony blanket of snow.

I picked up a paper at the shopping center in Roundhill and scanned it as I walked back to the Jeep.

MASSIVE AVALANCHE AT EMERALD BAY
Vehicle Found In Tree

A Caltrans employee found a huge snowslide at Emerald Bay yesterday evening. The worker, Greg Zendal, had closed the highway gate near Camp Richardson and was making his check run up to the north gate near Bliss State

Park. Zendal turned back when he encountered an avalanche that had buried the road.

When the blizzard let up for a moment, Zendal spotted something dark down below the highway. "It looked like a strange tree with a bare trunk leading up to a big chunk of metal, all caked with snow and frozen solid," Zendal said.

The Caltrans worker got out and hiked up onto the frozen slide debris that buried the highway. As he got closer to the tree with the strange crown he discovered that it was a pickup truck. The truck had apparently left the highway at high speed, flown through the air and hit the tree. The impact was so forceful that the rest of the tree was broken off and the truck was impaled on the remaining tree trunk.

Another Caltrans truck responded to the scene with a powerful searchlight, which they trained down through the blowing snow onto the truck. Although uncertain, both men thought it appeared that the pickup in the tree had no occupants in it. By late in the evening, enough snow had fallen that Caltrans vehicles could no longer get out to Emerald Bay. Authorities called off further searching until daylight when snowmobiles could be used to access the site.

The article concluded by saying that the authorities would not speculate as to whether the truck's driver had lost control, or if the avalanche itself could have hurled the truck onto the tree. At press time there was no news of the driver.

I remembered that I needed a few groceries, so I tossed the paper in the Jeep. Spot still had his head out the window despite the snowfall that had resumed. His only acknowledgment of the snow was his regular head shaking to get the tickle out of his ears. I gave him a vigorous head rub and headed to the store.

"Owen McKenna?" The voice sounded muffled and distant through the heavy snowfall, but still I could hear its deep and raspy resonance. The man needed to clear his throat.

I turned and scanned the parking lot, but saw nothing except white mounds of snow that indicated parked vehicles.

"Owen McKenna?" the voice said again. This time it was closer, behind me to my right.

I turned.

A big man with a complexion like a rusted fender was coming toward me on metal crutches, his fingers clutching the handgrips. The leather sleeves of his expensive coat were gathered in wrinkles where the metal rings of the crutches encircled his lower arms. He shifted his weight to his left and held out his right hand, the crutch hanging from his arm.

"Bill Esteban," he said. "Sorry to chase you down like this." Behind him was the open door of a pearlescent Escalade, its engine running, wipers sweeping the huge windshield. The sweet happy rhythms of the Buena Vista Social Club harmonized from the speakers hidden among the tucks and folds of the leather interior. On the roof was a scant two inches of white stuff. Unlike me, he must have had a garage at home or office or both.

I shook Esteban's outstretched hand. He hung onto my hand a full five seconds too long, one of those awkward people who never figured out personal boundaries.

"I went to your office but you weren't there. I was going up to visit a friend in Zephyr Cove and saw you just as you were pulling into this center. One of the cops I talked to this morning said you had a Harlequin Great Dane. When I saw your giant dog hanging its head out the window I figured it had to be you. Am I right?" He turned and looked at Spot. "He's a big fella. Probably takes up the whole back of your car, huh? Steams up the windows in this weather, I bet?" He stared at me through thick glasses with circular metallic rims the color of dull steel. His eyes were black and hard-looking and set close together. Rimmed by the dark metal they reminded me of the business end of the antique double-barreled shotgun that my friend Diamond owned. The gun's firing pins had been removed, but the sight of those barrels made me aware of the power it once possessed.

"Can I talk to you for a minute?" Esteban said. "I'll park my truck and come with you inside. Just give me a sec?"

Before I could answer, he turned back to his Cadillac SUV and shoved his crutches across to the passenger seat. Teetering on unstable legs, he propped the heel of his left hand on the armrest of the door, grabbed the steering wheel with his right hand and boosted himself up into his luxury boat-on-wheels. Esteban gunned the engine and slid into a spot halfway down the row. I waited and he hobbled up a minute later. We walked at a slow pace toward the supermarket entrance, his crutches making creaking sounds as he shifted his substantial weight from side to side.

"Sorry to intrude on your shopping like this," he said. When we got to the entrance, he stamped his feet to try to shake off the snow. There were metal bars that rose from the soles of his shoes, past his ankles, and up alongside his legs under his slacks. In spite of the metal bracing, his shoes looked sophisticated and expensive. In such weather, they indicated tourist or wealthy vacation home-owner.

"What can I help you with, Bill?" I stopped near the racks of real estate booklets and turned to face him.

"Don't let me stop your shopping," he said. "I'll just tag along."

"We can talk here."

He stood three inches shorter than my six-six, and when he looked up at me, his eyes searching my face, I thought that in spite of his hard countenance, he looked like he was about to cry.

"It's about my nephew. March Carrera. He's gone missing. I think he died in that big avalanche last night."

TWO

"I didn't hear that any victims were found," I said.

"They haven't really looked," Esteban said with a rising voice.

"Yet."

"Right. But I don't see why not. The weather eased off hours ago. I stopped at the El Dorado Sheriff's Department and made a missing persons report. I asked if there was a way to speed up a search and they told me I could try you. Then I called the U.S. Forest Service and the CDF and Caltrans." Bill was cranked up, emotion in his words. "All they said was that they're using those big rotary plows to dig their way down the road. They said there's been no indication that anyone had been buried in the slide. But they found a truck in a tree. What more do they want? March drove a truck. I wanted to go out there. See if it was his. But they wouldn't let me. So I gave them my number and told them..."

"Easy, Bill," I interrupted. His rough face was red with stress. "They'll eventually figure out whose truck is in the tree and then you'll know one way or the other."

"How hard can that be? All you have to do is take a look to know the model and the license plate."

"Maybe it's covered in snow."

Bill thought about it. "Anyway, March left me a note, yesterday. I brought it with me." He leaned against the wall to stabilize himself. With both crutches swinging from his lower arms, he pulled out his wallet and removed a small piece of white paper and unfolded it. It was about 4 x 6 and was ripped along the top edge where it had been torn off of a tablet. He handed it to me.

The lettering was scrawled in blue ballpoint pen.

> 'Uncle, heading out to Tahoe City. The Guru of the Sierra is going to be at a little group there. I'll stay overnight. Back tomorrow early, weather permitting. March'

I refolded the paper and handed it back to him. "This seems a weak reason to think your nephew was in the slide."

Bill swallowed and said, "That and the fact that he didn't call and didn't answer his cell."

"It's still early in the day."

"Yeah. But I know my nephew. He would have called first thing this morning."

Maybe I gave him a look.

"I'm not saying he's some kind of perfect kid. But he wouldn't make me wonder. He'd call." Then, after a pause, Bill said, "I'd like to hire you."

"Hire me to do what?"

"Look into it. Find out if he died."

"Bill, aren't you getting ahead of yourself? A nephew gone missing for a day does not necessarily mean he died. Even if he did die in an avalanche, it would be an accident. What would I do?"

"I just want to know what happened. That kid was every-thing to me."

"*Was* everything to you? Isn't that a little premature?"

Bill frowned so hard, you could store toothpicks in the folds of his brow. "You do that, right?" he said. "Track people down? Find out where they went, what happened?"

"Yeah, but first we need to wait to find out if the truck in the tree was his. If he is in it, that will answer the question. That note doesn't mention him going to Tahoe City with anyone else. Do you think he went by himself? If not, you could talk to the people he might have ridden with. Or people he may have told his plans to. See if they know whether he made it through or not."

"I called the few friends of his that I know. His buddy Will Adams was March's main ski partner. Will thought that March probably drove to Tahoe City alone because he didn't think any of their South Shore group knew the people March was visiting."

"Does March have a girlfriend?"

Bill shook his head. "No. March doesn't want to be tied down."

"Is he dating anyone?"

"Not that I know of. He used to see a girl from Reno, Samantha Peachtree. I called her. She said she hasn't heard from March in a year."

"What about the guru of the Sierra that he mentions in his note?"

"I don't know who that is. I asked Will if he'd heard of this guru guy, and he said he had no idea who March was referring to. So I asked him who else I should call. He said I should try Paul Riceman and Carmen Nicholas. I called them, but they didn't know March was going to Tahoe City."

Bill's face was contorted with worry. A Cuban drumbeat came from his coat. He pulled out a cell phone.

"Hello?" Bill said.

I could hear a faint tinny voice talking between Bill's sentences, but I couldn't make out the words.

"Yeah, this is Bill Esteban...Yes, Sergeant. What did you find out?...Yes, that's what he drove. A red Toyota...You could see the plates?...He was thrown out?...I don't understand."

Bill listened for a time, then said, "Call me when you learn something more? Thanks."

He hung up and looked at me, his face grim. "That was Sergeant Bains with the El Dorado Sheriff's Department. They had a climber who got up the nearest tree. Took some pictures. They ran the plate. It's March's truck perched on the broken tree. But March isn't inside."

"March was thrown out in the impact?" I said.

"It looks like he wasn't inside when the avalanche hit. Both doors were caved in. Sergeant Bains said the driver's door was probably caved in from the avalanche. The passenger door's got marks that look like they match a guardrail. He said that stretch of road has guardrails, but they can't check them because they're buried under fifteen feet of snow that's set up like concrete."

"So the truck got smashed between the avalanche and the guardrail before it was hurled into the tree," I said.

"Sounds like it. But March is nowhere to be seen."

"Suggesting that March was not in his truck when the avalanche hit."

"Yeah," Bill said. "Maybe March got stuck on the road. He got out of the truck, sensed the avalanche coming and ran to safety."

I raised my eyebrows. "Possible," I said.

Bill's face got darker. "Or he got out of his truck and was swept away just like the truck."

I didn't say anything.

"Either way, I'd like to hire you to look into it. The cop I talked to in South Lake Tahoe said you're good. I'll pay whatever your rate is."

I shook my head. "I investigate crimes, not accidents," I said.

Bill looked wounded. "Why not? Can't you just give me one day? Make some calls, ask around or whatever it is you do?"

"Sorry. There's meat in investigating crime. A bad guy to catch. But accident investigations are always about trying to establish negligence, even when common sense says there isn't any. It always leads to a lawsuit, and I won't be part of that."

Bill had picked up one of the real estate booklets and was rolling it into a tight tube, wringing it hard enough that his knuckles were white. He shut his eyes a long time, took a deep breath, held it, then breathed out slowly. "I'm not interested in suing anybody, Caltrans or otherwise, you have my word on that."

I didn't say anything.

Bill slumped a little against the wall, taking some of the weight off his arms and crutches. His eyes suggested a lot more age than his driver's license would probably show. Weariness and sadness and pain.

Bill turned and looked at me. "I wouldn't know where to start," he said. "If he's buried, what do I do? Do they have a way of finding bodies in the snow? Or do the bears get to him first, like carrion, like rotting venison? Do I just wait until spring and hike around looking for his bones?" Bill's eyes were red and puffy.

"You're not from here, are you?" I said, glancing at his city shoes and coat.

"No, I live in Houston. But I have a house in the Tahoe Keys. I come whenever I can. March lived at my house."

"You have a card?"

He fished one out of his wallet and handed it to me. "Addresses, phone numbers, it's all there. I wasn't going to go back to Texas 'til Saturday. Maybe I won't at all, now."

"Let me make some calls," I said. "I'll call you tomorrow."

THREE

I went to my office on Kingsbury Grade, called the El Dorado Sheriff's Department and was put on hold for a long time.

I had left an art book from the library on my desk. It was about East Asian art. I didn't know anything about art east of the Ural Mountains and west of San Francisco, but I'd paged through it at the library and was fascinated by the way the Chinese made fog and clouds and rain and snow with a wash of ink off a brush. I paged through it now, courtesy of the county's phone system, and saw that the stormy Tahoe landscape had already been painted a thousand years ago in a country on the other side of the planet. Eventually, Sergeant Bains picked up the phone.

"I've heard of you," he said. "You were with San Francisco PD, right? Now you work private?"

"Yeah. I was talking to Bill Esteban a half hour ago when you called him about the truck that belonged to his nephew March Carerra."

"Was that something or what?" Bains said. "Who ever heard of a truck on top of a broken-off tree? Must have been one hell of a slide to throw that truck out into space like that."

"Any word on the owner, March Carerra?"

"Nothing. But the whole area is covered by frozen snow from the avalanche. Ten or more feet deep everywhere. If Carerra is buried under there, who knows when we'll ever find the body. Caltrans has a rotary on it. But it could be a day or two before it punches through the slide. Those rotaries take a bite six feet high, but the slide is twice that deep in places. They've got a front-end loader helping to break it up. Hate to think of what happens if a rotary hits a body. But then, considering what the slide did to the truck, it figures Carrera's body would've been thrown way down the mountain. Might be a long time before we find him."

"Any plan to bring in search and rescue dogs?" I asked.

"Several of the county SAR team members have dogs, but at this moment they're working a search on the West Slope. A couple of backcountry skiers were caught in the storm. They called in on their cell, and we got a good read on their location off the cell GPS. But we still haven't got to them yet. The skiers are alive and this pickup driver at Emerald Bay probably isn't, so I don't think the SAR team will be bringing their dogs this way anytime soon."

"Mind if I bring in a dog and do my own search?"

Bains paused before answering. "I'm thinking you wouldn't get in the way and cause any further problems, so be my guest. If you can find the body, it'll save the taxpayers money. I'll clear it with Caltrans, get you past the gate."

I thanked him, hung up and dialed Ellie Ibsen.

While Spot had some search training, it would be much faster to get professional canine help. Which meant calling on the most famous dog trainer in the West.

"Ellie, darling, Owen McKenna," I said when she answered.

She hesitated, her brain no doubt scrambling to place my name, not surprising for a person not far from ninety. "Owen! Where have you been? I've gone months without hearing your voice. Do you think I'm going to live forever?"

"If not you, Ellie, who?"

"And you only call when you want to use my dogs," she kidded me. "Let me guess. You're calling about that avalanche at Emerald Bay. I saw it on the news. They showed pictures of a truck up in a tree."

"Yeah. Our hope is that the driver got out of the truck before the avalanche. Maybe he got a ride from someone. But he may have been buried in the slide."

There was silence on the line. Finally, Ellie spoke in a subdued voice. "Avalanche victims who are buried rarely live more than fifteen minutes, so if he was buried, he's almost certainly dead. My best avalanche dog reacts badly to that. I try games and such, but not much works to cheer him up."

"What about a live find?"

"Yes, that helps."

"Then I'll arrange it if necessary."

Ellie didn't respond immediately. I knew she was remembering all the times over the years when her dogs had been out on search and rescue missions in the Sierra or even flown to earthquakes or other disasters around the globe. There had been many times when people had been found too late. Some dogs experience depression when their enthusiastic search work results in a body instead of the reward of finding a living person.

"Which dog is your best in avalanches?" I said, trying to redirect her thoughts.

"I have a couple. You remember Natasha, of course. You worked with her on that forest fire. She's great in snow, but she's laid up with a torn tendon. My newest, however, is going to be a star. Honey G is only two years old, but you won't believe how that dog works a territory."

"Honey G?"

"Yes. Stands for honey-colored Golden Retriever. I've had him out on many searches now, and he's amazing. I've never seen a dog air-track a scent better than Honey G." She paused, then said, "When will you pick us up?"

"First thing tomorrow morning? Say, six o'clock?"

"You should know it's supposed to start raining down here again tonight. So that will slow you down even after you get out of the snow."

"I'll leave extra early."

"Will you bring his largeness?"

"If he found out I visited you and didn't bring him along, there'd be repercussions."

"Good. I'll be waiting," Ellie said, eager as a Central Valley kid coming up to ski the mountains.

"Ellie, this slide is large and very deep, and by the time we get there it will have been set up for thirty-six hours. It will be like sending Honey G out to sniff through acres of concrete. Is there much hope of finding a scent in that situation?"

"Maybe not. But we still have to try."

"Right. See you in the morning."

I called Bill Esteban and told him I would work his case for a day or so, and I'd report tomorrow night. He was appreciative and said he'd wait to hear.

I left the next morning at 4:30 a.m. Spot sat up in the backseat as we drove through the darkened town. Caltrans had a long row of dump trucks occupying one lane. At the head of the line a rotary was eating the huge snow berm that the graders had deposited in the center of the four-lane road. The driver angled the chute to fill the lead dump truck. It took only twenty seconds. Then the truck pulled away and the rotary operator paused as the next dump truck pulled into position. Snow removal on this scale is a large, expensive operation, but it is the only option in Tahoe where most snowfalls are measured in feet, not inches.

Spot's ears were forward, his huge panting tongue flipping drops of saliva here and there around the backseat. He stuck his nose on the window and made a big smear across the opaque condensation.

"It's snowing outside," I said. "Most pets would be glad to be in a warm, dry car."

Spot licked the window.

"Your choice," I said. I hit the button to roll down the rear window just as another snow squall swept down the highway.

Spot stuck his head as far out into the snowstorm as he could, staring at the dump trucks. If he didn't have 170 pounds of ballast and studded paws gripping the seat fabric, I'd worry that he'd fall out. Instead, I put the windshield wipers on high, turned up the heat on the defroster, ignored my dog and concentrated on driving.

I went through town and climbed up the thousand vertical

feet to Echo Summit. Eventually, Spot pulled his snow-encrusted head inside and went to sleep.

It was very slow going around the big curves down to Twin Bridges. At Strawberry the snow became slushy and stuccoed the windshield. The wipers began to ride up over the ice rather than scrape it off. I rolled down the window and reached out to scrape the buildup off with my hand.

Because this storm off the Pacific was relatively warm, we drove out of the snow and into cold rain when we came down to 4000 feet at Kyburz. The rain never let up as I followed the tight curving highway. Eventually, the road left the American River and climbed back up the ridge to Pollock Pines. Once again at 4000 feet we popped up into heavy snow, but then re-entered the rain as we wound down to Placerville. I turned north on 49 and headed toward Coloma where the gold discovery in 1849 started the mad rush. The turnoff to Ellie's Three-Bar Ranch was only a few miles ahead.

Spot somehow knew where he was, and he was standing, excited, in the back seat as I pulled down the perfect drive to the perfect ranch home. It was still very dark and the short post lights lining the drive reflected on the wet asphalt. I parked where the drive looped around, got out and opened the back door. Spot charged out and zoomed around like a puppy on amphetamines.

Ellie came out wearing a raincoat and a backpack and carrying an umbrella in one hand and snowshoes in the other. With her was a Golden Retriever. The retriever ran to meet Spot and the two of them sniffed each other, tails high and wagging, then ran around for a couple of minutes.

We loaded Ellie's snowshoes and pack into the Jeep just as the rain began to let up.

"Owen, I want you to meet Honey G," she said to me as her Golden Retriever jumped into the Jeep, smelling, as all wet Goldens do, so ripe that I wondered how he could possibly sniff out any other scent. I reached around and gave Honey G a pet.

"You said Honey G is male, right?"

"Yes," Ellie said. "You think it is a feminine name?"

"Well, it does sound like an NFL cheerleader. He doesn't have gender confusion?"

Ellie touched my shoulder. "A little gender confusion is good for males of most species. Keeps them sensitive."

"Ah," I said.

"You could probably learn something from Honey G."

"No doubt," I said.

Ellie and I talked of old times as we drove. She asked about Street Casey. I asked about her dogs.

Winter moisture off the Pacific often comes in waves. We found ourselves between two waves and we followed the seren-dipitous lull in precipitation all the way back to Tahoe.

"Do you need a break?" I asked Ellie as we came over Echo Summit at dawn and coasted down the cliff edge toward the big lake that shimmered deep blue between rolling storm clouds. "Or should we go directly out to Emerald Bay?"

"We should get to work, don't you think?" she said. "We can rest tonight."

I drove out the Emerald Bay Highway and stopped where the Caltrans worker was stationed at the gate. He stared past me at Ellie as I explained who we were. He was no doubt wondering what a tiny old woman was doing on a search and rescue. "Sher-iff's Department said you're okay," he said as he let us through.

FOUR

I drove out the highway through four inches of fresh snow. We powered up the switchbacks in four-wheel-drive and stopped near the Emerald Bay overlook. The parking lot hadn't been plowed, but I parked at a wide spot on the highway where a grader had pushed snow to the side.

We put on our snowshoes and I pulled on my small just-in-case backpack with the windproof anoraks, space blanket, energy bars and water, then grabbed my shovel.

We headed down the road, the dogs running loops around us. The slide loomed like a glacier that flowed down the mountain toward the lake and completely covered the highway.

There was a narrow channel cut into the slide, following the highway. At the far end of the eight-foot-wide groove was a rotary plow looking like a giant insect chewing its way through the snow and belching diesel smoke. It spit out snow like a thousand snowblowers combined, its locomotive roar muffled by the walls of compacted snow on either side of it. A huge arc of snow shot 100 feet out of its chute, up and over the rest of the slide.

I helped Ellie up off the road and onto the roadside snowbank. From there we headed into the woods off to the lower side of the highway where the mountain dropped away in a steep plunge.

The dogs loped through the deep powder, Honey G having particular difficulty with the snow depth. I slogged ahead, breaking trail, and Ellie followed in my tracks. The deep snow was still work for her, but manageable. If her age or the high altitude made it more difficult, one would never know.

A tenth of a mile down we walked up onto the compressed snow of the slide and, although it was a very steep slope, it was like stepping from water onto land. Hiking was much easier, with a hard surface cushioned by the carpet of snow that had fallen over the last day. In places, the wind had blown the new snow off the slide, leaving the exposed hardpack slippery enough that if you fell, you'd slide a long way down. But our snowshoes had cleats, and they kept us from slipping.

The dogs charged ahead, toenails digging in, glad for the mobility provided by hardpack snow.

"Look," Ellie said. She pointed down the mountain.

I followed her line of sight and saw the truck sitting on top of a tree trunk. The truck sat well below the highway, and was firmly perched on a smooth straight Ponderosa pine trunk that had broken cleanly off. It looked like a post-modern, post-apocalypse tree-house, three stories high. The ground below was solid with the compacted snow left by the avalanche, much like a ski run that had been groomed multiple times. The nearby trees that survived the slide were devoid of all branches from the ground up to maybe fifty feet in the air. Clouds raced by above. A snow shower gave way to a fast-opening vertical tunnel with gray for walls and blue sky at the top. In seconds, the tunnel folded and collapsed and another burst of snow came where sunlight had stabbed down to the earth a moment before.

"Where should we start our search?" I asked.

Ellie stopped and surveyed the landscape. "Assuming that the boy was out of his pickup when the avalanche hit, his body could be nearly anywhere." She pointed up toward the highway. "I suppose it's possible that someone swept off the highway could have been rolled under the slide and deposited just below the guardrail with the bulk of the snow rushing by overhead. But it's more likely that a person would have been carried far down the mountain, maybe even most of the way toward the beach at Emerald Bay." She pointed down to the blue water, so beautiful and so deadly cold.

"In an avalanche search," I said, "what works best for a dog trying to find a scent? Starting at the top and working down, or going from the bottom up?"

Ellie was shaking her head. "It's not about the lay of the land. It's about the wind. When a victim is buried in snow, there is no trail for a dog to track. It is an air-scenting exercise. The best strategy is to start with the dog downwind, which provides the best chance that the dog finds a scent."

We both stopped and lifted our heads to the breeze.

"The wind is out of the west or southwest," I said. I turned and pointed northeast down the slope toward where the Vikingsholm Castle sat hidden in the trees. "Somewhere down there, at the farthest point of the slide, would be the downwind point. Should we hike all the way down before we start?"

"That would be best. A buried victim gives off a scent that percolates up through the snow. Once the scent comes out of the snow it moves out with the wind, gradually expanding, in the shape of a cone. We need to get the dog into that scent cone."

We started down the mountain. I looked across the slide, a surprisingly hard river of snow. "Seems like this snow is so compacted and dense that no scent would come through," I said.

"The deeper and denser the snow, the slower the percolation rate of the scent," Ellie said. "But the nose of a dog is an astonishing thing. Dogs are often able to pick up smells where common sense would suggest no smell exists."

"What about a victim that's dead compared to one that's alive?" I asked.

"I don't know of any scientific studies that have been done on that," Ellie said. "But anecdotal evidence suggests that dogs are almost as good at finding the dead as the living."

"They just don't like it as much?" I said.

"No, they don't."

We hiked in silence for a while, the dogs running ahead.

Ellie was huffing a little as she stepped her snowshoes with care to avoid falling. I stayed a little downslope from her, just in case she slipped and fell and slid.

"An interesting bit of search and rescue trivia," Ellie said, "is that when a dog alerts on the scent of a buried human and digs toward the person, they often go directly to the person's head. We don't even know what, exactly, the dogs are smelling."

"Could it be the scent they track only comes off the head?"

"Seems like it. Or maybe our entire bodies radiate the scent, but the strongest concentration comes off our heads."

Fifteen minutes later we were at the lowest reaches of the slide. A little above and north of us the river from Eagle Lake spilled over the falls before its last rush to Tahoe's only bay. Past the river, hidden in the huge pines, was the Vikingsholm Castle, dark and quiet until the onslaught of next summer's tourists.

Ellie looked up the mountain. "This is a good place to start." She turned toward where Honey G and Spot were running through a stand of fir trees.

Ellie whistled, then called out in her very small voice, "Honey G, come!"

It was amazing to watch the response as Honey G immediately stopped and charged up toward Ellie. Honey G stopped in front of Ellie, his wagging eager, his panting like a happy smile.

Ellie, as limber as I am, kneeled down in the snow in front of the retriever. She turned him to face up the mountain, then put one gloved hand on the back of his neck and the other hand on the front of his chest.

She spoke loud, her voice intense and excited. "Honey G, there is a victim in the snow!" she said, passing her excitement on to Honey G. "I want you to find the victim. Do you know what I want?" She vibrated her hands on his body. "I want you to find the victim."

Ellie stood and turned toward the vast area of the slide. She made an obvious pointing motion with her arm. "Find, Honey G! Find!" She tapped him on his back, and he took off.

Honey G ran across the snow at medium speed, his nose in the air. Spot loped along after him, aware that Honey G had a mission but not quite knowing what it was. I'd done some search training with Spot in the past, but always gave him a human scent to start with. Searching for a buried human without a starter scent was new territory for him.

Honey G went up at an angle to the right, his head still high, swinging back and forth. In thirty yards he came to the edge of the slide and plunged into the deep undisturbed snow. He stopped, turned and looked at us. Ellie made an exaggerated pointing motion with her arm. Honey G ran the way she directed him, back up onto the slide residue, and he ran to a point directly above us. He looked to Ellie again. She made another hand signal and Honey G zigzagged his way across the slide, gradually moving up the mountain. Ellie and I hiked up after him, taking a gentle angle up and across the mountain.

"When I give Spot a scent off clothing," I said to Ellie, "I can send him on a fairly effective search. But I've never tried a search without a starting scent."

"But he *does* have a scent to search for," Ellie said. "In our training he's learned that the command 'find the victim' means to find any human scent that isn't what's coming from the people he's with. It's actually quite easy to train a dog in that way. You just set up the standard situation where a person hides under the snow and you use the command 'find the victim.' A smart dog figures it out after his first successful find. He doesn't even have to think about it. We don't technically know if the dog searches for a scent that is distinct from the scents of the people around him or not. But it is easy to see that as soon as he gets the command, he knows what his job is, to find the scent of a person who's lost or buried.

"And when you give Spot a scent off someone's clothing," Ellie continued, "he may not be as focused on that particular scent as much as you think. Don't get me wrong. Dogs can certainly distinguish individual human scents. A blind-folded dog can easily pick his owner out of a group of people without any voice to help him. But in most search situations, it may be mostly that the clothing just lets him know that you want him to find a human scent."

"Ah," I said. "I could have him scent any hat, then send him onto the avalanche area and he'd go find the buried person whether the hat belonged to the person or not?"

"Right. Remember when the arsonist was setting the forest fires? We gave Natasha the scent of a drop of gasoline. We wanted to prime her to search for any fire accelerants. She understood that any similar smells were her target. Gasoline, kerosene, or any other volatile organic compounds. The point of having her sniff gasoline in the beginning was just to let her know it was an accelerant search and not another lost person search.

"With an avalanche dog, we train him to do the search without using any scent as a starting point. It's like when you get up in the morning and tell your dog to find the Frisbee. The dog finds it without being given any advance smell."

Ellie paused to watch Honey G. He'd turned yet again and was coming back across the slide when he stopped again. He looked down at us. Ellie pointed to the left and he went in that direction, slower now. Spot had stopped below Honey G and watched, no doubt catching his breath.

"Looks like Honey G's interest is waning," I said.

"No. He's winded, but he's a real worker. Even as a puppy, if I told him to search for his tennis ball, he'd never give up until either he found it or a different tennis ball or I called him off. He's even more dedicated when searching for a person."

Ellie and I had been traversing the slope at a gentle angle. We came to the edge of the slide, turned and started back across. "Good to turn," Ellie said. "It's hard on my ankles and knees to always lean one way."

"Me, too."

Honey G came back across the slide again, his focus intense.

Spot continued to watch him, but after Honey G's fifth or sixth zigzag across the landscape, Spot figured it out. When Honey G struck out on yet another circuit across the mountain, Spot ambled straight up the slope and then stopped. Sure enough, Honey G's next circuit brought him right to where Spot was waiting.

More than most dogs, Spot was at home in the snowy mountain woods, familiar with its secrets and surprises. But watching him observe Honey G was like watching the street-smart kid on the playground who is unable to understand the drive and purpose of the class valedictorian.

Ellie and I continued to follow Honey G and headed up the mountain. Straight up the mountain above us sat the truck in the tree.

"Should we rest a little?" I asked.

"That would be good," Ellie said. She was breathing hard, and I realized I'd waited too long to stop.

"What about Honey G," I said. "Does he need to rest?"

"Honey G is an overachiever," Ellie said. "He doesn't rest. He just keeps working. The job is what gives him purpose."

Above us loomed the mountains that wrap around Emerald Bay. Storm clouds encircled their peaks, but the 3000-foot icy rock walls sheltered the bay from the wind. A gentle drift of flakes came quietly, muffling the distant sound of the rotary up above us on the highway.

"The breeze is gentle but steady," Ellie said, looking at the even drift of falling snowflakes. "If there is any kind of scent cone on this mountain, Honey G should have found it by now."

"If we get back to the top and he hasn't alerted yet, do you think there could still be someone buried here?"

Ellie was shaking her head. "I doubt it."

"Even considering how thick and solid the slide is?"

"It's possible, but I still doubt it. Honey G would find him."

We started up the mountain again. Twenty minutes later, we were almost directly under the pickup in the tree. I was looking up at the mangled, ice-encrusted shape when Ellie spoke.

"Here we go!" she said. She pointed toward Honey G. The dog had his nose in the air, zigzagging across the surface with frantic intensity. "He's alerting! He found a scent!"

FIVE

Honey G ran up the slope, moving back and forth, sniffing the air and narrowing in on an area thirty yards above us. He stopped abruptly, dug a couple of strokes with his paws, stuck his nose into the little hole and sniffed hard. He made a high bark and started digging furiously.

Ellie went up the slope with the energy of a teenager. She kneeled next to him. "Good boy, Honey G!"

Honey G dug like a trenching machine, snow flying out between his rear legs.

"The compressed snow is very hard," I said as I unstrapped my shovel.

Ellie nodded. "Be careful not to hit his paws."

I started four feet away. I had to swing hard with the shovel to penetrate the frozen surface. It felt uncomfortable to stab down with such fervor, because although I was certain that March Carrera would be dead, I nevertheless didn't want to plunge my shovel into a body.

When I started digging, Spot, too, came over, no doubt remembering the couple of times he and I had done search training on snow. He moved around, sniffing at the snow. He must have found a promising scent for he started digging with vigor midway from me to Honey G.

While Honey G dug remarkably well, Spot's size and his very long legs allowed him to go down twice as fast.

My shovel was even more effective. In ten minutes I hit a fallen tree about five feet down. The tree must have cast a kind of impact shadow, for the snow in the area below it and down the slope was much less compacted. Some loose snow fell away and my shovel went into a small space.

I called out, "Ellie? Can you get Honey G down here? I found a softer area, and I think he can go laterally from here."

She appeared above me. "Honey G," she said. "Down there." She pointed down at me.

"C'mere, Honey G," I said. "Take a sniff down here."

Honey G looked at Ellie for reassurance, then jumped down next to my feet.

"Find the victim, Honey G!" I said.

Honey G turned around, sniffing the walls of my snow cave, then stuck his nose under the tree trunk. He made another yip and dove under the tree, digging frantically.

The space was too small to get my shovel in without hitting Honey G, so I worked on the sides of the hole, widening my snow pit, careful to throw the snow up and away from where Ellie was standing. Spot stood next to her, his brow furrowed as he stared at where Honey G had disappeared under the tree.

In a minute I heard Honey G stop digging. My snow cave was now wide enough that I could get down on my hands and knees and look under the tree trunk. It was too dark to see anything but a vague shape of Honey G. I pulled off my backpack, got out my small flashlight and shined it toward Honey G. He turned around to look toward me, his eyes flashing in my light beam. He whimpered.

"Honey G, come out of there." I patted my thigh. He turned around and dug some more, then stopped and cried. "Ellie?" I said loudly. "Can you call Honey G? I think he's found the body. I need him to move so I can have a look."

"Honey G, come here," she said.

Honey G crawled out of the hole, out from under the tree trunk and jumped out of the snow pit.

I didn't look up toward Ellie because I wanted my eyes to adjust to darkness. I got down on my belly, held the flashlight in my teeth and squirmed under the tree trunk toward the dark hole.

It was a tight fit. I moved forward inches at a time, my jacket catching on the bark of the tree. I took the light out of my mouth and shined it ahead of me. My eyes gradually adjusted, and I saw snow and branches and more snow. There was nothing that looked like a body.

I belly-crawled forward until I could scrape away at the snow where Honey G had been digging. I dug through branches and twigs and snow until I hit something with a different consistency. Thin and solid, but flexible. Like a carrot. I scraped at more snow. It was hard enough that I could barely abrade it with my gloved hand.

I was trying to inch forward when the top of my tiny worm-hole tunnel collapsed. The snow buried my head and arms and my flashlight. I was trapped in the dark, my arms pinned. I felt like an idiot, remembering that compacted snow from a slide makes a good solid material for digging snow caves. Difficult to dig, but strong. Whereas the loose snow, protected from the slide by the tree I was under, hadn't been compacted. The very quality that made this snow easy to dig through also made it dangerously unstable.

My butt and legs were still under the tree trunk. I wormed my way backward. I got just far enough that I could pull my arms free. Again, I held the flashlight with my mouth and used both hands to try to sweep the snow free.

There was less room than before. I moved my head to try to get the light angled just so. But I couldn't see anything. The most sensible approach was to squeeze back out of the tunnel, climb out and dig down from above.

But I was so close. If I could just verify that it was in fact the body that Honey G had discovered, then we'd know that March Carerra hadn't escaped the avalanche. I wouldn't have to dig. I could leave him there, call the El Dorado Sheriff's Department and let them do the hard work.

Once again I squirmed forward, gouging at the snow with my fingers, pulling it away, trying to compact it to the side so it didn't fill my space. I made a little progress, then moved forward another couple inches.

My tunnel was nearly full, so I pounded at the snow with my fists, trying to compress it down and to the sides. I made a little more space. Inched forward. Dug some more.

The first thing I uncovered was hair, matted into the snow, glinting in the beam from my flashlight. I wasn't eager to go further, but I had to be certain I hadn't uncovered an animal. A mountain lion or a bear could get caught in an avalanche just as easily as a person.

I scraped away at the snow and found the carrot. It was a finger. The position of the fingers next to the matted hair suggested his hand was cupped around his face.

I twisted my head trying to angle the light with my mouth. I panted with effort and sucked air through my teeth around the flashlight. My breath made clouds of steam that filled my tiny space with fog.

By gently pulling on his head with one hand and using my other hand to push away at the frozen snow around his hand, I was able to expose his head.

The flashlight was still in my mouth. I shifted my jaw and got the flashlight beam to shine directly on his face.

Her face.

The body belonged to a young woman.

SIX

The body buried under the avalanche had a thin delicate jaw. The snow and ice had pressed one corner of her mouth back into a frozen half-smile. She had good teeth. Graceful arched eyebrows. One eye was shut, the other eye was peeking out as if trying to see what things looked like from the perspective of death. Now I understood why the hair had glinted in my flashlight. It was blond. I guessed her to be in her early twenties.

I wormed my way back out of the tunnel and climbed out of the snow pit.

It was obvious that Spot had smelled the death. He eyed me with drooping eyes and limp ears. His tail didn't move, and he didn't come forward to greet me as I got out of the snow cave. Honey G sat next to Ellie. His head hung low, his energy and enthusiasm gone.

"Honey G found the driver of the pickup, didn't he?" Ellie said.

I walked to Ellie's side and put my arm around her. "He found a body, yes, but it's a young woman."

Ellie gasped. "But you said they identified the truck as belonging to a young man. And the boy's uncle said his nephew had driven off in it, right?"

I nodded.

"Then who is the young woman?"

"I have no idea, Ellie."

I pulled out my cell. There was no reception.

"Let's go up to the highway. I can try calling the Sheriff's

Department from up there."

We hiked up slowly, drained after the depressing discovery. Spot stayed next to me, not looking around, walking like a refugee. Honey G hung back behind Ellie. Ellie tried to cheer him up, using her glove to entice him into a game of tug-of-war, but he wasn't interested.

Back in the Jeep I started the engine and turned on the heat. I pulled energy bars and dog cookies out of my pack and handed them to Ellie. While she waited with the dogs, I walked down the highway until I found some cell reception and got Sergeant Bains on the phone.

"I'm out at Emerald Bay," I said. "I brought Ellie Ibsen, the search dog trainer. Her dog found a young woman's body buried about a third of the way down to the water. Not far below the truck in the tree."

"Whoa, whoa, whoa. You said woman?"

"Yes. Early twenties, I'd guess. Buried in the slide about eight feet down."

"She have identification on her?"

"Don't know. She's still buried. I dug a pit, then the dog tunneled a little distance sideways. I went in and just managed to get to her head before I backed out. You'll have to dig down from above to get her out."

Forty minutes later I was snowshoeing back down the mountain with Bains and two deputies. Ellie had decided to stay with the Jeep and the dogs.

One deputy towed a toboggan behind him. On the toboggan were two shovels and a variety of gear. I showed the cops my snow pit and then walked over to where I thought they should dig.

Bains and I stood to the side while the younger men dug.

"You got a take on this?" Bains said.

"Not a clear one. The simplest explanation is that March Carrera drove off with the girl. He got stuck and they got out to walk. The slide caught both of them. We found her. Now we still have to find him."

"Why do you say you don't have clear take on this?"

"When I talked to the uncle he said March had no girlfriend and wasn't dating. March's friends didn't know of anyone, male or female, who might have ridden with him to Tahoe City. Something about this feels wrong."

Bains looked at me and chewed his lip. "You worked homicide for the SFPD, right?"

"Yeah," I said.

Bains nodded thoughtfully. "Okay. Your warning lights are good enough for me." He stepped over to where the men were digging.

"Boys, when you get to the girl, go slow and easy so you don't disturb her. We're going to treat this as a potential homicide."

The men stopped digging and looked at Bains.

"I want a large excavation, photos at each stage. Bag her hands and feet. Any snow stuck to her goes into the body bag with her. Sift all nearby snow and dirt. You know the drill."

It took ten minutes to reach her, another twenty to carefully excavate around her.

They were very thorough with the scene, carefully following Bains' instructions.

I left as they were strapping the body bag onto the toboggan.

SEVEN

"We should go back for the boy," Ellie said when I returned to the Jeep.

"We're tired, the dogs are depressed, and it's already mid-afternoon. You've put in a long day."

"As you look at the slide below the highway, Honey G never searched the upper right quadrant." Ellie said. She slouched with weariness, but her eyes were clear and intense.

"Shouldn't I be taking you out for a hot meal?"

"We stopped where he found the girl. We never went past that point," she said.

"I know a good restaurant with tables by the fireplace," I said.

"If that young man is buried, Honey G will find him," she said.

"Grilled salmon, a good pinot noir," I said.

Ellie opened the back door of the Jeep and spoke to the dogs. "Okay, boys, nap time is over."

On our way back down we passed Bains and his men. They'd hauled the toboggan almost up to their SUVs. The toboggan would just fit in the one with the rear seat folded down.

"Going back to look for March Carrera," I said.

Bains looked at Ellie, then at me.

"At her insistence," I said.

"You know where to call."

Ellie was less effective at getting Honey G excited the second time around. But he did his job, hiking up the slide at an angle, nose in the air. Periodically, he turned and looked back for Ellie's hand signals.

Without saying a word, she maneuvered him across the portion of the slide we hadn't searched. He zigzagged his way up past the tree with the truck in it. Ellie and I hiked slowly up the slope. I was tired. Ellie's stamina was amazing. Spot followed us.

In ten minutes, Honey G alerted.

He put his nose to the snow, ran several feet away and stopped so quickly it was as if he'd hit the end of a leash. Then he started digging.

Spot finally got interested, trotted up and again found his own place to dig a few feet away. I joined them with my shovel and we reached March Carrera fifteen minutes later. His body was smoothly curved around a tree trunk as if, like a rag doll, it had no bones.

Ellie tried to praise and reward the dogs, but they were listless. Again, we walked up the mountain until I got cell reception. Bains answered immediately.

"Found March Carrera's body about six feet down."

"The boys and I are in town. We just dropped off the girl at the mortuary where she can stay the night. I was making arrangements to have her brought to Sacramento. Now you want us to come back? You think we're running a morgue shuttle service?"

"Something like that."

"You have similar suspicions on this one?"

"Maybe."

I heard Bains sigh. "Back soon," he said.

EIGHT

"Time for a meal?" I said as we drove back to town.

"First, we have to cheer up the dogs."

"Got it," I said, my stomach growling.

I called Street Casey at her bug lab. I told her about our day and asked if she would get lost for the dogs.

"Of course, but I can't bury myself in snow. I'd need help. And I'm not exactly dressed for it."

"A variation would work. I'm thinking about that giant boulder out back of your lab. It's got that overhang?"

"Good idea," she said. "I've got my snowshoes in the car trunk. When should I head out?"

"Now?"

"Advance notice is so helpful. Okay, let me turn off the scope and put these samples back in the incubator. I'll bring my cell and call you when I'm in position."

Ellie and I were waiting in my office parking lot just up the street on Kingsbury Grade when my phone rang.

"It's very cold and dark under this ledge of rock," Street said. "The dogs better find me soon."

"Three or four minutes, max," I said.

We drove down the block to Street's lab.

"In the interest of not breaking pattern, I'll follow my normal procedure," I said to Ellie. I knocked on Street's lab door, called out her name, opened the door with my key, called Street's name again. "She's not here," I said. Spot looked at me, puzzled. Honey G stood nearby.

Without turning, I said to Ellie, "She's hiding in the woods about a tenth of a mile directly behind me. If you look at the big Jeffrey pine where lightning split the top, she's just down to the left."

"I see it," Ellie said. "There's no breeze over on this side of the lake, so it's not clear what kind of scent cone he might find. But we'll send him out. Honey G, come."

Honey G obeyed as before, albeit with no enthusiasm. He sat and Ellie held his chest and gave him an intense vibrating shake. "Find the victim, Honey G. Find!" She pointed toward the boulder and sent him on a search. He did a kind of slow leaping canter through the deep snow.

I kneeled down and gave Spot the same command.

Spot acted bored as if the exercise were a waste of time. Nevertheless, he followed Honey G at a fast walk.

In a minute Honey G had veered far to the left and Ellie corrected him when he looked back. In another minute he stuck his nose straight up and stood up on his hind legs for a moment. Then he ran out into the woods, leaping like a deer through the snow. Spot ran after him.

Honey G's enthusiastic sprint was 45 degrees off from Street's location, and I worried that he had picked up someone else's scent. But then he turned in a big gradual arc and homed in on Street's boulder as if he knew exactly where she was.

Spot figured it out, too, and they both converged on the boulder and dived out of sight under the overhang.

Street emerged from behind the boulder, romping with the dogs, their moods completely changed.

Ellie turned to me. "Thank you."

"No. Thank you."

NINE

We drove back down to the foothills and finally found food at a roadhouse near Placerville, a comfortable five or six minutes before I would have expired. We dropped Ellie and Honey G at the Three Bar Ranch and headed back up the mountain. I called Sergeant Bains and volunteered to tell Bill Esteban about his nephew's death. But it was late when we arrived home. It could wait.

The next morning I headed to the Tahoe Keys. Bill Esteban's house was a big modern box on one of the inland canals, a short boat ride to the freedoms of the big lake. It had a three-car garage with all the doors open. Inside were his Escalade, a Seville and a snowmobile trailer with two machines on it.

It took Bill a couple of minutes to get to the door. He ushered me in and up the stairs. Many Keys houses have the bedrooms on the ground floor and the living area upstairs to take in the views of lake and mountains and sky. Bill had me go first.

The living room was huge and lavish. Teak furniture glowed against Prussian blue carpet.

We sat on two of six opposing chairs. Between the chairs were small tables. On the one next to Bill was a chessboard with a game in progress. The black king was well guarded. The white queen cavorted with the bishop while the white king stood like a lonely pariah in the corner.

From where I sat I could see out one window toward Heavenly with its network of ski runs and out another window toward Mt. Tallac. We were in a break between storm fronts, and the variegated clouds were sparse and high allowing a view of the mountain peaks. A plume of blowing snow streaked off the summit of Mt. Tallac into the blue sky. It was relatively warm down at lake level, but that plume indicated deadly weather at 10,000 feet.

A giant garish TV screen showed the Vikings butting heads with the Cowboys. The volume was turned down.

"You came unannounced," Bill said. "I suppose that means you've learned something about March?" He braced himself, hands on the arms of his chair.

"Yes. I'm very sorry to say that he died."

Bill looked like he'd been sucker punched. He exhaled hard and didn't breathe back in for a long time. His eyes seemed focused somewhere far beyond the house. Then he suddenly inhaled and gasped for air as if he'd been a long time under water.

"I brought in an avalanche search dog and he found March's body buried under six feet of snow. They got him unburied late yesterday. His body is at the morgue in Sacramento. Eventually, they'll get the truck out of the tree. Perhaps there will be something more we can learn about what happened."

"You think it was an accident?" Bill was sitting on the very edge of his chair, elbows on his bad knees, his eyes large and dark and wet and imploring behind his glasses.

"Hard for an avalanche not to be. Why do you ask?"

"It's just that March was careful. He took risks, but he was smart about it."

"It wasn't very smart for him to be out driving in the storm that night."

"No." Bill leaned back in his chair. He forced a deep breath in an effort to stay calm. "But I can't see him stopping and getting out in the path of an avalanche. He was a backcountry skier. He knew the risks."

Bill started breathing hard again. "What do I do now? I feel like I'm responsible."

"Why?"

"I don't know. I should've done things different."

"Like what?"

"I don't know. Something." Bill was panting, his chest heaving. "I was March's closest family. Maybe his closest friend. He was buried and suffocating in that avalanche while I was oblivious. I should have been there for him." Bill gasped like a drowning man. His face was red. He looked like he would have a heart attack any moment.

I walked over in front of him. "Bill, you're hyperventilating. Hold your breath."

Bill gasped harder than before.

"Bill, stop breathing and hold your breath!"

My shout startled him. He reached up and clamped his thumb and fingers over his nose like a little kid. His cheeks puffed out. There were bits of dried blood in the cracks of his cuticles. His fingernails were chewed back so far it was as if he had done it to inflict pain on himself.

"Good. Hold it a little while longer. That will calm you down. A little more. Okay, let your breath out slowly. Now take a small short breath."

"I have anxiety medication," he whispered. "In the cabinet in the bathroom. Brown bottle."

I fetched the pills and brought him a glass of water. He shook one out and swallowed it.

"Sorry," he said after a minute. "Death in the family... it's something I..."

"What?" I said.

Bill didn't respond.

"Death in the family is what?"

Bill hesitated. I waited.

"It's very hard," he finally said.

When he calmed, I said, "March have other family?"

"Just April, his sister, and me. No other relatives."

"March wasn't alone in the slide."

Bill jerked.

"There was a young woman. Her body was also buried in the slide. We found her about fifty yards away."

"Do you know her name? What did she look like?"

"Thin and delicate, with blond hair. I'd guess she was younger than March by a couple years. We don't know her name, yet."

Bill looked ill. "They're going to do autopsies, aren't they? They'll want permission from March's closest of kin. That's his sister April. I don't know how they can even reach her."

"They will give April or you a courtesy call. But they don't need permission to do an autopsy in California."

In time, Bill calmed, got up on his crutches and moved around. "Get you something to drink?" Bill said.

"Whatever you're having," I said.

"I don't touch alcohol, but I keep beer for visitors."

"Sure."

I looked out the windows while Bill fetched libations. Down in the drive, Spot had his head stuck out of my Jeep's rear window. Snow was blowing off Bill's roof onto Spot, tickling his ears. Spot shook his head. Snow and saliva flew and his jowls and ears flapped and he turned and looked up at me.

Bill came and stuck a tall glass of amber in my hand. He sat down on a different chair, sipped what looked like iced tea and, with a struggle, got his bad legs up on the matching hassock. He glanced at the TV, two rows of giant men lined up to trample each other into the turf, then turned back to me.

"Do you want me to keep looking into March's death?"

"Yeah."

"Even though I'm unlikely to uncover anything other than more details about an accidental death?"

"Yeah."

"I will have lots of questions and it may take a long time."

Bill looked at me and raised up scratchy misshapen eyebrows that looked like two-inch pieces of barbed wire. His face was still red.

"That's okay," he said.

"March lived with you?" I asked.

"Yeah."

"He spend much time with you?"

"Some. We ate dinner together a few times a week."

"He confide in you?"

Bill frowned. "You mean, like tell me his personal problems? No. He was a man. He could figure things out himself."

"So he slept here, ate a few meals here, but that was it. You didn't really know him well?"

Bill stared at me, his rough complexion looking like 40-grit sandpaper in the morning sunlight. "Christ, this is what it turns into, doesn't it? One minute, I've got a nephew who is everything to me. Then he's dead and I need to talk about what he ate and who he knew and his personal habits…"

I waited for Bill to see the sense of it.

"Sorry," Bill said. "No, I guess I didn't really know him well. He was mostly here alone. I live in Houston."

"You've had this place long?"

He looked around at the room. "I picked this up six years ago. It was built by another guy from Houston. A customer of mine. I came here a few times to vacation with him and his wife. I was always interested in Tahoe because I had a Washoe grandmother who visited my sister Maria and me when we were young. Grandma was an incredible basket weaver from Carson Valley. She told us stories about Tahoe, the sacred lake where her ancestors hunted and fished. I wanted to come to Tahoe just because of her stories.

"One thing led to another and my customer made me a good deal on this house. I thought, what the hell, I've got the money. It's a nice place and I don't need any more stocks. God, I can't believe he's gone." He looked around in desperation, his eyes settling on the chess board, then on the TV. The Cowboys' quarterback drilled a ten-yard bullet into the end zone. The receiver plucked it out of the air like he was catching a coasting butterfly.

Bill took a breath, staring at the receiver, then breathed out. "March asked to come out here while he was in college. He was a snowboarder. A rider, as he used to say. But he recently switched to skis. He said the new ones are amazing in junk snow."

Bill drank some tea. He picked up the white queen and

moved her diagonally one square, next to a group of pawns, even farther from the king. "March met some people here and came back several times. After college, he worked in Houston for a while, one of those IT companies, they make human resource software for other companies. But he didn't like it. So he quit and asked me if he could stay here in Tahoe for a while. He wanted out of software engineering. He said he wanted to figure out his brain. I said sure. That was two years ago."

"What did he do for income?"

"He worked for awhile at a snowboard shop. What they call a custom boot fitter, I guess. But he quit after a few months. He said there was some tension with the guys after he stopped riding and switched to skis. So he was back to living off his savings from his software job. There's also a trust fund for both him and his sister. It's not huge, but enough to pay for the basics."

"What happens to the income now?"

"I haven't thought about it. I guess it would go to his sister."

"Where does his sister live?"

"April? Who knows? First, she's in Houston right out of college, working as a secretary. It was the only work she could get because she majored in American History. What was she thinking? But she's got a real thing for the Civil War. Always talking about Grant and Lee, Lincoln and Davis and Armstrong.

"She came and stayed with us last fall, then left a month or so ago. I don't know where she is now. March talked to her, but he didn't much mention it to me. He knew we don't get along. Once, he said April was going to the Dominican Republic. Part of some charity group that builds shelters for women. I've tried calling her cell, but all I get is voicemail. She never calls back. I'll call her again. She should know about March."

"What's her number?"

Bill told me and I wrote it on a business card. I wondered how many uncles would know a niece's phone number by heart.

"March and April?" I said.

"Yeah, the names are kind of different. They're twins. Born on either side of midnight, March thirty-first."

"Their parents?"

"Their mama was my sister. Maria Carrera. She died twenty-two years ago. The kids were three. Maria was sweet and kind and soft-spoken and beautiful..." Bill stopped talking and looked out the window. The snow had resumed falling. His dark eyes were moist. "Like I said, death in the family is hard."

"What about their father?"

"Maria married a crook. John Carrera. He was around for a couple months, then left. I heard he went to Mexico and was involved in a chop shop. Cut up stolen cars to sell the parts. Probably in prison, now. Bottom line is the kids never had a father. He'd already been gone for half a year when they were born. Then, three years later, they didn't have a mother, either."

"Who raised them?"

"Maria's best friend Gabriella Mendoza took them in. Gabriella was poor and single, but she has a good heart. She did right by them. I tried to help, but they were out in Dust Devil, Texas, and I was in Houston. And my business pretty much consumed me."

"Are you retired?"

"No, I still have the nightclub, but I have a good team. I can get away, now. I couldn't the whole time those kids were growing up. I regret that. But what can you do?" He looked at the TV, then outside as if searching for something calming. He squinted and blinked and found Kleenex in his pocket to blow his nose.

"Who paid the bills for the kids?"

"Gabriella is a frugal woman. I helped some. And the kids have the trust fund from my mother, bless her soul."

"Why don't you get along with April?"

"It could take some time to tell. She's a hothead for one. Where March was calm, April flies off on every little thing. For example, I had a little party here about six weeks back. March and April and their friends. Everyone was having a good time. April started talking about when they cut all the trees in Tahoe to shore up the mine tunnels in Virginia City. She said that the silver from the Comstock Lode was part of how the Union Army was financed, so the trees of Tahoe were instrumental in helping the

Union defeat the Confederates. Did you know that? That Tahoe lumber helped Lincoln hold the country together? I didn't know that." Bill picked up a black knight and moved it one square forward, two to the left, closer to the white king.

Bill continued, "So it was a real interesting party conversation. But then April blew it all apart."

"What happened?" I asked.

"April was saying something about General Grant and Armstrong, and how after the war, Armstrong had something to do with the Carson City Mint. But Paul Riceman said he didn't think Armstrong was important enough to even talk about. Then April said she could talk about Armstrong as much as she wanted. It was the silliest of disagreements. I don't even know who Armstrong was. Then they got in an argument and April got up and stormed out and drove away. It was like some kid having a temper tantrum. Imagine that. You've got these young kids who are smart enough they're talking about the Civil War for chrissakes. But they still get in a petty argument. Ruined my party."

Bill turned his head and stared toward Heavenly, now obscured by clouds. Perhaps he was imagining the trails that March had ridden.

"Paul Riceman was one of March's friends," I said.

"Right. Works in construction."

"How'd March react to the argument?"

"He acted like it was no big deal."

"You ever witness Paul argue with April before?"

"No." Bill shook his head.

"Paul and March do much together?"

"They were pretty good buddies," Bill said.

"Who else was at your dinner party?"

"Let me think. Besides March and April and Paul, there was Packer and Carmen. Packer works in the same shop where March worked. They all have passes at the local areas. Except Carmen. She wants to learn to ski, but she's afraid she'll get hurt."

"April and March get along?" I said.

"Everyone got along with March."

"And you think April is in the Dominican Republic?"

"Like I said, I don't know. That's what March told me."

I heard the pain of rejection in his voice.

Bill looked back at the TV screen. The Vikings were in a huddle. They smacked each other on the butt and ran back to the line. The Vikings' center snapped the ball, and the Cowboys ran over their front line and smashed the quarterback to the ground.

Bill watched it, then picked up the white rook and moved it four squares to the left, taking out one of the black pawns. Bill handled the pieces with aggression as if he didn't realize they were just pieces of carved wood.

"Your earlier comments," I said, "sounded like you suspected that something bad might happen to March. He'd been gone barely twelve hours, and you wanted me to investigate. Why?"

Bill looked at me. He picked up a ballpoint pen off an end table and clicked it in and out. "Call it a feeling I had. Maybe it's because he said something unusual about a month ago."

I waited.

"He asked me if I knew any financial advisors who are good. So I said, 'Sure, why?' Because we both knew that March didn't have any surplus of funds. His savings from his previous job was running low. And the trust fund is locked up. He can't touch any of it other than his monthly check."

"What did he say when you asked why?"

"He said something like, 'I'm twenty-five and I was thinking I should make a plan one of these years.'"

"Why does it stand out?" I said.

"I'm not sure. I suppose it's just that March wasn't a planner. He lived a day at a time. When he asked me about a financial planner, it didn't fit. I worried that he was into something bad. He also came home with a book on the stock market and one on coin collecting and Fortune magazine. It was strange, this sudden focus on investing." Bill paused. "There's another reason why I worried that something bad was going to happen to March."

"What's that?"

"You have to come downstairs to March's bedroom."

TEN

Bill hoisted himself to his feet and led me down the stairs, his pace labored, his crutches groaning. We went down a hall where Bill reached into one of the doorways and flipped on a light switch. I followed him in.

It was an unremarkable bedroom. The bed was unmade, and there were some clothes strewn about. A snowboard leaned in one corner next to a pair of snowboard boots. The closet door stood open, revealing some clothes on hangers and more piled on the floor. On the wall were topographical maps assembled to show the lake and surrounding mountains. In another corner stood a pair of skis.

"What made you worry about March?"

Bill pointed at the doorknob on the closet. A necklace of sorts hung from the knob. "He didn't wear his star," Bill said.

"What does that mean?"

Bill took it off the doorknob and handed it to me. "It is an amulet that brings the protection of the Guardian Spirit."

It was a small circular pendent, about an inch in diameter and woven of some kind of grass. It had exquisite details and a design of interlocking triangles. Some of the grass strands were died black, some gray and some left natural buff. The pendant hung on a thin leather cord.

"It was woven by my grandmother. She called it the Washoe Star. She said it was a design that came from her mother, my great grandmother."

"It looks a little like the designs I've seen on Washoe baskets,"

I said.

"Yeah, except it isn't a traditional Washoe design. Great grandma was a young woman when she met one of the Chinese laborers who came to the Sierra to work on the railroads and in the mines during the Nineteenth Century. She got close to this young man. They couldn't speak each other's language. But she showed him her woven baskets with her beautiful designs. Then he drew her several mandalas, which are concentric geometric shapes based on Chinese deities. Great grandma joined his designs with hers and wove what she called the Washoe Star. She said it would represent the Guardian Spirit, and she passed the design on to her daughter, our Grandma.

"Before Maria died she told Grandma how the storms in Texas were so bad that the paper called them Muerte Cielo, or Death Sky, and that her babies cried at the thunder. So Grandma wove a Washoe Star for March and another one for April so the Guardian Spirit would look out for them."

"But March left his at home," I said.

Bill looked at me, no doubt wondering what I thought about it.

I didn't believe that a woven amulet could, by itself, protect someone from an avalanche. But I did believe that an amulet's presence could make someone more self-aware and, in subtle ways too numerous to count, make them more careful and more inclined to better judgement, thus achieving the intended effect.

"Did March wear his Washoe Star often?" I asked.

Bill nodded. "You know how objects can come to take on important symbolism and meaning?" Bill said.

"Yeah."

"March wore his most every day. It was a prized possession." Bill reached under his shirt collar and pulled out his own Washoe Star. "I'll wear mine every day that I'm in this life."

I hung March's star back on the doorknob, and we went back upstairs to the living room.

"What about April?"

"April is a spoiled brat. I can't stand to be around her. If she were more of a planner than March, I would never know it."

"Did March spend a lot of money recently?"

"No. He was generous, but he didn't have a lot extra to throw around."

"He have any recent fights or disputes or disagreements with anyone?"

Bill shook his head.

"Does he hang out in bars or with guys you don't like?"

"What do you mean?"

"Guys that make you worry. Guys who are unemployed and un-ambitious."

"No."

"Is he on good terms with ex-girlfriends?

Bill nodded. "There's just the Peachtree girl, and they're good friends."

"What about drugs?"

"He wouldn't even try coffee until he was in his twenties."

ELEVEN

"You were asking about March's friends. I forgot to mention Will. He was at the party, too."

"Tell me about him," I said.

"Will Adams is March's main ski buddy. Lives over on the East Side. Zephyr Cove. He's a computer guy. Fixes your computer when it crashes. He refers to himself as a rent-a-geek. He's the guy I was going to see with my laptop the day I saw you at the shopping center."

"Do you have any photos I can look at?"

"Of March and April? Sure. I also have a photo we took the day of my party. I'll get it." Bill hoisted himself up and hobbled over behind a couch to some shelves with electronic gear. He found some snapshots and was coming back when he caught his left crutch on the couch leg. He sprawled onto the floor, landing with a house-shaking thud.

I ran over and bent down to him. "Bill, are you okay? That was a helluva hard fall."

Bill turned his head toward me, shock and confusion in his eyes. "Yeah, I'm okay," he said in an airy voice.

"Let me help you up." I reached for his arm.

"No. Don't touch me."

"Easy, Bill. Just trying to help." I stayed bent, my arm in the air, wondering if he had major injuries.

"Get away. I'll get up myself."

I backed away. It was painful to watch Bill get to his elbows and knees, grimacing in pain. He scrabbled forward, braced ankles scraping the carpet as he worked his way to the end of the couch. He got his hands onto the couch and heaved himself over it, crutches flopping, grunting like a large animal. I turned away and went over to the window to look out. Spot had pulled his head inside the Jeep. I heard the clink of crutches and more grunting behind me. Eventually, came the sounds and sighs of someone sitting down after a grueling exercise. I turned and saw Bill sitting in his chair, his chest heaving as he breathed.

I sat down.

"I might be a crip," Bill said, his voice an angry growl, "but I can do the crabwalk, fend for myself. You use crutches, the whole world divides into two groups. One group ignores you, looks right the hell through you like you don't exist. The other group is falling all over themselves trying to open doors and helping you up stairs and spreading your damn peanut butter."

"I won't go near your damn peanut butter," I said.

Bill stared at me. He was still panting. He looked up at the TV. It showed the scoreboard. It was a rout. "I played college ball at Texas A&M. I was good. Not pro material. Too small. But they gave me a scholarship."

"That how you messed up your legs?"

Bill nodded vacantly. "Yeah. Got hit from the front when my feet were pretty well anchored." He looked down at the chessboard. "Ripped out the knee ligaments and broke the head of my left tibia up like it was made of cheap pottery. Lots of pieces. The docs got some of them back in place, but they said I wouldn't walk again without crutches. Here I am, decades later, still proving them right. Life can change in a big way in a very short moment. Most people don't realize that until it happens to them. Surprise. One minute you're a good athlete. The next minute the only game you'll ever play again is something like chess. Then you can re-enact how easy it is to lose important pieces, pieces you can never get back."

Bill was still breathing hard. When he calmed, he pulled the snapshot out of his pocket.

I took it from him. It showed six young people standing on

Bill's deck, snow piled high on the deck railing, the canal and a few snow-covered sailboats behind them. They were in a row with arms over each other's shoulders, boy, girl, boy, girl, boy, boy.

"Left to right, if I remember, is March, April, Will, Carmen, Packer and Paul."

March was a big kid, trim and fit like a strong swimmer, a mop of hair over a square face, a smile suitable for toothpaste commercials. He radiated confidence. His arm around his sister squeezed her with enthusiasm.

His twin sister was the opposite. She was a foot shorter, not particularly fit looking, with a darker complexion and no smile at all. Her hair was stringy straight and most people would never notice her in a group. Yet I could see a fierce intelligence in her eyes. It reminded me of when you see a coyote staring out of the forest and you realize that nothing escapes its notice.

The next person was Will. "You said Will's a computer geek. Is he self-employed?" In the picture he wore jeans and a sweatshirt, a scruffy haircut combed straight up and a grin like Honey G the retriever, happy and eager.

"I guess so, because when he fixed my firewall problem he had me write the check out to his name."

"What's he like?"

Bill thought a minute. "He's the easy guy, everyone's friend, no rough edges."

"Like March?"

"Yeah, except March was more passionate. When they hiked up Mt. Tallac to ski the cross, March was very driven about it, focused on every detail of what to bring and exactly where to hike and what the best strategy was for skiing down. Then he raved about it afterward. Whereas Will acted like it was no big deal."

"The image of a geek isn't usually someone so athletic that they ski the cross," I said.

"No."

"Will have a girlfriend?" I asked.

"Not real close, I don't think. I believe he and Carmen used to date. Now they're friends."

It was hard to see the details of Carmen's face in the picture, because she'd been moving, but her smile was huge. She was short and stout and looked like she was having the best time of her life.

"Tell me about Carmen. What's her last name?"

"Carmen Nicholas," he said, his voice suddenly warm. "A real sweetheart. We only just met at that party. She's been over here several times since and she's brought me little gifts each time. Homemade cookies, a refrigerator magnet with a team picture of the Cowboys, a bottle of my favorite barbecue sauce." He smiled. "I didn't think I'd ever get attracted to anyone again."

"She's what, about thirty years younger than you?"

"Yeah. Don't get me wrong. I'm not stupid. I know she'll never really love an old crip like me. But she likes me. And I can provide something for her. I have some money. That sounds crass, but it is a currency of relationships more often than people like to think."

"Her job?"

"She's a casino cocktail waitress at Harrah's. I've never visited her there, but I've kind of wondered about it because they wear those skimpy dresses and, frankly, I can't quite see Carmen like that. She's pretty plump, and she's got legs like Whitebark pines, thick and strong as hell. But who am I to judge?"

"What about Packer?" In the photo he looked like a punk rocker. Angular and sullen, with big bones and a heavy brow. He wore jeans so torn up it would be hard to pull them on without your foot going out the wrong hole. His black hair was greased straight back, and he had a pointed goatee below two lip rings.

"The guy at the snowboard shop. He used to be March's riding partner before March switched to skis. Packer's a rough kind of guy. Smokes a lot of pot, drinks a lot of beer, talks loud, doesn't care if people don't like him."

"His last name?"

"Mills. Packer Mills."

"Packer have a girlfriend?"

Bill frowned. "I don't understand all the questions about girl-friends and boyfriends. What is that with you? Does this have to do with the girl in the avalanche?"

"Some," I said. "But March's disappearance bothered you immediately. When I looked into it I found March and a second body. I would normally assume both deaths were accidental. But your immediate worry when March didn't come home makes me wonder otherwise. If either death wasn't accidental, then the first place to start looking is friends and family of the deceased. You want me to stop?"

"No, no. If March didn't die an accidental death, I want you to find out what happened." Bill looked away. "I don't know if Packer had a girlfriend. I don't think he was the steady type. More of a one-night-stand kind of guy."

"One-nighters with any of March's friends?"

Bill shook his head. "Not that March ever said."

"April?"

Bill flashed a look at me, fire in his eyes. "Absolutely, not."

"Why do you care? You don't like her."

"Right. I don't like her. Doesn't mean I want my niece doing it with that jerk." He grabbed a black pawn and moved it forward one square, setting it down hard enough that the rest of the pieces jumped sideways. "And don't even think about Carmen," he said with anger.

"You mentioned Paul," I said. He was on the right in the photo. He was the only one with light hair, so light it looked like it had been triple bleached.

"Yeah. Paul Riceman. A contractor up on Kingsbury Grade."

The TV, still silent, was showing a figure skating contest. Bill picked up the remote and turned it off.

"Paul and March ski together a lot?" I asked.

"Just now and then."

"Does Paul do much with the others?"

"Not to my knowledge. I don't think he'd even met Packer before he came to my party."

"Who else should I talk to? People who weren't at your party?"

"I invited all of March's best friends. But I remember one other girl who is a friend of April's. I guess she knows March, but not real well. Her name is Ada. I don't know the last name."

"She live in Tahoe?"

"I assume so," he said.

"How'd you meet her?

"April brought her to the house. A real firecracker. Smart as they make 'em."

"How would I contact her?" I asked.

"Through April, but April doesn't answer her phone."

"Anyone else you can think of?"

"No one comes to mind. Hey, it's getting late," he said, "and you haven't had any lunch. Can I make you a sandwich? I learned some good tricks in my club after all those years."

I stood. "No thanks. I'll save my appetite. Got a date with my sweetheart for dinner."

"That would be Street Casey? You can always bring her over here, if you want. I'm even better at dinner than I am at lunch."

"We'll do that some time. How do you know her name?"

Bill looked uncomfortable. "I don't know. I guess I must have heard it around somewhere. When I was asking the cops about you, maybe."

We looked at each other. I tried to see past his eyes, wet and dark as a seal's. I wanted to see the gears turning, servo-mechanisms whirring. Always, you look for the glitches, the grit stuck in the gear teeth, the broken connectors, the leaking pipes, the frayed cables, the stripped and shorted wires. But I couldn't see past the dark eyes, past the weary sadness.

"I'll give you a call when I learn something new," I said and left.

TWELVE

I called Street at her lab while I drove home and asked if she'd like dinner at my place.

"What's on the menu?"

"To be decided. But as you are a woman of elegant tastes, I should warn you that it would likely be humble."

"Humble works."

I next called the number Bill gave me for April's cell. Her voicemail answered, a quiet voice that nevertheless sounded tough and angry. "If you want to leave a message for April, go ahead. Maybe I'll call back."

"April, this is Detective Owen McKenna. I am investigating an avalanche at Emerald Bay that March was involved in. I have some questions you can help me with. Please give me a call." I left my number and hung up. I didn't want to say anything in my phone message that would suggest that March had died. Best to do that in person. But maybe Bill called April as soon as I left his house. Or maybe April heard about the slide from someone in Tahoe.

I had a good hour before Street would show up, and I'd been thinking about Ellie's perfectly trained dog.

"Spot," I said as I pulled up to our cabin and got out of the Jeep. He jumped out and looked at me, anticipation mixed with boredom. I could tell he was making those calculations that dogs use to predict the chances that their owner is about to produce food. "Do you want to emulate Honey G?" I said. "Do you pine for search-and-rescue fluency? Are you plagued by feelings of inadequacy?"

I opened the front door. Spot walked in, went directly over to his bed and lay down, ignoring me. The food calculations must have given him a negative answer.

"I think we should brush up on your tracking skills."

Spot didn't move except to sigh.

I'd been thinking about hand commands like Ellie used with Honey G. I was also envisioning a scent tracking exercise. I found an old rag and tore it in two. For a distinctive scent I rubbed the pieces with deodorant. I could hide one and use the other to scent Spot on. I stuffed them in my pocket.

To get Spot's attention I opened the cupboard over the fridge and pulled out my secret tube of potato chips. They were the manufactured kind, regular even discs of salty processed potatoes, perfect for edible Frisbee exercise.

Spot jumped up, suddenly alert. His eyes were intense and his ears made little adjustments like radar antennae tweaking their position for maximum reception.

"Outside before you drool," I said, opening the door.

Spot raced out in anticipation. I shot a disc out across the snow and he went after it like it held the key to eternal bliss. I heard his jaws snap and the chip was no more. Several rounds later it was clear that, as with humans, a dog would never stop eating them until the source was taken away. I put the chips back in their hiding place.

I fetched my gloves and went back outside. Spot sniffed my gloves, just in case I still had a chip left.

I began to roll up large snowballs and built three snowmen outside my cabin. One was near the deck, one by the parking pad, and one on the corner of my small lot. It was a difficult project because Spot kept jumping on my snowballs as I rolled them.

The snowmen were each separated by fifteen feet or more, but all were in view from the front door. I wanted Spot to see them all together.

Despite their forked-stick arms, I was pleased to have achieved such an impressive human likeness, with indentations for eyes, pine cones for ears, and protruding lumps of snow for noses.

When I was done, I called Spot over.

Because we'd been doing search-and-rescue work, I thought we should expand to suspect work.

I called him over to my front door and had him sit like any good student.

"The critical thing to remember in suspect apprehension," I told him, "is to get the correct person. Are you with me?"

Spot stretched his head forward and sniffed at my gloves again.

"Later, Spot. Now I want you to focus."

Spot stood up, stretched his front legs out so that his chest lowered down, but kept his butt in the air. His eyes looked demonic. He had snow on his nose and between his ears. His tail was a high-speed metronome. He didn't know what we were going to do, but he knew we were going to do something. Dogs like to do stuff.

"So watch me very carefully," I said. I was going to work on directing him with a hand command.

Spot lowered farther so that his chest was down in the snow. He was about to spring on me.

I turned away, hoping to cool his excitement and lessen the chance that he would leap his 170 pounds onto me. One of the problems I'd always had in training Spot was that he thought everything was about having fun. Good to have enthusiasm, but I sometimes envied trainers who worked with Goldens, Labs, German Shepherds and other breeds that took their doggie work more seriously than do Great Danes.

I was aware, however, of a small advantage that Danes have when doing both suspect apprehension and search and rescue. Suspect apprehension requires aggressiveness. Search and rescue requires gentleness. Some breeds, after they've been trained as police dogs, are not suited to search and rescue because they may forget that finding the victim is not the same as finding the suspect. The last thing a lost hiker needs is a dog finding them and then holding them with his teeth until his handler comes.

Great Danes are inclined to think that both activities are a game. And they need almost no aggressiveness to intimidate a suspect. Their size alone does the job.

"Okay, Spot," I said. I squatted down at the front door. It was still snowing lightly and the dormer over the door gave a little shelter. "Turn around," I said. I reached my arms around his chest and with some effort shifted him 180 degrees. "Spot, do you see the suspect? Do you?" I put some excitement and tension in my voice.

Spot turned his head and looked at me, his eyes intense. Finally, we were going to do stuff.

Kneeling next to Spot, our heads were the same height. I put my arm around his neck, grabbed his head with both hands and pointed him toward the snowman on the right. "There's the suspect! Do you see, Spot?" I tensed my hands on his head so that he was pointed directly at the right snowman. Then I extended my arm next to his head and pointed at the guilty snowman. I figured it would be obvious to him that I was indicating the snowman and not something near it because of the recent activity of building it. Even so, I was careful to make certain that Spot could not misunderstand which snowman I was pointing at. "Take down the suspect, Spot! Take him down!"

Spot shot away from me, his head pointed toward the snowman on the right. Three long fast leaps later he launched into the air on a rising arc. He opened his giant mouth and closed it on the snowman's head, ripping it off the snowman. His chest hit the snowman in a full body block and the snowman was smashed into a sorry lump of snow.

I felt a momentary smugness with my training success, but only until Spot got up running, picking up speed in a wide arc and closed in on the next snowman. He repeated his attack, destroying the second snowman, and then attacked the third with increasing precision. After that, he raced around in circles, pleased with his accomplishment.

I walked over to the lump of snow that had been the correct

suspect, beckoned Spot and praised him lavishly. Then we went to the second snowman and, using my scolding voice, I told Spot it was bad to kill innocent bystanders. Same for the third snowman, but I don't think Spot believed me considering that these were snow people and not quite like the real thing.

Undaunted, I proceeded to rebuild the snowmen. This time I buried one of the deodorant rags in the neck of the center snowman.

Back at the front door, we faced away from the snowmen. I took the remaining portion of the rag and let Spot sniff it.

"Do you have the scent, Spot? Do you?" He didn't seem to care.

I stuck the rag against his nose. "Smell it, Spot. Do you have the scent? Find the suspect!"

I made no hand signals. I just gave him a little smack on his rear and he took off. He shot straight for the center snowman, ripped off his head and crushed his body.

As he came around to ravage the second and third snowmen, I was already sprinting toward him, my arms out wide. I flapped them madly, feinting left, then right, pretending I could stop him if he wanted to make mischief.

I saw motion to the side and turned to see Street Casey pulling her VW beetle into the drive, tire chains on all four wheels.

Spot ran to meet her.

She got out, looking sleek and glamorous in her long black coat. She had on narrow-cut black pants and boots that were slim and stylish despite their non-skid soles for snow and ice. Her hair was pulled up and back in a bun and her gold earrings sparkled. She'd put on some makeup that emphasized her cheekbones. Her lipstick was the shade of red that said, kiss me, you idiot.

I dropped my arms to my side and stood panting.

Spot jumped around her, his greeting skills as enthusiastic as his other tricks.

"Oh, sweetheart," Street said to me. "You were practicing for flight? You have such nice technique, but I think you need a little more plumage for proper lift."

"We were practicing suspect apprehension," I said.

"Of course. I've seen it on TV, right? Cops see a bad guy, first thing they do is run and flap their arms like flightless turkeys."

"First thing. Scares the crap out of crooks."

Street walked to the front door and stood under the overhang. She looked like the perfect enticement to come inside and get out of the snow.

"If you were willing to take a break," she said, "from this flapping apprehension thing, we could go inside and have a glass of wine and commune with your fire before we commune with your dinner."

"My fire? Or the fire in the woodstove?"

Street wrapped her arms around me, her hands exploring. "Both," she said. She pulled the remaining deodorant-rag out of my pocket. She sniffed it, frowning. "Is this an apprehension accessory?"

"Bad guys often smell bad," I said.

"And good guys smell good?"

"Always."

"We better check," she said, opening the door and dragging me inside.

Later, I pulled two wine glasses from my collection of four.

"The fire was hot," Street said, "but we have a wine emergency." She wore my old terry cloth bathrobe. It wrapped around her nearly twice and dragged on the floor like a wedding dress. "I noticed your wine rack when I came in. You are completely out. I thought of going to the store right then, but your ardor was, um, quite spirited. I didn't want to interrupt."

"I can run to the store now if your post-coital needs are dire," I said.

"They are."

So I did.

THIRTEEN

First thing in the morning, Glenda Gorman from the Tahoe Herald walked into my office. She walked over to where Spot lay in the corner, gave him a pet, then sat down in one of my visitor's chairs and did a staccato rat-a-tat with her boots on the floor. "Burrrrrr, it's cold," she growled through clenched teeth. She wore a fake fur coat, fawn brown, which set off her blond curls. The curls were just so, as with the little eyeliner that emphasized the blue of her eyes. She looked good and she knew it.

"Some places, Glennie, twenty degrees in January is considered warm," I said.

"Where?"

"Bunch of M states. Minnesota. Montana. Maine. Michigan, Manitoba."

"Masochists," she said. "And isn't Manitoba a province?"

I shrugged. "Hard for us Tahoe types to keep track of anything east of Reno."

"Anyway, I've got some hot news. I received a phone call you'll want to know about. A guy claims he set the avalanche at Emerald Bay."

"Why do you think I want to know?"

"My business, ace reporter and all. You're working for the kid's uncle." She put her boots up on the edge of my desk and rocked her chair back, balancing on its rear legs. "I have informants all over this metropolis."

"You mean you're nosy as hell."

"Like I said, my business. I called Mallory, and he called the

El Dorado Sheriff's Department, and a sergeant named Bains called me back, and in exchange for info about my mysterious phone call, he told me that you went out with the dog trainer lady and her dog and found the bodies. Anyway, I gave Bains the number of the avalanche psycho off my caller ID. Then he pulled some strings or called in some favors and got a trace on the call in, like, five minutes. Amazing. Have you met this guy in person?"

"Yeah."

"Is he cute? He sounds cute."

"Ichabod Crane meets the Phantom of the Opera without his mask."

Glennie stood up and glowered at me across my desk. Her eyes were just barely higher than mine were sitting. "McKenna, you are not the only handsome guy in this town."

"You're right. George Clooney meets Pierce Brosnan."

"Better. Much better."

"What did the phone trace show?"

Glennie sat back down. "The avalanche psycho called from a pay phone in Reno. Bains told the Washoe Sheriff's Department. They dusted the phone, but it was wiped clean."

I nodded.

"Aren't you going to ask me what the guy said?"

"What did the guy say?"

Glennie pulled out a little notebook, green paper with a pink spiral binding at the top. "I take notes as I talk on the phone. I don't think I missed more than two words of what he said."

She flipped a few pages, then spoke. "The phone rang and I picked it up and said, 'Glenda Gorman.'"

"He said, 'I set the avalanche at Emerald Bay.'"

"I said, 'Who's calling?'"

"He said, 'None of your business. All you need to know is there's going to be more avalanches. Payback for ruining the pristine Tahoe landscape. Tahoe belonged to the Washoe Indians, and they kept Tahoe clean and pure for thousands of years. White man has nearly destroyed Tahoe in just a few decades. Now Tahoe will start destroying white man in a just a few weeks.'"

Glennie shut her notebook. "He hung up before I got a chance to ask another question."

"Can I copy your notes?"

Glennie thought about it. She handed me the notebook. I got up and made copies.

"What did his voice sound like?"

"His enunciation was spotty and inconsistent. He was trying to sound dumber than he was. Emerald was two syllables and he didn't pronounce the D. He just ran the words together. 'Em'ralbay.' When he said, 'None of your business,' he didn't pronounce the word of. Your was yer and business was missing the middle S. Like, 'None uh yer biness.'"

"You rattle that off like a linguist."

"Like I said, it's my job."

"He's trying to disguise himself," I said.

"Yeah. But he's doing a poor job. He sounds dumb but uses the word pristine. Just the kind of word that would be run-of-the-mill for a smart guy, so run-of-the-mill that he doesn't think to edit it out. Same with the word nearly."

"A dumb guy doesn't know the word nearly?"

"Knows, but doesn't use," Glennie said. "The biggest giveaway that it is a fairly smart guy is the self-conscious couplet, 'White man destroyed Tahoe in a few decades. Now Tahoe will destroy white man in a few weeks.' A dumb guy wouldn't think of that construction. He'd just say, 'You wrecked Tahoe, so I'm gonna kill your asses.'"

"So we've got a smart guy trying to sound dumb. But he's not really smart or he would have done a better job of sounding dumb."

Glennie nodded.

"You study speech characteristics when you could be home baking cookies," I said.

"Part of my business is to divine a person's inner workings by the way they talk."

"I like chocolate chip, if it matters," I said.

"You think women can curry favors with cookies?"

"Curry? I didn't think anyone under forty knew that word."

"It's my favorite spice. I could put it in your cookies."

"Maybe you should stick with linguistics. You think the payback thing is true? That he's some kind of eco-terrorist, like the Earth Liberation Front group that burns down buildings around the country?"

"Could be," Glennie said. "Could also be he just gets off making snow slide. Like a firestarter who tries to frame his kinkiness in some grander intellectual concept. I know that the Earth Liberation Front issues press releases taking credit for their burns. They haven't said anything about this avalanche. For that matter, we don't actually know that anyone caused the avalanche, do we?"

"No," I said. "I'm going to try to find out."

"Let me know? I'm late. I gotta run."

My phone rang and I answered it. It was Sergeant Bains.

"Hey Bains," I said. Glennie was at my door. She stopped.

"You were right," he said in my ear. "The girl in the slide was murdered before the avalanche ever started. By suffocation. But the guy was killed by the avalanche."

"You got an explanation that fits?" I said.

"Not even close. Hey, I'm not far away. You going to be there? I'll give you the details in person. Besides, I love to take my cruiser across the state line. It always tweaks the Nevada deputies when they see us on their turf."

"I'll be here."

Glennie was still at the door as I hung up. "That was Sergeant Bains?" she said. "George Clooney meets Pierce Brosnan?"

I nodded.

She looked at her watch again. "Damn, I gotta go," she said and hurried out.

FOURTEEN

The morning sun had risen enough that it was now shining on the left side of my desk. I took the little poinsettia Street had given me and slid it into the sunlight. Its leaves were as brilliant as fresh-polished fire engines. It shimmered with joy.

A tiny triangle of sun missed the desk and poinsettia and hit the bottom of the wall by the door. Spot spied it, got up, walked over and sniffed it. He lay down hard against the wall so that the patch of sun shined on him. My door opened. Sergeant Bains walked in and saw Spot. "Sorry to interrupt his nap. Not like he's upset, though."

"Like a poinsettia in sunlight, he shimmers with joy."

Bains looked at me. "I don't buy you're a poet."

"What was the giveaway?" I said. "Shimmers?"

"Probably got that word from your girlfriend. She's the bug scientist, right? The medical examiner in Sac wants to speak to her. Some kind of bug question."

"Did you ID the girl?"

"Yeah. A Lorraine Simon from San Fran. Lived in one of those mansions over by the Presidio. Twenty-two years old. The girl, not the house. I drove down last night to inform her parents. They were out. They have a baby-sitter, sits for their Pomeranians. I told him a white lie about some stolen property that belonged to his employers. In the fifteen minutes I waited for them to come home I learned more than you'd want to know about Lorraine's parents.

"Girl's old man is a guy named Samuel Simon. Wife is

Clarice. Simple Simons they ain't. They own a company that does hydro-dynamic research. Under contract to ship builders. Something about laminar flow. Don't ask me what that means. They employ eighteen engineers. And I almost forgot. In their spare time, he's a radiologist and she's an attorney. And, oh yeah, she's served two terms in the state legislature. Lunches with the Guv. And the doc is on the board of one of those cancer foundations."

Bains hitched up one trouser leg and perched his thigh on the corner of my desk. "Finally, they came home and I told them about their daughter."

"How'd they take it?"

"Mom was pretty strong, dad went shaky and the dog-sitter had a meltdown. Dr. Simon had to give him a sedative. Then he popped some pills himself."

"You learn what Lorraine was doing in Tahoe?"

"Only that she'd graduated from college and was taking a year off. Dad's words. Snowboarding and mountain biking."

"What does mom say?"

"I couldn't tell. Mom talks like one of those life coaches. Who knows what it means. Stuff like Lori was self-actualizing her true potential, and she was flowering, and she was on a spirit quest."

"You tell them how she died?"

"Earlier in the day, when I talked to the ME, he said his findings were preliminary, so I just told the parents their daughter's body was found in an avalanche."

"They say anything revealing?"

Bains shook his head. "Nothing. What about the uncle of the kid? Esteban. You talked to him more than I have so far. He seemed awfully tense to me."

"Esteban's wired tight as they come. He'd redline any kind of meter you strapped on him. I think it's his frustration at being handicapped. He was an athlete as a young man and he was crippled by an accident on the gridiron. He's still angry as hell. I think his handicap contributed to his reaction to his nephew going missing."

"And now that he knows his nephew is dead, how's he reacting to that?"

"He seems to blame himself. He said March suddenly got interested in investing, and he thinks that means the kid was into something bad. Esteban feels that he should have done something about it. He had an anxiety attack when I was there."

"What's the thing about investing?" Bains was fishing.

"He only said that March asked him about financial planners and it stood out as strange because March wasn't the planning type."

"You gonna share when you find out anything else?"

"Bains, never mind that I'm working a case in your territory, for twenty years I was a cop same as you. I know that I-help-you is the best way to make for you-help-me."

Willie Nelson started singing On The Road Again out of Bains's shirt pocket. Bains pulled out his cell phone.

"Bains," he said.

I heard a woman's voice talking.

"Thanks," Bains said and hung up. He pulled his radio off his belt, inspected it and swore. He turned to me. "Radio isn't working. Office called to say there was a big slide on the Nevada side. Hit a section of road near Sand Harbor. A witness said a car was buried."

FIFTEEN

I called Diamond Martinez.

"Have you heard about a slide at Sand Harbor?"

"Yeah. A possible vehicle involved. The Washoe Sheriff's Department will have more in the morning."

"Coffee at my cabin?"

"If I can get up your road. Weather report says another foot by morning. How many is that this month? Twenty feet?" Diamond sounded disgusted.

"Good thing it keeps settling. You on duty in the morning?"

"Yeah."

"Then your Douglas County SUV should be up to it."

We hung up.

We were in one of those wet weather patterns. El Nino and La Nina were doing their courtship dance out in the Pacific. To impress the girl, El Nino hurled a blast of moisture at the coast of Northern California every twenty-four hours. The rain bumped across the coastal ranges, dropped down for a quick wet sprint over the Central Valley, then made the long climb up the west slope of the Sierra. Frostbitten by the ascent, the storm clouds got angry and lashed Tahoe with snow. I doubt La Nina even noticed.

I leaned back and put my feet up on the desk to think. The phone rang. I stopped thinking.

"Owen McKenna."

"Mr. McKenna, my name is April Carrera." She sounded tentative. Frightened. With stuffed-up sinuses like she'd just gotten over a bout of crying and cranked herself up to call me.

"Thanks for calling, April. Your uncle is worried."

She took a moment to answer. "Uncle Bill doesn't worry about me. He exudes anxiety about me."

"Is that why you went to the Dominican Republic?"

"Did Uncle Bill tell you that's where I went?"

"That's what March told him," I said. "Are you there now?"

Another pause. "Yeah. But don't ask what town. You might tell Uncle Bill, the last person on earth I'd want to know."

"April, have you heard about your brother?"

"Yes. March died in an avalanche. Uncle Bill said it on my voicemail. That's sensitive, isn't it? A real soft touch, ol' Bill. 'Hey, April, where you been, you never return my calls, by the way, March was killed in an avalanche.'" She started crying.

"I'm sorry, April," I said. "If there's anything I..."

"If there's anything you can do... I guess I've heard that one before, haven't I? Everybody's sorry. Everybody wants to help. Yeah, well it's too late for that, isn't it?"

"I understand your anger."

"No, you don't! And don't ever think you understand anything else about me, either! Do I make myself clear?" She hung up.

Later, I was driving past the shopping center near Stateline when I noticed an Escalade that looked familiar, so I pulled in. Bill Esteban was sitting in the front seat. The engine was running, and he was looking away from me, toward the supermarket. He made no moves to suggest he was going into the store or had just come out.

It seemed peculiar to me, so I stopped behind a large panel van and watched.

Bill continued to stare at the doors of the supermarket.

After a couple of minutes I noticed him shift. He moved his head as if watching someone. Then he shifted into reverse and began to back out of his space.

I pulled out and followed him. Spot was lying down sleeping in back, so I wasn't obvious.

Bill drove down to the end of the parking row and stopped. I stopped where I could see him. The only person clearly in his view was a young woman who was loading a baby into a car seat in the back of an old beat-up Chevy. She shut the back door and began putting her groceries into the trunk. I couldn't see her well, but she appeared to be in her late teens or early twenties. She was very small, probably weighing 100 pounds. Except for her Asian heritage, her size and apparent fragility reminded me of Lori Simon, the girl whose body we'd found in the avalanche.

The girl pushed her empty cart through the snow and left it in the cart drop-off area, then got in her car. It started with a large puff of blue smoke. She backed out and drove away.

Bill followed her. I followed Bill.

The girl drove across Lake Tahoe Boulevard and took the back streets behind the motels to a small trailer park. There she transferred her baby and the groceries into a small trailer that had been badly remodeled into two half-trailer apartments, with a door for each side and a scar on the outside where a second bathroom had been grafted side-to-side onto the original bathroom.

I stayed well back, watching Bill as he watched the girl. When the girl was inside, Bill drove away. I followed him as far as Tahoe Keys Boulevard where he turned to go home.

I called Bains as I turned around.

When he answered, I said, "I just saw Bill Esteban at the supermarket. He watched a young girl with a child come out of the store. When she drove away, he followed at a distance, then watched from a distance as she unloaded her baby and groceries into her trailer apartment. After she was inside he drove away."

"What's your read?" Bains said.

"The girl didn't know he was there. Maybe they know each other, maybe not. But he didn't just follow the first girl who came out of the store. He was watching and waiting for her."

"So if he knows her, he could be checking to make sure she got home okay," Bains said.

"Yeah."

"Or he could be a stalker."

"That, too," I said.

"If he's a stalker and the girl hasn't had any contact from him, that's a problem for us, huh?" Bains said.

"Yeah. No crime watching someone in public. No crime following someone in public."

"Anything you notice about her?" Bains asked. "She a hottie or something?"

"No. Only thing that strikes me is she's tiny. Like Lori Simon, the girl in the avalanche."

I gave Bains the girl's address and description and we hung up.

Spot and I made a quick trip to Carson City for some things you can't get in Tahoe, then went to Street's condo for dinner. Spot lay in front of her fire. I'd brought a Fat Cat cab that I got at Trader Joe's. I opened it and poured half the bottle into Street's fancy wine glasses, the ones that hold about sixteen ounces each.

We sat in front of the fire and tasted the wine while I told Street about April calling me and oozing grief-stricken, angry-young-woman frustration. Then I told her about Esteban following the girl from the grocery store.

"You've got two people dead in an avalanche and maybe more in the Sand Harbor slide and a stalker client whose remaining niece is estranged from him, and she's yelling at you for calling and saying you care. Great business, this detecting."

"Yeah."

I moved to one of the barstools in her kitchen when Street began to cook. She was sautéing chicken strips in olive oil with garlic. "I'm making chicken stir fry," Street said, glancing at the Fat Cat cab. "Some people think a cab is too hearty for chicken."

"Those are the same people who think you can't go out running unless you're wearing a shiny skintight running uniform."

"But I wear a shiny skintight running uniform when I run."

"Something I've always wondered about," I said.

"You want me not to wear it?"

"No, you should definitely wear it," I said.

"Why, if it's part of the conformist world of uniforms?"

"Next time you put on your uniform, look in the mirror."

"Are you saying that people who look, uh, trim, should wear shiny skintight uniforms even as you demean their use? But that's ageist and sexist and fatist."

"Fatist?"

"Okay, awkward word," she said. "Anyway, people should be able to wear whatever they want."

"Absolutely," I said.

"But you..." Street stopped. "Oh, got it. You wear a baggy old sweatshirt when you run and you drink a hearty cab when you eat chicken stir fry. And the people in the uniforms are the ones who make up rules about behavior."

"Always been my observation," I said. "But you should stay with the uniform even if you eschew the rule-making." I drank some more Fat Cat. I gave it an eight on my taste-to-cost scale. Street had touched her wine with her lips and maybe even her tongue, but I couldn't see that the level had dropped in her glass.

She added strips of green pepper and red pepper and yellow pepper. She arranged the strips in a decorative pattern in the pan, then held it out for me to look at. The food was a culinary kaleidoscope and smelled like heaven. Then she stirred in the strips.

Street began talking about April's phone call.

"Many discomforts between people are the result of a structural problem, not ill will," Street said. "April was obviously hurting and feeling alone, and she snapped at you on the phone. It doesn't mean you did anything wrong. And it doesn't mean she is a bad person."

"Thank you, Dr. Casey."

"Okay, so my specialty is insects. It doesn't mean I can't pronounce on topics outside my field."

"But I'd pay more attention to your pronouncements if you put on the uniform."

"So you could take it right off? Men don't make any sense."

"Never said we did."

SIXTEEN

Heavy snow was coming down at a 30-degree angle when I creaked and groaned my way out of bed. My deck had accumulated another foot of snow on it since I'd shoveled the night before. My world's-greatest-view across Lake Tahoe had been reduced to the deck railing.

My breath made clouds in the frigid air of the living room. My indoor wood supply was down to two pieces of kindling and one split log. All the rest of my fuel was outside, relishing the frozen storm.

I decided I wasn't that brave first thing out of bed. So I bunched up a pile of newspaper in the woodstove, criss-crossed the two sticks and munched the chunk of Lodgepole pine onto the pile. I struck a wooden match under the newsprint, then swung the stove door so that it was open only one-half inch. My insufficient pile would fail any Boy Scout survival-fire merit-badge test. But what the Boy Scouts don't tell you is that a stove with good draft and a not-quite-shut door will turn damp newspaper and a green log into a blast furnace in a few minutes.

With the growing rush of air fueling the fire, I took the three steps to my kitchen nook and pushed the button on the coffee maker I'd loaded the night before.

Spot hadn't budged. He was curled up in his corner. His nose was under his right front paw, just visible under the edge of the big polyester sleeping bag I'd flopped over him the night before. He hadn't moved since.

"Hey, largeness," I mumbled.

I thought I could hear him breathing, but otherwise there was no sign of life. Great Danes have short hair and belong in large houses with central heating, not 500-square-foot log cabins with woodstoves. I knew Spot would eventually unfurl when the temperature in the cabin climbed from Tahoe to Tahiti.

I poured coffee into a mug that Street had given me. The mug had lettering that said, "Bugs Love Global Warming." Spot probably would, too.

I drank coffee. Spot slept. Someone knocked on the door. Spot didn't budge. Great watchdog.

I opened the door.

Diamond stood in a ski parka, hood pulled down to his eyes, drawstring tightened under his chin. "I grew up in Mexico City," he said, shivering. "If you were to take me in out of this weather, I might be your friend for life."

I held up my mug for him to read the lettering.

"Me, too," Diamond said.

Diamond sat with me at my little kitchen table. I gave him coffee. He never took off his jacket, or even his hood, as he drank it. The snow on top of his hood was melting. It dripped into his coffee.

"On duty?" I said.

He nodded.

"Can't see your uniform under the parka."

He nodded again. "Can't see your dog under his sleeping bag. They make heaters. Burn natural gas or propane. Keep entire houses warm at night."

"Woodstove has worked ever since Ben Franklin," I said. "All I'm missing is fuel that isn't caked with ice and snow." I set about preparing a morning feast. Some days I have three cups of coffee for breakfast. Others, cold ones, I get serious at the cooktop. I put burger and onion into a fry pan and turned the propane burner on high. Diamond didn't even glance at my efforts, unaware that my culinary dance moves could probably get me an audition for Rachael Ray's TV show. A few minutes later I cracked two eggs and mixed them into the burger and onion.

Then I spooned the mixture out of the fry pan and onto tortillas, added cheddar cheese and salsa and rolled them up.

"Smells like Mexican cooking," Diamond said.

"Breakfast burrito?" I said. "Got an extra. You want one?" I put the burritos into the microwave.

"Welsh, Scottish type like you," Diamond said, "I'd think you'd be frying up some haggis with bashed neeps on the side and laver bread for your carbs."

"What's all that?"

"Sausage made of offal and cooked in a sheep's stomach, mashed turnips on the side and seaweed pancake to give you energy."

"You mean offal like I think you mean it?"

"Sure. Ears, lips, noses. Scots are frugal."

"I'll stick with Mexican." I pulled out the burritos, put them on plates and shoved one toward Diamond. "Coffee?"

He nodded.

I poured another cup and slid it toward him.

Diamond attacked his burrito. His hood was pulled down so far I could barely see him eat.

"You got that much enthusiasm for haggis and bashed neeps and laver bread?" I said.

Diamond shook his head as he chewed.

"Then why do you know about food from my ancestors' part of the world?"

"Like to eat," Diamond mumbled. "Like to learn about food. Helps me find out which foods not to eat."

"More you learn, more you realize that Mexican food is better than most, right?" I said.

"Born and raised in Mexico City. What do you expect." Diamond finished his burrito.

I was still on my second bite. "You eat like Spot," I said.

Spot lifted his head from his sleeping bag and looked up. His nostrils were flexing.

"What did you find out about the avalanche at Sand Harbor?" I asked.

"Not big, but brutal if you're the guy driving the old Blazer."

"Somebody got squashed?"

"May as well drop boulders on him," Diamond said. "Those other burritos for the hound?"

"I'll use some to flavor his sawdust chunks."

"The rest?"

I put two more burritos in the microwave, then slid one onto Diamond's plate when it was done. He bent over it, his hood still obscuring his face.

"They get an ID?"

"Yeah," Diamond said through a full mouth. "Guy in the Blazer was from Incline Village. Someone named Astor Domino. Funny names you gringos got. Sounds like the name of that football stadium."

"Learn anything about him?"

"Just that he was a student at Sierra Nevada College in Incline Village."

SEVENTEEN

Diamond left after breakfast.

I called Bill.

"Did March have a friend named Astor Domino?" I asked.

"Never heard the name before, why?"

"He died in a slide at Sand Harbor, yesterday."

"Christ. It's murder, isn't it?"

"Maybe," I said. "I'll call you when I know more."

I wanted to pursue Astor Domino, but Street and I had an appointment in Sacramento. Spot and I picked her up at her condo, and we were in palm tree country two hours later.

We met the Medical Examiner in the Sacramento morgue, a modern building that looked more like the home of a high-tech medical company than a place to examine bodies.

"Jack Kylie," the man said, extending his hand. He had a small nose and narrow-set eyes that sat above and behind a jaw so broad and heavy, it was like looking at a super tanker head-on, with the bridge dwarfed by the ship's prow.

"I appreciate your coming down from Tahoe," he said. "As you may know, El Dorado County lacks sufficient morgue facilities. So they contract with Sacramento County for morgue service when their facilities are full."

"Sergeant Bains said the young woman was suffocated," I said.

"Yes." The doctor looked at Street. "You two aren't squeamish, right? No, of course you wouldn't be. Let's go into the cooler. I'll show you what I've found. And I have a forensic-ento-mologist question for Dr. Casey as well."

He took us down a hall and through a door with a sign above it that said, "As you are, we once were. As we are, you will be."

We went into a room where we donned gloves and masks, hair covers, goggles and white coats. The doctor then took us through a series of large rooms that looked like those in a modern hospital. The floors were polished tile and the walls were painted white. There were many of the tools and instruments of a stan-dard operating room. Everywhere were specialized machines from electronic and analytical devices to forklifts for lifting carts with bodies on them.

"We have six autopsy bays plus an infectious disease room and," Dr. Kylie paused with a little flourish as he opened a door, "a homicide room."

The area was chilled and was permeated with the sickly odors of death. There were two rolling carts draped with white sheets like a painter's drop cloths carefully arranged over couches.

Kylie flipped on some bright lights and rolled one of the carts out to the center of the room. He pulled back the cloth revealing the girl's head and neck.

Although she was grayish white and looked very much dead, I tried to imagine life in the thin fragile face, a musical laugh, a furi-ous frown, the imperious arch of the well-shaped eyebrows.

"Here's where I began my investigation," the doctor said, pointing to the girl's mouth. "The young woman's lips and nose show some abrasion and signs of nascent frostbite from when she was still alive." He lifted her top lip. The girl had beautiful teeth. "Here, too, we see frostbite and abrasion on her upper gums. On her forehead are light contusions and what looks like faint marks on her temples. The marks would be consistent with an attacker wearing thick gloves.

"The cause of death was asphyxia, and there was a small amount of water in her lungs. I believe someone held her down on her back in the snow, perhaps with a leg over her arms and chest to keep her from moving. He then held her head like this, with his left hand, fingers across her forehead, thumb gripping her temple." The doctor demonstrated with his hand across the girl's forehead. "I say 'he,' because few women have hands large enough to span this distance. With his right hand he held a glove-full of snow and smothered her."

I said, "An unsophisticated attempt to make it so he could put her body in the way of an avalanche and hope we'd think the avalanche killed her?"

"Yes." Kylie pulled the cloth back over her head and moved to her other side. He lifted the cloth to expose her arm. "I found contusions on her arm, such as the bruising that might occur from her struggles while she was being suffocated. The marks are very faint, no doubt because of the padding of the killer's gloves and of her insulated jacket. The girl is quite small, five-three and one hundred ten pounds. A strong, average-sized man could have suffocated her easily."

"Were there other injuries?" I asked.

"Yes, and they add credence to my scenario. She has two broken ribs on her back under her left scapula. Her jacket was ripped in that area and there were bits of bark in the fabric as if she'd struck a tree. But the breaks came postmortem. You know of course that our bodies don't die all at once. Long after the heart stops and brain activity ceases, our digestive system is still working on our last meal, our fingernails and hair are still growing, et cetera. But these rib fractures show no physiological reaction to trauma in the bone or the surrounding flesh. No bruising, no blood clotting, no beginning stages of tissue repair. I think these ribs were broken in the avalanche, but I think she had been dead for at least several hours or even most of a day prior to the slide."

We were quiet a moment.

"You said you had a question for me?" Street said.

"Yes, yes, thank you, I almost forgot." Kylie opened a cabinet and pulled out a small glass jar with a medium-sized bug in it. "I was hoping you could identify this."

Street held it up to the light. "It looks like a Boat-backed Ground beetle. A type of insect from the order Coleoptera and a member of the family Carabidae."

"Oh good," Kylie said. "This is a gift to me that you recognize this. What can you tell us about it?"

"I'm not positive of the exact species. But it is a predatory beetle. Many beetles eat plant material or decomposing matter or even dung, but this carabid is a carnivore. He attacks and eats animals."

"By animals, you mean other insects," Kylie said.

"It's true that many carabids eat insects. But in this case, I mean animals. Snails, in particular. He finds a snail, dives inside its shell opening and attacks and eats the resident. His larger cousins can actually crush the shells of small snails and eat them without crawling inside. Many of these eat slugs as well."

Street set the jar down. "Carabids are nowhere near as scary looking as huge beetles like the Elephant Stags, but they are nevertheless the T-Rexes of the beetle world. Even in larval form, they will hide in a burrow, and if an insect comes near, they will jump out, impale the creature with their knife-like mouth parts, and then eat it."

"Tell me," Kylie said, his face showing some discontent, "not to segue from my questions, but are these beetles very rare?"

Street laughed. "I hate to tell you, but they are everywhere. Fortunately, they focus on small prey. They won't hurt you unless you poke a finger in their face."

Dr. Kylie was nodding without smiling. "I have another question about this beetle, although this is a bit of a reach. To me the beetle smells unpleasant, perhaps somewhat bitter and of course, now that it has been dead for some time, there is also the smell of decomposition. However, when I first found it, there was a very biting smell, very caustic. I couldn't imagine that the beetle could have produced the smell, but if the smell came from something else, then I should really have a puzzle to solve. Have you ever heard about unusual smells from these carabids?"

"Yes," Street said. "In addition to vicious offensive techniques, certain carabids, the Bombardier beetles, for example, have a clever and effective defensive tactic. If they feel threatened, they will squirt hot acid at you from their anal glands. And, yes, the acid has a strong smell. The liquid vaporizes into noxious cloud puffs that are quite effective at driving predators off."

Kylie looked a little pale. "But you didn't think this was a Bombardier beetle. Are you saying a Boat-backed Ground beetle would also squirt hot acid?"

"Not that we know of."

"Then perhaps I'm missing something."

"Sorry," Street said. "I should back up and explain something. Entomologists have no idea how many beetle species there are. We do know that beetles are the most common form of life on the planet. We've identified a few hundred thousand species. Based only on those, we can say that every fourth species of life on earth is a beetle. But here's the catch. Many entomologists, perhaps most of them, estimate that there are ten or twenty times as many beetle species out there as what we've cataloged. If that is even close to true, then there are more kinds of beetles than all other kinds of life, plant or animal, added together. Maybe two times as many. Maybe four times as many."

"You're saying that beetles are the most successful manifestation of life on the planet." Kylie raised one eyebrow.

"By numbers of species, yes," Street said. "Where I'm going with all of this is that it leaves us with an important implication. If most of the species have yet to be identified, then it's very likely that there are uncountable kinds of characteristics that we haven't yet observed. So if you have a beetle that looks like a Boat-backed Ground beetle and it fires hot acid like a Bombardier beetle, I, along with many of my colleagues, won't doubt you. We'll just think that you've probably found a species that hasn't been cataloged yet."

"Are carabids normally found in Tahoe?" Kylie asked.

"Carabids are everywhere on earth, but I don't think this particular guy is in Tahoe. Judging by his narrow mouth parts, I think he dives into a type of snail that only lives at lower elevations. Where did you find him?"

"In the poor girl's lungs."

EIGHTEEN

"I hate to think of this bug crawling around inside the girl's lungs," I said. "You think she inhaled him?"

"I'd guess not," Dr. Kylie said. "If she had, she would have tried to violently cough him back out. There was no sign of that. I think he came postmortem."

"He crawled in?"

"I think so." The doctor turned to Street. "Would this kind of bug do that? Crawl into a moist dark tunnel?"

"I've learned that there is no behavior that the odd bug won't do. But I wonder why he didn't crawl back out."

"She was moved. Her neck was flexed a little, collapsing his escape route. He died in her lungs."

"So the girl was killed with snow," I said. "Perhaps there was sufficient snow at a lower elevation where this bug resides. But she could have been killed in Tahoe and then the body was brought down to a lower elevation. Street, are these bugs found relatively near Tahoe?"

"I haven't studied them, so I can only guess. The snails these bugs are after are plentiful in temperate soils. One might find them in the foothills, as high as two or three thousand feet of elevation."

"What about the possibility of the bug hitching a ride up to Tahoe?" I said. "Let's say the murderer kills the girl and puts her in the trunk of a car where this bug has been hitchhiking."

"I think it's possible," Street said. "If this bug were brought up to the cold of Tahoe, it might not die in a somewhat-warm car trunk. And it might seize the opportunity to get warm inside the mouth and throat of a fresh corpse."

I turned to Kylie. "Jack, have you come to any conclusions about the time of death?"

"The condition of the body suggests she was killed approximately eighteen to twenty-four hours prior to being frozen. The time range is primarily due to not having knowledge of the body's temperature during that period. I should point out that while her body likely became substantially frozen when it was left in the avalanche path at Emerald Bay, it is also possible that it was very chilled or partially frozen a few days before that."

"Couldn't she have been killed even earlier and her body frozen shortly after that, preserved this whole time?"

"No, because even a frozen body undergoes dessication. Freeze drying, if you will. I see none of that." Kylie pulled out another jar with a few white dots floating in a clear liquid. He handed the jar to Street. "I found these in her sinus cavity."

"So there was some blow fly activity," Street said, holding the jar up to the light.

"Apparently. Although I must confess to being very negligent in how I handled these. I carefully collected every one I found and preserved them."

"In a solution that kills them," Street said, still looking at the jar.

"Yes. Only later did I remember the importance of keeping some alive so that the species can be identified after they mature. I'm so sorry."

"Don't worry," Street said. "Handling entomological evidence is still a young science. Many coroners are not up to speed on it. Do you have a lens?"

Kylie found a magnifier and handed it to her.

Street studied them under the lens. "These are first instar maggots. At eighty degrees, a blow fly will likely lay eggs on a body within ten minutes of death. The eggs will often hatch within ten to thirty hours. The maggots will grow from the first instar stage to the second within another ten to forty hours. At the earliest, first instar maggots can grow to this size in approximately twenty-four hours from the time the fly laid the eggs.

"Of course, in the middle of winter it is hard to find eighty degree weather anywhere close to Tahoe, but a nice warm winter day in Sacramento can get up to seventy. And the sinus provides a warm environment for several hours after death, quite insulated from the weather. If the body had been down in the Central Valley, and a blow fly had done her duty and got into the girl's nostrils very quickly, then these maggots could have hatched and grown to this small size in twenty-four hours. Probably not less time. Very likely more time."

"Makes sense," Kylie said. "Then the low end of your estimate based on the maggots and the high end of my estimate based on the state of the body match up at about twenty-four hours."

Street nodded.

"There is one more bit of evidence," Kylie said. "On the back of the girl's left hand and on the palm and fingertips of the right was dirt. But her fingernails were clean. The pattern would be consistent with dumping a body on its left side in the dirt. Like this." He demonstrated a sideways sleeping position, on his left side, with the back of the left hand and the palm of the right hand striking the ground. "If she'd been alive and conscious, she would have clenched her right hand and gotten dirt under her fingernails. With no dirt under her fingernails, I surmise that she was dead when she hit the ground."

Kylie pulled a glass slide out of a drawer and slid it into a microscope. "There was only enough dirt on her hands to leave stains, but I collected what I could." He gestured toward the microscope. "If you could have a look, Street?"

Street sat down at the scope. "I know what to look for in bugs," she said. "But I'm not very dirt savvy."

"Just tell me what you think," Kylie said.

"There are some very tiny grains of what look like crushed granite particles," Street said. "But most of what I see is much darker and has fibrous components. It looks like humus, decomposed plant and animal material. The portion of the soil that gives it the most nutrients and makes it fertile." Street turned from the microscope. "Humus is where one finds carabids."

"Thanks," Kylie said. "That confirms my thoughts."

"What about the male victim?" I asked.

"That case is much simpler," Kylie said. "He died from blunt-force trauma to the chest. The damage to his chest was consistent with hitting a tree. The blow ruptured his aorta. Brain death would occur within a few minutes. The back side of his body, especially his back and the back side of his head, shows a great deal of snow abrasion such as what would happen if an avalanche hurled him into a tree and then continued to flow over him from behind."

"So his death appears to be accidental," I said.

"Unless someone can play God with avalanches, yes."

NINETEEN

"You think that someone caused the two avalanches?" Street said as we drove back to Tahoe.

It was raining in the Central Valley, a very light drizzle that had me switching the wipers from a constant sweep of the windshield to intermittent and back again. Spot slept in the back seat, something he often does when it is raining and he can't see well out the window.

"It's possible. Glennie's caller claimed to have set the first one."

"Is starting an avalanche that easy?"

"Maybe. I've read that avalanche victims cause most of the slides that kill them. Their ski tracks cut the slope and release the snow. But that doesn't mean it would be easy to start a slide whenever and wherever you wanted. You'd have to have a slope that was ready to slide. And if you wanted to increase the odds of starting a slide, you'd have to use explosives the way ski patrollers do at the ski areas."

"The victim at Sand Harbor was in his car," Street said. "In theory, the killer need only force the car to stop, then trigger the avalanche. But how would it work? Does the killer wait up on the mountain, shoot out the victim's tires to make him stop, and then toss the explosive to start the slide? Shooting the tires on a moving car would be difficult. Getting a slide to be so precise that it buries the stopped car seems equally difficult. And that still wouldn't explain how March Carrera died, out of his truck, wrapped around a tree."

We were silent, thinking.

Street continued, "Doctor Kylie's discovery that the girl was killed by suffocation and later positioned to be in the avalanche breaks the pattern. Why would that be? If Glennie's caller were telling the truth, that the slides he is causing are some kind of eco-terrorist payback, then it would imply that March Carrera was accidentally caught in the slide. But the suffocated girl suggests that whomever triggered the Emerald Bay avalanche was the girl's killer, which suggests that murder rather than eco-terrorism was the goal. In which case, you need to find a connection between March Carrera, Lorraine Simon and Astor Domino."

Street drew a shape in the condensation on the inside of her side window. It looked like a mountain. Then she used the palm of her hand to sweep a big path down the center. "Unless the girl's death and the mens' deaths were caused by two men," she continued. "The girl's death would be unrelated to the others, and her killer just happened to dump her body where the second perpetrator set his avalanche."

Street turned to me. "What do you think?"

"I'm trying to keep track of your ideas, but I ran out of neurons."

"That's a guy problem, huh?"

"No doubt," I said.

"You should ask Mare about the avalanches," Street said.

"I'll do that."

I dropped Street off at her condo and headed up the long private drive to my cabin. There was a plain envelope push-pinned to my front door. I went inside, fed and watered Spot, then opened the envelope. There was a single sheet of paper inside, computer printed, Times Roman, double-spaced.

> McKenna – Our dispute with the people
> destroying Tahoe doesn't concern you.
> Stay out of it. If you don't you will find
> yourself in the center of future battles.

I called Diamond and told him about it.

"Did you ask your neighbors if anybody saw the person who delivered it?"

"They're all gone at their primary homes."

"You sure?" Diamond asked.

"No tire tracks on the road going past my cabin for two weeks except the guy who plows."

"You want me to send the note to the crime lab?"

"It's your call to spend taxpayer dollars," I said. "I'd bet there are no prints or any other evidence on it. Looks like standard paper and envelope and push pin available from any office supply store. I'll hang onto it."

"Okay," Diamond said. "Keep your head down."

TWENTY

Street had reminded me about our avalanche-expert friend.

Mariposa Pearl had been a ski patroller at Heavenly Ski Resort ever since she moved up from Big Bear, outside of L.A., six years ago. Her friends knew her as a sweet, feminine, 29-year-old kid with a sophisticated sense of humor.

But to the rest of the world, at six-two and one hundred ninety pounds of solid muscle, she was Pearl-The-Powerhouse. Once, when Street and I were skiing with her, we saw two skiers recklessly speeding on one of the beginner runs. They ran over the skis of some little kids taking a group lesson. They came so close to those children, it was a miracle none of them was hit, a collision that could have been fatal.

When Mariposa caught up to the speeders at the base of the chair, it turned out they were college-aged and linebacker-sized and they'd had more than a few beers. They were as belligerent as they were big, but after Mare gave them a dose of Pearl Power, they meekly handed over their lift tickets, red-faced, embarrassed, and possibly even chagrined at their stupidity.

I dialed her number at eight o'clock that evening. She answered on the third ring.

"Mmm, mello?" she mumbled through a full mouth.

I remembered that her hobby was cooking. "Owen McKenna calling to make sure you're getting enough vegetables in your diet."

"Owen! How long it has been? Hold the phone. I can swallow if I drink milk."

I heard drinking sounds, then a glass banging on the counter.

"Okay," she said. "If I count the beans and rice and onion stuffed in the green pepper, that makes four vegetables."

"Rice is a vegetable?"

"After my day on the mountain, toothpaste is a vegetable."

"I thought ski patrollers were just in it for the free skiing."

"If it would stop snowing for five minutes, I could do that." I could hear her fork clinking on a plate followed by the sounds of eating. "But this year, all I do is work, clearing snow, digging snow pits, doing avalanche control. It never stops. A week of blue sky would be like a vacation back home."

"You working tomorrow?" I asked.

"Yeah. But I'm off the day after that. I'm going to sleep late, then lounge around and drink tea all day."

"What kind of fee would get you out for a backcountry ski trek?"

"On my day off?"

"On your day off."

"Where would we be going?"

"Up Maggie's Peaks, the north mountain, to do some forensic avalanche analysis."

"Forensic like on TV?"

"Yeah. Figure out the past snow by studying the present snow."

"You're investigating the slide at Emerald Bay? Is the truck still in the tree?"

"Yeah and yeah," I said.

"And you'd pay my regular wage plus a forensic bonus?"

"Depends on the bonus. Would donuts cover it?"

She was silent for a moment. Thinking, maybe. Or eating more stuffed pepper. "Just to be sure I understand, you want me to analyze the slide?"

"Yeah."

"But it's snowed another foot or two since the slide. How would I see anything?"

"You do avalanche control at Heavenly."

"Me and the guys."

"So you're an expert," I said. "I could go up myself and stare at the snow and think about the view. But you might see something else."

"Under two feet of snow."

"Yeah," I said.

She ate some more. "I think the donuts will cover breakfast, but dinner at Evans would complete the bonus nicely."

"They serve beans and rice?" I said.

"They serve the whole rainbow of vegetables plus a filet mignon medium rare. And Street will join us?"

"I always bring her along. What time do I pick you up?"

"Seven? Day after tomorrow?" she said.

"I'll be there."

TWENTY-ONE

I woke up hard from a dream about Bill Esteban following a girl. I didn't like the dream, and I didn't like wondering about Bill.

After I coffeed up and took Spot out for an early morning run, I prepared for a stakeout over in the Tahoe Keys. I made a bag lunch, a thermos of coffee, took my cell phone so I could do some business phone calls and my book on East Asian Art in case I wanted to get smart.

I didn't know if Bill was even home, so I drove over to his house. The garage door was shut. I couldn't see the Escalade. Only way to tell was to knock on the door. Maybe a surprise visit would shake something up.

A woman who looked like the photo of Carmen Nicholas answered the door.

"Hello," she said in a pleasant voice and cheerful demeanor. She was short and round and poured into a tight yellow summer dress that showed off her substantial chest. On her feet were summer sandals, thin little straps that bit into pudgy flesh.

"Hi, I'm Owen McKenna, here to see Bill, please."

"Oh, of course. I'm Carmen Nicholas. Bill has told me all about you. He is so glad you are helping him." She lowered her voice. "This has been so hard on him, but he won't talk about it much. I'm just glad he has you to lean..." She looked past me and saw Spot with his big head hanging out the window. "Oh, my God! That is the most beautiful dog!" She ran out into the snow and immediately hugged him. No fear. No hesitation. She ran her hands up and down his neck, and when he unburied his face from the depths of her bosom, he looked rapturous.

"What is his name?" Carmen shouted back toward me.

"Spot."

"Oh, Spot, you gorgeous creature! Come out of there and play with me." She opened the back door without asking permission and Spot jumped out. He didn't even try to walk away, but just stood still, tail wagging, loving Carmen's hugs and kisses.

"Spot, you have to come inside," she said. "I can't believe that Mr. Owen is such a meany that he leaves you in the car when you should be eating cookies with us!" Carmen turned and beamed at me. Spot often had a magical effect on people, but I couldn't remember ever seeing anyone happier with him than Carmen was at that moment.

Carmen kept her hand around his neck and he walked at her side to the door. "Bill?" she called out when she was inside the front door. "Owen McKenna is here and I'm bringing his dog in. Is that okay? You'll love him, I'm sure."

She went up the stairs with Spot, and I followed, and when I saw Bill's face I knew that he wasn't wild about the idea of a dog in his nice house. But it was equally obvious that he was eager to keep Carmen happy. When he looked at her it was like he was a nervous kid beholding the girl of his dreams.

"Bill, meet Spot," she proclaimed. "The most handsome dog in Tahoe." She bent over just a little so that her head was next to Spot's and hugged him again. His eyes went half shut with bliss.

I looked at Bill and shrugged my shoulders. "Not my fault," I said. "I left him in the car."

Bill made a sweet smile. "It's fine."

"Can I feed him a treat, Mr. McKenna? Please?"

"Owen, please, and yes, if you are nice to Spot, he will sometimes eat a cookie just to be polite. But I should warn you, I just fed him. Don't be disappointed if he is too full."

Carmen turned her back to Spot, held her hand at her chest so only I could see and pointed at the plate of scones that she and Bill had been eating. She mouthed words at me. 'Would it be okay to give him a scone?'

"Sure, but I don't know if he likes them. He's very picky. He might just sniff it and walk away."

Carmen picked up a scone and turned to face Spot. He immediately understood her intentions and his sudden focus on the scone in her hand was so intense it unnerved her. She started to hold it out to him, and then, fearful of losing her fingers, gave it a little toss.

None of us actually saw him eat it. There was a blur of movement, the clicking snap of teeth and the scone went from being in the air to being gone, replaced by a drop of saliva that arced through the living room and landed on the carpet near the fireplace.

Carmen's eyes got as wide as eyes get and she started giggling, then sat in Bill's lap and threw her arms around his neck. "Oh, Bill, we should get a dog like that. Did you see him eat that? It was magnificent! Let's go puppy shopping!"

"Yes, Carmy," Bill said. "He's a nice dog. Maybe we'll get a dog someday." Bill winced. "My knees. I... "

Carmen jumped up. "Oh, I'm so sorry. I didn't realize what I was doing. I know I'm heavy. I must have hurt your knees bad."

Bill murmured that it was okay, and she bent down so they were cheek to cheek. She held his head and they made clucking sounds.

"It's nice of you to stop by, Owen," Bill eventually said as Carmen stood up. "Unfortunately, I have to get Carmen back from our little breakfast soiree. Was there anything you needed?"

"No. I was just in the area and thought I'd stop by and say hi. I have to get going as well."

Carmen went back to Spot and wrapped her arms around him and lay her head against the back of his neck. It didn't look like I'd have much luck separating them, but eventually I pried them apart. We all said goodbye and Carmen blew Spot little kisses as we left.

It was hard to watch Esteban's house and not be seen. His windows looked out from above and provided a good view of the street.

So I pulled into the lot of the Tahoe Keys commercial center several blocks away. I found two other Jeeps near each other and parked in the space between them. When Bill and Carmen left, they'd have to come down to where Tahoe Keys Boulevard crossed Venice. As long as I didn't fall asleep, I'd see them go by.

I figured it wouldn't be long. I turned on NPR and listened to political discussions, part of my attempt to get smart. When Bill and Carmen hadn't gone by in an hour, I ate my lunch. Later, I used my art book to get even smarter, careful to hold it so that any Escalade going by would register in my peripheral vision. At 4:00 p.m. I turned on All Things Considered, listened to the first hour, then gave up and left.

I stopped at my office to check messages. There was another envelope on my office door. It looked identical to the one that was on my cabin door the previous evening. I realized it could have been put on my office door at any time during the preceding 24 hours. This time I used gloves to open it.

> You obviously don't believe how
> serious we are, McKenna. Consider
> this a cease and desist order.

I talked to Street about the notes over dinner.

Street got pale. "Two notes in a row scares me," she said.

I nodded as I chewed pizza. I washed it down with a Crane Lake Merlot, cheaper than Fat Cat cab and about as good, thus 8.5 on the taste-to-cost scale. "Scares me, too."

"But you won't quit," Street said.

"I've provoked a murderer. That may help me catch him." I ate more pizza, drank more wine. "All I can do is pay attention and be careful."

"Somebody's watching you. Somebody who has killed three people. I need you to not be so casual."

"Sorry. I will watch and listen and stay alert."

Street made a little nod, but she did not look happy.

TWENTY-TWO

The next morning, Spot and I picked up Mariposa Pearl at her condo building a couple blocks from Heavenly's Stagecoach Lodge. Mariposa's rented home was in an old tacky 6-plex. It perched on a steep slope with half of the building propped up by warped, peeling posts held together with flimsy X-bracing. It was an eyesore that would eventually be torn down. But it provided cheap rent, a rare commodity in Tahoe, and something Mariposa desperately needed.

Mariposa's mother had large medical bills. Because Mare had arranged for her to come across the border for surgery in San Diego, Mare had signed a guarantee of payment. It was a debt that would take decades to pay off.

Street and I had talked about setting up some kind of fund, but when Street ran the idea by Mariposa, she wouldn't hear of it. I asked Diamond about it and he just shrugged and said, "Mexican pride. Nothing you can do."

Mare came out with a pack and boots over one shoulder and her skis and poles over the other. I put the skis and poles on the roof rack while she tossed her gear in back.

We ate donuts as I drove down the Grade and out through South Lake Tahoe toward Emerald Bay. Spot leaned over the seat-backs, wondering if we were going to eat all the donuts. Caltrans had opened the highway to Emerald Bay a short while ago, but it was snowing again. They might close it at any time.

I found a wide spot in the road near the Bay View Camp-ground and parked next to the vertical wall of snow left by the rotary plow.

Mariposa and Spot ran to the lake side of the highway. They found a place to scramble up the snow embankment and look down at the slide below. I heard Mare whoop with amazement.

"Like stunt driving in a movie!" she said when she got back to the Jeep. "Park your truck in a tree. It would take some cojones to take that ride, no? I saw it in the paper, but had to see it myself."

I unlatched the ski rack, lifted our skis and poles off the roof and stabbed them into the snow. Mariposa put on her boots and her pack with the folding shovel strapped to it. She stood waiting.

I was ready in another minute.

"I brought electronics," she said. "This is your transceiver." She handed me a device about the size of an old cell phone. "You know how it works?"

"Got a lesson a few years back." I worked the controls. "This switch is off and on. This is transmit, this is receive, right? We leave them on transmit when we ski. If you were to be buried, I'd set it to receive. The readout will point the direction of your transceiver, and the beeping will get faster as I get closer to you."

"Correct," she said.

I put my transceiver in its cloth pouch, pulled the support straps over my shoulders and adjusted them so the transceiver was in the center of my chest.

"How do you want to do this investigation?"

"I want you to think about how you would set off an avalanche that would bury the highway," I said. "Which way would you go up the mountain. What would you look for. Where would you toss a charge to trigger the slide. That sort of thing."

I swung my pack and shovel up on my back.

"You really believe that the slide was set on purpose?"

"It's looking like that."

We carried our skis up the embankment on the mountain side of the highway. The road below looked like a tunnel, crawling around the bay. The cars on the highway had nothing to look at but ten-foot walls of white ice.

We dropped our skis off our shoulders and clicked into the

bindings.

"A few instructions," Mariposa said. "Maybe you know them already."

"I'm all ears."

"We stay off all slopes that like to slide. Those are everything between thirty and forty-five degrees. Shallower than thirty is usually okay because the snow doesn't slide. Steeper than forty-five is usually okay because those slopes constantly sluff the snow off." Mariposa made a motion like she was shaking a jacket off of her back. "Everything in between is suspect.

"We also stay off all of the leeward slopes. That's everything that faces between north and clockwise around to the southeast. The prevailing winds are from the west and southwest. They blow snow off the west-facing slopes. As the wind comes over the mountain the snow drops out onto the leeward slopes. The snow-loading on these slopes after a long wind is huge. Southern slopes are also a concern when the sun comes out. Sun-warming loosens adhesion between snow layers." Mare looked up at the cloudy sky. "But we obviously don't have to worry about that now."

"Couple days ago I watched a steady plume of snow coming off the top of Tallac," I said. "It occurred to me at the time that it would add up to tons of snow in a small spot below."

"Yeah. Those plumes are like a dozen snow-making guns. The cross on Tallac can grow to thirty or fifty feet deep. When that snow releases, it makes one big-ass slide." She grinned. "I'll break trail. You follow. When possible we stay in the trees. Tree cover is no guarantee of avalanche protection, but standing trees indicate areas where strong avalanches are rare. The trees also help pin the snow down and inhibit slides. But you often find small slides in the trees. It only takes a couple yards of snow to completely bury a person. Guess how much a single cubic yard of snow weighs after it's been compressed in an avalanche?"

"I'm not going to like the answer, huh?"

"Over eight hundred pounds. Often a thousand pounds. Get a couple of yards over you and you're not going anyplace." Mare looked up at the mountain. "On any questionable slope we also keep some distance between us."

"Got it," I said. "Nothing more stupid than both being buried in the same avalanche."

Mare winked at me. "Now that I've given you the rules, I have to tell you that we are going to break two of them."

"Which ones?"

"The main ones. Our first slope is steeper than thirty degrees. And it faces east."

"No other way up?"

"No. Both north and south Maggies are too steep. But I've been here before. There is a lot of lumber on the slope. I think it will hold the snow."

She strode off at a fast pace, her bindings set for free-heel motion. Backcountry gear is a blend between cross-country equipment and downhill gear. In free-heel mode, you can kick and stride your way up the slope. Then, for descent, you lock your bindings down and they give you the same control that regular downhill equipment provides.

Mare demonstrated a hint of Pearl Power as she went up through the Bay View Campground, which was now buried under ten feet of snow. She got to the base of the mountain and began to traverse up through the heavily forested slope. She didn't race, but her pace was strong, and she was breaking trail in ridiculously deep snow. Spot stayed with her. I fell behind. Mare switchbacked here and there, never pausing. She seemed unaware that her traveling companion was older and less fit. Eventually, she and Spot stopped and they waited for me. When I finally caught up, she said, "Are you tired?"

"You said we shouldn't be too close lest we get caught in the same slide," I said, huffing.

"Right. That was for down below. But this part of the slope is shallower. You can stop worrying."

When we were well up on the mountain, she turned into an area where the trees were more sparse, and I recognized that the summer hiking trail was ten or twelve feet below our skis.

Soon, we came out to an overlook above the rockslide where

the mountain gave way a half-century before. The area was bare of trees and very steep. This was where the avalanche had slid five days before. But it was hard to see exactly where because so much snow had fallen since. Clouds swirled around us and below us and occasionally opened up to give us a clear view down to Emerald Bay below. I got out my camera and took several pictures.

"Like a tourist, you can't resist?" Mare said.

"No. Just documenting a potential crime scene."

Mare nodded. "I want you to lock your bindings into downhill mode," Mare said. "Then ski to just above that tree." She pointed. "If you and Spot stay there you will be safe from any slide. I'm going to ski across here, above the point where snow would normally release. My skis will make a cut and I can feel how the snow acts."

"What will you feel for?"

"Settling, cracking, whumping noises, any sensation of movement." She pointed again. "As I crest the bulge right there, I'll be able to see farther down. I'll stop at those other trees on the far side of the rock slide."

"And my job..." I said.

"You should stay put until I make an assessment. Unless, of course, something goes wrong and I end up buried. Then come and find me and dig me out."

I locked down my bindings and skied to the tree. Then Mariposa skied across.

She went through the clearing fast and sure and didn't stop until she reached the trees on the other side. She did a 180-degree kick turn, then side-stepped up the mountain. I was struck by how easily she did it. I'd always found that side-stepping up was nearly impossible in bottomless powder.

When she'd gone straight up far enough to traverse back, she skied back toward me and stopped halfway. She stuck her pole down into the snow a couple of feet in several places, then skied the rest of the way to me.

"Did you notice what's wrong?" she said.

"The snow isn't very deep."

"Right. There's about two feet of fresh snow on top of hard-pack. I was on the slide residue. Which means the slide didn't break off at the logical point where the slope gets steep. It must have come from up in those trees, gathering strength when it burst out into the open. Then it grew to a massive slide by the time it hit the highway below."

"Unusual for it to start in the trees?" I said.

"Yeah. Common avalanche tracks won't let trees grow to any size. You can spot them when you look up at treed mountains. They are always the vertical stripes without trees."

"Looks like your forensic skills are pretty good even after two feet of new snow."

Mariposa smiled. "We've got more climbing to do."

I followed her up into the trees. She traversed back and forth, feeling with skis and poles for where the snow was only two feet deep. When she hit a drop-off into bottomless powder, she knew she'd found the edge of the slide.

We'd gone up a long ways when she stopped. She studied the landscape, skied back and forth and poked around with her poles. Then she unfolded her shovel and began digging. Spot ran to her, sniffing, wondering what Mare had alerted on.

I skied up. "Unearthing clues?"

"I think you are right. Someone did start this avalanche. With explosives."

She was tossing the fresh light powder snow to the side, gradually making a dish-shaped hole. She felt with her shovel, going slowly, taking care about what snow she scooped up.

"A crater from dynamite?" I asked, snapping more pictures.

"Yes. I took out all the new snow. What remains is the pit that an avalanche bomb leaves. About six feet across and several feet deep." She brushed at the snow with her glove. "You can see where some of the snow was darkened from the dynamite."

"If someone tossed an explosive here, they'd never be able to see their victim on the highway below."

"Right. All three of the bombs were set off by remote control."

TWENTY-THREE

"Three bombs?" I said.

Mariposa pointed to the left and right. "See the other pit over there by that tree and that one by that boulder? This guy used three bombs. If you look at the lay of the land you'll see it makes a steep funnel. He figured out that even though this area is in the trees and doesn't make big slides, he could put three bombs up here and start a slide in three places at once. The bombs would bring the snow in this funnel area down on converging paths."

She pointed below us. "Down there where the trees stop, the snow would burst out, all its energy focused by the shape of the land."

I said, "And it would give the slide a big head-start by the time it got out into the open above the rock slide."

"Exactly."

"How would this guy place these charges?"

"He'd just ski up here like we did and drop them in."

"What kind of triggers could be done remotely?" I asked.

"I don't know. Some kind of transmitter, a garage door opener or something, that could be rigged to a receiver that fires off the detonator, which blows the charge."

"Garage door opener," I said. "You've got a good mind for this stuff."

Mare put her hand on her waist and cocked her substantial hip. "You said you wanted avalanche forensics. I could get a business card. Mariposa Forensics. Sounds pretty good, huh?"

"It does. Anything up here that we could use as solid evidence? Something I could take to the sheriff's department?"

Mare held up her gloved hand. She had a little piece of brown paper between her thumb and forefinger. "This looks like part of the wrapping off a three-by-eight."

"Which is?"

"The bombs we toss in avalanche control. It's three short sticks tied together."

"And a short stick is what?"

"In mining they use a long stick of dynamite. In avalanche control our three-by-eights are shorter sticks. The pack of three is great for tossing some distance by hand."

I got pictures of several pieces of the wrapping that were scattered in the snow where Mare had dug, then collected them in a zip lock bag to give to Sergeant Bains.

TWENTY-FOUR

Spot and I dropped Mariposa off with two leftover donuts, a check for services and a promise of dinner at Evan's.

It was still early in the afternoon, so I stopped by my office. The phone was ringing as I walked in. It was Glennie.

"The slide up at Sand Harbor," she said. "I got another call from the avalanche psycho. Claims he triggered that slide as well. I told him he should be proud that he'd killed three people. Want to know what he said?"

"What did he say?"

"He said, 'good,' and hung up."

"Nasty guy," I said.

"I'll say."

"Same number on the caller ID?"

"No," Glennie said. "So I called George Clooney meets Pierce Brosnan and gave it to him. He's running a trace as we speak."

"Thanks for the info."

"You got something to trade?" she said.

"Yeah. But first I gotta clear it with Bains. If he says yes, we're good to go."

"He'll say yes. I told him he sounded cute. He practically melted and flowed right out of those speaker holes on my phone."

"He might be married, Glennie."

"Might is a word with a lot of room in it."

We said goodbye and I dialed Bains.

"The slide at Emerald Bay was set with three dynamite

charges," I told him when he answered. "They were placed up above the rock slide and designed to focus the avalanche energy."

I heard Bains slurping on a drink at the other end of the line.

"How do you know it was dynamite? You got a sample or what?"

"They were what ski patrollers call three-by-eights. Three short sticks of dynamite, wrapped together. The dynamite left craters of darkened snow. And, yes, I have evidence. A little brown piece of the wrapping paper."

"So you place a perp up on the mountain, and he sees cars coming in the distance, climbing up the highway to Emerald Bay. He does a little count to get the timing right, then throws three charges and gets to watch what happens."

"Probably not. He couldn't see the highway from up there. We're thinking it was remote control. Some kind of a receiver and a transmitter like a garage door opener. Guy sits down by the highway and pushes a button at the right time."

"Hey, that's good McKenna. A garage door opener."

"It was Mariposa Pearl, avalanche control specialist at Heavenly, who figured it out."

"Okay," Bains said. "I can call her, get the details."

"I got a call from Glenda Gorman at the Herald," I said. "You okay with me passing this along?"

"Sure. She's the one goes by Glennie, right? She called me. Told me I sounded cute."

"Is that a surprise to you?" I said.

"I don't know. Should it be? Do you think I'm cute?" he said.

"George Clooney meets Pierce Brosnan," I said.

"Hey, McKenna, you're not pulling my leg, are you? You really think that?"

I didn't know what to say.

"So what about this Glennie broad?" Bains said. "Is she good looking?"

"Marilyn Monroe meets Michelle Pfeiffer," I said.

"Come on McKenna. No one looks like that. Tell me the truth."

"The truth, sergeant, is that Glennie is smart, beautiful, and sexy. You should take her out to dinner at the earliest opportunity."

"But I haven't even met her," Bains said.

"You're going to let that get in your way? My friend, Sergeant Diamond Martinez in Douglas County, will probably get to her first, then."

"Who's he?" Bains said.

"Antonio Banderas meets Johnny Depp."

"Oh, Christ, McKenna. Hang up and free up this line. I gotta make a call."

I hung up and dialed Glennie, but her number was already busy.

I drove over to Esteban's house, thinking I'd get him talking, see if I could learn anything that might illuminate why he was following the girl. I could confront him about it directly, but then he might clam up. Better to get him talking and see where he'd slip.

He let me in and, as before, insisted that I go up the stairs first while he followed. There was a light on in a room by the base of the stairs. The laundry room. The laundry tub was half full of water. Sitting in the tub was a broom, bristle end down in the water, the handle propped up by the pipes above.

"Head on up," Bill said, gesturing at the stairs.

I went up. Soft music filled the living room. Jazz trumpet. It sounded like Arturo Sandoval.

"Come sit here," Bill said as he hobbled over to the kitchen island. On the counter was a glass, a napkin, a plate and a long skinny fork. I pulled out a barstool and sat on it. There were several blocks of cheese that Bill had been cutting. He returned to his task.

"I've been putting together the fixings for a little fondu party. Got the cheese cut, and the bread is fresh out of the oven."

"Thank you, but I don't want to crash your get-together. I didn't have anything important." I stood up and pushed the barstool back.

"No, please stay. There's nothing to crash. It was a party of one. Now it's two." Bill fetched a second plate, fork, glass and napkin. He poured me a beer and milk for himself and continued with his food prep.

"March was good company. But now it's just me again. Carmen has been keeping me company some. She's a sweetheart, but she's got a life to live."

"Have you always lived alone?"

"Yeah. There've been some women who paid me attention when I was young. I was real close to one. Fay Perkins. I even asked her to marry me." Bill sipped his milk. He adjusted the flame under the fondu pot. "She said no. It was probably best. She was a psychologist who specialized in grief counseling. I told her I believed I would make her a good husband, but that I probably couldn't talk shop much. The nightclub is boring and I've got too many demons to hear about grief cases during dinner. Who knows if that was what turned her away. Could've been the gimped-up legs. Not like she was into skiing or anything real physical, though." Bill stirred the cheese as it began to bubble, then shut the flame vents.

"I'd think a psychologist would be able to look past a physical handicap," I said. I was thinking that if Bill was sick enough to be a stalker, the psychologist probably sensed it.

"You'd think," Bill said as he cut the bread into chunks. He stabbed one with his fork, dipped it in the cheese and popped it in his mouth. He pointed at me and the food as he chewed.

I joined in.

"Someone bumped their car door into Fay's at the supermarket once," Bill said. "It was a really tiny dent. Most people would just live with it. But she had that door replaced."

I nodded, ate more bread and cheese, drank beer.

"Other than the kids' friends, I don't really know anyone in this town," he said. "That's part of why I appreciate Carmen."

We continued to eat and make awkward conversation. He never asked why I stopped by. He never said anything that had anything to do with the girl he followed.

After an hour I left.

When I pulled into my driveway I saw a strange shape in the snow not far from my front door. I got out and let Spot out of the back. I pulled out my pack and was walking to the cabin when I realized that someone had done a little snow sculpture. Maybe one of my rich vacation-home neighbors had come up with kids and they had gone around the neighborhood making shapes in the snow.

But the sculpture looked more sophisticated than something kids built. As I got closer I saw that it had four legs, a tail, a deep chest and large head.

Spot saw it too, and he went to investigate at the same time that I remembered Street's words about being careful.

"Spot! No!" I leaped forward and caught him from the side in a full tackle, driving him away and down into the snow as the sculpture blew up in a blinding flash and ear-thumping boom.

TWENTY-FIVE

I was horizontal in the snow on top of Spot as the bomb went off near my feet. The shockwave hit so hard it was as if someone had swung a baseball bat at the soles of my shoes. The blast numbed my ears and stung the right side of my face.

I checked Spot. He seemed okay except for a small wound on his ear. I wobbled on unstable legs into my cabin. I called Diamond and explained what happened. I could barely hear him over the ringing in my ears. Two Douglas County Deputies arrived in fifteen minutes and Diamond came a few minutes later with Street in his cruiser. She looked horrified when she saw me.

"My God, Owen, your face is torn open!"

"I felt something sting," I said, touching the side of my face. Warm, wet blood flowed from my temple down under the edge of my jaw. "I must have got hit by a piece of shrapnel or ice."

"I'll get a compress." She fetched a washcloth. "You're cut bad. You'll need to get stitched up. Hold this on it until we can get you cleaned up."

I pressed the cloth against the wound as Street hugged me. She then held Spot who was almost as shaky as she was.

I went over the details with the cops while Street called Doc Lee. The cops collected lots of bits of brown dynamite wrapping as well as two tiny shards of what looked like black plastic. They searched the area for ski or snowmobile tracks and found nothing but tire treadmarks exactly like those from Diamond's Explorer, which meant the marks also matched a huge number of other SUVs and pickups throughout Tahoe.

The person who did the snow sculpture wore the most common type of snow boots, available in lots of stores. The only thing of note was that they were large, size twelve or thirteen.

"Where do you think the bomber waited?" Diamond asked.

"Somewhere up there." I waved my arm at the vast expanse of mountain that rose up behind my cabin all the way to Genoa Peak and stretched off for miles to the north and south.

"Lotta wilderness," Diamond said. "Hard to search."

"Almost no point. If the bomber was on a snowmobile, he could already have the machine in a garage or on a trailer heading out of town. A person on skis could silently ski out of the forest anywhere. He could even ski over the back side of Genoa Peak and drop all the way down to Carson Valley."

Diamond nodded. "Be safe. I don't think this guy is finished."

Spot and I stayed at Street's that night. More for her comfort than mine. I knew the killer could put a bomb at her place just as easily as at mine. Doc Lee came with his bag and stitched me up, telling me that the scar would be thin but over four inches long. He looked at Spot's ear, which Street had scrubbed. "Got a little hole here," Doc Lee said. "Perfect for an earring. But it will heal."

The next morning, Street and I were up early, discussing our options. She thought that Spot would be safer with her. While she knew that a threat to her or Spot would be the ultimate way to bend me to the killer's wishes, her instincts told her that the killer wanted to make the impression on me directly.

"Call it an ego thing," she said. "The sculpture bomb was a performance. This guy is beating his chest to impress you. Coming after me when you're gone wouldn't satisfy him."

I agreed with her and left Spot in her care.

I left at 7:00 a.m. and got to Sacramento just after the rush hour. I turned off in Vallejo and went north around the bay on 37 to Marin County and was on the Golden Gate by 11:00 o'clock.

I found the Simon mansion on a curving manicured street above China Beach on El Camino del Mar in Seacliff, not far from the Presidio. I squeezed in between a new Jaguar and an old Rolls, its lugubrious countenance looking unhappy in the rain.

The Simon's front door was a five-foot-wide slab of hand-carved oak. I pushed the button and heard the same ponderous chimes as they probably use at the Queen's Palace in London.

A tall elegant woman in her late forties answered the door. She wore a black pantsuit with a see-through knit wrap over it. Two little dogs, one light gray, the other mottled, charged out beneath her feet. They jumped up on my legs, almost reaching my knees. Their barks could shatter wine glasses.

"Are you Mr. McKenna?" She shouted over the dog barks. She looked with alarm at the bandage on the side of my face. "I'm Clarice Simon. And these are our girls, Salt and Pepper. They're Pomeranians. Salt! Pepper! Quiet!" The dogs barked even louder. "So good of you to come," Clarice shouted. As she shook my hand, diamonds sparkled on her fingers and on her wrists and in her ears and around her neck and probably on the fringes of her underwear. "Please come in. Sam and I are so glad you are looking into our daughter's death. After you called us, we did a little checking and found that you are highly recommended." She emphasized the word highly.

We walked through the cavernous entry with the dogs barking and skittering around my feet. I bent over and snatched the one named Pepper off of the floor. I held her tight to my chest, my hand around her neck so her head was immobilized and she couldn't bite. Astonished, she stopped barking. Salt sensed the change, ran on ahead of Clarice, spun around and stopped, a tiny high growl warbling in her throat.

After we traversed the entry, we went through the central hall for awhile, eventually arriving at a living room a little too small to host the G-8 summit.

"Sam, this is Mr. McKenna."

"Owen, please," I said.

Sam was a lanky man, and his rumpled clothes looked ill-fitting to the same degree as his wife's clothes looked perfect. When he stood up from a deep upholstered chair his right pant leg stayed up, the hem stuck on the top of his sock. The bulge where his knee had been ballooned forward. He reached out without taking a step, leaning improbably far forward. I set Pepper down and hurried to meet his outstretched hand before he could fall on his face. He seemed waxen and glazed-over, still in shock.

"The officer told us about our daughter three days ago. But it was just last night that we found out she was murdered," he said.

"I'm so sorry," I said.

Pepper was on her hind legs, doing a little pirouette, pawing at my legs, wanting me to pick her up again. Salt had jumped up on a distant chair and she eyed me with suspicion.

"We should have known," Clarice said. "The policeman drove all the way down from Tahoe to give us the news of her death. That seems unlikely if it had been an accident. He didn't say it was murder. But he must have suspected it. However, now that you are on the case, perhaps there will be some justice. Don't worry about your fee. Whatever it is, we don't mind."

"There is no fee. I'm not working for you."

"But I don't understand," Clarice said. "You called. You came down. The officer I talked to said he was certain you would find the killer if they didn't find him first."

"I may find the killer, but I'm working for another client. His nephew was killed in the same avalanche."

"His nephew was murdered like our daughter?"

"Not suffocated, no. He was actually killed by the avalanche. But I believe their deaths are connected."

"God, this really sucks," Simon said. He walked over to a sideboard, pulled a glass stopper out of a decanter and poured whiskey into a crystal glass, filling it to the brim. He drank it down partway, poured it back up to the brim and carried it to his chair. "You bust your ass to give your daughter everything in the world and some scumbag kills her. Why? She was good and pure and kind. She never hurt a soul. Was it something we did? Was it my business? Did someone kill her because she had the misfortune to be born into a successful household?"

"Sam," his wife said. "Calm down. It's going to be okay. Lori was a free spirit. She's finally found her freedom."

Sam shouted, "Did someone resent her riches or her opportunities or her beauty? Why did they prey on an innocent girl?!"

Clarice sat down on the arm of the chair as Sam downed the rest of his drink. She touched his shoulder. "Sam, honey..."

"Don't honey me!" He brushed her hand off his shoulder. "If you'd ever been here, spent time as a mother instead of sweet-talking the governor and the legislators and the voters..."

"Sam, don't talk to me like that! I've done good work! Lori would tell you that she wanted me doing that work, making this state a better place." Clarice was crying, tears flowing freely.

"You were a politician, not a mother!" Sam hissed.

Clarice jumped up off the chair arm and faced him. "You weren't a father! You were a doctor, an engineer, a financier! Who took that child to dance lessons and swimming lessons?! Who coached her through algebra and geometry?! Who got three state legislators to write her letters of recommendation?! Who went and saw her dorm at Humboldt State? Who, Sam?! Who?!"

"It was always about you, Clarice. Do you even know what she studied in college? Do you know her major?"

"Of course I do. How dare you."

"What was it?"

"It was... It was communications. I got my secretary to help her with her papers. Or sociology. Maybe that's what Herm helped her write about. Oh, God, I don't know! She started out in biology or some worthless science, and how can I keep track when she was always switching! The girl was a complete flake!"

Sam was weeping. "When Lori went to that study camp in Costa Rica, what was it they studied?" Now his voice was so soft it was nearly unintelligible.

"I don't know," Clarice whispered.

"That girl's family who took her to Vail the week we had to be in Paris to talk to those ship builders, who was that family?"

"I don't remember," Clarice said.

He reached up and Clarice fell into his arms and they held each other and sobbed. I found my way back through the palace and let myself out the huge wooden door.

TWENTY-SIX

There was still plenty of afternoon left when I got back to Tahoe. I was remembering the photo Uncle Bill had shown me of his party. March's best friends were Will Adams the computer geek, Carmen Nicholas the cocktail waitress-turned-Bill's new paramour, Packer Mills the snowboarder, and Paul Riceman the contractor who lived up on Kingsbury Grade. The one person that Bill thought of who wasn't in the photo was April's friend Ada, last name and whereabouts unknown.

I drove to the snowboard shop where Packer Mills worked.

There were two kids at the front counter, holding opposite ends of a snowboard. They had it up at eye level so they could sight down its base. They had weird hair and metal coming out of their skin, and their ratty pants were hanging so low that, if they hadn't been wearing boxer shorts, they would have lowered the bar to a new plumber's-butt standard. They spoke English, but it was the arcane language of snowboard and skateboard speak, filled with inscrutable phrases and unusual idiom. I couldn't understand anything they said. I could tell they were smart, but they belonged to a group whose very purpose was to be unfathomable to society in general and adults in particular. But like a generation of ex-hippies, they now seemed to be the majority, and most of them had grown up, so their raison d'être had lost its point. Eventually, the rest of us would die off, and the world would be theirs. Then they would have to cope with a new, younger generation that defined itself by speaking, acting, and dressing unlike those pesky old board riders.

I waited. One of them looked at me and stared at my bandage.

"Help you?"

"I'm here to see Packer. Is he in?"

"In back." The kid gestured toward a doorway behind him.

I walked into the back of the shop where they worked on snowboards. Packer was bent over a huge machine made for grinding, sharpening and polishing board bases. The machine had a large sand belt and a stone wheel, all cooled with a constant spray of water. There was an LED readout with red numbers and a keypad for inputting information.

Packer wore goggles and an iPod and he held a snowboard against the machine. Sparks flew off the metal edges of the board. The noise was deafening. Packer's head nodded to the beat in his ears.

He looked like he did in Bill's photo, big and rangy with black hair polished against his scalp. The goatee was scraggly and the lip metal was tarnished.

After a few minutes, he hit a switch and the machine began to wind down like a jet after landing. He set the board down, turned and saw me. He picked his iPod off his belt and dialed back the volume.

"Hey," he said. He was the first person I'd seen who didn't seem to notice the wound on my face.

"Hey," I said. "I'm Owen McKenna, a private investigator. March's uncle hired me to look into March's death. He gave me your name. Said you would be able to fill me in a little on March's life."

"Uncle Bill, he of the bourgeois oppressor state."

"Marx goes around and comes around, doesn't he?" I said.

"Actually, the whole of politics leaves me limp. I'm just a poet prole, looking for love on the mountain."

"Who are your main influences?" I said. I didn't know jack about poetry, but it seemed like a way into this kid.

"Ferlinghetti, Ginsburg, Snyder, lotta the beats."

"You write that kind of verse?" I asked.

"I'm working on my chops, but I wouldn't use my name and theirs in the same sentence. You into poetry?"

"I'm one of the philistines. I think I know what I like, but I don't know anything about it. I like Frost. Does he rate on your scale?"

"The god of formalism? No, he's like a realist painter. Everything nice and neat and pretty. And totally predictable."

"So you write more like the way Pollock or DeKooning painted," I said.

"Hey, not bad."

"Or Kline or Rauschenberg?"

"Exactly. Poetry should be visceral. It should have surprise. What's your medium? Oil? Acrylic? Watercolor?"

"I have some art books. But I don't have the talent to do art."

"Anyone with books in this post-literate world gets my time," he said. "What can I tell you about March?"

"There was a girl's body in the slide. Lori Simon. She was killed and then put in the way of the avalanche. March was killed by the avalanche. I'm looking for a connection between them."

Packer was shaking his head. "I read about it in the paper. But I'd never heard of her before."

"March never mentioned a girl he'd been seeing?"

"Not to me. Although Benson out front, you probably saw him when you came in, he said he saw March with some girl down in Reno a week to two ago. You could ask him about it. Maybe that was Lori."

"The slide up at Sand Harbor," I said. "The guy killed in his Blazer was named Astor Domino. Ever heard of him?"

"No," Packer said.

"Any idea where April is?"

"Nope. Haven't talked to her in weeks."

"March left his uncle a note saying that he was going to meet the Guru of the Sierra in Tahoe City. Does that mean anything to you?"

"No. But you should know that March and I didn't spend that much time together. He's pretty far out of my circle. We met on the mountain, we worked together for a few months, and we've seen each other at a kegger or two, but that's about it. He didn't understand poetry. 'Course, no one does. Then he switched over to skis, and my buds are all riders. Frankly, I was surprised that Uncle Bill invited me over there in November. But I guess March still thought we were buds. Hell, maybe we were."

I pointed at his iPod. "What you got on there?"

Packer raised his eyebrows. Maybe the first time someone outside of his group had ever asked.

"Bunch of Charlie Parker and Dizzy Gillespie tunes. They were inspiration for the beats."

"Good stuff," I said. "I noticed you've got Dizzy's beard."

Packer grinned. Then he turned and looked at a stack of snowboards. "Good to talk, man, but I gotta get all these tuned before I can go home tonight. Check with Benson on your way out. See if he knows that girl."

I thanked him and went back out front.

One of the kids who'd been looking down the snowboard was handing a credit card slip to a young woman.

She said, "Thanks."

He said, "Hey, no problem."

She left.

"Are you Benson?" I said.

"Yeah."

"Packer said you saw March with a girl down in Reno some time back."

"Yeah."

"Ever seen her before?"

"No."

"Did March say who she was?"

"No," Benson said. "I didn't talk to him. Not like we hang together. I just saw him and this girl at a microbrew bar next to a snowboard shop. I was going in to check out the shop 'cause I'm thinking of moving to Reno. They got a great skate park. And I saw March through the window. I waved, but he didn't see me."

"What did the girl look like?"

"It was dark in there and they were sitting in a booth so I couldn't really see. Kind of normal, I guess. Medium hair."

"Medium length? Or medium color?"

"Both, I think."

"Short, tall, skinny, fat?" I said.

"Um, medium height, medium thickness."

"Anything about her strike you?" I asked.

"What do you mean?"

"You know how sometimes you see a girl and something sticks with you. Like, she seemed too young to be drinking beer. Or, she's so pretty, how'd that guy get her to go out with him? Or, she smiled on only one side of her mouth. Something you remember."

Benson shook his head. "Sorry, I don't remember anything."

"You ever hear of the Guru of the Sierra?"

"Guru? You mean like the Dalai Lama?"

"I don't know. March called him that. The Guru of the Sierra."

"Guess I ain't much help."

I thanked him and left.

TWENTY-SEVEN

It was dark when I left the shop. Cocktail hour. Which meant Carmen might be at her job.

I parked in one of the big lots behind Harrah's casino, walked in and cruised the tables. I asked another waitress and she said she didn't know anyone named Carmen Nicholas.

I kept working the casino floor. After five minutes of searching I saw her handing a beer to a lone man at a blackjack table. She turned away, carrying a tray with two martinis on it.

Her confidence wearing the summer dress at Bill's house was nothing compared to what it took to put on her current outfit. She obviously figured that if she dressed and acted like she was hot stuff, she'd actually be hot stuff and get tips to match.

She was poured into a short little silver lame wrap three sizes too small. But it squeezed and kneaded and pulled her body into a figure of sorts, and if her muscular legs were a bit clunky in their lace stockings and spiked heels and her belly a little too obtrusive in the sparkly dress, her breasts were served up as if on a platter, and they upstaged everything else.

I came up behind her.

"Hi Carmen."

She spun around. "Oh, Mr. McKenna! What happened to your face? You scared me."

"Slipped in the snow and bumped my cheek on the ice."

"It looks very painful. I hope you are all better soon." She reached up and gave me a gentle pat near my bandage.

"Any chance you could take a moment? You could help me

with a couple questions I have about March's death."

Carmen breathed out and her entire physique sagged. Her tray tilted, the martinis sliding sideways. She reached out with her other hand to grab a big brass railing for support.

"This is only my second day back on the job. I was out for most of a week after I heard the news. I can't stand it, poor March being buried like that. Crushed in an avalanche. I've gone over to Bill's three times since March died. It's like we both need the other to prop us up. The other day when you came by was the best Bill has been." She stopped to breathe, bowing her head.

Her hair was lacquered up like an Egyptian vase that balanced on top of her head. It wobbled dangerously close to the martinis.

"Were you close to March?" I asked.

Carmen's eyes teared up. Her lower lip quivered. Her breath was short. If it was acting, she could do better on stage than hustling cocktails.

"I think I loved him," she said in a voice barely above a whisper. "I first met him here at work. He and Will stopped in at the Olive and Spear after the Crosby, Stills and Nash show. I was on that night. They had beers and they talked to me. March was so nice, so gracious. He told me that I was good at my job. No one ever told me that before.

"I fell for him that first night. A few days later I saw him at Baldwin Beach. He was playing Frisbee with this handsome guy who I got to meet. Paul Riceman. I've seen Paul a few times since including at a party that Bill had. Anyway, March and Paul invited me to join them and we played three-way Frisbee. They were so good, but they never made me feel bad when I missed."

"Did March know how you felt about him?"

"No. It was a one-way love."

"Does Bill know you loved March?"

"No. Please don't tell him. Bill is such a dear. I would never want to hurt him. I originally went over there just to feel closer to March. But I've grown to really like Bill."

"Did you ever meet or hear of a girl named Lorraine Simon?"

"The girl in the avalanche. I read about it in the paper. Is it true, the rumors I've heard? That March didn't die accidentally? That he was murdered and the avalanche was, like, the murderer's weapon?"

"Where did you hear that?"

"One of the other waitresses heard a bunch of people talking about it at one of the tables.

"What about the girl? Did you ever hear of her?"

She shook her head. "No."

"How about Astor Domino? Did you know him?"

"The man killed in the Sand Harbor avalanche? No. Do you think he was murdered, too? The paper said a caller took credit for setting both avalanches. Is it true? Can you make avalanches go where you want so you can kill people with them?"

"I don't know, Carmen."

She lowered the tray with the martinis and set one edge of it on the railing. "Is there any way I can help you catch March's killer?"

"I'm looking for a connection between the victims. If you hear of anyone who knew March, Lorraine, and Astor, let me know?" I handed her a card.

Carmen nodded, her eyes serious. She tucked the card under the pile of napkins on her tray.

"Have you lived in Tahoe long?" I asked.

"It'll be a year next month. I came down from Eureka. Everyone thinks living on the coast is so wonderful, but you have fog all summer and storms all winter and there's, like, six days in the spring and fall when the weather is perfect. Here, it's sunny all the time. Well, except when it's snowing. And it does snow, sometimes, doesn't it?" She tried to force a grin through her sadness.

"Sometimes. Do you have family in Eureka?"

"Just my father and sister. My mother split with a logger from Oregon fourteen years ago. Fourteen years and three months ago. My poor daddy had to finish raising both me and sis. Now my dad's got prostate cancer real bad. He's sixty-seven. They say it's real common at that age, but I think that it came from the stress with him and mom and all that. I really believe that the mind and body are connected. If the mind undergoes stress, the body shows it. Do you believe that?"

"It can probably happen."

"If you aren't happy, your energy fields get mis-aligned. Then you get sick. I used to drive him to Redding to get his treatments. Radiation, chemo, the whole package. Every month they inject him with a mix of stuff. He calls it the cancer cocktail. Now dad jokes that he and I both live off cocktails.

"Anyway, I saw an ad in our local paper for jobs in this hotel and casino. I guess it works for Tahoe companies to advertise in the small towns around the state. There are lots of good workers who like the idea of a more exciting life. 'Course, the reality of slinging drinks at night isn't quite the same as what you expect from looking at the pictures of Tahoe in the brochures. But I thought I'd apply. I knew the pay would be way more than I got in the gift store.

"And my sister was just moving back from Portland. She was a secretary for a business that installs home irrigation systems. In Portland where it rains all the time. Is that weird or what? They went out of business in about two years."

"This is a good job?" I said.

"Oh, yeah. I get an hourly base plus tips and benefits. There's enough for me to get by and still send some gas money back to dad and sis. She drives him to Redding, now, and gas is getting so expensive." Carmen's eyes opened wide again as she noticed the martinis. "Oh, my God, I forgot these drinks." She lifted the tray and turned to scan the tables. "Those men probably gave up on me. I have to go. Call me if you have any more questions?"

I got out another card and a pen. "Your number?"

She gave it to me and I wrote it down.

TWENTY-EIGHT

The next morning, Spot and I drove up the East Shore.

The slide that buried the road near Sand Harbor was small but obvious. The rotaries had made a clean cut through the frozen river of snow, leaving vertical walls of white ice seven or eight feet high on both sides of the curving highway. I drove through the passage, pulled off the highway on the far side and got out.

The slide was maybe thirty feet wide and a little deeper than I was tall. It didn't look like much compared to the larger and deeper Emerald Bay slide.

I got my snowshoes out of the back and let Spot out. We climbed up on the slide residue. Because the east side of the Tahoe Basin gets only a third as much snow as the west side, there was only a half-foot of fresh snow on the slide.

The long thick bulge of residue looked like someone had peeled it out of the snow carpet on the upper mountain and laid the piece down like a rug on the lower mountain.

There was a scattering of large trees. Based on what Mariposa had told me, this slope was steep enough to slide, but not big enough to regularly produce large avalanches with tree-breaking power.

So I played a little game of 'what if' as I looked at the land-scape.

What if it was a variation of the Emerald Bay technique? A charge could have started the slide up in the trees. Then two charges could have been placed farther down, releasing snow that would come in from the side. With thoughtful placement and careful timing, the killer could probably create three small slides that would converge as they descended. The gathering river of white might have enough momentum to easily punch across the shallower slope just above the highway and bury the road.

As Mariposa had suggested with the Emerald Bay avalanche, it was conceivable that the killer could have been driving his vehicle up the highway with the victim following. Maybe the victim knew the killer and was following him on purpose. Or maybe the victim didn't know that the killer was in the car ahead of him. Either way, the killer could slow to a stop, forcing the victim to stop behind, and then fire the explosions by remote control.

The victim had been pointing north when they dug out his vehicle. Any vehicle that forced him to stop would have to be north of the point where the avalanche came down.

I climbed back down onto the highway and walked to where the obstructing vehicle would likely stop. Spot stayed up on the slide and stood with his toes at the edge of the fresh-cut wall. He looked down on me, his head lowered, his jowls flopping open.

I heard a car approaching from the north and moved to the edge of the road. "Stay there," I said to Spot.

The car rushed by, unaware that a large animal was directly above him, watching the car's movement.

I climbed back onto the slide track and hiked up the river of white. Spot ran ahead.

At the top I found a depression in the snow, similar to what Mariposa had found at the top of the Emerald Bay slide. Twenty-five yards down, I found two more depressions, one on either side.

I thought about Lori Simon.

Was it possible that there was a second body in this slide as well?

I could drive back to Ellie's Three Bar Ranch, borrow Honey G and see what he could find.

As before, it would take an entire day for two round trips to the foothills and a thorough search of the slide. Honey G was clearly superb at Search-and-Rescue. But I had a dog by my side who had just taken a refresher course from the master. It would only take a few minutes to give him a try.

I knelt down next to him, put one hand on his chest and the other on his back, just as Ellie had with Honey G. I gave him a little vibration to get him excited.

"Find the victim, Spot! Find!"

I gave him a pat and he ran off.

It was nothing like the organized, methodical search that Honey G had demonstrated. Spot meandered here and there, ranging up the slide path a good fifty yards and then coming back down. When he veered off the slide residue into the bottomless powder to the side, he seemed to understand that a victim wouldn't be there, and he climbed back onto firmer snow.

Spot's staying power was greater than mine. After wandering the slide on both sides of the highway, I was ready to give up before he was. I couldn't be certain, but I believed there wasn't another body in the slide.

I called Spot and praised him lavishly as we walked back to the car.

TWENTY-NINE

I'd gotten the Sand Harbor victim's address and description from the Washoe Sheriff's Department.

Astor Domino was twenty-seven, originally from Brooklyn, New York. The old Blazer he drove belonged to his parents who still lived in Brooklyn. The Washoe lieutenant said that the parents had been informed that their son had died in an avalanche. The lieutenant also said that Astor was in his last year at Sierra Nevada College in Incline Village. His major was Ecology, and he was on track to graduate with honors in the spring. He lived near the college.

I was in Incline Village before noon.

The address was on Lakeshore Drive, which went with names like Lexus and Mercedes, not with Chevy Blazer. But unlike the ritzy lakeshore residents who paid $100,000 a running foot for their lots on the beach, Astor's address number was on the slightly poorer side of the street.

There was a stone fence draped with snow. Part way down the fence was a solid plank, double wooden gate with heavy wrought iron hardware in a King Ludwig design. The gate was open. I pulled in.

The drive was made of warm, creamy brick and laid in a repeating half-circle pattern. It was moist and clear of snow and as the flakes landed they instantly melted. A gentle mist rose from the heated surface.

Adjacent to the front gate was a gray stucco caretaker's residence. It had a steep roof that curved at the edges and wrapped underneath at the eaves, which were supported by robust, rough-cut beams in a timber-frame style. The windows were small and made up of dozens of small panes. A heavy brick chimney wrapped in leafless vines rose from one end of the house.

I continued down the drive.

The creamy brick road curved like a fairy tale around the caretaker's house. It wound through thick plantings and artful arrangements of boulders toward a mansion that loomed over the yard. I pulled up and parked under a drive-through portico. On one side of my Jeep was a wall of rock down which a fountain cascaded. Steam rose from the water, but I couldn't tell if the water came out heated or if the rocks were heated like the driveway brick. Either way, it was good to know that the rich were doing their part to keep the energy companies' market cap up and the atmosphere filling with greenhouse gases.

I looked for a doorbell. There was a small brass diorama where a door knocker would normally be. A bear bent over a stream. I reached for the bear, trying to figure out how it worked. The bear turned back and forth, and his paw swiped at a fish in the stream. From the recesses of the house came a tabernacle choir hitting a high chord. The owners of this house and Lorraine Simon's parents in their Seacliff mansion must have downloaded their doorbell sounds from the same website.

The door opened and a seventy-something gentleman answered the door. "Good afternoon, sir," he said. He glanced at my bandage and then studiously concentrated on my eyes.

He didn't wear white gloves, but he had on a dark blue suit over a light blue shirt with a dark blue bow tie. His white hair was perfectly combed and his white moustache trimmed in a Clark Gable cut. I forgave him the untrimmed nose hairs as a feature of declining vision.

"I'm Detective Owen McKenna. I'm investigating the death of Astor Domino and I have this as his address."

"Our caretaker, yes. A terrible thing, what happened. He was a good boy." The man made a surreptitious glance behind him. "But it would be out of place for me to talk to you without

Mrs. King's permission. If you will wait inside, please, I'll tell her you're here."

He went to the far side of the foyer, stepped through French doors and shut them behind him. The doors had little panes with distorting glass that allowed light but no clear image to pass through. I saw movement and then nothing. A few minutes later he returned.

"Mrs. King is in the pool for her morning ablution. She'd like you to visit her there. And she requested that you bring your dog. That is, if he isn't dangerous."

"No, he's not," I said, thinking that the security cameras were too well hidden. Like a marked squad car, an obvious security camera is much more effective at deterring break-ins than a hidden one.

The butler held the front door while I let Spot out of the Jeep. He trotted through the portico, sniffed the heated water cascade, inspected the creamy heated bricks and looked up at the columns that supported the portico roof. "Come on, Spot," I said.

"Does he, um, need to perform restroom duty?" the butler said. "He's so huge I'd worry if..." The butler stopped talking.

"No, I'm sure he'll be fine."

"This way then," the butler gestured.

Spot walked up to the butler and sniffed him just below his chin. The butler froze, and his eyes showed more white than is customary.

"A little pet between the ears and he'll love you," I said.

The butler was still frozen.

"It doesn't have to be much of a pet. It's the gesture that counts."

"I don't mind if he loves me, but I'd prefer he didn't lick me," the butler said in a small tight voice.

"He only licks if he senses you want it," I said.

"How would he know?" the butler said, tentatively raising his arm, his hand poised to touch Spot between the ears.

"I don't know," I said. "He can just sense whether you'd be receptive. Some kind of internal lick meter, I suppose."

The butler was still frozen, hand in the air. "Did you say lick meter?"

"Yeah. But don't worry. I think he's getting a negative reading off you. I think you'll be safe."

It took ten seconds for the butler to slowly lower his hand. His fingers were straight out, stiff as a board. He touched Spot between the ears and then made a little petting motion before raising his hand back up in the air and holding it there suspended.

"There," the butler said. "Will that be sufficient? He will love me but not lick me?"

"I believe so," I said, privately remembering the will-he-love-me-but-not-lick-me line in case I gave up investigations to become a lyricist.

"Then perhaps we shall proceed to see Mrs. King," he said. His hand was still up in the air.

"Yes, let's proceed," I said.

THIRTY

The trip to the poolroom was similar to the walking tour I took through the Simon mansion in San Francisco. The butler took me past and through a wide range of rooms of excessive size and insufficient purpose. My favorite room was the one with the most focus. No doubt based on a museum gallery, the room contained a large number of glass display cases, artfully illuminated and displaying a large collection of gold coins.

The pool was twenty by thirty feet and in a glass-walled room twice that size. The water was electric turquoise, and the air was moist and warm and smelled like chlorinated orchids. Potted palm trees stood fifteen feet high. It was like walking into the tropics.

Mrs. King was maybe ten years younger than her butler. She was on her back in the pool. She wore a black one-piece swimming suit with a plunging neckline. On her feet were small blue swim fins. On her hands were blue webbed gloves. She was facing me, back-paddling away toward the far side of the pool as the butler brought us into the poolroom.

"That is the biggest and most magnificently spotted hound I've ever seen." She erupted in a loud raucous laugh that reverberated in the large rectangular room. "Does he swim?"

Spot walked around to the far side of the pool.

I nodded. "He'd probably jump off the board, if you wanted."

"You're kidding!" she said. "You must be kidding."

I shook my head. The butler was trying to disguise his look

of alarm. He took baby steps backward, toward the door. He made an effort to look out the wall of windows toward the walled garden behind the house. The garden had a curving path through the snow. Like the drive, it was made of the creamy bricks. Steam rose from the wet surface.

Mrs. King reached the far side of the pool, turned around and paddled back toward me, again on her back, her head facing away from me. "I bet your dog has never swum in a pool, has he," she said.

"Actually, he loves pools and their clear water. He puts his head under water and looks around."

"Oh, this I have to see." She stopped paddling, turned and treaded water. She added, "But Jamesie, dear, I'm sure you won't want to see this."

"No, I'm sure I won't," he said. "Thank you, ma'am." He turned and left, shutting the poolroom door behind him.

"Jamesie?" I said.

"I know. It is a bit much. His real name is Wayne. But I asked him if I could call him James. You know, sort of a celebration of having a butler. And he said, 'Whatever you wish, Mrs. King.' Can you believe that? He went to butler school after he retired from teaching high school social studies. They taught him to talk like that. It must work, because after meeting Jamesie, two of my friends decided to get butlers. They called the school for referrals. Tell me, is the head wound de rigueur for a private detective?" she asked.

"Of course." I gave her a small grin.

"Well, you look tough enough to be a brawler."

"Have you had Jamesie a long time, Mrs. King?"

"Only since I semi-retired and bought this house. And, please, call me Josie. Jamesie only calls me Mrs. King because they hammered that into him at the BA."

I raised my eyebrows.

"Sorry. Butler Academy."

"What line of business are you in?" I asked.

She looked around at the cavernous room. "I know. Everyone wants to know, am I married and what kind of work does he do. I was married. He was a bum. Charming and good looking. Not half bad in bed, either. But a bum. Played cards and drank martinis by day and fooled around with girls half my age at night when I was traveling. So I made him a settlement offer before I took my company public. Ten years later the stock had risen, split, risen and split again. I groomed a very smart young woman to take over as CEO. When the time was right, I walked away. I still have fifty-one percent, and I'm still Chairman. Never give up control until you're ready to give up, I always say. But sorry, you asked what my line of business is.

"If you go out and look under the hood of your car," she continued, "and you know where to look, you'll find a tiny plastic box with some electronics in it. It's not the car's so-called computer. More like an accessory. It's complicated, but suffice to say it helps regulate some engine functions.

"I actually got the idea back when I was an engineer at Honeywell. We were working on auxiliary power units for the space shuttle. One night at home, I had one of those light-bulb moments. The thing I imagined wouldn't have done Honeywell any good, but I always remembered it. A few years later I took an early retirement option and worked on my idea.

"First I got a patent. Then I moved to San Jose and got in touch with some investors. They saw it clearly, and we started my company. Needless to say, it worked out well for everyone."

"This is in lots of cars?"

"Just cars made in the last ten years. Every car in the world, though. My company only gets about ten dollars per unit. But the world's car production is somewhere north of forty million cars a year. It all adds up." She stopped swimming at the shallow end of the pool and stood up. "I think your dog still wants a swim."

I walked over to Spot. "Do you want to go swimming, boy?"

Spot looked up at me, his eyes taut with excitement.

I got up on the diving board. "Up here, Spot." I pointed at my feet. He stepped up on the board. The board sagged under our combined weight. "Sit-stay," I said. He sat on the diving board. I walked around the pool to the shallow end. I bent down and splashed my hand in the water. Josie moved to the side. "Come, Spot! Jump in." I smacked my hand on the water's surface.

Spot stood up, stepped off the diving board onto the terrace, and trotted around the pool toward us, wagging, pleased with himself. "Good boy," I said. "But I mean, go in the water." I pointed at the water.

He lowered his head and stuck his nose in it.

"Okay, let's try it again." I took him back to the board, had him sit and called him from the shallow end once more.

Spot stood up, walked to the end of the board and hesitated. "Come on, boy. Jump in."

"He knows what you want," Josie said. "He's just not sure if he wants it." She turned to me, pulled off her webbed gloves and absently handed them to me.

I saw a movement in my side vision. The diving board made the sound of snap and recoil. Then came a monstrous splash.

Josie screamed.

A wall of water erupted from the pool and knocked over two of the potted palm trees before it doused the windows.

Josie shrieked with joy as she turned to see Spot churning toward her.

I spoke in a loud voice. "Move to his side as he approaches or his front paws will scrape at you. His nails are nasty."

Josie did so and then romped with Spot, hugging him, turning in circles, climbing on his back and pushing him under.

Spot came up the steps and climbed out. He shook, one of those thorough twisty shakes that starts at his ears and works its way down to his tail. Then he took a running jump and leaped in again.

I sat down in a lounge chair to watch. As Josie and Spot played, I saw the door to the rest of the house open a bit. Jamesie peeked out. I don't think he saw me off to the side. But the light from the pool caught his face. This time, his face wasn't worried or concerned but gripped with malevolence. Some emotions are hard to read. But hate and rage are usually clear.

THIRTY-ONE

It was like watching a physical therapy class where people frolic with dolphins. Swim With The Great Dane.

In time, Josie King tired, got out and put on a thick robe. She sat on a lounge chair next to me. Spot got out after her and found a Red Cross ring hanging on a wall hook. He lifted it off and brought it to Josie, who threw it into the water. Spot leaped in to fetch it. Water splashed out everywhere. The pool was down six inches.

I knew Spot would never tire of the pool, so after a couple of rounds of fetch, I called him out of the water.

"You are going to need a special permit from the Public Utilities Board to refill this pool after Spot is done," I said.

"Ah," Josie said. "That was fun. I swim for mental therapy. But that was much better. I totally forgot myself. But you didn't come to talk about me. Astor is the problem du jour. Correct?"

"Yes." I snapped my fingers to get Spot's attention. "Lie down." I pointed. He lowered himself to the tiled terrace and lay with his nose hanging over the edge of the pool. "Astor Domino was your caretaker?"

"Yes. I met him at a fundraiser for the Sierra Nevada College ski team this past fall. We were at the same dinner table. He was a strange young man, very reserved in general, but loquacious at times.

"Near the end of the evening it came out that he needed a place to stay, so I said my caretaker's house was available. There would be some duties attached, but the rent would be relatively cheap. He explained that he was quite poor but that his prospects would likely change come spring. I don't know what he had planned other than graduating, but it's a shame that he didn't live to see any dreams come true. What a tragic and unlikely death!"

"What duties did he perform?"

"The main responsibility is snowblowing. My friends all have commercial services do it, but my drive is delicate. I need someone who respects the fragile nature of the bricks as well as the border and the nearby landscaping. A snow-removal contractor would gouge up my drive."

"Your driveway is heated."

"True. But any heavy snowfall over five or six inches over-whelms the heating system. When we got that first three-foot snowfall I had innumerable small heated caverns under an uneven blanket of frozen snow chunks. It took hard labor to chop it up and shovel it away. Getting the bulk off with the blower right after it falls is the way to go."

"Did Astor do a good job?"

"Yes, he was an ideal caretaker. Don't get me wrong. Astor Domino was not particularly likable. I didn't cry when I heard of his death. He didn't ingratiate himself with me or anyone else. He didn't smile. But I was sad for him. He had a certain honor. He did what he said."

"Any friends?"

"Not that I know of. He kept to himself. Studied and watched TV. And he loved to ski. Had a pass at Diamond Peak. I have no idea what he intended to do after college. Although he obviously thought he was going to make some money. Maybe ecology degrees are more lucrative than they used to be?" Josie chuckled.

"The Washoe Sheriff's Department told me he was twenty-seven," I said. "Any idea what he did before college?"

"Only that he worked in a library in Brooklyn where he was raised. I think his father is a road worker of some kind for the state of New York. I forget about his mother. I think the family had money problems."

"We suspect that the avalanche that killed him might have been triggered on purpose."

"I heard that on the news. What an extraordinary circumstance to have someone do some kind of terrorist act or whatever it was and then have an innocent person die by it."

"We also suspect that Astor might have been the target, that it wasn't an act of environmental terrorism, but an act of murder."

"What?" She stared at me. "Even if someone wanted to kill with an avalanche, how would they do it? Force him to sit in his car while they sent an avalanche down on him?"

"Something like that," I said.

"But wouldn't it be exceptionally difficult? Would he realize it was coming? They make noise or something, don't they? I'm sure he would get out and run out of the path. He wasn't the kind to sit in a car and think about a possible avalanche. He was impulsive. He would act on it."

"Did he know about avalanches?"

"I would think so. He was taking a class to become a ski patroller. They must teach patrollers about avalanches, right?"

THIRTY-TWO

"The victims in the Emerald Bay avalanche were March Carrera and Lorraine Simon. Did Astor ever mention them?"

Josie King shook her head.

"March had some friends he used to ski with. Will Adams, a computer guy, and Packer Mills, a poet."

"Never heard of them," she said.

"How about a cocktail waitress named Carmen Nicholas?"

Josie shook her head.

"A contractor named Paul Riceman?

Another head shake.

"Bill Esteban? April Carrera?"

"Sorry."

I was thinking about the acid look that the butler gave Josie when she was swimming in the pool. "Your butler," I said. "How did he and Astor get along?"

"I would say they were cordial, not particularly friendly. One time when I was looking for Jamesie it turned out he'd been over talking to Astor for some time."

"Jamesie lives here?" I asked.

"He has the third floor."

"What about time off?"

"Yes, of course. He works a 40-hour week, with flexible hours. I give him the schedule three weeks in advance so he can make plans. If I don't have a gathering in the evening or some other special occasion, then he is on nine to five and eats his lunch while he's on duty."

"So he is free to go out in the evening."

"Absolutely. He doesn't even have to stay here over night, but I like advance notice from him in case he's planning to be gone."

"Did Astor have hours?" I asked.

"No. He paid rent, albeit much below market. Our arrangement was only about work required, snowblowing, some shoveling, some yard work next summer. As long as the work is done, his hours were his own."

"So he could have had a significant relationship off premises with Jamesie or anyone else if he wanted."

"Well, yes, I suppose," Josie said.

"What did Astor do for a living?"

Josie looked down and seemed to study her fingers. She held her hand out, fingers spread. She wore four rings, two on each of her index fingers. "I actually don't know. When he moved in he said his parents were paying all of his expenses until he finished college. But later, when I asked about his parents, he was vague. A couple of times I've seen him around this town with a range of people, people who didn't act like his friends. Once, at the gas station, I saw him with two other guys and they exchanged something. It looked like he handed them a small bag and one of them gave him some money. So I've wondered if he sold drugs."

"Did it look like a bag of pot or like a bag of pills?"

"It was dark and bulkier than what you'd think with pills. So I thought it was probably pot."

"Would you mind if I spoke to your butler?"

"No, but why do you ask about him and Astor?"

"I'm only filling in blanks. Astor lived with you and your butler. You would both be good sources of information."

Josie nodded.

"Have Astor's lodgings been changed since he died?"

"No. Several cops from the sheriff's department came through. I don't know if they moved anything. But I haven't even been over there."

"Any news from Astor's family?"

"His father called. Said he'd been told by the cops. He asked me to send him anything personal. I assured him I would, but that is too much for me to cope with right now."

"What about Jamesie? Has he moved any of Astor's things?"

"I wouldn't think so. I'm sure he would ask me before he did anything to Astor's things."

"But he might neaten things up a bit?" I asked.

"He might neaten up, yes."

"May I look at where Astor lived?"

"The cottage? Certainly. Jamesie will show you there." She reached over to the table between the lounge chairs in which we sat, picked up a remote and pressed two buttons.

The door opened in a minute and the butler said, "Yes, Mrs. King?"

"Owen would like to see where Astor lived. Would you please show him?"

"Yes, ma'am."

I stood up to leave. "May I call or visit you again?"

"If you bring your hound."

Spot and I followed Jamesie through the house to the front door. "It is snowing hard," he said. "Would you like to use an umbrella? Or perhaps you'd care to drive to the cottage?"

I looked at the caretaker's house, which was just a doggie bone's throw through the trees. "Walking will be fine. I have an umbrella in the car."

While Jamesie took a red umbrella out of a large pottery floor vase, I pulled a card out of my pocket. As he turned to the door, I dropped the card behind a side table that was draped in a long red cloth. I heard the small sound of the card hitting the floor, but it was not visible behind the floor-length cloth.

We stepped outside. While Jamesie opened his umbrella, I fetched mine from under the passenger seat of my Jeep. I made a lot of movement as I popped my umbrella open, action designed to obscure my search for security cameras.

I saw only two. They peeked out from above the large crown moulding that ran around the inside of the portico roof.

One was trained toward the drive and would record anyone approaching. The other faced the opposite direction and pointed toward the front door.

"Ready," I said to Jamesie. He nodded and stepped out into the snow.

When we got to the cottage, I was careful to be behind and to his side so I could memorize the key combination when he punched it into the electronic door lock. Seven, six, five, one, two three. He pushed on the door. The weather stripping was so tight it made a whooshing noise as it opened.

"Okay if I leave Spot outside?"

Jamesie frowned. "I presume you mean he now needs to perform restroom duty. I should like to know where so I can pick it up."

"If you would be so kind, you could watch him," I said. "If there is anything to pick up, I'll take care of it after I take a quick look around the cottage."

The butler looked concerned. "Some dogs become agitated when their owner is out of sight. Will yours mind being alone with me?"

"No. He will love you but not lick you." I shut the door behind me.

The cottage could be a spread in Country Home magazine. The furnishings had no doubt been chosen by a designer, and Josie had rented it out furnished. Thick upholstered furniture was arranged in front of the gas fireplace. There were woven blankets on the arms of the couch and thick rugs on the slate floor. The kitchen was large and open to the dining and living areas. There was a short hallway that led to a half bath on one end and a luxurious bedroom to the side. Inside the bedroom was a large bath with separate tub and glassed-in shower.

I glanced around, saw nothing personal to Astor, then climbed the steep shipboard ladder to the second floor loft.

There were two bedrooms with sloped ceilings and between them a large tiled bath. One bedroom was used as an office. He had books on the shelves and desk things on the desk, and there were files in the file drawer.

I looked for any items that weren't common to all offices. There were two things that caught my attention.

The first were several histories of the Sierra Nevada. They were stacked on a corner of the desk. I flipped through them, looking for notes in the margins or pieces of paper stuck in the pages. There was nothing. They looked like something to augment a standard college class. The books appeared to have been read, but they didn't look worn. Like many books intended for class, they may have been purchased used and never read at all.

The second item that stood out was a roll of paper. I unrolled it across the desk and saw that it was a topographical map of Tahoe, showing detailed elevation lines, which revealed all the mountains and passes and valleys in fine detail to anyone who was familiar with such maps. It appeared to be identical to the topo map I'd seen in March Carrera's bedroom. Like March's map, this one had no extra markings.

I climbed down the shipboard ladder and let myself out.

Spot was bounding around the deep snow. He ran across the drive and jumped into the snow on the other side. At the focal point of his movement, in the middle of the creamy brick road, stood Jamesie, his arms stiff at his side, his legs locked, his body frozen. Spot leaped toward him, stretched out his front legs and sank his chest into the snow. His butt was in the air and his tail wagged at high speed. Then he bounded up into the air, jumped past Jamesie again, flew across the drive and dove back into the snow.

I walked down the creamy brick road toward Jamesie who stood motionless.

"He's just playing," I said. "He hasn't touched you, has he?"

Jamesie didn't move. He spoke through clenched teeth. "No. Please call him off. I have to go inside and lie down."

I called Spot over. Jamesie waited until I had my hand on Spot's neck. Then he walked stiffly toward the portico and disappeared inside.

THIRTY-THREE

Spot and I got into the Jeep and left. After I pulled out of the gate I stopped and took an empty Starbucks coffee cup from the cup holder. I used my pocketknife to slice the bottom off the cup, leaving me with a conical tube. Then I sliced the tube lengthwise so that it opened into a gentle arc of paper. I folded it and slid it into my jacket pocket.

The snow was falling thick enough that it was hard to see as I shifted into reverse and slowly cruised backward into the drive. I stopped where the drive began to curve around into the portico. Anyone wondering why I didn't continue into the shelter of the portico would assume that I couldn't easily see through the snow on the rear windshield to navigate the curve in the driveway. They wouldn't realize that I only did it to justify pulling out my umbrella again. I turned off the engine and got out, closing the door as soundlessly as possible.

I knew the security cameras had recorded my movements. But unless someone rigorously kept track of the time, my movements would seem benign. They would just record me getting out of the car, popping open my umbrella and walking up to the front door. The camera would show that I stayed at the front door for some time, but anyone viewing the recording would merely think that the extended time frame meant I had a long wait before someone came to the door.

The umbrella stayed between me and the camera that pointed at the door. I pulled out the modified coffee cup and re-rolled it into a pronounced cone. The small end went into my ear.

The large end went against the door. It was a primitive but effective sound amplifier. While the shouted voices from far within the house were hard to hear, I could still make out the words. Josie was the one yelling.

"...because anyone with half a brain would have thought to say I was out of town. How could you be so dense!"

"If he'd been watching, he would have seen you come in," Jamesie said, his voice loud and sounding righteous. "If he'd looked in the garage, he would have seen your car. Nothing would arouse his suspicions faster than if I'd appeared to be evasive. He probably knew you were home before he knocked on the door."

"Then why didn't you tell him I was in the shower or taking a conference call?"

"I didn't think of it! And anyway, you were the idiot who gave him details about Astor! You should have just said that the boy got his money from his parents. Telling that detective about Astor selling pot will only raise his suspicions further. He's a goddamn cop!"

"But he did sell pot!" Josie shouted. "You think McKenna's stupid? When he asks around and finds out that I told him the truth, he'll think I was completely forthcoming because I revealed something uncomfortable, that we had a suspected drug dealer living in our house. If a cop has to squeeze you to get that kind of information, he will assume you are hiding something worse. But if you offer it up, he'll assume you have nothing to hide! Now get out of here and let me think!"

I heard a door slam. With the umbrella still hiding me from the security camera, I folded the cup, put it in my pocket. I still had to justify my second appearance on the security camera. I worked the door knocker.

I heard footsteps approach. The door opened. Jamesie stood glowering at me. He looked past me toward the Jeep.

"What is it now?" he said, forgetting his composure.

"I'm sorry to bother you. When I got out my keys as I was leaving earlier, I think a card fell from my pocket. It had a phone number on it that I need. When I didn't see it on the floor, I assumed I was wrong and that I'd left it in my Jeep. But it's not there. Do you mind if I have another look here?"

Jamesie stared at me, then stepped back, looking at the floor. "Well, I don't see anything on the floor. Could it have flipped into the umbrella vase?" He glanced down into the group of umbrellas and canes.

"Maybe," I said. I leaned my umbrella against the wall of the house as I stepped inside. I made a little show of looking in the corners, then squatted down and lifted the tablecloth. "Oh, here it is." I reached under the table and pulled out the card. I stood up and put the card in my pocket. "Very glad I found that," I said. "Sorry to bother you. Thank you for your time."

The butler nodded at me and shut the door behind me.

THIRTY-FOUR

"I had several errands to run today, from a meeting at UNR to a library in Auburn," Street said during dinner at her condo. "So I took my tools and sample jars."

"Bug lady on patrol?" I said.

"The Carabid Sherlock," she said.

"And the result?"

"Initially, not good. First, I shoveled away the snow behind my lab where there are some bushes at the base of a group of Lodgepole pines. Like most of Tahoe in a good snow year, the ground doesn't really freeze because the snow insulates the ground from the nighttime cold. I dug around in the dirt and found a good bit of humus. A good place for Carabid beetles. Beetles live everywhere and leave behind lots of evidence. But I didn't find anything like Doctor Kylie's sample. Only a single specimen of a much different species, and an abandoned carabid larval tunnel, dating from last summer."

"People must wonder about a woman digging in the dirt in the middle of winter," I said.

"No one saw me here, in Tahoe. But I was quite the attraction at the park in downtown Reno. There were three little kids who kept following me around as I scratched at the ground and studied the dirt with my magnifying glass."

"Any luck?"

Street shook her head. "Reno is only forty-four hundred feet of elevation, but it is nearly as cold as Tahoe, so I wasn't surprised. After I was done at UNR, I headed up Interstate Eighty. I pulled off before I got into the Truckee River canyon and drove to a field that is used for ranching. The soil was much richer than in the Reno park, and I found several species of beetles. But they were mostly dung beetles."

"None like the little guy who took refuge in that girl's lungs," I said.

"No. From there I went through Truckee, up over Donner Pass and stopped on the West Slope when I got down to about the same elevation as the ranch land outside of Reno. I'm guessing it was maybe five thousand feet. Because the West Slope of the Sierra gets so much precipitation, the soil is completely different. More beetles, and plenty of Carabids, but still nothing quite like Doctor Kylie's."

"You did all this driving just to help me? I'm touched."

"Actually, no. The library in Auburn has an out-of-print entomology title that doesn't circulate and I've been meaning to look up something in it for years. But I got close in Auburn. I walked over to a vacant lot where there are a couple of Black oaks and a Knobcone pine or two. Under there I found something very similar to Kylie's beetle."

"But not the same," I said.

"Not the same, but a Ground beetle with the same morphology, mouth parts adapted for eating snails and other similar traits. Close enough that I think it serves as a model for Kylie's beetle."

I'd nearly finished my stir-fried beef and peapods while Street had been talking. "By model, you mean that Kylie's beetle could have been found in the foothills at a similar elevation?"

"Yeah. What is Auburn, anyway? Twelve hundred feet?"

"Something like that," I said. "Highway Forty-nine runs from Auburn south to Placerville and on toward the foothills below Yosemite. So our beetle could have been found anywhere in those vicinities."

Street seemed hesitant. "Maybe. Let's just call it a hunch."

We spent the evening in conversation, making detours around the subject of the snow-dog sculpture with the bomb inside, trying to stay with cheerful subjects. But always, the vision of Spot or me walking into a bomb haunted the room.

Eventually, I said goodnight, feeling awkward as always about living in separate quarters from the woman who knew me so well and loved me so deliciously and yet still had enough childhood baggage that she couldn't give up her independence.

Street got up and fetched her purse. "I almost forgot. I stopped in a store in Auburn and they had a counter display with studs."

She handed me a small piece of jewelry like what kids put in their noses and lips.

"It's just a rhinestone, but I think it will make Spot look very hip, don't you?"

I held it up and looked over at Spot. "For his ear?"

"Of course. His ear has mostly healed, and if I wash the stud well, it should be safe." She took it from me, washed it with detergent and walked over to where Spot snoozed on Street's thick floor rug. He was so out of it that he barely lifted his head when she put it in the little hole left by the bomb shrapnel. He flicked his ear a couple of times. The pretend diamond caught the light and made a twinkling sparkle an inch back from the tip of his ear.

"Come on, boy," I said. "Time for bed."

He reluctantly got up to accompany me home, his ear still flicking a little, the diamond making little curlicue tracer sparkles.

"Pretty stylish, huh?" Street said.

"Yeah. He looks like a rap star."

THIRTY-FIVE

Over morning coffee I looked up the address for March's friend Paul Riceman.

There was a listing for Paul Riceman Construction & Painting at the top of Kingsbury Grade. I dialed the number and got his voice on a machine. I left a short message.

With that task done, I'd finished the only item on my list for the day and I hadn't even poured my second cup of coffee. Everything else I could think of was busy work and unlikely to be fruitful.

I decided to repeat my stakeout of Uncle Bill and see if he would follow any more young women.

I found a parking place with a good view of the intersection of Venice and Tahoe Keys Boulevard. I turned on the radio, poured a cup of coffee and opened my art book on the passenger seat. I'd barely taken a sip when Bill came along in his Escalade. I set my coffee in the cup holder and pulled out to follow. As we approached Highway 50, I started to move toward the left turn lane, anticipating another stop at the trailer where the Asian girl lived. But Bill turned right. He drove a block and turned left on Third, heading toward the hospital. He made two more turns and parked on the street in front of a dilapidated house.

I stopped far enough back that he couldn't see me. I couldn't see what he was doing, so I got out, walked forward slowly and stopped behind a young fir that was encroaching on the sidewalk.

Bill got out of his SUV, gathered his crutches and hobbled off across the sidewalk. He went down a narrow shoveled path to the house, turned and followed another path to the back of the house. As he moved out of my sight, I ran into the lot where I was standing, past a small 4-plex surrounded by a wooden fence on the sides and in back.

I boosted myself up on the fence trying to see across to the house where Bill had gone. Similar fences enclosed the nearby yards. With all the fences, I couldn't be sure how far down Bill was. I vaulted the fence, ran across the next yard and vaulted its fence. A dog erupted in one of the yards. Fortunately, he wasn't sharing the yard with me.

At the next fence I paused and looked over. It looked like the house that Bill had gone to was now two houses away. The fence I was leaning on was wobbly, and it felt like it would break if I put much weight on it.

Twenty feet away was a wine barrel planter near the fence. I took an awkward run through the deep snow, made a running leap up onto the planter and pushed off like a gymnast doing a vault.

My pacing was off and my hand hit the top rail at a bad angle. My other foot caught as I went over. I didn't break the fence, but I sprawled into the snow on the other side, going down on a knee as I twisted and then crashing down on my side. If it weren't for the cushion of the snow I would have been dazed and maybe injured. As it was, I got up slowly, worrying that the noise I made had alerted Bill to my presence.

I stepped through the yard as quietly as possible. I still wasn't certain if Bill was in the next yard or the one after that. I kept my head low, approached the back corner of the yard and slowly raised up to peek over.

Bill was bending down at the back door of the next house, his crutches dangling. He leaned against the doorjamb with his left hand and slid an envelope under the door with his right hand. It didn't want to go in. He worked it back and forth until it disappeared.

Bill straightened up, slid his hands onto his crutch handles and hobbled back up the narrow shoveled path that led along the side of the house. With his crutches, he was barely able to fit along the path.

I stayed put. In time, I heard the big engine of the Escalade come to life. Leaning over the fence, I saw Bill cruise down the street and drive away.

This time I carefully vaulted the fence and walked through the deep snow toward the house. It was a small house, not much bigger than my cabin. The front portion had a second floor with a low, gabled roofline. The back part was single story. I guessed that the back was a mother-in-law apartment.

I walked up to the door and bent down. I could see light through the space between the door and the doorsill. Whatever Bill had put in the envelope must have been relatively thick to make it hard to slide under the door. I walked down the narrow little sidewalk the way Bill had come and gone. With Bill gone, the Jeep was farther away than it needed to be for surveillance of the house, so I drove forward a half block.

From where I sat I could see if anyone approached the house. The coffee in my cup was cold. I dumped it out the window and poured another cup, then started on my lunch. I ate leisurely, making it last, while I ruminated on what Bill was up to. After lunch I listened to the radio, aware that if I got entranced in my book I might notice an Escalade in my peripheral vision, but not a person, especially if it was a small person.

Eventually, I tired of NPR's too-thorough report of all the terrible things in the news, and I started scanning music stations. I found pop rock, oldies rock, punk rock, classic rock, seventies rock, new age rock, top 40 rock, hard rock, country rock and eighties rock. There was one classical station and one that played Mexican ballads. But no jazz. No reggae. No polka. No Asian music. No blues. No bluegrass. No Cuban. No Indian. No Zydeco. Such is the depth and breadth of mainstream culture.

I stopped my music tour when my scan came back to the classical station, and I listened to the London Philharmonic working over Gershwin while I stared at the house before me.

An old Honda with a drooping bumper slowed to a stop in

the middle of the road. The passenger door opened and a girl got out. She reached in and pulled forward on the back of the passenger seat. Another girl got out carrying a child of maybe one or two, an age about which I'm not expert. There was no car seat. Neither the child nor the child's young mother had winter jackets or footwear appropriate for snow.

The first girl handed the mother an old backpack that was stuffed full. As the first girl got back into the car, the mother swung the strap over one shoulder and hoisted the child up onto her hip. She said something in Spanish to the first girl and the boy who was driving. The boy shouted, "Be cool, girl," and they left.

The girl walked over to the house and down the narrow path on the side, the backpack dragging into the deep snow on the side of the path. She disappeared around the back.

I gave her a minute, then went around to the back and knocked.

The girl was exclaiming at high volume as she opened the door. When she saw me instead of the friends she'd obviously expected, she held the envelope behind her back, went silent and frowned. She looked afraid of me.

"Hola," I said in a cheery voice. "A man was here. He put an envelope under your door."

The girl shook her head, her eyes showing fright.

"Don't worry," I said. "I just had a question. Have you seen the man before? Do you know him?"

The girl stared at me. I couldn't tell if she comprehended what I was saying, even though I was certain that, like all the other immigrants in Tahoe, she knew at least a basic amount of English.

"Has he ever bothered you?"

She started to close the door, no doubt worried that I might stop her.

"I'm not going to make trouble," I said. "Don't be afraid. Can you tell me what was in the envelope?"

She shut the door. I heard a bolt slide.

THIRTY-SIX

The girl lived in the city limits of South Lake Tahoe, so I called Mallory.

"Commander, it's McKenna," I said when he answered.

"I heard you're on the avalanche thing," he said, brusque as usual. "And someone tried to blow you up."

"They were only trying to scare me off."

"Good," he said.

I was grateful that Mallory didn't wrap his thoughts in carefully padded statements designed to cushion the impact. The memory of the inaccurate search warrant and no-knock entry I sent him on last fall would last for a long time.

"Got a situation you should know about. It doesn't require you to act on anything."

"I'm listening."

I told him about Esteban and the young mothers. I also gave him the addresses.

"You got a reason to think this guy is off?" Mallory said.

"No. But I don't understand his behavior. I'll let you know as I learn more."

"Right," Mallory said. "Hey, McKenna."

"Yeah?"

"Be careful of that bomber."

When I got back home, I let Spot out to charge around while I tried Paul Riceman Construction again. Still no answer. I still had half the afternoon left, so I thought I'd check it out.

Spot and I drove through snow flurries on the way up the Grade. Near the top of the pass, I turned off Kingsbury and drove slowly, then turned when I saw the street name I found in the phone book. A hundred yards down was a long, concrete block building, built decades ago with no detail designed to make it more attractive.

There were six narrow units, each with a human door, a garage door and a small window. I found Riceman's number. The door said Paul Riceman Construction in red vinyl letters. Someone had tried to peel the letters off, but the letters had torn into vinyl slivers. I tried the door. It was locked.

I knocked. Waited. Knocked again. I looked in the window. There was a lighted clock on a desk and light coming out of an open bathroom door, but otherwise it was dark.

The door on the next unit said Angie's Shape and Style. No one had tried to peel her letters. I opened the door. The woman closest to me had her head in a big bubble dryer. She was reading a magazine with close-up pictures of celebrity cellulite on the cover. At the far end of the room, a thick woman who chewed gum as if she were auditioning for a gum-chewing movie role was teasing the platinum hair of a tall skinny woman. The woman in the chair wore a frilly blouse that was tucked into tight jeans. The chair had been lowered, but still the skinny woman was tall enough that the hairdresser had a hard time reaching the top of her client's head.

"Yeah?" the gum-chewer said.

"I'm looking for Paul Riceman next door. His office is closed. Any idea when he's usually in?"

The hairdresser looked puzzled. She smacked her gum and then stopped. Too hard to think and chew at the same time.

When the tall skinny woman answered in a voice nearly as deep as mine, I thought maybe she was a drag queen.

"Moved out," she said. "He told me it was the bureaucrats and all the rules that did him in. He used to have two employees. A secretary and a helper. But the government made it impossible to have employees any longer. I remember what he used to say.

'Ridiculous rules, prodigious paperwork, terrible taxes and friggin' forms.' So now he's running solo."

"Are you a friend?" I said.

"Sweetheart, I'm a friend of anyone who'll have me. I used to swing a hammer for Paul. Are you lonely? I could swing a hammer for you."

"Any idea where to find him?"

"Sure, he offices out of his house, now. The A-frame at the end of the road. I know he's there 'cuz I saw his big truck down there when I pulled up. The red Ford. You should sit in it. The seats feel so good on your thighs."

"I'll bet they do," I said and left.

THIRTY-SEVEN

I parked next to the Ford pickup. It loomed over my Jeep as if I'd parked next to a small building. It was the perfect vehicle for hauling commercial air-conditioning units or jet engines for medium-sized planes. Anything smaller, and it was an absurd waste of equipment and gas.

I left Spot in the Jeep, walked past an old single-car garage that wouldn't even shelter the back end of the pickup, and headed across a walkway that had been shoveled in the last couple hours. The walkway had two or three inches of fresh snow that showed several sets of tracks. Although the walkway was elevated above the surrounding ground, the piles of snow left by shoveling came up to my chin on either side of the walk.

The A-frame house sat at an angle to me. I walked under the deep roof overhang at the end of the house and knocked on the door.

In time, I knocked again. "Hello? Paul Riceman?"

I tried the door. It was unlocked. I opened it a few inches and called out again.

Still no answer.

I went back outside and looked around. The layer of snow on his truck was thin. He'd driven it recently. The tire tracks from his truck paralleled the tracks from my Jeep. There were no other tracks nearby.

I studied the foot tracks on the walkway. They were hard to decipher and my own tracks had made it more difficult. In time I decided that Paul had driven home and walked from his truck to the house through the fresh snow. After that, someone else had walked in from the street and then back out. Those tracks were smaller than Paul's large boots. The fresh snow was dry enough that it didn't take a good impression of either person's boots. There were other tracks near the house that didn't show purpose, as if Paul and his visitor had milled about on the walkway.

I found a cigarette butt in the snow. Maybe they'd just shared a smoke, talked about the weather, remarked about the never-ending snow. Some of the heaviest concentration of tracks were at a place on the walkway that faced the side of the house. I looked up at the house.

The peak of the roof was thirty or more feet tall. Huge wind-sculpted cornices of snow curled off the back side of the roof. The side that faced me was barren on the top, as the snow had slid to the ground in a pile that rose in a steep slope fifteen feet up the roof. I looked at the slide residue. There was almost no fresh snow on it. It had happened within the last half hour or so.

I noticed that some foot tracks went off the walkway, through the snow and disappeared where the snow had slid off the roof. My breath caught, and I ran, slipping, back down the walkway and out to the Jeep.

I jerked open the back door.

"Spot, come!"

He jumped out and raced past me as I ran back up the walk and off into the snow toward the roof slide. I grabbed Spot, pointed his head toward the small slide and gave him a concentrated shake.

"Find the victim, Spot! Find!"

Spot's eyes got intense as he pulled away from me, leaping through the deep snow. His paws hit the firm snow where it had slid down onto the lower part of the roof. He jumped forward up onto the steep slide, climbing up the roof. He spun around, nose in the air, then scrambled toward the far end of the house. He went down the short slope, turned again and ran toward me. Then stopped.

He stuck his nose on the snow and without pause started digging.

I remembered my shovel back in the Jeep and sprinted back down the walkway.

When I came back with the shovel, Spot had dug down a foot. I moved to his side and shoveled at a furious pace. What had Ellie said? That most avalanche victims only survive fifteen minutes before the oxygen in the surrounding snow is exhausted and the victim's warm breath glazes the snow around their head and prevents more oxygen from permeating the snow.

In my rush, I made the mistake of shoveling too hard, too fast. I felt that mix of rapid pulse and rapid respiration and darkening vision that can combine to knock one unconscious. I slowed, gasping for air, then pulled out my cell and dialed 9-1-1.

"Paul Riceman's house!" I shouted when the 9-1-1 call center answered. I gave them the address. "Send an ambulance for an avalanche victim!"

I hung up and went back to shoveling at a more sustainable rate.

Spot found him first. He made a sound like a grunt and a whine, and I moved to where he was digging.

"Let me in there, boy," I said. Spot moved and I got my shovel into his hole and widened it. Spot had dug directly to Riceman's head, at least one toenail scrape visible across the man's temple.

"Paul!" I yelled. "Can you hear me?"

There was no response. It appeared that he wasn't breathing. But I had a lot more digging to do before I could get him uncovered enough to give him CPR.

I worked hard with the shovel. But the snow had already set up like cement. My shovel cracked as I tried to lever snow up and out of the hole. I eased off, but there was another crack and the entire blade broke off.

I dropped down on my knees and used the blade with my hands. Without the handle there was no leverage. It was excruciating work, swinging the broken blade with my hands, chipping away at the icy snow, scooping it out of the hole. I grabbed the broken handle and stabbed it into the snow, levering it around to break it up into chunks. Then I switched back to the blade to scoop it up.

In the distance grew the keening wail of a siren and then a second siren.

I kept stabbing and levering and scooping. I had Paul's head and shoulders exposed.

A Douglas County Sheriff's SUV was the first to arrive. Diamond jumped out, pulled a shovel out of the back and ran down the walkway as a fire department rescue ambulance pulled up after him. Two men got out of the ambulance.

"Over here!" I shouted at them. "I've got a buried victim. I don't think he is breathing."

I kept digging.

Diamond joined me in shoveling. We spoke no words, just worked as fast as we could. When the paramedics ran up, we had enough snow cleared away. They intubated him and started CPR.

Diamond and I kept digging. We got Paul's body free and the paramedics lifted him onto their stretcher and ran with him to the ambulance.

They slid the stretcher in the back and shut the rear door as Diamond and I came up behind the ambulance. The big van started to back up. The wheels spun on ice and the van stopped moving. The driver was a woman, and she glanced at me in her side mirror, her eyes wide with that universal look of fear that the tragedy that was about to unfold would be partly caused by her. She put it into drive, gave it gas, then put it into reverse, rocking the van back and forth. She got the van moving, but it would only shift five feet before the wheels dropped into a frozen depression and it got stuck again.

I saw the medics through the back window as the van went forward.

The van lurched back. When it lurched forward again, I got another view into the rear window. They had Riceman's shirt cut away, his pink chest bared. The medic had the defibrillator on his chest. Riceman jerked. The van came back. The driver did not shift, but kept trying to go backward, burning the wheels down through the ice in an effort to reach pavement. The spinning tires hummed at high pitch, grinding away at the ice.

Diamond and I ran around in front of the van, put our hands against the grill and pushed. The van inched backward. The driver locked eyes with me, her teeth gritted, worry and fear passing between us like electric current. I dug my boots into the snow, turned my head and Diamond and I pushed as if to restart Paul's heart with our effort.

The van's tires found purchase, and it pulled away from us. The driver backed into the street, stopped and lurched forward, tires again spinning. The big van skidded around and rushed down the street toward the boulevard, its siren rising and its flashing lights as staccato and unsynchronized as a fibrillating heartbeat.

When the ambulance siren receded into the distance it was deathly quiet, the gentle snowfall in stark contrast to an atmosphere so tense that I could feel it prickle my skin.

Diamond stood near me, still panting with his effort, his legs and arms stiff as boards, his grip on his snow shovel so tight there was no color in his fingers. And in the street, next to Spot, was the drag queen. She kneeled in the slush, her shivering visible from a distance, her shaking arms clinging to Spot like he was a life preserver.

THIRTY-EIGHT

Diamond got into his cruiser and got on the radio to make a report.

I turned to the drag queen who was still waiting, shivering, next to Spot. I was still hot from shoveling. So I took off my jacket and gave it to her.

"Here, put it on," I said. "Let's get in the Jeep and get you warmed up."

She pulled on the jacket and got in the passenger seat while I let Spot in back. She shivered. I was sweating. I started the engine and turned the heater on high. I directed the vents toward her and rolled down the window on my side.

"I'm Owen McKenna," I said.

"So very pleased to meet you." We shook hands. "I'm Terrance Burns."

"How well do you know Paul?" I said.

"I was just one of the girls to him. He knows lots of girls."

"But you said you swung a hammer for him. Did the other girls swing hammers for him?"

"No. So I guess I wasn't exactly like one of the girls. But he thought of me as a she, not a he."

"How long did you work for him?"

"Let me guess. You're a cop?"

"Ex-cop. Private investigator, now."

"Paul do something wrong?"

"Not that I know of. How long did you work for him?" I asked again.

"About six months, two summers ago. He mostly uses sub-contractors, but he was in a jam on a remodeling job. The framing sub was overbooked, and Paul had to do it himself. But he couldn't get it done on time without help. I used to work for a framing contractor down in Southern Cal, so Paul hired me. But now I'm a banker. I'm actually using my college degree from USC."

"How long have you known Paul?"

"We met the summer before I worked for him. So three years, I guess. The girls and I had a volleyball thing going at the beach every Sunday that summer. Paul and some of his guy friends used to watch. I was the spike king because, well, you know why. Anyway, they would cheer me on when I would spike the ball. But the girls all agreed that every point won on my spike was only worth a third of a point. It was complicated. So Paul and his buddies would keep track of the thirds. They'd always yell out the score, calling my team The Terrance Girls and the other team The All Girls."

"Did you ever meet any of his ski buddies?"

"No. That was his winter side. Me and the girls were his summer side. The two parts of him were completely different. He hung with different people in the winter. His personality was like that, too. He'd be all dark one day and sunny and cheery the next. I'd make up names for him that were light and dark. I'd say, 'Hey, coffee and cream, hand me that nail gun.'"

"You've probably heard about the avalanches where people died," I said.

Terrance nodded, her face serious.

"Did you know any of the victims or hear Paul ever mention them?"

"What were their names again?"

"March Carrera, Lori Simon and Astor Domino."

"No. I'm sure Paul never mentioned them. And they're just names to me."

"There are some other names I'd like to mention. See if you ever heard of them or if Paul ever mentioned them. Packer Mills and Carmen Nicholas? A girl named Ada? Bill Esteban? April Carrera?"

"No," Terrance said. "Never heard of them, either."

We talked for another twenty minutes. Terrance filled me in on everything she knew about Paul, his business, and his friends, male, female and in between. She told me about Paul's current project, a solo gig building an off-grid cabin north of Truckee.

We'd gotten out of my Jeep and Terrance had taken off my jacket when my cell phone rang.

"Owen McKenna," I said.

"It's Mallory."

"Commander," I said.

"Paul Riceman didn't make it. The ambulance guy said they were able to trigger a weak heartbeat, but that it kept cutting out, or something like that. Something to do with a low body temperature. They brought him over here to our ER. They tried everything, but his heart kept stopping. After a while they couldn't restart it."

"Sorry to hear it," I said.

"One thing I forgot to ask. Do you know Riceman's next of kin?"

"No. But hold on. I'm talking to Terrance Burns, a friend of his." I turned to Terrance.

"He died?" Terrance said.

"Yes. Do you know his next of kin?"

"Oh, God, that's terrible. That's so terrible." Terrance was leaning against the Jeep. She began to sag.

"Do you know if Paul had any next of kin?" I said again.

"I don't know," Terrance said. "He never mentioned any family."

I spoke into the phone. "No next of kin that we know of. I'll call you if I learn of any."

THIRTY-NINE

Terrance Burns went to tell the girls the news about her ex-boss. Spot lay in the Jeep, depressed at finding yet another lifeless body. I got two pairs of latex gloves out of the box under my seat.

Diamond headed for Riceman's house, and I started with his truck. I searched in, around, and under both front and back seats, through the glove box, in the cup holders, under the floor mats. I found nothing but the usual items, fast food wrappers, a stray mint, some spilled toothpicks.

I went around back, opened the topper latch and pulled down the rear gate. The truck bed was empty except for some dirt in the grooves of the bed liner. I was closing it back up when I realized what I'd seen. I called Street.

"Working on something important?" I said when she answered.

"Updating my Tahoe Basin insect catalog. Why?"

"I'm up at the top of the Grade. Spot found Paul Riceman's body buried where the snow slid off his roof."

Street inhaled. "Murder or an accident?"

"I'd guess murder. I also found a little bit of dirt in the back of Riceman's pickup. I wonder if you could look at it. See if it is similar to the kind of dirt those beetles live in."

"Give me twenty minutes."

I told Street where the home was, and we hung up.

I joined Diamond in the house. We took our time and left nothing out except those areas that would require destruction to get to. We opened jars in his fridge, but we didn't cut the couch cushions apart. We pulled out everything in his drawers and closets, but we didn't pry up floorboards. We took off switch plate covers, but we didn't take apart his computer or his printer. We lifted up throw rugs, but we didn't pull up carpet.

We had no idea what we were looking for other than something that Riceman may have taken the trouble to hide or something that would connect him to any of the other avalanche victims or their friends.

Paul's house contained nothing unusual except several large working models of biplanes from the barnstorming days. They had five-foot wingspans and gas-powered engines. They hung in custom slings from hooks in the lofty A-frame ceiling. On a shelf sat the radio remotes for flying the planes from the ground. I picked one up.

"You think a guy could use one of those transmitters to fire an avalanche from a distance?" Diamond asked.

"I don't know. But I have an idea who to call to find out." Someone knocked at the door.

It was Street. She stood with her toolbox in one hand and a sample jar in the other. She held up the jar. "I already looked in the back of the pickup. No beetles. But I'll take this dirt sample back to the lab and scan it under the scope to look for any signs of carabid presence."

I gave her a hug and walked her out to her car. She pointed at the slide and the hole we'd dug to pull out Riceman. "How do you think it was caused?" she asked.

"Don't know, yet."

I thanked her, and she drove away.

Two hours later, Diamond and I had found only two things worth noting.

One was a topo map of Tahoe that looked identical to the one I found in March's bedroom and in the caretaker's cottage where Astor lived. Like the others, it had no hand-made markings on it.

The second item I noticed was a Post-it note stuck on Paul's desk phone. It was written in pen in barely legible cursive, hand-writing that I'd seen elsewhere in the house and was certain belonged to Paul.

"Look at this," I said to Diamond. I read from the Post-it, "'Three by eight seems a good size, and what about AC for the project?'"

"Any number of things on a construction job might be cut to three by eight feet or three by eight inches," Diamond said. "But I don't get the AC reference. Alternating current, right? Why would a contractor even refer to the question of whether AC would be the way to go on a construction project?"

"When you were calling in your report, I talked to Terrance Burns, the drag queen. Burns said that Riceman was building an off-grid cabin. I've read a little about off-grid power. Most off-grid houses use inverters to convert the low-voltage direct current from solar cells into higher-voltage alternating current for normal household use. But apparently, inverters waste a little bit of juice. So some very small projects use DC exclusively because it's more efficient and it works well if you're just running a few lights and not plugging in household appliances."

Diamond nodded.

"But I can think of other translations of the note," I continued. "The words 'three by eight seems a good size' could refer to the three-by-eight explosives that Mariposa Pearl said are the preferred size for avalanche control."

"You got an alternate explanation for AC?"

"AC could refer to March's sister, April Carrera," I said.

Diamond thought about that. "You think Riceman's death was an accident?"

"Let's take another look."

We went outside and looked at the large pile of snow from which we pulled Paul. It sloped at a steep angle from the ground up the side of the roof. The other side of the roof still had a curling cornice of snow six feet deep and fifty feet long, clinging precariously to the ridge of the roof. It looked like it could slide at any moment.

"You wouldn't want to be under it when that cornice goes," Diamond said.

"No. How do you figure it could be done? Let's say you get Paul to walk below it. You could toss something important where he'll see it and then go fetch it. But you have to make the roof release at exactly that moment."

Diamond shook his head. He studied the roof, then walked down the slide residue, looking up at the roof ridge.

I walked around the other side, staying a good distance from the roof in case the remaining snow gave way. Before I got around the house, Diamond whistled. I continued my circuit through the deep snow.

Diamond stood looking up at the back end of the house. He pointed toward the peak and the deck that projected out under it.

I looked up toward the shadowed overhang. The waning light of late afternoon was flat. The house was a dark triangle against a dull gray sky smudged with the light gray falling snow.

"What do you see?" I asked.

"The rope," Diamond said.

"Where?"

"From the peak of the roof, going down into the snow. Stretched tight, right along the roof's edge."

"Oh, I see it," I said.

"Looks like there was a dark-colored rope where someone hung a flower pot or one of those plastic owls that are supposed to keep songbirds from building nests under the eave."

Diamond still had his arm up, pointing. He drew in the air with his index finger. "Someone got up on that deck and attached a long coil of nylon cord. They took the coiled rope and hiked out to that rise over there, pulling the rope tight so it went over the snow on the roof. They walked in a big arc until they got the cord to the front of the roof's ridge."

Diamond walked that direction and sighted along the roof. "Except, it doesn't look like that rise over there is high enough. You'd have to get the rope another twenty feet up to clear the cornice."

I went to the front of the house. "You could use the utility lines in the street," I said. "Tie a rock to your rope and toss it over the lower lines. Those are the cable TV lines. The high voltage lines are the ones at the top. As long as you stayed away from those you wouldn't light yourself up."

"That'd be better," Diamond said, "but I still don't think you could get your rope high enough."

"Remember that time we camped before they invented those bear-proof food containers? And there wasn't a tree high enough to string up our food?"

"Yeah," Diamond said. "We used a three-point suspension between three trees and hung that pack out over a gully. Someone could do that here."

I looked up at a big Jeffrey pine that shaded Paul's walkway. The lowest branches were a good forty feet in the air. "If someone could get a rope up over that first branch, then it could be used to hoist the other rope coming from the cable TV utility line. Adjust the tension here and there and you could drop your cord down onto the roof snow right where you want."

"So you agree with me," Diamond said.

"Yeah."

"Once the perp had the cord running the length of the roof, he tucked the end of it down into the snow where the roof edge is near the front door. Later, after Paul came home, he knocked on the door." Diamond was moving around, acting out his scenario. "Paul answered, and the perp talked to him and then pretended to see what he'd already left in the snow below the roof. Paul looked and saw the item and went over to get it.

"At just the right moment, the perp pulled the cord out of the snow where he'd tucked it out of sight, and he ran down the walkway, jerking it so hard that it cut into the snow on the roof and released it down onto Paul."

"Makes sense to me," I said.

FORTY

Diamond left, and I made phone calls as I drove back to my cabin, to Street to arrange dinner, to Sergeant Bains to tell him about Paul Riceman's death and our suspicions that it was murder. Then I called Bill Esteban.

"March's friend Paul Riceman was killed in an avalanche today," I told him.

"What? Mother Mary. Was it a murder?"

"I think so. Can I stop by in the morning?"

"Yes, of course. I'll be here."

That evening Street told me that the dirt in Riceman's truck looked promising as a home for a carabid like the one found in Lori Simon's lungs. Street sensed that our evening discussion was going to descend into darker events and darker human motivations. So she invoked the one-glass rule, which meant that we could only discuss the crime during our first glass of wine. After that we had to switch to pleasant topics.

As always, it was a good policy, and after a simple baked salmon and asparagus dinner, she decided on a sleepover, and we eventually went to bed and watched a DVD movie on my laptop.

In the morning, I called information for Dust Devil, Texas, and got the number for Gabriella Mendoza, the woman who was the best friend of Maria Carrera, March and April's mother.

Gabriella answered on the fifth ring. "Hola."

"My name is Detective Owen McKenna. I'm calling from

California where I'm working for Bill Esteban. You probably are aware that March Carrera died in an avalanche."

"Si. William called me. It is a fright to my soul. The poor boy. And April. She is on the island all alone."

"We think someone caused the avalanche. We think that person knew March."

"It gets worse," Gabriella said. "Where is my creator in this?"

"I have a couple of questions about when March and April were little. You took care of them."

"I did my best. And what has come of it? March is gone. William has kicked April out. She is having a struggle."

"Did April live with Bill in Tahoe or in Texas?"

"With March and William. In Tahoe."

"Why did Bill kick her out?" I asked.

"William has a temper. April has the same temper. They are like two cats who cannot live in peace. But why call me? You think the avalanche was made by a person from Texas?"

"I don't know," I said. "Can you think of any friends of March and April who moved out west? Anyone from your community who now lives in California or Nevada?"

"No."

"Have you heard of anyone from your town who became a skier or snowboarder?"

"No. You must understand, our town is very poor. The meat packing plant is the only job. Same now as then. Maria did her best. But when she died, she had nothing. With money, she could have made the car brakes repaired. She would have been able to stop the car. She died because she was poor. I did my best. William helped some. But it was very difficult. The other people in town are the same. No one has money for ski or snowboard."

"What about Maria and Bill's mother? She had money."

"No, it is not true. Elena was poor. Very poor. She helped me with her grandchildren. But it was the baking. And the clothes. She was good at clothes making."

"Bill said she set up a trust fund for the grandchildren. He said March and April have had a small but steady income."

"April and March have talked of this trust fund. But I cannot understand. Elena could not help when the children got the food poison. They were very sick. But there was no doctor. If she had money, there would have been a doctor."

"Gabriella, when the kids were growing up, except for being poor, did they have a normal childhood?"

"There was not much worry. They missed their mother so much at first. But children adjust. They ran around and rode on the bicycle of their friend. They laughed and played. The most stress was the storms. We live in trailers. Every year or two the tornadoes blow at the trailers. Some are ruined. Some vanish. The paper called it Muerte Cielo. When the clouds turned black, people would shout Muerte Cielo! That was the only worry."

I thanked Gabriella for her time and hung up.

I dropped Spot at Street's lab and was heading toward the Keys at 9:00 a.m. The clouds parted, and I was blinded by dazzling sunshine on the snow. I reached into the glove box for my sunglasses and an envelope fell out. There was no name on it, but it was sealed like the other warning notes. I thought about the times I'd left the Jeep unlocked. I pulled over, put on my gloves and opened it.

> McKenna, save yourself and your dog.
> Tell the guy with the crutches you're
> no longer working the investigation.
> If you don't, the first bomb will rip
> your dog apart and the second one will
> tear you in half.

I stayed parked at the side of the road as I considered my options. I'd thought that Paul was the killer. I had thought that he wrote the other notes and built the snow sculpture bomb. But this note had a similar message, and the envelope, paper, type, and formatting all looked the same. So either I'd focused on the wrong guy and Paul was innocent, or he'd had a partner who killed him and was taking over his mission.

The practical, sensible thing for me to do would be to stop. Give up the case and preserve my dog and myself. But I realized that I must be close to knowing who the killer was. Otherwise, the killer wouldn't be concerned.

I decided that Street was right, that the killer was just after me and Spot. So I'd watch for bombs everywhere I went. I'd keep careful track of Spot. And I'd keep after the killer until one of us stumbled.

I pulled back onto the road and drove over to Uncle Bill's.

The garage door was open and he was getting three bags of groceries out of his Escalade as I pulled up.

"May as well come through the garage," he said. Then he saw my face. "Christ, McKenna, you look like hell. I heard about the explosion. I'm so sorry."

"Help you carry those bags?" I said.

"Nope. I may be a crip, but I can carry my own groceries." The words were rough, the voice rougher.

I understood that his disability was a sensitive subject. Unfortunately, what he thought was acceptable behavior from others was only clear to him. Which meant that the rest of the world would forever have to tiptoe around him.

I wasn't good at tiptoeing.

Hanging on the garage wall was one of those ski sleds made for handicapped people. It had a blue plastic seat and straps to hold down someone's legs. The seat sat on a framework that was mounted to a ski.

Also hanging on the wall were two short outrigger skis. They had crutch-like handles that wrapped around the rider's lower arms, similar to Bill's regular crutches.

"Do you ride the ski sled?" I asked.

"Hell, no."

"Why do you have it?"

"April fancies herself a do-gooder, a cripple-fixer. She can't just let other people be. Sees something wrong and considers it her duty to fix it. Problem is, what she thinks is wrong isn't the same as what other people think is wrong. The world would be better off if she'd mind her own business and fix what's wrong with her."

"Are you saying that she got the sled for you?"

"She's like a burr under a crip's saddle." He mimicked her, speaking in a high voice. "'Uncle Bill, there's a reclining bicycle they make that you can pedal with your hands. You should get those new crutches that fold so you can get them in the car easier. My friend is studying physical therapy, and she says you should be going to therapy at least every other day. And here is a leg exerciser that you can use in bed. Oh, and Uncle Bill, here's a ski sled for physically challenged people. I also bought you a season pass at Heavenly, and I arranged for lessons, and I printed out the race schedule so you can work toward the handicapped Olympics.'"

"She sounds very thoughtful, very supportive."

"She sounds like a meddling little bitch. She should stay with her ghetto shacks in the Dominican Republic or wherever she is and leave me out of her life." Bill put all his grocery bags over one arm and, letting his crutches dangle from his arms, pulled himself up the stairs using the handrails on each side.

My impulse again was to offer to help him, but I kept my mouth shut and slowly followed him up the steps.

I parked myself in one of the living room's big leather chairs and waited while he unloaded groceries. Eventually, he hobbled into the living room and sat down.

"Both avalanches were set on purpose," I said. "And it appears that the slide off Paul's roof was intentional." I didn't mention the new warning note. "Did March ever say anything unusual about Paul?"

Bill shook his head. "Nothing that stands out. They skied together now and then, that's all."

"He ever say anything about three-by-eights?"

Bill shook his head. "What are three-by-eights?"

"A charge that ski patrols use for avalanche control."

"Oh. Never heard of them."

"Did he ever refer to April as AC?" I asked.

"You mean, using her initials? Not that I know of."

"Did March ever talk about ski patrollers?"

Bill shook his head. "You got a lot of questions."

"That's a problem? You've got a dead nephew who was probably murdered. That's a problem, too."

"Yeah, but I'm paying you to find out who started the avalanche. Instead, you're asking me questions like I've got some key to March's death. I lay awake night after night trying to think of anything else March might have said. Trying to help you do your job. But I already told you everything I know."

"Did you? You didn't tell me that April lived here, and that you kicked her out."

Bill started to speak, then stopped. "She's always been an ungrateful kid. She was impertinent. She acted like I owed her. Like my home was her home and she didn't have to earn a damn thing. I had to practically wait on her. She never lifted a finger."

"If she had, you would have jumped on her for patronizing a cripple."

Bill glared at me.

"Gabriella also told me that your mother was broke," I said. "If she was broke, where did she get the money for a trust fund for her grandchildren?"

Bill hesitated. "She was broke because she put all her money into the trust fund."

I walked over to where Bill sat. "Bullshit, Bill. According to Gabriella, your mother couldn't even pay the doctor when the children got sick. If she had money for a trust fund for the kids, she would have gladly used it for the kid's medical expenses."

Bill's naturally red face was turning redder. I leaned over him. "What are you hiding? Why did you lie?"

"Go away," Bill said. "Quit prying into my life." Bill pushed down on the chair arms, raising himself up. "Out of my way," he said.

I didn't move.

He realized he couldn't get up with me in the way. He flopped back down into the chair, astonished. "Move, you sonovabitch!" He struggled again to get up. I stayed put.

"Goddamn, you, McKenna!" He yelled loud enough that the neighbors would be able to hear. "Let me up!"

"I will when you tell me the truth."

"I did!"

"No. I want it all. Let's start with the money. You set up the trust fund for March and April, didn't you?"

Bill stared at me.

"Didn't you!" I shouted.

Bill jerked at my yell. He stared for another second, then looked down. The stiff anger in his face melted away and then turned to sadness and then grief. He began to cry. At first his lip quivered and then his face scrunched up and tears came down. He bent over, arms on his broken knees, his big head nearly covering his arms. His chest heaved and his sobs were wrenching.

I walked into the kitchen while Bill cried like a howling animal. I looked out the kitchen window at mountains wrapped in the dark clouds that delivered the snow, precipitation that brought money to some, death to others. In time I found a glass in the cupboard, filled it with water and brought it back to Bill.

It took a long time for him to calm. Gradually, his sobbing grew quieter, the muscular spasms less severe. Eventually, he went silent, and I could barely see him breathing. He pushed against his legs and flopped back against the back of the chair. His head lolled sideways, his face crimson and wet. Bill wiped off his glasses with his hand and stared toward the wall, toward the framed picture of his sister Maria and the two toddlers sitting on her lap, March on her right knee, April on her left.

I set the glass of water on the table next to Bill, then sat down and waited.

When Bill spoke his voice was low and monotone. There was no emotion, no feeling. Just reportage. Just the simple recitation that makes a horrible revelation even more devastating.

"I was driving the car that night, not Maria. She was in the passenger seat. The kids were in back. I was drunk. I caused the accident that killed March and April's mother."

FORTY-ONE

I sat down, leaning forward, elbows on my knees.

Bill didn't move, his head still lolled sideways, like he had no muscle control, like someone in a coma.

"It was two in the morning. Maria and I had just closed up my club. She was my manager, my head waitress, my chief accountant. I was the man at the door greeting the guests, and the man behind the bar pouring the stiff drinks that we became known for, the young entrepreneur who was so full of himself that he couldn't see why he shouldn't celebrate his success every night.

"Maria gathered up the kids from the cots in the back room where they were asleep, wrapped them in sleeping bags and carried them one at a time out to her car. She came back in to tell me there was a sleet storm rising up and would I drive her home? She'd slid off an icy road once and ever since had been petrified of driving on ice and snow. She had an old Chevy from the early sixties. It didn't even have seatbelts, and I think that added to her fear.

"I told her I couldn't drive her, that I had work to do at home. Of course, I didn't have a life outside of the club. The only work I had to do at home was to watch late movies and drink myself further into oblivion.

"So she went back outside. I didn't hear her car start up. Eventually, I looked out, and she was standing under the eave by the back door of the club. The parking lot light shined on her face, and I saw her looking up at the sky, her eyes wet with fear, as the freezing rain coated everything. It was a winter version of Muerte

Cielo.

"So I thought I'd be big about it. Help my little sister home. It was like I'd completely forgot that she'd moved in from the country with her kids and rented an apartment just to help me run the club. I was good at driving in the snow and ice. Of course, I'd been drinking a little here and there, just as I always did during work. Maybe it added up to six or seven drinks, quick shots of tequila, nothing serious like the double martinis that were popular with my customers.

"So I downed a couple more for the road. Nothing that would mess with my brain, just a little pick-me-up.

"She thanked me and wiped her eyes and thanked me again and I felt so important. She ran through the ice storm and got the scraper out from under the seat. But I said I'd do it because I had my gloves on. Mr. Nice Guy.

"So I scraped the ice off the windshield. The babies were sound asleep in back, all wrapped up in their sleeping bags. They never made a sound as I drove them home.

"It was only about three miles to her apartment. But the road was dark and icy and there was a curve to the left, not real sharp, the kind of thing a good driver can take without slowing down. I took my foot off the gas just because I was such a good driver that I knew not to push it on ice. And it wasn't the ice that got me.

"It was my vision, my goddamn drunken blurry vision. I was trying to see the line, trying to blink away the double image in my brain, when I caught the tire on the shoulder.

"It was like being sucked off the road by a giant vacuum cleaner. The car seemed to get pulled down the embankment and it rolled all the way over twice. I felt metal from the dash smash into my knees, and I heard Maria scream, and the passenger door popped open, and then it was still.

"The babies were still in back, still in their bags, but awake and crying. I pulled myself out of the driver's door, my legs on fire, and I crawled to Maria who was lying in the dirt. Her body was face down, but her head was sideways. Too far sideways. I knew there wasn't any hope.

"With Maria dead, all that mattered was the kids, their safety, their lives. I knew my knees were messed up, but that didn't matter. I had some decision making to do. I'd been picked up for drunken driving in the past. I knew they'd convict me of manslaughter, and I'd go to prison.

"I was sitting there in the dark, in the wet dirt next to my dead sister, trying to make a decision. Freezing rain was soaking everything with icy slush. There was no sound but the wind howling like Maria's ghost and the babies crying and the sobbing of a stupid drunk trying to figure out how he messed up so bad.

"The choice was simple. If I turned myself in, justice would be served, and the kids would be dirt poor, raised by my mother or by one of Maria's friends or by some foster home chosen by the state. The kids might never go to college, might never have a job other than working in the meat packing plant, might never live better than in a rusted trailer on the bluff.

"But if I didn't turn myself in, and if I didn't get caught, I might be able help give the kids a better life. I was all the kids had left. I didn't amount to much. I had no home, no savings, no education. But the club was doing well, and I could see that in a few years I'd be able to pay off my debts. If the club stayed busy, I'd eventually be able to make good money. I could help the kids a little now, a lot more in the future.

"They would suffer the loss of not having a mother, and it would be a terrible loss because they didn't have a father, either. But they would have an uncle who would help."

Bill stopped talking. He was breathing the long deep breaths of someone who has just confessed his darkest secret and is undergoing seismic emotional shifts as a result.

"I know it seems convenient that I had these justifications for why I didn't turn myself in. I've beaten myself up about it continuously ever since. Constantly wondering if I did the wrong thing, constantly questioning my reasoning. Every time I hear of someone successful who came from nothing, someone who was adopted or was an orphan and they made something of themselves, then I realize that they could be March or April, that my presence wasn't necessarily any help at all.

"And in my deepest despair about my actions I have the self-pitying thought that if I'd gone to prison I might have been able to let myself off the hook a little bit for what I did. The state says that prison is how you pay your debt to society for the crime that you commit. But does prison help you pay your debt to yourself and your loved ones? Probably not. But if it did, then I wish I'd gone."

Bill paused. He turned his head from the picture of Maria and looked at me for the first time since he'd begun talking, perhaps wondering what would come of telling me.

"You left the kids at the scene and walked back to your nightclub?" I asked.

"Yes. I'd worn gloves, so my prints weren't on Maria's car. I figured it would look like she had been driving. She was nearly as tall as me, so I hadn't moved the seat position. I stumbled through the dark, my knees screaming. There were some trees just down the road and there was a broken branch on the ground. I used it like a crutch and walked a mile back to the club. Only one car came by, crawling along, its wipers on high speed. I got down in the ditch, and it went by without seeing me.

"Back at the nightclub I called the cops, told them that my sister and I were working late and she'd left an hour or so ago but didn't answer her phone, and I was worried that she hadn't made it home okay. They went and found the accident and called me at the club with the sad news. I was up in the storeroom when the phone rang. Later, to the best of their understanding, they thought that the news was so upsetting that I tried to sit down on one of the cardboard boxes up there, but it collapsed and I tumbled down the stairway. They heard the racket over the phone and they came."

"They thought the fall down the stairs ruined your knees?"

"Yes. And it did. What started out as a bad injury in the car accident became much worse. I was in the hospital for two weeks. They did three surgeries, trying to reconstruct the broken bones and torn ligaments. They spoke of amputating the right leg. In the years since, I asked about having both knees replaced. But they say there isn't anything to anchor a knee joint to. It would be like a car mechanic trying to bolt a new wheel onto a pile of rust."

"Maybe just as well," I said. "If you could get new knees, it would ease your punishment," I said. "Take you off the hooks you're hanging from."

"Right. I'm glad I can't get them replaced. Being a crip is my penance. Without that I might be completely destroyed by my sins."

"So the kids moved back to Dust Devil, Texas, and Gabriella raised them?" I asked.

He nodded. "I sent her some money now and then. And I started investing in what would later become the kids' trust fund. And when I die they get everything. But I wasn't around much. That bothers me more than I can say."

"Did March or April ever suspect that you were at fault?"

"Not to my knowledge." Esteban looked at me, his eyes dark as ink. His rough complexion was blotchy as if shame were pooling under his skin. "You are the only person I've ever told."

We sat in silence for a minute. Bill lay his head back against his chair. He stared at the ceiling. His hands clutched the chair arms as if his grip were all that kept him from plunging into a despair that would crush what was left of his life.

"Life is so short," he said. "You only get a few chances to make things go right. We all make lots of small mistakes. But some of us make real big mistakes, ones you'd pay any price to take back. But you can't. So you gather up the leftover pieces of your life and reassemble them as best you can. But you make a mess with the glue, and the cracks still show and there are big holes where the missing pieces used to be."

"Tell me about the girls you've been following."

Bill jerked his eyes wide open. He stared at me, speechless. "You've been following me. I can't believe that you've been following me. I've done nothing wrong. Nothing. It probably looks bad, me following them, but I can explain. I'm sure I haven't broken any laws even if I'm a little unorthodox."

"Bill, you're digging yourself in real deep. Stop talking in circles and tell me about the girls."

He looked stricken. "It's a private thing. Between me and my maker."

I waited. Maybe my look was stern, because Bill started to shiver.

"I saw the first girl last summer," he said. "At the grocery store. She was very young. Probably sixteen or seventeen. She had a little girl she carried on her hip. She reminded me of Maria. So thin and pretty. And no husband to help. She had to hold the baby with one hand and get the groceries into her cart with the other. Just like when Maria had March and April.

"Something happened to me, I don't know how to describe it. I waited out in the parking lot, and when she came out I followed her. I wanted to see where she lived.

"A cab came to pick her up. I followed it over to an apartment building near the Y intersection. She got out, and it was heartbreaking to watch her struggle to carry all her bags of groceries and her baby, too. I wanted to help, but I was afraid to approach because I was certain she would be afraid of me. She was Mexican and I speak Spanish, but I kept my distance. I watched her disappear inside the building and I left.

"I drove home and worried about her. I couldn't sleep, and I sat up most of the night thinking about her and about Maria and how she had no help when her kids were little. And I thought about Gabriella who did most of the work and had no help, either.

"Before my Washoe grandmother died, she taught me a little about how to weave grass. But when I wanted to try to weave the Washoe Star, I couldn't find anything like those grass fibers. So I learned to soak floor brooms. After a few days I could use the bristles. For dies I used ink. My first three were terrible. On my fourth try I started to get the technique.

"I knew if I could make it beautiful, it would engage the Guardian Spirit and help protect the girl. So I put the Washoe Star in an envelope and waited near her apartment building. The second day the cab dropped her off. I followed at a distance, inside and up the stairs. I think she saw me. Maybe she was worried. But I saw which door she went in.

"The next morning, I went back into the apartment building and slipped the envelope under her door."

Bill stopped talking. He seemed embarrassed. Exhausted.

"What else was in the envelope?"

"What do you mean?"

"I saw you put an envelope under one of the doors. It was thicker than the star. You could barely get it under the door."

Bill's jaw muscles bulged. "I wrapped the star in some money."

"How much?"

"Five hundred dollars."

"So this is private charity."

"Yes," he said. "It's enough to help with groceries or rent. Not enough to get into real trouble."

"Because they remind you of Maria."

"Yes."

"And you've had no other contact with the girls?"

"No. I follow them to see where they live. Then, when they are gone, I go back with the Washoe Star and money. I believe the star will help the most. I don't know about the Guardian Spirit or Mother Nature or God, whatever you call it. But the amulet is handmade. Each one takes hours. It is one person bringing energy to another person in need. If she actually wears it, if she senses the time and energy that someone put into dyeing the fibers and weaving the designs, it will help her. I really believe that."

"How many times do you bring each girl money?"

"I've only gone once to each girl."

"How many girls?"

"Since I started last year?" Bill thought about it. "A little over thirty."

"Thirty times five hundred each is fifteen thousand dollars."

"I've done some real damage in the world," Bill said. "I'm trying to make it a little better."

I didn't speak.

"Some people look at me and think I've got it all. A business and house near Houston, a house in Tahoe, money in the bank. Maybe they've got their own hell to live, but they'll never know my hell because I can't tell them. I killed my sister, and I sense that, in some critical way, I'm responsible for March's death, too."

"In what way?"

"I don't know. I should have been more involved. A better role model. I could have taught him better judgement. Maria would have. But after I took her away from him and April, I didn't step into the void. I should have quit the business, gotten a regular job with regular hours and raised those kids myself." Bill took several deep breaths. "I read something once in a novel by John D. MacDonald. He had these characters, Travis and Meyer, and there was this thing called Meyer's Law. It basically said that whenever someone is faced with a terrible emotional dilemma, the right course of action is the one that is the most difficult to take.

"I always took the easy way out. Still do. When April acted like a spoiled brat, I kicked her out instead of working with her. It was inconvenient to have her acting immature in my house. Much more convenient to send her into the street.

"Now March is dead, and she's all I have. But she's gone. And she despises me. When will I learn? I'm helping girls I've never met and letting my own niece flounder. Am I going to go to the grave being this stupid?" Bill stared at me. The flesh around his eyes was red and swollen.

"What are you going to do about it?" I asked.

It was a long moment before Bill spoke. "You think I should call her and apologize? Start over with her? But I don't know if I can make myself say the words."

"Meyer's Law," I said.

FORTY-TWO

After I left, I called information and asked for Terrance Burns. They didn't have a listing. So I got the number for Angie's Shape and Style, the hairdresser near Paul Riceman's house.

"Angie," a voice said. She was still chewing gum, smacking it loudly in my ear.

"Owen McKenna," I said. "I stopped by there yesterday and talked to Terrance Burns."

"Yeah, I remember. I was giving her the Chorus Girl tease. It's one of my specialties, kind of a local fave, actually. She told me what happened to that contractor. Imagine getting killed by a slide off your own house! That's unbelievable."

"Yeah," I said. "I've got another question for Terrance. Any idea how to reach her?"

"Well, I normally wouldn't put you on to one of my customers, but I know she would have a hissy fit if I didn't give *you* her number. Hold on, it's in my appointment book."

I heard the phone bang down. An old Kinks song thumped in the background. "Ready?" the gum-chewer smacked in my ear.

"Yeah."

She gave me the number. "This is her work number, so get ready."

"Thanks."

I hung up and dialed.

"Northern Cal Trust Company," a woman answered.

"May I speak to Terrance Burns, please."

"I'm sorry, he's with a client. Oh, hold on, it looks like he's just finishing up." She put me on hold. The music in the phone sounded like a Madonnawannabe but with an even flatter baby-girl voice.

"Terrance Burns," a voice said, deeper than the previous Terrance Burns, no obvious inflection.

"Owen McKenna calling. Are you the Terrance Burns I spoke to the other day?"

"Yes, sir. Good to hear from you." Then, in a softer voice that wouldn't be overheard, "Trousers, wingtips, jock-type wig, suit and tie. I even talk sports. Hey, how 'bout those forty-niners, huh?" Then, in an even quieter voice, he said, "That's the one with the pointed ball, right?"

"The bifurcated life of a drag queen banker is confusing, huh?" I said.

"Let me tell you. Half the time I can't even remember which way I'm dressing today. But the banker thing pays the bills, I'll give it that. Oops, here comes the boss on his regular route." He went back to the louder voice. "What can I do for you, Mr. Mc-Kenna? Are you still interested in that fifteen-year mortgage? I'm authorized to reduce the points to zero if you decide to lock in now."

"I have a question about Paul Riceman."

"Mortgages are confusing. Don't hesitate to ask anything you like."

"Did he ever mention taking an outdoor avalanche class?"

"Funny that you should ask that. Let me think. Yes, it was last fall, wasn't it? November. I remember it was just after we'd gotten that first series of storms. In fact, we'll still stay with the ear-lier rate quote."

"Has Riceman acted strange or done anything unusual recently?

"Well, I kept wondering, why would he go to Utah a couple of weeks ago to visit the area where he used to be a ski instructor when we have so much more snow here? But I told him that if he finds property there, we can do mortgages out of state just as easily as in state."

"What about someone known as the Guru of the Sierra?" I said.

"I recall hearing that. But you know how it is with a co-signer. At this point, I don't know who it is. Until I know who it is, I can't even make a preliminary judgment."

"Did Paul ever mention anyone else who took the avalanche class?"

"I actually know a client in Truckee who fits the bill perfectly. She was a friend of Paul and got the same type of mortgage on our referral program. I'm sure she's happy with it, but you are welcome to ask her yourself. Of course, you'll understand our standard policy of not giving out phone numbers or addresses. But our referral program can be a nice little bonus to those who decide to participate. Let me look in my computer and see if she opted in after she got her mortgage. Well, wouldn't you know, yes, she did. The way it works is like this. I can give you her first name, which is Amy, and her email address. You contact her and if you decide to go with us, she will get a sweet little check. Who knows, maybe she'll take you out to dinner with it. Do you have a pen?" He read off the email address. Then his voice got quiet again. "I can talk normal, now. Write this down, too," he said and read off Amy's phone number.

"Another question?"

"Sure."

"Did Paul ever talk about doing any avalanche control like ski patrollers do?"

"Not that I recall. But he learned about it in that class. He went on at some length about how they can use dynamite to start slides."

"Thanks, Terrance. You've been more helpful than you know. And if I ever need a mortgage, I will call you first."

"Honey, you need anything on Kingsbury Grade, I'm your girl."

FORTY-THREE

I called Amy and made an appointment to meet her a few minutes after 4:00 p.m., the time she got off her shift at the supermarket in Truckee.

A young woman came into the coffeehouse on Truckee's main street at five minutes after.

"Amy?"

She nodded as she looked at my bandage and frowned.

"Hi, I'm Owen McKenna. Thanks for meeting me."

"Amy Brewer." She shook my hand. "You're a friend of Terrance's?"

"He's been very helpful," I said. "She's been."

"Is she a dear, or what? Most men are such jerks. Why can't more men be like her?"

"Got me there," I said.

We sat at a table near the window. Amy got a fancy drink; I had black coffee. The snow had resumed and blew at a 45-degree angle, blurring the view of the buildings across the street. A steady stream of cars and trucks cruised down the street, wipers on, headlights on, chains clinking against fenders on the unfortunate cars without four-wheel-drive.

"Tell me about the Guru of the Sierra," I said.

"He's, like, kind of a strange dude," Amy said. "I mean, I think he's nice deep down, just very different. But he knows his stuff, I'll give him that." She had a straw in her drink. She pulled it out with her lips and used her fingers to steer the bottom of the straw around the top of her drink. She carefully sucked up the foam that wanted to roll down the outside of the cup. The noise was irritating. An elderly woman at the next table stared, her lips pinched.

"How did the class work?"

"The class I took was, like, three years ago. We met at the park here in town. They have this little area with three park benches and that was our classroom. Can you believe it? But I guess it makes sense because we only met there twice, and the rest of the time our meetings were up on the mountain."

"How long did the class last?"

"Six straight days. Monday through Saturday."

"How many students?"

"There were six of us in the class. I remember because Claude – that's the guy's name – he would say things like, 'come, my little six-pack, and let me show you the ways of the snow gods.'"

"Claude's last name?" I asked.

"Sisuug. Claude Sisuug. I remember because he told us this whole story that included his name."

"Do you remember it?"

"More or less. See, he's a pretty wild guy with one of those real big personalities." Amy sucked the rest of the foam off her drink. "You know how sometimes you meet a group of people and afterward you just keep thinking about one person? Not because you're attracted to them or anything, but because they sort of command everyone's attention? That's how Claude was in our class. I'd wake up in the middle of the night and go over everything he said, just because he was so out there.

"Plus, he's kind of passive-aggressive. It goes on and off like a switch. You never know when he's going to erupt, so you kind of pay attention just because of that. He even has one blue eye and one brown eye. It went with his personality. Anyway, back to his name. Claude's father was Eskimo and his mother was a French-Canadian who had moved from Montreal to their little village in Northwest Canada to teach.

"He told us that Sisuug is an Inuit name that means snow-slide. During our first class he described how an avalanche had struck his parents as they snow-shoed across a slope not far from the cabin where they lived in the Yukon. The snow ripped baby Claude from the sling on his mother's front, and - while they all survived - the impact turned Claude's left eye from the deep brown of the Inuit to the soft cerulean blue of his French-Canadian mother. I still remember him saying that. Cerulean. What a great word for blue, huh? Anyway, can you believe that? I can't believe that. But that's what he said. Who knows? Maybe it's true."

"How did you find out about this class?" I asked.

"Claude put a note up on the bulletin board at work. He sometimes shops at the store. Not real often, but just to get basics. You should see what he buys. Bulk oatmeal, bulk flour, bulk sugar, bulk granola. Salt, sausage, jerky. God, no lattes for him. And candles. He bought lots of candles. He's like the pioneers or something. He carries all his groceries in a big pack. I think he owns a truck, but I don't think he uses it much."

"Do you know where he lives?"

"I've heard rumors that he lives in a mountain man cabin in the Granite Chief Wilderness. You can't drive there."

"Near Squaw Valley?" I said.

"Behind there. Between Squaw and Sugarbowl, I think. He mountain-bikes in and out during the summer. One time in the winter he came to our store on his backcountry skis. Like he'd skied all the way. Imagine that."

"How did the class work?" I asked.

"You mean structure and stuff?" Amy mumbled as she sucked at her drink. "Well, when we met at the park for the first two classes, he went over academic avalanche stuff. He called it avalanche science. After the first two classes, we started meeting up on the mountain. We went to this place off Donner Summit. It was a long way to ski up there from the parking area. We had four classes up there doing hands-on stuff."

"Can you remember what you studied?"

"Oh sure. Claude had a way, you know? He was so wild about it that it stuck in your brain. Plus, I'm a good student. I got nothing but As and Bs at the community college. I took nursing prep classes. Biology and chemistry. I might go down to Sac State and get a degree."

"Tell me about the avalanche class?" I said.

"Well, we studied snow and weather and slope angles and stuff because those are the things that make snow slide down mountains. We even dug these deep snowpits to study the snow. They were eight or ten feet deep. I thought it was ridiculous. But then I got to go down in there. It was like a blue cave. We identified the weak layers 'cause those are where the snow above can separate and slide. After that I realized it made sense to dig the pits. But what a lot of work!" She focused on her drink.

"Was that the main way Claude determined if a slope would slide? To dig a pit and look for weak layers?"

"Oh, no! There were so many factors, I can't begin to think of them all. Like, we examined snow crystals. We actually put them on this piece of dark velvet and looked at them with a magnifier to see if they had agglomerated. Is that a word or what? I still remember."

"You mean they stick together?"

"Yeah. Well, maybe not if they stick. More like if they're just grouped. The crystals get all rounded. Sometimes, if that happens and then new snow falls on top, it can easily slide off. I forget some of the details. I know we also looked for cohesion. That would be more about stickiness. Claude said that even if you find mostly cohesive layers, sometimes the very bottom layer at the ground can still be weak. Then all of the snow can slide even though it's stuck together. That's called a slab avalanche. They're really dangerous because they can get going really, really fast. A slab like that will take out everything in its way. Buildings, trees, chairlifts, you name it."

"You learned a lot."

"There's more, too." Amy was excited now, recalling the details. "We stuck these density things into the snow. That told us how heavy the snow was. Denso-meters? No, wait, I think they're called densitometers. And we measured temperature gradients and learned how to determine slope angles. That's important because if a slope is between thirty and forty-five degrees, watch out.

"We also studied the different kinds of mountain faces. Claude always said how we had to notice which were windward and which were leeward. That means when the mountain faces away from the wind. It's just like sailing. Isn't that cool?

"Anyway, I remember that that's important because the wind can blow most of the snow off a windward face and drop it on a leeward face. They can be just yards apart and one will have almost no snow and the other might have a hundred feet of snow. And guess which one will slide!"

"Do you remember any of the other people in the class?"

"Just Paul Riceman who you mentioned on the phone. And my boyfriend. Only, he's not my boyfriend any more. We still get along, but he's not my kind of guy. I want a regular guy, you know, regular job and all that. Reliable. But my boyfriend was kind of exciting, and I thought it would be fun to take the class together. He's big into the backcountry thing. Always takes his snowboard and rides down. You know Mt. Tallac on the South Shore, right? Well, he rides down the cross. I think he's crazy. It's like this narrow gully between the cliffs. And super steep. That's part of why I broke up with him. I would never go with him on those dangerous rides because I'm too sensible, as he puts it. He always would say, 'You're so sensible. How can you live like that, always sensible?' It drove me nuts. I took the avalanche class. Is that sensible? Climbing up on some ridiculous mountain and digging snow pits? Like I'm going to use that in my job?

"My boyfriend was the opposite of me. He was totally interested in avalanches and how they work. Plus, he was into the whole control thing. How to rig up detonators and toss the dynamite."

"Do you have his number? I'd like to call him."

"Yeah, I still remember it. His name is Packer Mills. He's a poet. Talk about not being sensible. No wonder he wanted to break up with me. Here, I'll write the number down on my napkin."

Amy and I talked some more, finished our coffees and left.

"You're going that way?" she said. "That would be leeward. I'm going windward. See, I told you I was a good student."

I gave her my card. "If you hear of Claude, give me a call?"

"Sure," she said. She was walking backward down the sidewalk, facing me as she moved away. The wind whistled around from behind her head, blowing her hair out toward me. She wiggled her fingers at me. "Hey, Mr. McKenna," she called out, yelling over the wind. "What I said about more men should be like Terrance Burns? I wouldn't want that for you. If you want to do coffee again, I would, too."

I nodded at her. "Thanks."

She turned around, leaned windward, and trudged up the sidewalk into the blowing snow.

FORTY-FOUR

I drove down the East Shore. Street had left her lab and gone home, so I picked up Spot from her condo.

I caught Packer Mills just as he was leaving the snowboard shop. He had his key in the shop door, the glass of which was a color-burst of decals. The only light came from a light pole at the street and the neon signs of a nearby bar.

We exchanged 'Heys.'

I said, "I met a girl named Amy Brewer who said she used to be your girlfriend and that you and she took an avalanche class together three years ago. She said the teacher was called the guru of the Sierra."

"So?"

"You said you'd never heard of him."

"I hadn't," Packer said. "This is the first I've ever heard him called that."

"How come you never mentioned taking the class?"

"You never asked. I didn't think it mattered. Half of Tahoe's serious boarders and skiers have taken avalanche classes. I've skied and hiked above Emerald Bay, too. Does that matter?"

"Did you hear that Paul Riceman died yesterday?" I asked.

"No," Packer said, no surprise in his voice. "How?"

"Buried in an avalanche off his roof."

"Really? Must have been a lot of snow on his roof."

"Were you and he close?" I asked.

Packer shook his head. "Barely knew him." Packer's dull lip metal caught the streetlight and sparkled as if it were polished.

"Amy still in Truckee?" he asked.

"She still works there, anyway," I said.

Packer nodded. He picked up a snowboard that was leaning against the outside wall of the shop and walked toward his pickup.

"She say anything about me?"

"Like?" I said.

"How she regrets leaving one of the last true poets?"

"She did mention that you were a silver-tongued, mellifluous-voiced maestro of verse and walking out on you was the stupidest mistake she ever made. But other than that, no."

"Good," Packer said. He dumped his board in the back of his pickup. It clattered against the metal bed.

"Just curious," I said. "You spend a lot of time grinding and polishing snowboard bases, trying to make them perfect."

"So? Same with skis," he said.

"Then you toss them down without regard to how they get banged up. And some boarders ride rails in the terrain parks, and on off-hours they ride down stairway railings. One day at the mountain I saw several guys riding down a long series of concrete steps. There was no snow on the steps, no cushion at all. A single trick like that must pretty much destroy the base of the board that you worked so hard to polish. What am I missing?"

Packer made a little smile of frustration, then went serious, looked at the ground and shook his head. To him I was a geezer, incapable of understanding an artist.

"It's experience. It's process. It's about finding authentic expression. Ginsburg had an amazing command of the language. You could say he worked on his chops the way I work on the base of the board. But he didn't write Howl because he wanted to celebrate polished English. No way, man. It was about finding a gut-level experience and then translating it into words. The more raw, the better. Think of it as a voice of the viscera. That's what the boarders are doing. They don't all know about Dizzy and Pollack and Kerouack. They just know that when they get on their skateboards and snowboards they have a true experience, raw and unpolished. If the rails are rough enough to rip up their boards, it's like Ginsburg's obscenity. The gouged bases and trashed edges become the marks of authentic experience."

"You ever think about teaching?" I said. "Some of those kids could benefit from learning the antecedents to their passions."

"I could teach, but I couldn't handle the administrators. I've got a friend who teaches creative writing at UNR. He says the rules he operates under and the creativity he's supposed to teach are mutually exclusive. That's why Claude had to run his own avalanche gig. The schools, they all have outdoor programs, now. It's the new big thing. Sure, we'd love to have you teach, they tell you, but you gotta teach our way."

Packer leaned back against his pickup. "No way. I'd rather grind bases and get plastic lung disease."

"Is Claude Sisuug an artist?"

Packer nodded. "Absolutely. The mountains are his subject, the snow is his language."

"You keep in touch with him?"

"Nobody keeps in touch with him. He comes into a community at the beginning of a story and he rides back out at the end. Claude is the classic existential loner. His entire life is like a Western. He lives by his code, and he doesn't care what other people think."

"Any idea where I could find him?"

"Like I said, I haven't heard from him since we took his class.

"Amy said he supposedly lived in a hut in the Granite Chief Wilderness. Any idea where?"

"Not exactly. I remember him mentioning that he had an old miner's shack not far from the Pacific Crest Trail. Somewhere between Donner Pass and Squaw. He talked about how he could get to his place from either the north or the south. He said the hike from Donner on the north was about ten miles farther but it didn't have much elevation gain. Whereas the shorter route in from Squaw on the south side had a climb of fifteen hundred feet. No big deal with a day pack, but when you're hauling all your food in on your back, it adds up. He said hauling water was the worst part. That country is mostly volcanic in origin. Snowmelt doesn't stick around like in granite country. It just runs down through the rock and disappears. But like I said, for all I know he could be back in Montana. Or the Yukon."

"Where in Montana?"

"I remember him talking about the Beartooth Range. Near Red Lodge. He said they're real big mountains. Not like ours."

"Anybody else you know who took his class?"

Packer shook his head. "It was a pain driving up to the North Shore every time, fighting the weather. There wasn't anyone else from the South Shore to share the drive with."

"Has Claude taught any other classes since?"

"I don't know. Probably. I don't think he has any other way of earning money. It's not like he could get a job."

"Why?"

Packer laughed. "You'll know if you ever meet him. He's a mountain man, a real piece of work."

"You mean unkempt and strange?"

"Yes and yes. Wild eyes. Amy said he was creepy. I would say he was passionate."

"Amy told me that you were really into the avalanche control stuff. Detonators and explosives."

"Sure. Who wouldn't be? The explosives are powerful. The slides they dislodge are even more powerful."

"That would be raw, authentic experience?" I said.

"You catch on fast for an adult."

"You think you could find Claude's shack?"

Packer shook his head. "Maybe. Maybe not. I got the idea it was pretty well hidden because he didn't worry that hikers would stumble upon his stuff. Oh, one more thing. He said that he would take his morning coffee up to his lookout rock. From there he could see the top of one of the chairlifts in the distance. I don't know if that would help you. You thinking of going there?"

"Maybe. Want to come along?"

"Just say when."

FORTY-FIVE

I headed across town, stopped at my office and called Teddy Post in Oakland. I'd met him back when I worked homicide in San Francisco. Turntable Teddy, as he was known, was a pink-faced guy in his forties, about five feet tall and nearly as wide, and he lived in his mother's basement in one of Oakland's roughest neighborhoods. The basement had its own entry at the bottom of a broken concrete stairwell that had been dug out on the side of the limestone foundation maybe fifty years after the 19th Century house was built. Teddy had a regular stream of visitors who carried their aged, non-functioning electronic gear up and down those steps. In an era when most music libraries had shifted onto iPods, Bay Area vinyl record holdouts increasingly found their way to Teddy to keep their turntables spinning and their old amplifiers humming. I also knew that Teddy had a long history of fencing for small time burglars with electronics to unload.

"Hey Turntable," I said when Teddy answered. "Owen McKenna."

"I dint do it," he said in his squeaky voice.

"But an electronic guy like you can help me find who did."

"Okay, but careful what you say. You-know-who might be listening."

"Right," I said, remembering that he always made the joke about his mother listening in on his phone calls. "I'm looking for a way to make a detonator go off with one of those radio-controlled model airplane devices."

"You know I don't do bombs," Teddy said. "I'm clean. I fix

record players."

"Of course. But you're smart. You can help me figure this out."

Teddy sighed. "Tell me what you know. Maybe I'll have a thought."

"Guy set off some avalanches using dynamite. The avalanche charges were up on a mountain. I think he fired them from down below. He was also into those model airplanes you fly from the ground. I wondered about a connection."

"I dunno. Not much like making vinyl sing out of old speakers. Model airplanes are line-of-sight stuff. Not like you could fly them where you couldn't see them, right? We're not talking military drones run by satellite uplinks. So, while the frequencies the model airplanes use might work at a distance and out of line-of-sight, the power level would probably be too low to send a signal way up a mountain."

"What would have enough power?"

"Anything that can communicate over distance," Teddy said. "Like cell phones."

"I don't think this guy used cell phones," I said. "They can be traced."

"Right. And the receiving end would get blown up. Okay, walkie talkies. The expensive kind that operate on the GMRS frequencies. They will transmit for a mile or two. Technically, you have to have a license to use them, but it's not like anybody who buys a set at Walmart is going to register with the feds."

"How would a walkie talkie fire a detonator?"

"Like I said, I don't do bombs. Talk to Mr. Lee across the bay."

"Lee have a first name?"

"Yeah," Teddy said. "Mister."

"How would I reach him?"

"I dunno. I've never talked to him. But I've heard about him."

"What's his business?"

"Import, export. Stuff that ain't his. He specializes in electronics. But he brokers anything that you can't buy legally. From what I heard, if you want some military-grade night vision equipment, Mr. Lee might be the person to talk to. If you want to buy some explosive contraband, Mr. Lee might be the person to talk to for that, too."

"You think he would know about firing detonators with walkie talkies?"

"I'm a vinyl guy," Teddy said. "What would I know about relays?"

"What's a relay?"

"A switch that gets a low-power message and turns on a higher power circuit. Like all the stuff in your car. You turn on the headlight switch, it sends a little current to the relay, which handles the big current for the headlights. Probably need a relay to make a walkie talkie run a detonator."

"You think Mr. Lee knows about relays and detonators?"

There was a pause. "I heard the feds went to Lee when they were trying to solve the bombing of the Milton Building in L.A."

"Any idea where to find him?"

"He's in the Tenderloin. That's all I know."

"White guy or Asian guy?"

Teddy had to think about it. "Chinese, I think."

"Okay, thanks."

I hung up and dialed the San Francisco PD. Both Kim Hu and Billy Fong were sergeants back when I was a homicide inspector. I asked the receptionist if either of them was working the night shift. The receptionist said that Lieutenant Fong was in.

"Hey, Inspector," he said in my ear.

"So you got promoted. Congrats."

"Thanks," he said. "Now, instead of working the streets, keeping track of what's going on, I sit on my ass and do paperwork. What's that like, going private, spending your days skiing and sailing up at the lake? Sounds pretty sweet to a paperweight like me."

"Sure thing. I'm on the chairlift as we speak." I touched the lever under my desk chair, dropped it a couple inches, put my feet up on the desk. "I wonder if you can tell me anything about a Mr. Lee in the Tenderloin. Import, export, electronics, might know something about how to wire a walkie talkie to fire a detonator."

"My name is Fong, sure, but I was born in Arizona. I'm not much more Chinese than you. Not like I speak Mandarin."

"You've got born-in-China family in The City, right?"

"Chinatown, not the Tenderloin," he said.

"Maybe make a call or two? For old time's sake?"

"Comp me a lift ticket next time I'm up the hill?"

"Sure."

"Okay, I'll call you back."

I ate chips and a beer from my micro fridge while Spot demonstrated his napping expertise, on his side, his back solidly against the office door, a loud snore to intimidate potential visitors. The phone rang thirty minutes later.

"First I checked his background. Mr. Lee's name has come up in over a dozen investigations over the years," Billy Fong said. "But he has sat at the defense table in a courtroom exactly once."

"Acquittal?"

"Not only that, he got the ACLU involved on his behalf in a suit against The City about civil liberties violations. He lost that, but the DA's afraid to touch him ever since."

"You see anything that would help me get to him? I don't want to muscle him. I just want information."

"I made some calls. Got an aunt who knew of him but wouldn't say much. She thought the best way in to Lee and his guys is to invoke the competition. Be a friend or a foe, your choice. Gets their attention, either way."

"Who's the competition?"

"There's a Japanese group run by a Bill Smith. He's been pushing into Lee's business for a few years. Had some success from what I heard."

"An anglo running a Japanese mob?"

"No. He's Japanese. He can't even speak English. He looks like a Samurai warrior. The Bill Smith moniker is just part of the act. Good marketing. Everybody remembers the name, and it cranks up the fear factor."

"What makes Lee and Smith competitors?" I asked.

"Part of it is the usual. They're both hustling import contraband. But I heard there's something else going on. Some kind of art dispute."

"Asian mobsters care about art?"

"Right. Guy in the department said they've got some weird intellectual disagreement. Don't ask me what, but I guess it's got them cranked up."

"Your aunt have any thoughts about how to contact Lee?"

"Lee owns a bunch of electronics stores. Some in Chinatown, a couple in the Tenderloin, one down in East Palo Alto. You could call around, see what shakes loose."

"He speak English?"

"My aunt said Lee has a guy who translates at all meetings. But she says he speaks English.

"Is Lee from China?"

"Born and raised there, but moved to San Francisco in his late teens. Worked in the family bakery. Then he decided he wanted to make real money, so he went into business for himself."

"How does your aunt know Lee?"

"Worked at the same bakery with him."

FORTY-SIX

I thanked Billy Fong, then called Doc Lee at the hospital. I waited on hold, talked to a second person, waited again. Eventually, someone named Sue at the ER desk told me that if I waited she might be able to grab him after he finished setting a broken leg.

Five minutes of Mannheim Steamroller later he came to the phone.

"Owen," Doc said. "Are the stitches in your face ready to come out?"

"Got me. Hey, Doc, how's your Mandarin?" I said.

"Funny question to ask a health professional."

"It could be critical to someone's health. I need to talk to a Mr. Lee, no relation I'm sure. He's in the Tenderloin. Mandarin would help me get through the layers he keeps around him."

"The Tenderloin? This is a bad guy you want me to talk to?" Although Doc Lee had said that he once wanted to be a cop, he was small and sensitive and lived a quiet, thoughtful life in the mountains. He didn't like commotion and noise and never even drove into the Bay Area unless a new boyfriend beckoned him there. Over the years of practicing ER medicine, he realized he wanted nothing to do with people who perpetrated some of the trauma he saw at work.

"Yes, he's a bad guy," I said. "But you wouldn't have to have anything to do with him. I just need you to make some phone calls to some electronics shops and ask after Mr. Lee. I'm guessing that he may be more forthcoming if the inquiries are in Mandarin.

You can do it from my phone. There'd be no way to connect you to anything."

"Whose health is this critical to?"

"I don't know their names. But the avalanches were set using the kind of electronic devices that Mr. Lee knows about and possibly sells. If we can learn more about them, maybe we can catch the killer. The health of the next victim is at stake."

"I see. I go off my shift in twenty minutes. I'll come to your office?"

"Thanks, Doc."

Spot had shifted to his other side for the second stage of his nap, but was still in front of the door when Doc Lee knocked. He lifted his head and cranked it sideways to stare up at the closed door. He made a little pretend woof and kept his head in the air, his jowly lip swinging free from his mouth.

"Typically, your largeness, when someone knocks at the door you get up out of the way so they can come in."

Spot didn't move, an indication that our visitor was someone he knew. How he knew was a mystery to me. Spot was lying, legs outstretched, on the rug, which was on the slippery tile floor. So I grabbed one front leg and one back leg and pulled. The rug and Spot slid away from the door. He never changed position, still held his head up at the funny angle.

I opened the door and Doc Lee walked in.

Spot smacked the floor with a single tail wag, then put his head back down. Doc Lee gave him a pet, and sat down.

"You never said how your Mandarin is," I said.

"Pretty fluent. My parents don't speak English. If I want mom to keep sending me her homemade eggrolls, I have to communicate in Mandarin."

"Are they good? I love eggrolls."

"Too many mushrooms, but good. I'll bring you one." He gestured at my desk phone. "Isn't it late to call?"

"These numbers are electronic stores, Chinatown style. They stay open late. Mr. Lee owns several of them, some in Chinatown, some in the Tenderloin."

"The Tenderloin is a tough neighborhood for those kind of stores, isn't it?" Doc Lee said.

"I'd think so. But Lee is probably a tough guy. Word on the street would be enough to scare the petty thieves."

"You mean, break my window, I break your neck?"

"Yeah. Anyway, all I want is to talk with him and get some information. I thought calling in English would get me nowhere. But you would have better luck getting through to him."

I handed him a list of stores and phone numbers I'd gotten off the Internet. "Start at the top. Say you're calling for Owen McKenna and that I wish to speak to Mr. Lee."

Doc said, "If the person who answers says they don't know of a Mr. Lee, I won't be able to tell if they're telling the truth," Doc said.

"Correct. If that happens, say that McKenna has something very important to discuss with Mr. Lee and if either McKenna or Mr. Lee finds out that the person on the phone was obstructing this discussion, the repercussions will be severe. That should at least bring a manager or a supervisor."

"What do I say if I get Mr. Lee or his representative?"

"Say I found Mr. Lee's name at Paul Riceman's house. I have evidence that Paul Riceman used some kind of electronic detonator device to set off avalanches. You can stress that I have no interest in pursuing Mr. Lee. I only want confirmation that Riceman used such a device, what kind of device it was and that it would work at a distance of one mile."

Doc Lee frowned. "What if Lee or his subordinates refuse to confirm or even discuss this with you?"

"Tell him Bill Smith is willing to partner with me to bring him down. Then remind him of Dong Wang. Tell him I was the inspector who caught him. Tell him this is a personal thing with me and I'd be happy to do a repeat performance for anyone peddling illegal detonators or stolen electronics."

"Who's Dong Wang?"

"Gangster from the same neighborhood, a dozen years ago.

Well-enough entrenched that he thought I couldn't backtrack an execution-style murder to him. But I scraped up enough evidence to get a warrant. He had so much protection that I couldn't go in with a team without alerting him and giving him time to get out through one of his underground tunnels, so I went in at night by myself. He had two bodyguards who resisted, and when I got past them to Dong, he resisted as well. It got physical and someone flashed pictures when I pulled him out of the building where he had his penthouse. He was still alive, but he was a mess. The neighborhood rag printed them on the front page."

"I thought the police department frowned on Dirty Harry showmanship."

"Hell, yes. They dragged me through every kind of public humiliation and disciplinary action. I was the Chronicle's headline two days in a row."

"But they didn't fire you?"

"They held a private thank-you party for me up on Russian Hill at a house that belonged to one of the mayor's golfing buddies."

Doc Lee nodded and swallowed. "Okay, let's do it."

I dialed the first number and handed Doc the phone.

Someone answered and Doc spoke in Chinese, and I noticed as always how it wasn't just the words that are different, but the tonal quality changes as well. I can recognize a familiar voice speaking an unfamiliar language, like when Street speaks French. But with Chinese, it is as if the speaker changes the shape of their throat and the sounds move up into the back of their sinus cavity. It didn't sound like Doc Lee's voice until he hung up and spoke to me in English.

"A young woman answered. She sounded sincere when she said there was no Mr. Lee connected to the store. Same for when I told her there'd be repercussions if she was lying."

I nodded.

Doc picked up the phone and dialed the next number. His next conversation seemed a little longer before he hung up. "A guy said they have a kid who works stock and gopher and garbage and his name is Lee, but they have no other Lee. I believe him."

I nodded.

It was the same for the third and fourth and fifth store Doc Lee called. The sixth store was different.

Doc spoke on and off several times, then listened for a long thirty seconds. Then Doc raised his voice, irritated and intense. Someone shouted something in Chinese loud enough that I could hear it from five feet away. Doc Lee stood up and paced back and forth at the length of the phone cord, shouting back. He yelled my name and the name of Bill Smith and Dong Wang all in a Chinese accent. He stopped, then shouted a blistering barrage of Chinese that included Paul Riceman's name and lasted most of a minute.

In a moment he stopped and sat back down, still holding the phone at his ear.

I raised my eyebrows at him.

Doc Lee held up a finger. "I'm holding." In a minute he telegraphed that someone was talking, then he handed the phone to me. "Mr. Lee wants to talk to you."

"Owen McKenna," I said.

"This is John Sun. I am Mr. Lee's translator. Mr. Lee will see you tomorrow after lunch. Will one o'clock work for you?"

"Yes."

"Do you know Turk Street?"

"Yes."

"I'll give you the number."

I wrote as he gave it to me.

"The doorway has a metal gate over it. If you reach up high, you'll find a concealed doorbell button just to the side of the upper right corner of the gate."

I told him I'd be there, and we hung up.

FORTY-SEVEN

The next day I once again left Spot at his favorite place for interesting odors, Street's bug lab, and was in San Francisco a little after noon. I parked off Geary and walked through the Tenderloin, the one neighborhood that doesn't show up on the Things-To-Do tourist maps that show off the most beautiful city in the world.

In four short blocks I had to step over two homeless people who were passed out and lying across the sidewalk. Nearby, a large group of Asian teenaged boys wearing T-shirts that showed their muscles and tattoos gathered around a boombox blasting a rap, and two of them were doing an athletic street dance so inventive they maybe moonlighted as Cirque du Soleil performers at night. On the next block a trio of what I guessed were Guatemalan women sat cross-legged on a spectacular woven blanket with Mayan designs in shades of red and orange. The youngest one was nursing a baby. All three were singing a soft song in a language that sounded like a Native American language. Along one edge of the blanket were rows of handmade silver jewelry. My first thought was that they belonged on Union Square where they could actually make good money. But I realized that the Mayor's troops had probably scoured the shopping and theater district and pushed out all vendors who weren't licensed, scheduled on The City's calendar, and carrying proof of liability insurance.

But the police didn't like to venture into the Tenderloin. Even illegal alien jewelry makers could ply their wares.

A red-faced man with waist-length dreadlocks had pushed his

grocery cart full of belongings up so close to them that the cart's dirty wheels had tracked mud onto their perfect blanket. He was lecturing them about public access.

I tapped him on the shoulder.

"Wassup, man?"

"Your cart is dirtying their blanket." I pointed.

"They're on the public sidewalk, they gotta expect some dirt."

"Not your dirt," I said. I took the cart and dragged it off the curb. "Respect their beautiful work. If you ever did anything beautiful, they'd respect it."

"My speech is my work. I sing the praises of public access for all layers of society. I'm beautiful at it." He began to pull his cart back toward their blanket.

"You touch their blanket again, I'll put your cart over your head."

"So you're an Injun savior, huh? The government gives them all that free land, but still they come to our city and take over the sidewalk. Makes you feel like a real man picking on people like me, doesn't it?"

As I walked away, the two older women lifted their hands, palms together, and touched their thumbs to their noses. They bowed their heads to me.

Mr. Lee's building was half a block down. The ugly gated door was centered in a narrow run-down building that sat between a flophouse and a liquor store with month-to-month apartments above.

I reached up and felt around the upper right corner of the steel gate. I found the concealed button and pushed it.

Ten seconds later a voice came from a hidden speaker. "You are too tall for the camera. Please move back so we can see you."

I stepped back, looking but not seeing the hidden camera.

"Your name?"

"McKenna."

The door buzzed. I pulled open the gate, squeezed the door latch and pushed the door inward.

I stepped into a hallway that was an art piece. The floor was a mosaic of tiny tiles showing a vivid mural with scenes, I guessed, from Chinese history. The Great Wall was featured in some, charging armies on horseback in others. There were dragons and maidens and a large Buddha in the center.

The walls looked like dark polished ebony or mahogany. Every five feet were recesses in which were displayed magnificent hanging scrolls, Chinese landscapes, ink on silk, just like in my book. From the ceiling hung huge paper globes that radiated a warm orange-yellow light. On the globes were ink-wash paintings of inland seas reaching back to improbably steep mountains.

Two men stood waiting for me. They were small but their athleticism reminded me of Bruce Lee in his iconic martial-arts movies. I had the thought that I should make no sudden movements.

"I am John Sun," one of them said. "Your shoes, please." His English sounded American like he'd been raised on an Iowa farm. He pointed at a mat with other shoes on it.

I kicked off my shoes.

He then pointed to the wall. "Morris will pat you down."

I turned to the wall and put my hands on the wood. Morris was quick and efficient, paying special attention to my ankles as if I might have thin throwing knives hidden under an ace bandage.

"Please come," Sun said.

I followed him, and Morris followed me. We turned through an opening draped with fabric and went up a wooden stairway with a hand-carved railing. Two flights up he led me into a huge room that looked vaguely like the banquet rooms in elegant Chinese restaurants.

There were no walls, but there were several arrangements of furniture defining a sitting area, a bedroom, a kitchen and an office. I took the banquet room to be Mr. Lee's house. A house with invisible walls.

The room's perimeter walls had tall ornate windows with long elegant patterned drapes held aside with velvet pulls. Out each window was a different scene, and were I not in a building that was surrounded by other buildings, it would be easy to be fooled by the realistic murals painted to look like the Chinese countryside. The windows seemed to light the room, and I couldn't tell how the illusion was done. I decided that there must be lighting all around the windows, hidden beneath the drapes and shining on the painted surfaces.

In the area that the furniture defined as the office, sat a man I assumed to be Mr. Lee. He was behind a desk.

"Mr. McKenna," Sun said. "Meet Mr. Lee. Mr. Lee, Mr. McKenna."

Mr. Lee nodded at me but remained seated. He was thin like a sword is thin and the edges of his face were sharp enough that if you hit him on the edge of his jaw you'd expect to cut your hand. His eyes didn't gaze so much as they burned. And his eyebrows were angled and chiseled like cuts made in wood by a sword.

"Please have a seat, Mr. McKenna," John Sun said.

He pointed me toward the two chairs in front of Mr. Lee's desk.

"I am Mr. Lee's assistant," Sun said.

I sat. Sun sat next to me.

In an effort to ingratiate myself with Mr. Lee, I said, "You have beautiful hanging scrolls, Mr. Lee. I've been reading a book on Asian art and I've come to love those monochromatic Chinese landscapes. Something about the brushwork. Very detailed, but still soft."

Mr. Lee looked at me without expression. Lee, Sun and Morris were all silent.

"I also like the way the earlier Chinese painters used the silk itself to represent the mist in the mountains."

More silence. It occurred to me that I might be violating a basic custom. Maybe commenting on a Chinese person's art collection was unforgivable presumption.

"They're actually Japanese," John Sun finally said.

"Oh, sorry. I've never been very expert at art. But I enjoy them."

Sun said, "The Chinese invented landscape painting in the

Tenth Century. Hundreds of years later, Japanese artists became fixated on painting in the style of Chinese painters from the Sung Dynasty. The ones downstairs are by a Fifteenth Century Japanese master from the Ashikaga period. Like many Japanese intellectuals of the day, he was infatuated with all things Chinese. Buddhism. Tea rituals. Chinese landscapes. The Japanese were very studious in capturing every nuance and technique of their Chinese predecessors from five hundred years earlier. Some say the Japanese painted Sung period landscapes even better than the Chinese. But don't say that to a Chinese person."

Sun's mouth may have hinted at the tiniest of smiles, but I couldn't see it.

"Your Mandarin translator on the phone," he said, "mentioned Bill Smith by way of trying to convince us to meet with you."

"Yeah," I said. "A Japanese tough guy I could use to stick a pry bar into your resistance should you resist me. I understand he is trying to move in on your business."

"That," Sun said, "is true to some extent. But Mr. Smith's major problem with Mr. Lee is that Mr. Lee collects these Japanese paintings. Smith feels that it is an insult for a Chinese businessman to collect priceless artifacts of Japanese culture. Never mind that the paintings are copies of Chinese paintings. Smith has been apoplectic ever since he found out about it."

I nodded.

"We understand that you are a man of honor," Sun said.

"Thank you." I spoke toward Mr. Lee. "When I say I don't intend to pursue Mr. Lee for providing avalanche explosives or electronic detonators to Paul Riceman, I mean it. When I say I will make his life difficult if you don't help me, I also mean it. But I can't speak for other law enforcement. If other cops come after you, I can't stop them. If they ask me what I know, I will tell them. But I won't advertise what you tell me. My goal is to stop the person setting the avalanches. Other than that, you are outside of my purview."

Mr. Lee was still quiet.

I waited.

John Sun spoke. "Mr. Lee and his agents did not sell any explosives or detonators or electronic devices to anyone named Paul Riceman."

I sensed there was more and waited longer.

"One of Mr. Lee's agents did sell materials to a young woman from Tahoe. That agent understood that she was an instructor in a school that teaches avalanche control classes, and he arranged for her to come here."

"When was she here?"

"Two weeks ago," Sun said.

"What did she buy?"

"Two dozen electronic transmitters and detonators."

"No dynamite?"

"No dynamite," Sun said.

"What's the difference between an electronic detonator and a detonator with a fuse?" I asked

"The electronic detonator has a built-in receiver, like a pager. You must also have an accompanying transmitter. Like pagers, they operate on a radio frequency."

"Would the transmitters work at a distance of a mile or more?"

"Several miles, yes."

"Are they made for avalanche control?"

"They are designed for the Chinese military," Sun said. "But they are useful to other organizations as well."

"So you import them for avalanche control?"

"We import them to sell to the U.S. military. But they have proven attractive to a wide range of companies and individuals."

"How does it work," I said, "setting the transmitter to fire the detonator?"

"It's very simple. The detonators are stamped with a number corresponding to the appropriate transmission frequency and firing code. The transmitter has a standard digital readout. You pull up the appropriate menu and enter the number code for the detonator. There is a safety sequence to prevent accidental firing. It has proven to be foolproof."

"Do you sell them to anybody who asks?"

"No. We use discretion. Among other things, we require the purchaser to have a valid Blaster's license."

"And this young woman from Tahoe has a Blaster's license?"

Sun glanced at Mr. Lee. Mr. Lee's face didn't move. He still hadn't said a word. Nor had Sun translated anything into Chinese.

"Yes, she had a Blaster's license," Sun finally said.

"How old would you guess her to be?"

"Mid-twenties. Maybe older. Maybe younger."

"What did she look like?" I asked.

"She was fair, Caucasian, pretty and slightly built. Like a Chinese girl."

"Do women of that age often come in with Blaster's licenses?" I asked.

"No."

"Yet you believed it to be authentic?"

"It looked authentic," Sun said.

"Do you make photocopies of your customers' Blaster's licenses?" I asked.

"Of course," Sun said. "Her driver's license as well."

"Perhaps I could have a copy of your copy," I said.

Sun looked at Lee. Lee was motionless. Sun looked at Morris. I saw no expression, no communication, but Morris walked over to some office equipment behind Mr. Lee and pulled open a file drawer. He flipped through some files, pulled out two pieces of paper, put them on a copier. When the copier was done, Morris re-filed the originals and brought the copies to me.

I held them up to the light. One was a certificate with a fancy border and state seals and verbiage that looked official. At the top it said California Blaster's License. At the bottom it was validated by two different state functionaries. The name of the person to whom the certificate was awarded was written in a delicate cursive script. The other paper showed a California driver's license.

The name on both was Lorraine Simon.

FORTY-EIGHT

This time Sam Simon met me at the door of the palace in Sea-cliff. "Oh," he said, his face expressionless, his eyes dead. "It's you."

"Sorry to interrupt you like this. Something came up I'd like to ask you about."

The two little Pomeranians jumped around at my feet, yapping at me with their high-pitched barks. This time I snatched the other dog, Salt, off the floor and gently held her until she submitted. Pepper stopped barking and pawed at my legs, wanting another ride. I picked her up in my other arm.

Simon looked worse than the last time as if trying to adjust to his daughter's death became more difficult with time. His face was haggard and unshaven. His hair went in all directions, and he smelled like garbage. It was hard to imagine that he was a doctor and an entrepreneur, saving lives and handling business details and making a thousand decisions a day. Now he couldn't even manage a shower.

"I should get Clarice," Simon said, walking away.

I shut the door behind me. Because he hadn't given me a clear sense that I should wait, I followed him.

He made small steps, like someone recovering from a stroke, and we went on the long trip through the central part of the house to a study of sorts. There was a cozy sitting area of three small couches arranged in front of a stone fireplace with a gas insert. The gas flames curled around ceramic logs that looked about as much like real wood as a Barbie doll looks like a real woman.

There were two desks facing each other at one end of the

room, and Clarice Simon sat at one of them, typing on a laptop computer. She looked up with a serious frown as though Sam were a child who disobeyed an order never to enter her room when she was working. Then she saw me and wrestled her face into a phony smile.

I set the dogs down, and they both started jumping at my legs, begging to be held.

"Oh, Mr. McKenna, what a pleasant surprise," Clarice said. She pushed back from the desk and stood up. She didn't move toward me, but came around and sat on the edge of the desk, her long legs in navy dress pants stretched out in front of her. Her hands were to the sides of her hips, white fingers gripping the edge of the desk. I couldn't tell if she was simply awkward at my unannounced visit, or if she wanted to block my view of her desk.

"Have you new information about Lori's death?" she asked in the kind of cheery voice that one uses to say, 'did you have fun at the party?'

"I don't have much information. But I have some questions." I got out the copies of Lori Simon's Blaster's license and driver's license. "I wonder if you've seen these?" I walked past Sam and handed the papers to Clarice.

She took them, the sheets trembling in her hands. It took her a moment to read them.

"What is it?" Sam said.

"I don't understand," Clarice said, ignoring him.

"Did you know your daughter had a Blaster's license?"

"No. I don't even know what a Blaster's license is."

"It's what people obtain in order to buy explosives."

"That is ridiculous. My daughter did not work with explosives. She wasn't some kind of terrorist. This must be a forgery. Somebody is trying to implicate her in something nefarious. Postmortem. This is outrageous. Obscene." She flipped the papers toward me. They fluttered to the floor.

"A Chinese mobster sold your daughter electronic detonators and the transmitters that operate them. His description of her matched. She had to bring him her license before he would sell her anything. The license may have been forged, and she may have been put up to it, but it was not postmortem."

Clarice Simon narrowed her eyes at me as if I were the enemy. "And you've brought us this news to, what, destroy what's left of our memories of Lorraine?"

"I came to ask about her friends and acquaintances. Especially those in Tahoe."

"And what good will that do? She's dead. She moved to your fetid mountains with your twisted, squeal-like-a-pig rednecks and now she's dead. But instead of looking for the psycho who killed her, you're going to dig up some forged document and harass her parents? You are one razor-sharp cop, McKenna. No wonder they kicked you off the San Francisco Police Department." She was panting with anger.

I tried to leave that alone, but I couldn't. "Wrong information. I resigned. They wanted me to stay."

She ignored me. "Sam should never have taken that girl to Tahoe to ride horses," she continued. "Right, Sam? I knew it was a mistake. You knew it was a mistake. But you were weak. A civilized girl from a good family should study ballet and music, not be horsing around, Western Style, in the mountains like some ranch hand on a weekend bender. She met that boy there. You knew that would happen, Sam. You were the beginning of her problems."

Clarice pushed away from the desk and walked over to the window where she stood facing the lawn, her shoulders heaving as if she'd just run a hundred-meter sprint.

"What was the boy's name?"

"I don't know!" Clarice shouted at the glass.

"Do you know where he lived?"

"No. Tahoe someplace."

"What did he look like?"

"I told you, I don't know! I only saw him once, out the window, when he came to pick up Lori."

"Tall or short?" I asked.

"He was tall and big. I hate big men!"

"Hair color?"

"He had a baseball cap on."

"Did Lori talk about him?"

"No," Clarice said. "She knew we disapproved."

"What can you tell me about Lori's other friends from Tahoe?"

Neither of them answered me.

"Did Lori even have any other friends?"

"She had lots of friends, of course," Clarice said, still looking out the window. "Lori was always good at making friends."

"Can you give me any names?"

Clarice didn't move. Sam bent over and picked up the copy of the Blaster's license, sat down on one of the couches and stared at it.

"Names?" I said again.

"Well, there was a girl she went snowboarding with," Clarice said.

"Her name?"

"I... I forget. I'll think of it in a moment."

"Where did this girl live?"

"Tahoe. Where else?" Clarice sneered.

"Tahoe's a big place. Eight or ten times the size of San Francisco."

"I know how big Tahoe is!" Clarice was still yelling at her reflection. "I'm a state legislator. I was the liaison between the governor and the Tahoe Regional Planning Agency on that last property rights issue. You think I don't know Tahoe better than practically anyone in this state? I can quote chapter and verse on the history of Tahoe regulations and development! I have friends with places in Tahoe!"

"Yet you don't know the name of a single friend of your daughter's."

Clarice spun around and walked up to me. She stopped far enough from me that she wouldn't have to look up at too steep an angle. "You are an insolent, disrespectful cop who doesn't know his place. Instead of finding a murderer, you have the audacity to come into our house and question our parenting skills when we have practically broken our backs trying to provide everything for our only child." She pushed past me and hurried out of the room.

Sam was still sitting on the couch near the fireplace. He hadn't even looked up. I walked over and sat next to him, his overripe smell enveloping me. Salt and Pepper immediately jumped into my lap, desperate for affection.

"I'm sorry for your loss, Sam. I'm trying to find your daughter's killer."

"I know," he said in a soft voice, nearly a whisper. He had folded the Blaster's and Driver's license copies up, over and over, making the sheets as tiny as possible. "I don't know the name of Lori's boyfriend, but he drove a big red pickup truck. I think he worked construction."

"Did you meet him?"

"No. But Lori told me about him. She talked to me sometimes."

"What did she say about him?"

"Just that he was a great skier, and he was fun, and they were making some big plans together."

"She say what kind of plans?" I asked. "Were they getting married?"

"No, not like that. Some kind of financial plans. I remember because I told her we would provide for her finances and that she didn't need to worry about that. But she said that it was more exciting to provide for herself. And she had figured out a way to do that."

"With this guy," I said.

"Yeah."

"Did she tell you about other friends?" I said.

It was a moment before Sam spoke. "She told me about Ada. She was at Ada's place a couple of days before they found her in the avalanche. I know because she called me from there."

"Where's Ada's place?"

"Ada is the manager of her parents' vineyard and winery. I

haven't been there. Lori said it's in the foothills up above Auburn, up around twenty-eight hundred feet. They make pinots. The Sierra Red Winery. Someone had picked Lori up, and they were driving to Tahoe, and they stopped at Ada's winery."

"Do you know who picked Lori up?"

"No." Sam shook his head. "I wasn't home at the time she left. Maybe the guy with the pickup. Maybe someone else. But they stopped at Ada's on the way up." Sam made a slow shake of his head. He had a small smile on his face. "Lori was such a city girl. She still got excited when she saw snow. She expected snow when they got higher up the mountains, of course, but when they got to Ada's vineyard and it was snowing hard, Lori called to tell me about it. I still remember. She said that Ada was gone, but there was six inches of fresh snow. Lori said she ran into the vineyard and made snow-angels."

Sam rubbed his forehead with the heel of his hand. "I taught her how when she was a little girl. We were up at the lake one Christmas, and we laid down on the snowy beach, and I showed her how to move her arms and legs to make the wing shapes in the snow. Then I picked her up and held her high so she could see her angel. When I put her down, she ran circles around her angel, careful not to touch it."

Sam stopped and stared into the gas flames. "I'll never forget the joy on her face."

I stood up and put my hand on his shoulder. "Hang on to that thought, Sam." I left the room and let myself out.

I called Bains from my car.

"I've got a possible connection between Lori Simon and Paul Riceman."

"Besides the fact that they both died in slides?"

"Yeah." I told him about Lori's visit to Mr. Lee to buy detonators and Lori's boyfriend who fit Paul's description.

Bains said, "So the two of them could have been in on the avalanche plan from the very beginning, but then Paul maybe killed her after she got the detonators. Question is, who killed

Paul if his death wasn't accidental?"

"I'll let you know when I find out."

I followed Interstate 80 east through Sac and on toward Reno. I took one of the Auburn exits, stopped and made some calls to locate Sierra Red, the winery Sam Simon had mentioned. It was fifteen miles up into the foothills.

The road was a turny narrow asphalt ribbon that climbed up and over and down and around a deeply folded landscape. The entrance appeared on the left, just after a bridge that arched over a stream gushing with snowmelt.

The gate was not as imposing as those of Napa wineries, but it was nevertheless a grand design of brick and wrought iron. I headed down a long crushed-rock drive that made a meandering path through a vineyard that was about the size of a city block. The air coming in the window was crisp. The snow that Lori had told her dad about had melted, leaving the vineyard redolent of cold moist dirt.

At the end of the drive was a parking area big enough for a dozen cars. Two of the buildings looked like a cross between warehouses and barns. A large sliding door was open in one and I could see huge stainless steel tanks inside.

The third building looked like a large rambling ranch house with a steep roof interrupted with several gables. A sign said, Sierra Red Tasting Room.

I walked past an outdoor sitting area where an older couple was sitting, their coats bundled up against the cold breeze. Indoors were two other couples standing in front of a gas fireplace. Each person held a large glass with an inch of red wine. They were swirling the wine, sniffing it, sipping it, chewing it, and moving their mouths like chipmunks with tooth problems. They frowned and pursed their lips then raised their eyebrows and finally, after swallowing, they smiled and looked very pleased.

The young woman behind the wine bar set down the bottle and turned to me. "We're tasting several pinots, sir. Would you care to join us?" She gave me a seductive grin.

"No thanks, I'm here to see Ada. Is she in?"

"She's not in. Would you like to leave a message?"

"Any idea when she'll be back?"

"Three weeks from tomorrow."

"How about her parents? Are they in?"

"No, they're all in France, investigating some new varietals. Perhaps I could help you?"

"Did they leave just recently? Wasn't Ada here just last week?"

"They just left last night. The red-eye from San Francisco nonstop to Paris."

"Have you spoken recently to Ada's friends Lori Simon and Paul Riceman?"

"I'm sorry, I don't know who they are." She frowned at me. "Your business is..."

"I'm just a friend of the family," I said.

I thanked her and left.

I drove out and stopped at the gate. There was a plastic shopping bag in my door pocket. I used it to scoop a good bit of dirt out of the vineyard, then drove home.

I stopped at Street's, spent an hour telling her about my day, then took Spot and headed up our steep road through light snow.

I let Spot out, and he sniffed the driveway as if we'd had a visitor, which, in the winter, meant coyotes more often than people. Then I saw the book delivery at my door, next to the woodpile.

I'd ordered two out-of-print art books from one of the online companies. According to the description, they were in good shape and had nice color plates of a broad selection of Chinese landscapes spanning the Sung Dynasty.

But as I approached I was disappointed to see that the tape on the box had not sealed well. Blowing snow could have gotten in and damaged the books.

Then again...

I grabbed Spot and slammed him down as the world exploded.

FORTY-NINE

Split logs from the woodpile exploded our way. One hit my left arm. A sharp shard of wood split off from the log and pierced jacket and shirt sleeve and my biceps muscle. The sharp end of the spear stuck out five inches on the right side of my arm, and the thick end stuck out three inches on the left side.

The pain was that of a hot poker fresh out of the fire. I gritted my teeth to stifle a roar of pain and anger. I wanted that wood shard out in the next half second. But the visible portions of the wood were covered with fresh splinters on the left and bloody, broken splinters on the right. If I attempted to yank it out, it would rip more flesh and leave more wood behind. I needed a pain killer now and surgery very soon. Fortunately, the spear didn't appear to have struck the Brachial artery, which is a quick way to bleed out and die.

I pushed myself up off of Spot to see if he was okay. He cowered by the cabin wall, holding his head low, shaking it to try to get the pain out of his ears. The rhinestone stud sparkled. Seeing him like that, I had the desire for vengeance, and I wished I could find the bomber and send Spot to take him down.

Holding my arm out so that the rough wood spear wouldn't bump anything, I turned and saw that my front door was blown in, shattered in two with one piece hanging crookedly from a single hinge. The living room window was also broken. A few shards lined the edges, with the main portion gone. Snow continued to swirl around, now blowing into my cabin as well.

With my right arm, I coaxed Spot into the house. Wind

whipped through the missing door and window, depositing a dusting of snow on every surface. The living room floor was covered in broken glass.

As before, I dialed Diamond.

"Bomb number two took out my door and window and put a spear of wood through my arm," I said when he answered.

Diamond spoke, but my ears were still deafened.

"Can't hear you," I said.

"On my way," he shouted.

It was like the first time, but with twice as many deputies combing the area, studying tracks, bagging evidence. Street came and nearly fainted when she saw me. She wanted to come with me to the hospital. I comforted her and told her it would be best if she stayed with Spot. Diamond said he'd see what he could do about boarding up the window and door of my cabin, then told one of the deputies to drive me to the hospital.

Doc Lee wasn't on in the ER. I got a new doctor named Lily DuPree who looked like a fifteen-year-old cheerleader, but acted professional if nervous. She kept glancing at the stitches in my face as she and a nurse cut off my jacket and shirt.

"You should go to Reno for this," she said when she saw the spear up close, the bloody wood bulging the skin and flesh. "There could be vascular and nerve damage in addition to the muscle damage. We can have a chopper here in a few minutes."

"Dr. DuPree, I'm sure you are up to the challenge. It's just a flesh wound. No major arteries or veins."

She shook her head. "In all those years at medical school, we never went over large wood-shard penetrations."

"Doctor, I've been shot twice, stabbed once, and one time I was cut up by a man with a reciprocating saw. This is wood sliver. A little bigger than normal, but that's how you learn, right? If you like, we can call Doc Lee. He will tell you to give me a local anesthetic, get out the utility knife, horse needle, sixty pound test line, and then cut this thing out and sew me up. He will also tell you not to waste time being too careful. It'll just be one more set of scars out of many, and I've got a bomber to catch."

DuPree looked pasty, and then a flush rose in both of her cheeks. "I don't know."

"Where do you want to do it? Here?" I lay down on one of the examination tables, crossed my ankles and angled my arm across my chest so the wooden spear was front and center.

Diamond's deputy drove me home three hours later. I was stiff and sore, and my numb, bandaged arm hung in its sling like a dead weight at my side. DuPree sent me home with a bottle of pills. She assured me that it would feel like I had fire in my arm for the next few days. She also said that she was certain there were many more tiny slivers left in the muscle, but that they would soften, and, after many months or even years, dissolve.

Street and Diamond had cleaned up the broken glass. Diamond had found a piece of plywood under my deck and fashioned a crude door. Street had found plastic, and they had staple-gunned two layers of it over the missing window. They'd kept the woodstove hot. The layer of snow that had covered everything had turned to dew, which was gradually drying. It took some convincing to get Street and Diamond to go home to sleep.

Spot and I were left to get warm in front of the woodstove. I put on an Edward Elgar disk and listened to the evocative music over the whistle of the wind outside the plastic and blankets.

Using my right arm exclusively, I roasted hotdogs in the woodstove, two for each of us. Spot likes them the same as I do, with a slice of cheddar and lots of ketchup on whole wheat buns.

We spent a long time in front of the fire, Spot curled into an arc around the side of the stove, his rear legs hanging off the big rug so he could be in position to rest his head on my foot. I drank most of a bottle of my best Stag's Leap cab to celebrate our survival of the bomb and then finished off the rest of it to mourn the loss of my new used art books. The shipping box had looked big enough that the bomber may have been able to add a couple of three-by-eight charges to it, leaving the books inside. Or maybe he took the books with him. Either way, they were gone.

I didn't get to bed until three in the morning, but the raging fire inside my arm prevented sleep. I lay there, sleepless, trying unravel the threads that connected all the young people who died.

Eventually, I got up, made a pot of coffee, and was opening my East Asian art book on the dinette table when the phone rang.

I looked at the clock. 5:00 a.m.

"Hello?"

"Owen? Bill. Is this okay? You sound awake. Tell me I didn't jerk you out of bed. I hoped you would be an early riser."

"I was up. What do you want, Bill?"

"I don't know. I had a bad dream. Real bad. I don't know who else to call. I don't have any friends."

"It's okay. What's bothering you, Bill?"

"I don't know. When I was young I was working toward something. Build my business. Make some money. It's a creative thing. You start with nothing but your ambition, and you make something. You've done that. You know how it works." Bill's words sounded steady, but I could sense him shaking with fear.

"You should feel good about what you've made, Bill."

"Yeah. But I don't care about it anymore. In the beginning, when I played chess, I always constructed a fortress around the king. My favorite pieces were the knights and the bishops. The goal was to fight the fiercest war and be victorious. Now all I care about is the pawns. But I still keep losing them. Once they're gone, you can't get them back. That's what my dream was about. I lost my last pawn. I woke up with my heart on triple speed. I couldn't breathe. I'm still soaked with sweat."

I didn't know what to say. I was starting to realize that the reason Bill was so wired and tense was that he cared about every little thing more than most people cared about any big thing. He was a big rough-looking guy on the outside, but inside he was as fragile and sensitive as a flower. He was desperately trying to make up for his tragic mistake in the past. But no matter how much effort he put into making the world better and more comfortable, it was always going to be very hard being Bill Esteban.

"Could you give me some advice?" he said.

"I'm just an ex-cop, Bill. I don't have many answers."

"But you know stuff different than what I know. I'm wondering what you do when you have questions, when you – I don't know – when you have doubts."

"Bill, I'm out of my league, here. I don't have advice for anyone else. I just know what helps me."

"What's that?"

"I look in my art books. Sometimes I don't see anything that helps. Sometimes I do."

"I don't get it," Bill said. "You look at pictures?"

"Yeah."

"What do you see?"

"I don't know," I said. "I try to imagine how the artist figured out the painting."

"What does that mean, figure out a painting? Don't they just look at something and paint it? Like a nude model or a still life?"

"I think so. But they still have to figure out their composition and their palette and the values and the line quality. And content."

"What's content?"

"I'm not sure. The part that isn't just the paint on the canvas. What the painting means. Its point. Its usefulness."

"Does art help with loneliness?"

"I think art helps with everything."

After Bill hung up, I flipped through the reproductions in my book, stopping at an 11th Century painting by Kuo Hsi. It showed gnarled trees on imposing mountains both near and far. There were waterfalls and lakes and distant valleys and bluffs and cliffs and temples on the cliffs. The composition was as complex as a puzzle, and the connecting points and pathways were all obscured in mist. I stared at the painting like an explorer who glimpsed the fantastic landscape during a brief break in the clouds. And now, with only a few clues, I was trying to navigate without a map. I knew the trail was out there, but it was lost in the mist.

FIFTY

I didn't leave the next morning until the carpenter and the glass shop guys were there to make repairs. Spot and I drove to Street's. I brought the bag of dirt from Ada's family's vineyard. I handed it to her when she got in the Jeep. "Thank you! Some girls have to settle for roses. But I'm special. I get dirt."

We dropped the dirt at her lab, and went across Kingsbury Grade to the Red Hut where we met Mariposa Pearl and Packer Mills for breakfast.

I explained about the bombs and my wounds and then told Mare about Paul Riceman over our coffee. She was horrified. Packer still played it so cool that I couldn't read him. It could have been macho posturing. Or maybe he just didn't have much empathy for other people.

"What exactly is our objective?" Packer asked.

"We ski into the Granite Chief Wilderness and try to locate Claude Sisuug's cabin," I said. "I've got questions for him. If he's not there, we leave him a note. Because you are the only one of us who heard Sisuug describe his cabin and its location, I'm hopeful that you will help us find it."

"But I haven't been there and don't know where it is."

"Nevertheless, aspects of the terrain will make more sense to you than to us. The rest of us will be guessing, while you will filter what you see through Sisuug's words. For you, it will be a visceral thing, raw and authentic."

"Yeah, I get it. Do the rest of you have an assignment while I search for a beat experience up on the mountain?"

"Mariposa is our backcountry guide."

She raised her index finger. "I should point out that while I've hiked that country in the summer, I haven't skied it."

"But you are one with topo maps and piles of snow."

"Ah."

Street said, "And I'm along for?"

"Never know when a search party needs a bug expert."

"Of course."

Caltrans had again shut the Emerald Bay Highway because of the ongoing snowfall, so we drove up the East Shore and back down to Tahoe City. Street and Spot were with me in the Jeep. Mare and Packer were in his pickup.

In places, the clouds seemed to rest heavily on the surface of the lake as if they'd already struggled to rise 6200 feet above the Central Valley, and they weren't willing to go any higher. In other places, there were holes up to the sky, and the sun pierced through here and there creating intense pools of ultramarine blue dappling the huge expanse of gray water. The weather report was predicting that a powerful storm would hit the following day, but for now we were just supposed to have periodic snow showers.

In Tahoe City we headed out 89, down the Truckee River to Squaw Valley. Despite the constant freeze/thaw cycles that compress the snowpack, snow covered the valley floor five feet deep. The rail fences poked out in places but mostly created long white bulges that stretched into the distance.

We parked in the big lot. Using my right arm, I grabbed Spot's mule pack, which I'd stuffed with dog food, water canteen and a bowl. I put it over his back, clicking the snaplock straps around his chest. The rest of us put on our backpacks and carried our ski gear over our shoulders. It was a long hike up to the far side of the village.

Like a rock star stopping to sign autographs, Spot had to pause to let fans give him a pet and ogle his size and ask if he was carrying brandy in his pack.

Once we'd passed the pedestrian village, Mare stopped,

opened her pack and handed out transceivers. "These are borrowed. My job security depends on bringing them back in working order." We put the harnesses on and adjusted them. Mare went through the lesson in how to use the transceivers. She then checked her topo map, divining from the topo lines secrets the rest of us would miss. She put the map back in her pocket.

"No compass?" I said.

She shook her head. "I brought one, but I don't need it as long as I have visibility. Unlike when you're on the prairie, the topo lines make a three-dimensional picture of the mountains. Unless it is real foggy, I can just match up the map with the landscape. No need to wrestle with the compass. The mineral deposits in these mountains give you local variations on your compass readings, anyway. And that is in addition to magnetic declination. A compass in the Northern Sierra points about fifteen degrees east of true north. But you all probably know that."

"We all know that, right?" I said to the rest of the group.

"Of course," we all said, nodding at Mare. It occurred to me that Street probably knew about magnetic declination for the entire country, but she didn't say it.

Mare set off, and the rest of us trailed out behind her. Street and I skied, with me using only my right pole, while Packer wore snowshoes for the uphill trek and carried his snowboard for rides down.

Mare followed Squaw Creek for an hour and then angled off to the north. The trail went through a winter paradise, up a short rise to a shelf, and then it began to climb. Mare skied straight up. In the places where her skis didn't provide enough grip on the loose snow, she made up for it by propelling herself with her poles, her powerful shoulders and arms working like pistons.

None of us except Spot were in shape like Mare. But it was easy for Packer on his snowshoes, and Street and I had the benefit of following their fresh-broken trail.

In an hour we'd climbed to a ridge with sweeping views south to many of Squaw Valley's ski runs and chairlifts. To the west was the broad ridge that comprised the Pacific Crest Trail. In the distance to the southeast was the Tahoe Basin. We could see two bits of gray water peeking out from a roiling mass of clouds that spilled over the Sierra Crest and down into the basin.

Mare stopped and got out her map as the rest of us caught up. We gathered around her on the ridgetop. Despite the heavy swirl of clouds that alternately covered the mountains and then filled the valleys, it was very bright on the high-altitude snow, and we all wore dark sunglasses.

"We are here," Mare said, taking off her glove and pointing to the map, angling it so that Packer could see. "From what you said on the drive up, I figure there's a good chance this old shack could be located in one of these four areas."

Packer studied the map. "I'd vote for these two areas. They fit with what Claude said about the trip from Squaw having more elevation gain than the trip from Donner Summit." He pointed to the map. "And this area might allow for a view of Squaw."

"Okay, let's start here." Mare made a circle with her finger. "If Claude's cabin is in fact an old mine shack, that helps in identifying where it might be. Mine shacks were usually built on a slope so that the mine tunnel can go back into the mountain."

"I see," Packer said. He reached for the map. "So we'd want to start exploring down below the ridgeline here."

"Yeah. That's a windward slope, a good candidate."

"What about this slope?" Packer asked.

"Judging by the topo lines, that slope is about forty degrees. The slope also faces a couple ticks east of northeast. Meaning it's a leeward slope and very likely to accumulate big-time wind loading of snow. The map also shows that it has very little vegetation."

"So it would be dangerous."

"Yes," Mare said. "But more to the point, if anyone had built a mining shack on that slope, the first big slide would take it out. Any shack that's been around for a while would have to have been built in slide-safe territory."

Packer turned to us and pointed sideways at Mare. "She's pretty smart, huh?"

"Why we brought her," I said.

Mare headed off.

This leg of our trek was still generally up, but it had a few downs mixed in. Packer put on his board, and we all rode untracked powder down.

As with our treks up the slopes, Spot stayed in my tracks on the way down the slope. Because I was the heaviest member of the group, my track was the most compressed and gave him the best footing. Even so, he still sunk in past his chest. At the bottom, I turned around to see him running down in my S-curve tracks, his head barely visible.

When we came over the ridge, the windward slope below was vast and mostly treeless. Mare handed Packer the map. She pulled out her binoculars and studied the view.

"That ravine over by that distant stand of trees," Mare said. "That would be good place for a mining cabin."

"But I don't think there would be a lookout close enough that Claude would go there with his morning coffee," Packer said. "At least no lookout high enough to see one of Squaw's chairlifts."

"Good point," Mare said.

"So we go to this next area?" Packer handed her the map.

"Yeah. We'll approach from the southwest and traverse up toward this small valley."

As we approached, we saw an old shack on the side of the small valley. Close by on one side was a miniature butte projecting out of the snow. The coffee lookout.

We stayed in the open so that we wouldn't surprise anyone.

"Claude?" Packer called out. "Hey, Claude. You there?"

We stopped about fifteen yards away. Mare took off one ski and tested the snow by stepping down. We waited, all of us familiar with the experience of stepping off skis and sinking up to our armpits in soft snow.

"Windblown," she said. "Seems pretty firm."

We took off our skis. Packer walked up to the cabin. It was a ramshackle building built into the slope. The shack was clad in tree bark siding, and its steep roof slanted from high on the back to low on the front. There were a couple of small windows and a wide, sliding barn door, the better to roll out ore carts, I imagined. Nothing about it looked like a cozy mountain cabin that someone would live in. It had all the charm of a pile of dirty ore.

There was a bent sheet-metal smokestack that came out of one side and then went up through the roof eave. No smoke issued from it.

There were no fresh tracks in the snow, either, although there was a general depression under the snow not far from where we stood and a narrow depression leading to the door. It looked like someone had skied to the cabin within the last couple of days. Then the tracks were covered with compacted and drifted snow about a foot deep.

"Claude?" Packer called again. Spot trotted around sniffing the cabin and the nearby trees. Packer took off his snowshoes, stepped up to the door and knocked. "Claude, it's Packer. I took your class a few years ago."

There was no answer. Packer tried the latch.

"It's not locked," he said. "You think I should open it?"

"Yes. We mean well."

Packer unhooked the latch and tugged on the door. It slid sideways about 18 inches and stopped with a rusty-sounding screech.

"Claude?" he said again. He leaned into the cabin, turning his head both ways. "Looks empty," he called out to us. Spot ran up next to Packer, jamming his head in between Packer's waist and the doorjamb.

Packer stepped inside, then turned his head back toward us.

"Something here you might want to see," he called out the open door.

Street and Mare didn't move.

"It's not a body or anything," Packer called out. "Just that I didn't expect it."

I walked over and stepped into the musty dark interior.

"Check it out," Packer said. He pointed to a cardboard box on the floor. "It's full of dynamite."

FIFTY-ONE

"A box of three-by-eights," Mare said.

"I remember him showing us these in his class," Packer said.

"Probably six or eight in that box," Mare said.

Street moved back. "Is it safe?" she asked.

"Pretty much," Mare said. "They don't have detonators. Those will probably be around here somewhere. Let's not drop any sledge hammers until we find them."

"What do you mean, pretty much?" Street said. Spot was sniffing the box.

"Dynamite without a detonator is quite stable. It won't go off unless it gets a serious pop right next to it. A detonator or a bullet would do it. In theory, you and Spot could play fetch with those three-by-eights without danger. Don't know if he would like the taste, though."

"In theory," Street said.

Mare grinned at her. "This is the stuff I use at work. When you see what it can do, you don't want to sleep with a box of it under your bed. Safety becomes a theory you don't want to test." Mare turned to Packer. "Do you know if this guy has his Blaster's license?"

"No idea. He seemed to know the stuff well, but I don't think he's the kind of guy who cares much for rules."

"Why do you ask?" I said.

"Just that you don't generally walk into someone's cabin and find dynamite. It's supposed to be under supervision or lock and key."

"Any idea where this stuff may have come from?"

Mare shook her head.

"Let me pose a different question," I said. "If you wanted to get a supply of dynamite for criminal use, where would you look for a source?"

"Well, I'd steal it."

"Would that be hard?"

"You don't want to know the answer to that question," she said.

"Where would you steal it from?"

"I wouldn't steal it from around here, although it would be easy. I'd probably go to Colorado. They have lots of ski resorts. Lots of avalanche control."

"Lots of dynamite," I said.

Mare nodded.

"And you would know where to look for it," I said.

She nodded again.

I thought about Paul Riceman, former Utah ski instructor who, according to Terrance Burns, had recently gone back to visit the area where he taught.

We were all silent for a moment. Spot sensed it. He grabbed at my glove. Come on, let's do something.

Street was poking around at the counter that Claude used for his kitchen. There was a campstove and some propane canisters and some pots and pans. Mare walked over to a large shelf where bulk bags of granola, flour and oatmeal sat. On a small shelf, positioned over a makeshift sink, was a large water jug with a spigot.

"What I'm looking for," I said, "is something that points to any of the victims. We know that Paul Riceman took a class from Claude. We know that March Carrera was going to visit Claude in Tahoe City. March probably knew Claude or at the very least, knew of him. But March may also have taken a class from Claude. So Claude is a connection of sorts between March and Paul. If we can connect Claude to Astor Domino or Lori Simon, then Claude will be the nexus of all the avalanche victims."

"And your chief suspect," Packer said. He was leaning against a roof support post, showing no interest in looking around.

"And my chief suspect."

"But you still won't know he's guilty." Packer sounded indignant.

"No," I said.

Packer stared at me. I couldn't read his expression. I wondered if he felt an allegiance to Claude, or if there was another reason why he didn't like what we were doing.

"This was just a friendly visit to a backcountry expert," I said. "Now that we've seen that he's gone and he's got enough unprotected dynamite to blow up half the mountain, we're checking to see if he left a note or anything."

"A note that says, 'don't worry, guys, I'm okay?'" Packer's tone was sarcastic.

"Yeah," I said.

Street had been poking in the ash inside an old woodstove made from a large metal barrel. She held up a piece of kraft paper that looked like something torn from a grocery sack. It was partially burned.

"I found a note," she said. "But this doesn't make it look like things are okay." She handed it to me.

I took it from her and held it up to the light that came in a dusty, spider web-coated window. Mare and Packer walked over to look.

Spot came and wedged himself in between Street and me.

The note had the names of the avalanche victims, written in pencil. All caps. Badly formed letters.

Lori Simon

March Carrera

Astor Domino

Paul Riceman

April Carrera

"Everyone on the list is dead, except April," Street said.

FIFTY-TWO

"Owen," Street said. "You mentioned a young man who said he saw March with a girl. It could have been April. She may have been in town all this time and no one knew but March, and now she's in danger."

"The other guy who works in the snowboard shop," I said. "What's his name?"

"Benson," Packer said.

"Right. He told me he saw March with some girl, but he didn't know who she was. Does he know April?"

Packer shook his head. "I don't think so."

"I bet you're right, Street," I said. "I think they all took the same class in November. April has been here with the rest. That would explain why she was hesitant on the phone about her location. If she'd really been in the Dominican Republic, she would have been more direct about it. Instead, I suggested it to her and she agreed indirectly."

"I was back east visiting my parents," Packer said. "But why would none of them tell me they took the class? They knew I'd taken it three years ago. It would be natural to talk about it."

"Because something happened in that class that none of them wanted to talk about. Something that is getting them all killed."

"It doesn't make sense that Claude would kill his former students," Mare said. "What could possibly have happened that would drive Claude to such lengths?"

"I don't know," I said. I pulled out my cell. A single reception bar came up on the screen. I went through the menus and found her number. Her recording answered.

"April, this is Owen McKenna. I know you are in town. You are in danger. You need to immediately go to someplace public where no one would think to look for you. A supermarket or a coffee shop. Then give me a call. But leave first, then call."

I left my number again and hung up.

"Street, do you have Diamond's number in your phone?"

"Yes."

"Please call him and explain what has happened. He will connect you to someone in the Placer County Sheriff's Department who can make decisions about what we found here. Maybe they can get some detectives up here on snowmobiles if the snow isn't too deep. But Claude could come back at any time," I said. "Mare, if you and Street hid in those trees, you would have a sight line to this cabin, but no one would see you. Without your help, the cops may not find this place, it is so well hidden under the trees. You know the territory and the map better than they do. You can talk them over the mountains."

"Better than that," Mare said, reaching into her pack. "I've got a GPS. I'll give them the coordinates."

"Take a roundabout way over there so your tracks aren't obvious. If Claude comes back, you can warn the cops before they get here. Then you can leave in either direction, and circle around back over the ridge the way we came."

"What will you do?" Street said.

"Packer and I will go after April. If she calls, we'll be closer to her. If she doesn't call, we'll be knocking on doors trying to find her. Packer will know best who we should contact. In the event it approaches sunset and the cops still haven't come, I think you should ski back," I said.

"Absolutely," Mare said. "We won't risk a night on the mountain. Even though I always bring survival gear." She reached into her pack and brought out thin wind-proof anoraks.

I stepped into my ski bindings and locked them down for downhill travel. Packer got on his snowboard.

"Spot will stay with you," I said to Street.

She nodded, her face very serious.

"Packer, are you ready?"

"Wait," Mare said. She pulled out her map. "Remember the gentle way we came up and over the ridge? We made a big curve? There's a better, faster way down." She pointed at the map. "If you start out here, you'll find a gradual downward incline over to where this slope opens up. From there it will be a steeper, curving path, first to the east, then it loops around to the west, then south. But it is down all the way. You won't have to do any climbing."

"Sounds good to me," Packer said.

"Okay, we're off." I gave Street a quick hug and a kiss. "I'll ride with Packer. You have keys to the Jeep?"

She nodded and patted her zippered pocket.

"See you tonight."

Street pulled out her cell to call Diamond. I pushed off with my poles and Packer did the snowboard jerk to get going. We went down the gradual incline to the top of the slope that Mariposa had shown us on the map. We rode next to each other, our speed slow.

"You knew April?" I said.

"Yeah, but not well."

"Did you know she was in town?" I asked.

"No. March said she was doing a charity thing in the Caribbean."

"Any of this make sense to you, that March and April maybe took an avalanche class from Claude but didn't tell you or anyone else about it?"

"No," Packer said. "Like you said, something must've happened in the class."

"You took one of those classes. Can you imagine what could happen that would drive someone to murder?"

I saw Packer shake his head in my peripheral vision.

We came to the point where the mountain dropped down into a long, steep curving slope that narrowed as it descended.

Packer jerked his board, dropped over the edge, and I followed.

FIFTY-THREE

It took less than ten minutes for Packer and me to make the three-mile trip and twenty-five-hundred-foot descent. We shot out of the Squaw Creek drainage and skidded to a stop where the houses and the village began.

Packer moved fast. He pulled his snowboard off and took off running. I grabbed my skis and ran after him. He had the pickup running and was scraping snow and ice off the windshield when I caught up with him. I tossed my skis in the bed and jumped in. He drove while I worked the phone.

I called Uncle Bill first, explained what we'd learned. I tried to break it gently, but I didn't want to cover up the danger.

"April is here in town?" Bill said. "She's been here all along? Am I an idiot? How do I mess up so bad? No, I didn't hear about any avalanche class. How could they take a class and I didn't even know? If I hadn't kicked her out, maybe she wouldn't be in trouble. No, I have no idea where to look for her. No idea. I've destroyed everything I ever cared about."

"Bill," I interrupted, but he kept talking. "Bill! Shut up and listen! April is probably still alive. If we can find her, we can save her."

"What should I do?"

"Stay calm and think of where she might be. Go back over everything she said. Anything that seemed unusual or out of place. Anything that could suggest who she might be with."

"Okay. I'll try. I've failed her in every way."

"Bill! This isn't about you! Start thinking!"

I hung up and called Sergeant Bains, and told him about the connection between the victims.

"Claude Sisuug?" he said. "How do you spell that?"

"I don't know. Maybe Google different combinations along with the word avalanche. You'll turn up something."

"You got any other address for him besides the mountain shack?"

"No. The guy I'm with, Packer Mills, took Sisuug's class three years ago. He said that Sisuug is from the Yukon and spent time in the Beartooth Mountains near Red Lodge, Montana."

"Oh, that makes it real easy." Bains was silent, no doubt making notes. "Okay, I'll put the word out on April Carrera and see what I can find. Meantime, you're looking for her?" he said.

"Yeah. Packer knows her some. He'll take me around to anyone who knows her."

"You got her number?" He asked. "I can track it."

"Her cell, yeah. Let me find it again." I went through the menu and read it off to Bains.

"Hang on."

I waited. Packer was coming around Crystal Bay. The lake was completely socked in. Dense fog sat on the slate gray surface of the water. If I didn't know there was a giant lake out there, I might have thought we were driving next to a very long but narrow duck pond. In the sky were darker clouds making evanescent shapes that emerged from the fog and then disappeared back into it like the ink wash clouds the Chinese landscape artists painted a thousand years ago.

Bains came back in my ear. "Nothing on the Internet cell locator. No surprise, there. These mountains, they get in the way of cell towers and GPS satellites and everything else."

"Maybe she turns it off for privacy," I said.

"A true subversive, huh?"

"Stay in touch," I said.

"Right." Bains hung up.

FIFTY-FOUR

I called Street as Packer was driving past Spooner Lake. My call got routed to her voicemail. The questions banged around in my head. Was she on another call? Did her battery die? Did the weather change enough to kill her cell reception? I left a message saying I'd try again.

Packer came up to Highway 50, turned down the mountain toward Glenbrook. I tried Street again, got her voicemail again.

"Who can you think of who knows April?"

"Lots of people know April," he said.

"Names."

"March's friends, of course. Will Adams, me, Paul... Oh, sorry. I can't believe I named him."

"I haven't met Will."

"He's in Zephyr Cove. We can stop there, first."

"Who else?"

"Carmen Nicholas."

"Met her," I said.

"The Lieberman brothers, Mack and Checker."

"What's their connection to April?" I asked.

"They're just buddies. They do a stand-up routine. First at one of the open-mike gigs at a coffee shop, then they graduated to a little venue over at Harrah's. They open for the bigger comics that come through. They're pretty good, actually."

"How'd they meet March?"

"I think we were all out partying one time, and Carmen said we should see them perform. She knew them from hustling drinks."

"They live here on the South Shore?" I asked.

"No. They stay in an apartment when they perform during the summer."

"They ski? Or do backcountry treks? Take an avalanche course?"

"No. They're more into the summer beach babe scene. They come up from San Diego. I don't think they'll ever get used to snow and cold."

"Who's next?" I said.

"People who knew April... Well, there's a girl who lives down near Auburn. Ada something. I forget. Her parents have a cabin out near Camp Richardson. She comes up now and then. She's not real tight with our group, but April and her have done quite a bit of hiking and camping. She stopped in the shop yesterday. She's smart, but she's such a college girl I don't know if she'll ever grow up."

"She's the one who manages her parents' winery in the foothills."

"Yeah." Packer pushed his truck fast as he entered the Cave Rock tunnel.

"I was told she was in France," I said.

"Someone got mixed up," he said. "I sold her some base wax yesterday."

And April was supposed to be in the Dominican Republic, I thought.

"Does Ada do any snow sports?"

"She's real into cross-country skiing, the skinny-ski thing. Kick and glide in the groomed tracks. I've seen a picture of her and April skiing where April had on wool knickers just like the old days, and Ada wore her race clothes. Skin-tight blue nylon, top and bottom. She's skinny, just like those race skis. But she's got serious leg muscles. I guess that whole Nordic thing is major exercise."

My phone rang. It was Street.

"You're okay?" I said.

"Yeah. I was on the phone with the sheriff's department. They're coming on snowmobiles. They'll probably be here in the next hour. Mare and I are still waiting in the trees. We can see the mine shack. We've seen no one else."

"Are you warm enough?"

"Yeah. Mare's anoraks are great. Spot's a little frustrated, but he's behaving. Here, say something."

"Spot, be good!" I yelled into the phone.

I heard him whine in the background. Then Street was back. "I'll call when the cops get here and we leave."

We said goodbye.

"You want to call Will before we stop by, or surprise him?" Packer asked.

"Surprise," I said.

FIFTY-FIVE

Will Adams lived in Zephyr Cove, up a winding road and around a curve that put his place above the highway below.

"Tell me again what this guy does for a living?"

"Computer consultant," Packer said. "Went to UC San Francisco. Worked for an Internet startup for a while, then moved up here. Now he does the rent-a-geek thing. You got a computer problem or a network that needs setting up, he'll do it. Only a hundred fifty bucks an hour."

"Even paltry wages add up," I said.

Packer pulled into the drive and parked. He beeped the horn twice and got out.

Will opened the door as we walked up. His hair was combed straight up like in the photo Bill had shown me. He wore khakis and a dark brown sweater.

We exchanged greetings and Will took us inside to a big living room with a stone fireplace and a huge TV. The furniture was black leather on chrome.

"Beer?" Will said.

We nodded and Will went over to the kitchen, opened a stainless steel fridge and pulled out bottles of Fat Tire Ale. I sat on the couch that faced the fireplace. Inside were remnants of a real fire. A half-log glowed with embers. Will sat cross-legged on the floor. Packer stood leaning against fireplace stone.

"I'm sorry to tell you that your friend Paul Riceman was killed two days ago," I said.

Will looked shocked. "What happened?"

"He was next to his house when the snow slid off the roof. He was trapped and he suffocated."

"Like an avalanche..."

"We're looking for April Carrera. Any idea where she might be?"

I watched Will's reaction. His frown seemed genuine. "I thought she was in the Dominican Republic, building houses or something." He looked down at the carpet. "I didn't know Paul that well, but to die in the snow, like March... Is April okay?"

"I don't know. The only time I've spoken to her she was vague about her surroundings. At first, I thought she didn't want to be found. Now I believe it was because she was never there."

"Why the obfuscation?" Will said.

"One of the things I want to know. I also learned that Paul took an avalanche class last November. I think March and April took that same class. Did you ever hear them say anything about that?"

Will looked at Packer. "Like that class you took?"

"Yeah. Mine was three years ago," Packer said.

"I never heard about it. I'd think one of them would've said something." Will drank his beer, then balanced it on his knee.

"Where do you think April would stay in town if she didn't want to be seen?"

Will shook his head. "I don't know. I don't know her that well. Some friend, I guess. Or a motel."

My phone rang. It was Street's number. "Sorry, I need to take this," I said. I stood up and walked outside.

"Hi, sweetheart," I said.

"The cops are here, searching Claude's place. They said you should call them tomorrow."

"No sign of Claude?" I asked.

"No. We're going to head back down. Mare says we have plenty of time to get out of the high country before dark."

"Call me when you get down the mountain?"

"Will do."

I went back inside Will's house. Packer was talking to Will in earnest, his tone low and serious. He stopped in mid-sentence when he saw me.

"Any thoughts on how we might find April?" I asked.

Will shook his head. "Is she in danger?"

"Yes." I handed Will one of my cards. "Call me if you hear anything?"

"Yeah, sure. Of course."

We said goodbye and left.

"Next stop, Carmen," I said to Packer.

"She'll probably be at work," he said, starting his truck, and pulling out of Will's driveway.

"The avalanche class you took," I said as Packer drove. "Was there anything else that Sisuug covered? Stuff unrelated to avalanches?"

"Not really. Some wilderness survival stuff."

"What did that consist of?" I asked.

"Winter camping, backcountry travel in winter, what gear to bring, high energy foods, stuff like that. He also taught us how to dig a snow cave, and how to tow a toboggan in case we wanted to bring in gear to make a base camp."

"Why would he teach you to make a base camp?"

Packer thought about it. "I think Claude looked at all backcountry skills from the perspective of how to live in the wilderness. He was a natural mountain man. I don't think he understood that us students just wanted to hike in and ride the steep and deep and not get caught in a slide."

Packer parked behind Harrah's and we walked into the casino. I stopped one of the cocktail waitresses. "Excuse me, is Carmen on tonight?"

"I think so. But I haven't seen her. Better check with Sierra."

"Sierra?"

"At the wait station. You can't miss her. She's the one with hair that comes to a point. Like Mount Shasta."

The waitress pointed toward one end of the casino. We walked over and saw a woman whose rigid hair did look like

Mount Shasta. She was at a bar, talking to the bartender.

"Excuse me, is Carmen on tonight?" I asked her.

The woman glared at my face bandage and my arm sling. "Carmen is AWOL."

"She called in sick?" I asked.

"No. She called in saying her family was sick. This family leave stuff is ridiculous."

"Any idea where I'd find her?"

Sierra glared at me. "Like I would know?"

"Got it," I said.

"Know where she lives?" I said to Packer.

He nodded.

A few minutes later, he pulled in to an apartment building off Pioneer Trail near Stateline. He found a parking space and we walked up an outdoor stairway that was caked with ice. Packer knocked on Carmen's door. We waited. Down to the right was an apartment with lights on inside and loud Mexican music thumping through the walls. Leaning against the railing were four pair of old downhill skis. I knocked again and we waited some more.

"I've seen her talk to the woman who lives on that side," Packer said, pointing to the left. Another pair of downhill skis leaned against the building near the division between Carmen's apartment and the neighbor lady's apartment. "That woman might know where Carmen went. But the lady's kind of a witch and Carmen said that she won't talk to anybody. She just slams the door on anybody she doesn't know. You can try it, but I just want to warn you."

We stepped sideways past the skis. The door had dirty paint and a splintered doorjamb where someone had tried to pry it off its hinges. Inside came the howl of girl-group music from the sixties.

I knocked on the door, hard and loud.

In time the decibels inside were turned down. The door opened and a cloud of cigarette smoke billowed out.

A middle-aged woman wearing pink shorts and pink a T-shirt and fluffy pink slippers stood there, a lowball glass in her hand, hanging down by her hip. I expected the drink to be pink, but it was a strong amber. She didn't appear to notice my injuries. Maybe injuries were normal for her visitors.

"Hey there, ma'am, my name's Owen and this here's Packer and we're looking for Carmen. We were just getting our bump after work and Carm's not there like normal and her supervisor said that Carm was sick, so we came over to see how she was doing, but now she doesn't answer her door. And the light ain't even on and we know that with her usual schedule she wouldn't be in bed this early even if she was liking to die. In fact, we were here a couple months back when she called in sick and we brought her some soup and flowers and Packer bought her a card from the shop just down from the wait station. Remember, Packer? The one with green glitter on it and the joke about the devil and the margarita? Anyway, we sat with her and watched Leno. So her light should be on, unless she's really sick. Then we thought we should probably ask her neighbors, just to be sure everything's cool. Do you know if she's okay?"

The woman swirled the drink at her hip and regarded me the way a carabid beetle probably regards a snail. "I ain't seen Carmen since day before yesterday. She could be in Paris, France for all the times I looked out and seen snow piling up on this walk and me the only sucker around here stupid enough to shovel the crap off."

"Really," I said, trying to look interested.

The woman drank a large swallow. "But actually, she went home. She's got family in Eureka and her daddy's got the big C real bad. They got these special shots they give him over in Redding. Carmen said her sister has to go up to Oregon for a week and can't drive him, so Carmen went home to take him to get his shots."

"I'm sorry to hear that, ma'am. Real sorry. Well, at least Carm's not sick. I guess we'll see her when she gets back. Oh, one more question, if I may. We're also wondering about our friend April. She hasn't returned our calls. Do you know if she's been in contact with Carmen?"

"Never heard of April."

"Okay, thank you for your time."

The woman nodded and shut her door, and we left.

Packer looked at me as we walked to the stairs.

"Well, can't you charm the ladies."

"If they're drunk."

We made several other stops at places where Packer thought we might learn news of April. But no one knew anything of her whereabouts. My only other idea was to get hold of Carmen and see if she knew where April was.

I called information in Eureka. I got several listings for Nicholas, Carmen's surname. On my third call I reached a man who sounded very weary.

"May I speak to Carmen, please?"

"She's not here, yet. She called from the Starbucks in Redding an hour ago, so she'll be here before too long. You want to leave a message?"

"No thanks, I'll try again."

With no connection to Will or Carmen or anyone else, April was proving as elusive as the mist in a thousand-year-old Chinese landscape painting.

I had Packer swing by Street's lab. My Jeep was in the lot, so I thanked him for his help and got out. "Anything I can do to return the favor, let me know."

"When my poetry chapbook comes out, you can buy one."

I nodded at him. He drove away.

While Street and I ate a quick dinner, she explained that two cops had arrived on snowmobiles. They took a quick look in Claude's cabin, talked to Street and Mariposa, took the partially burned note and the dynamite, and then let them go. Street drove Mare home before coming back to her lab.

"What did you make of Claude's cabin?" I asked.

"I'm not sure. The note and dynamite certainly make Claude look like the murderer. But that's not enough to convict, right?"

"No. But if there is a way to match the dynamite used on the deadly slides with the dynamite in Claude's cabin or at my cabin, that would be very helpful. Much better would be finding Claude's fingerprints on pieces of the dynamite and detonators at the crime scenes. Add in a witness or two, and we'd have a tight case."

"It could be," Street said, "that all the witnesses have died under snow. Except April."

"But April might be a perpetrator instead of a witness. She's the one person who's been hiding all along. She and Paul could have done all the murders to make it look like Claude did them. Then she could have left the partially burned note in Claude's cabin and killed Paul to eliminate her only witness. The cops may eventually find Claude, and he will seem like a more likely perpetrator than April. Especially if the wild-man descriptions of him are true. But April and Paul may have killed Claude, too, and they may have made it look like an accident. Maybe in a way that has nothing to do with avalanches. If so, the DA might realize there isn't enough evidence to pursue April."

"But what is her motive?" Street asked. "What could have happened that is so bad that she would kill everyone in her avalanche class?"

"I don't know. The more I inquire, the more people die, and I'm no closer to knowing why."

"One thing that may help," Street said. "I looked at the dirt you brought home from the vineyard. I found a carabid beetle just like the one in Lori Simon's lungs. I also found several bits of insect detritus that match the dirt I collected from the back of Paul Riceman's pickup. It's not proof, but it satisfies me that someone murdered Lori in the vineyard or near there and loaded her body into Paul's truck."

Spot and I left after dinner.

FIFTY-SIX

My cell rang late in the evening. I was lying in bed, wide awake, alternately wondering and worrying about April.

"Hello?" I said.

"Mr. McKenna, it's April Carrera. That's a very strange message you left."

"April, where are you? Are you okay?"

"Of course, I'm okay. I just called you, didn't I? I'm sorry it's late."

"Are you alone?"

"Sure. What does it matter?"

"Where are you?" I said again.

"Didn't Uncle Bill tell you that I'm in the Dominican Republic? I thought he was spilling his guts out to his new friend. Anyway, I'm okay. There's nothing to worry about."

"Are you with Claude?

"Claude who?"

"Claude Sisuug."

I heard April do a kind of disgusted snort. "I can't imagine what you are suggesting."

"I told you. You're in danger. You need to tell me where you are and if anyone is with you. If someone is listening, hang up and call me back when you're alone."

"Mr. McKenna, you've been watching too many movies. I'm working for a charity. We build houses."

"April, please consider this. Wherever you are, look at everyone you know as a potential threat."

"Look McKenna, I've been through hell dealing with March's death. And Lori. I want to be left alone."

"How did you know Lori?"

"She was in... I met her at a party."

"You all took the avalanche class, together, didn't you? Claude Sisuug had a list of the names in his cabin."

"That's ridiculous. March and Lori died. But it was a horrible accident. Everyone else is fine."

"Astor's dead. Paul Riceman's dead. You're next."

There was silence on the phone. "I don't believe you," she finally said. She sounded insecure, but I couldn't tell if it was genuine or an act. "I just talked to Paul a couple days ago," she said. "I know he's alive."

"I found Paul myself. We dug his body out of a snowslide. It must have been right after you talked to him. It was on the local news."

More silence. "I haven't seen the local news. I told you, I'm out of town. I knew Astor shouldn't have told that woman. I need to think."

"What woman?"

She hung up before I could say anything else.

I dialed Sergeant Bains.

"April just called me," I said when he answered.

"You have any idea where she is, yet?"

"No. But she hasn't been in touch with local events. She may not have known that Astor Domino and Paul Riceman had died. She could be traveling somewhere. Or hiding at a friend's place. Someplace where she wouldn't get that news. You might be able to get her location off her phone."

"I punched it in when you first said you talked to her. But it's still coming up empty. She must have turned off the phone. Any idea what she's doing?"

"She started to mention a woman. Someone Astor talked to. I have an idea that the woman she's referring to may be Astor's landlord."

"You going out there in the morning?"

"No. I'm heading up there now. I'll let you know what I find out."

Spot and I got in the Jeep and headed up the East Shore toward Incline Village. My cell rang as I was approaching Sand Harbor. I had to steer with my knee to answer it.

"McKenna? Bill. Sorry it's so late. Did I wake you? You said I should call if I thought of anything unusual."

"I'm awake."

"Well, it's probably nothing, but remember how I said that April was into history and such?

"Yeah, you said she turned every conversation around to the Civil War era."

"Right. Anyway, I keep thinking about my party when she talked about the key players. Lincoln and Davis, Grant, Lee and Armstrong. It was like she thought they were the most important guys in the Nineteenth Century."

"I remember," I said.

"So, I Googled it. You get acres of stuff on all of them except Armstrong."

"What are you getting at?" I asked.

"There were a couple of different guys named Armstrong who show up in the Civil War histories. But none of them was significant. Nothing at all compared to Lincoln, Grant and Lee. It would be like a history about business trends today talking about Bill Gates, Steve Jobs, Oprah and Bill Esteban. My name doesn't belong with them. All the important stuff about the Civil War, it's all about Grant and Lee and Lincoln. No Armstrong."

"You have an idea why April talked about him?"

"I remember she was talking about after the war, when Armstrong was involved with the Carson City Mint, she turned and looked at March when she mentioned Armstrong's name. Paul got upset. And March gave her a big grin and winked. It was like they had some kind of private joke."

"What do you think it means?"

"I don't know. But I thought I should tell you."

I was driving, thinking. The twisty road had a thin layer of glitter on it. Tiny crystals sparkled in the headlights. Not big enough to be snow crystals. Air crystals. Water vapor coming out of the air. Like the ink-wash fog in the Chinese landscapes. I wondered if I was wrong in thinking that those paintings were about idyllic settings, with themes of peace, serenity and sacred beauty. Maybe those painters from a thousand years ago were instead painting scenes of intrigue, the elaborate landscapes merely a complex backdrop against which dark events could hide, concealed in shrouds of mist.

"McKenna? You still there?"

"Yeah. Thanks, Bill. I'll be in touch." I hung up as I pulled into Josie King's drive.

FIFTY-SEVEN

I cruised up the drive, swooped around the curve fast enough to almost skid out of control, and parked under the portico. Several motion lights came on. I got out and let Spot out of the back. He ran around, excited. I worked the bear-and-fish doorbell and pounded on the door with my hand.

There was no sound from within. Probably everyone was asleep. Imagine that at one in the morning.

I pounded again and worked the doorbell device over and over. Eventually, they would be up, staring at the video screens, wondering if I were somebody crazy. My hope was that they'd see Spot and realize who I was and decide that it wouldn't be too dangerous to open the door.

I kept pounding and then I heard a voice and the door opened up ten inches.

Jamesie stood squinting at me, awake but confused. He wore a mauve silk robe below which protruded skinny white ankles marbled with blue veins. His feet were mercifully covered in mauve slippers.

"What is it you want?" No 'how can I help you, sir.'

I put my arm out, pushed open the door and walked in. Jamesie flinched and jumped to the side as if worried for his physical safety. "Spot," I called. "Spot, come."

He came running through the snow in the side yard, ran under the portico, and leaped up and over the three steps and skidded into the entry, his claws scratching the slate floor.

I turned and shut the door. Jamesie flinched again.

"What I want is for the madam to get her butt out of bed and provide me with a quick concise explanation of your involvement with Astor and his fellow avalanche classmates."

"I'm sorry, but I couldn't possibly interrupt her sleep. She's taken a pill and she won't see anyone until ten in the morning."

"If the explanation is not thorough I will call in the posse and show them evidence linking her to the murders of three young men and one young woman. I know from experience that they will care little for what kind, or how many, pills she's taken."

Jamesie's eyes got real intense.

"Go wake her and get her down here in five minutes or I will find her in her bed."

Jamesie did a kind of physical stutter as he tried to decide what his body was to do next. Eventually, flight won out over fright and he disappeared into the back of the main hall, bypassing the main staircase, presumably to take the more discreet back staircase up from the kitchen.

Spot and I wandered the main hall, poking our heads into the living room with its King George finery, the sitting room with its Queen Anne chairs, the billiards room with the wet bar and the leather furniture, the great room with its grand rustic timber frame excess, and the den where the coin collection lay inside the glass cases, lit by a warm glow from recessed light strips.

I didn't have a clue what the coins were or how much they were worth, but I could tell they were important baubles for people who never worried about paying a mortgage or day care or college tuition. I understood that coins were an important window into the history of most cultures, and they provided a record of how people lived from King Tut to modern times.

But I suspected that Josie King's interest in numismatics was more about lust for gold than it was an anthropologist's inquiry.

I'd made two circuits of the display cases when Josie appeared, wearing a red robe not unlike Jamesie's mauve robe. She held a green bottle of Rolling Rock. She didn't appear steady on her feet and she leaned on one of the bookshelves for support.

"Am I allowed to sit down for my interrogation?" she said.

"You may."

She fell back into a chair. She held her robe so it wouldn't fall open as she crossed her rubbery legs and swigged some beer. Her slippers were big floppy leather affairs with open heels.

Spot saw her, walked over and sniffed her bare heel. Then he shook and the last of the melted snow flew off of him onto the rug and the display cases and Josie. She jerked and wiped her face with the back of her hand, but didn't say anything, impressive control for someone just roused from barbiturate-aided slumber. Spot lay down at her feet.

"What happened to your arm?"

"The person who murdered Astor has made two attempts on my life."

Her eyes widened. "I'm sorry. Jamesie said you suspected me." She shook her head. "It wasn't me." She looked at Spot. "I assume your hound will be instrumental in your questioning." She slurred the word instrumental but otherwise sounded fairly lucid.

"You've heard about animals and their sixth sense. He can distinguish truth from falsehood," I said.

"And how does he respond?"

"Tell a lie, he bites."

Josie King tried to smile but she looked concerned.

"Tell me about the murders," she said.

I walked up and stood over her. "Nearly everyone in Astor's avalanche class has been murdered. I have testimony," I lied, "that Astor told you what happened up on the mountain and you have tried to intervene."

"You think I killed those kids?"

"I believe that I can make the DA seriously consider bringing charges against you."

"Unless I do what?"

"Unless you start at the beginning and tell me everything."

"I'll need more beer."

"I'm sure Jamesie knows where to find it."

FIFTY-EIGHT

"In eighteen-seventy," Josie said, "the Carson City Mint began its first year of operation. Among other coins, it began issuing Double Eagle twenty dollar gold coins." Josie was still drinking her first beer, alternately holding it in her lap or setting it on the floor next to her chair. On the other side of her chair lay Spot, and her other hand dangled down to rest on his neck.

At Josie's request, Jamesie had brought her a second Rolling Rock. After taking a long look at Spot, he chose the chair farthest away and sat primly, hands on both chair arms.

Josie continued, "That first year they only struck three thousand, seven hundred and eighty-nine Double Eagle coins. Most of that very tiny run was lost or eventually melted down. The best guesses are that today no more than fifty of these spectacular coins remain in the world and perhaps as few as half that. Of those, fewer still are in good condition."

Josie pulled a reference book off the table next to her, flipped through it, found a page and stood up. She brought it over to me and pointed at two pictures showing the front and back of a beautiful gold coin. "This is an example of one in very fine condition. You'll see the date on the obverse and the tiny CC mark on the reverse, indicating it came from the Carson City Mint."

I understood that by the word obverse she meant the front of the coin, which showed the familiar Liberty Head image of a woman wearing a type of crown. Underneath was the date 1870. The reverse, or back side, had the familiar-looking eagle emblem that we know as the U.S. symbol. At the bottom was the tiny CC imprint she referred to.

"Why is it called a Double Eagle?" I asked. "There is only one eagle."

"The more common eagle was a ten dollar gold piece and it contained about a half ounce of gold. The twenty dollar coin had almost an ounce of gold. Because it contained twice as much gold as the Eagle coin, it was called a Double Eagle."

Josie left me with the book and returned to her chair. "Several U.S. mints produced Double Eagles, and they were much more productive than the Carson City Mint. In all the years that the Carson City Mint was in operation, it struck fewer than half of one percent of all the Double Eagles ever made."

I closed the book and set it down. "You're saying that any Double Eagle from the Carson City Mint was rare."

"Yes and those from eighteen-seventy were the rarest of all."

"Valuable?" I said.

"Oh, you wouldn't believe. One in bad condition would fetch tens of thousands of dollars. One in uncirculated condition has recently gone at auction for over three hundred thousand dollars. One in perfect condition, what we call Mint State, would be more valuable, still. Estimates range from three-quarters of a million to a million dollars."

"For a single coin," I said.

"Yes. Of course, no one knows if such a perfect eighteen-seventy Double Eagle exists."

"What does this have to do with the avalanches and the people who've died?"

Josie leaned her head back on her chair, shut her eyes and took a deep breath. "When I talked to Astor about moving here, he came over to discuss the situation and saw this room with my coin collection.

"He began asking me about coins, gradually getting more specific with his questions. He was wary and didn't do anything other than ask about coins until he'd agreed to move into the caretaker's house. We'd probably met six or seven times by that point.

"One day he said he had a coin he'd like me to look at and he pulled an eighteen-seventy CC Double Eagle gold piece out of his pocket as if it were a quarter.

"I gasped and asked him where he got it, but he wouldn't say. He just wanted to know what it was worth. I explained that I wasn't an expert, but I thought it looked like it was in very fine condition, which meant it would be worth perhaps a hundred thousand dollars.

"He immediately put it back in his pocket with his other change. I scolded him for such abuse and explained proper treatment for such a coin and asked him again where he got it, but he wouldn't tell me.

"He never showed it to me again, and I have no idea where he kept it. But one day several weeks later, I asked him about the coin again, and he told me the story.

"Astor and several other young people, who I now believe included March and April Carrera, Lori Simon and Paul Riceman took an avalanche class from a French-Canadian-Inuit man named Claude. I forget his last name.

"Among other things, they studied avalanche control, which, in my limited understanding, is a process where one throws dynamite into unstable snow to start a controlled slide on any slope where you don't want to be surprised by an uncontrolled slide.

"I'm not clear on the details of what happened, but in essence the charge they threw to start a controlled avalanche cracked loose not just ice and snow, but some rocks that had been piled up for who knows how long. As Astor explained it, the slope was very steep and had lots of loose rocks. It was prone to slide both snow and rocks. All it needed was a little push in just the right place. The resulting slide of earth and snow cleared an area right down to the ground. Above the newly bare area were more rocks and snow, and they could see that the situation was precarious and in danger of sliding farther.

"But in this bare area were some large bones like from a horse and some human bones and chunks of dried leather that looked something like the remains of a saddle."

"A horse and rider who'd been buried for a hundred years or

more and then suddenly became unburied by the slide of earth and snow?" I said.

"Yes. Astor darted down onto the bare area and poked around in the remains. He picked up what appeared to be a small, decomposed leather bag. It disintegrated in his hands and a dozen or more gold coins spilled out across the earth.

"As Astor reached to begin picking them up, the others shouted that the snow and rock above were giving way. Astor had picked up one coin when he realized what they were saying. So he scrambled to the side just as the whole works came down from above and reburied the bones and the coins."

"And the coin he grabbed," I said, "was the eighteen-seventy Double Eagle he showed you."

"Yes." Josie stared at me.

"How many coins did Astor think were in the leather bag?"

"He said that his best guess was more than twelve and fewer than twenty. He didn't get to count them or even get to really look at them on the ground, it all happened so fast."

"But he thought they were similar? All gold and such?"

"Actually, he said he got the clear sense that they were all the same Liberty Heads and Eagles, same brilliant golden hue."

"Did Astor tell you what the reaction of the group was?"

"He said that they had no idea just how valuable the coins might be, but they assumed the value would be significant. He said that Claude was convinced that the coins would make them all rich and that it was hard for any of them to stay calm with Claude being so agitated. Nevertheless, they discussed the situation at length and decided that they should all share equally."

"How did they plan to get at the coins?"

"Astor said that they realized that if they set to digging they might not be successful. There was the question of where exactly to dig. Also, when the snow and rock came down from above it probably scattered the coins as it reburied them. In addition, they thought that digging with snow shovels would be just as likely to scatter the coins as to uncover them.

"So they came to an agreement that they would wait until

summer when the snow was melting. Slowly melting snow would be less likely to move the coins than shoveling it away. The location of the coins faced northeast, which meant it would be one of the last areas to melt. Claude said that in most years the area was not clear of snow until late June. But in a very wet year like this winter, he thought that the snow will be so deep that it probably won't melt until August.

"So they shook hands on a verbal agreement. Claude had told them that a verbal agreement was a legally binding contract and that if anyone shirked the contract, the others would testify on behalf of the agreement.

"The agreement was that they would reconvene at a time acceptable to all in the group. They would hike as a group up to the location as the snow was getting thin. There they would make a group camp and, with the aid of shovels and metal detectors, find the coins and, again as a group, bring them to an appropriate broker who would sell them. They would split the proceeds. They seemed a tight enough group that Astor even agreed to include his initial coin in with whatever the group found."

"Tight enough," I said, "that somebody is murdering the others in hopes of getting the coins for himself."

"Yes."

"Did Astor ever say who and how many people were in the class?" I asked.

"No. I should have asked. He might have told me."

"Did he give any indication of where this took place?"

"No. That was part of the agreement. None of them could reveal the location to anyone else."

"Yet if someone did exactly that, then the murderer could be anyone," I said. "What is your involvement?"

Josie sighed. "After March Carrera died in the Emerald Bay avalanche, Astor told me that March had been part of the group. He also told me that it was possible that the unidentified girl who was also found dead in the Emerald Bay slide might have been in the class. But then Astor died three days after that. Later, it came out that the girl was someone named Lori Simon from San Francisco. Now Paul Riceman has died from being buried by snow that slid off his own roof. Unbelievable, it seems. Did you know about him?"

"Yes." I pointed at Spot. "Spot found the body."

Josie stared down at Spot, then drank beer.

"Even after the deaths, you didn't leave it alone," I said.

"No. I realized that regardless of Astor's agreement with other unidentified people, that agreement doesn't extend to me. I also believe that just because the coins were glimpsed for a moment before they were buried, that does not convey ownership to the people who glimpsed them. It is like learning of an ancient shipwreck at sea. Anyone who comes upon information suggesting the existence of the shipwreck may pursue finding it."

"You've pursued it?"

"Trying, without much luck. I hired a pilot from Reno to fly over Tahoe's mountains and take pictures of anything that looks like avalanche sites. He has a plane equipped with a camera. I asked him to shoot anything that could be an avalanche and rock-slide even if it is covered with more recent snowfall. He has taken hundreds of pictures and emailed them to me. I've been studying them to see if anything looks like what Astor described."

"Sounds like an expensive operation," I said.

"It is. But I don't care about the cost. I just want to hold them in my hands. I want to put the best ones in their own display case so I can see them every day. As you are aware, I don't need more money. But like lots of people, I covet extremely rare things. For some people, it's paintings or ancient pottery or ivory carvings or stamps. For me it's rare gold coins."

"Because you have an extensive knowledge of these coins, you must have formed an opinion about how a rider on horseback would come to own a bag of them. Although people still ride horses in the Tahoe mountains, we can surmise that the person with the coins was probably riding back in the era when the coins were produced, right?"

"I think so, yes," Josie said.

"If there were a dozen of them," I said, "that would be two

hundred and forty dollars. Two dozen would be almost five hundred dollars, a small fortune back in the eighteen-seventies. Why would a horseman be carrying them over the high mountains? The roads we have today follow the common routes of riders from back when white men first came upon Tahoe. But Claude could not have been demonstrating avalanche control near any of our current roads. So these coins were not only off the beaten path of today, they were probably off the beaten path of yesterday. Was this a thief trying to hide from pursuers? A miner who made a good amount of money and then wanted to ride away where no one else would follow? What do you think?"

"I've wondered all of those things," Josie said. So I did some more reading. It turns out that in eighteen seventy-one, a year after the Carson City Mint opened, there were allegations of improprieties and discrepancies at the mint. Although the superintendent of the mint claimed the accusations were politically motivated, he lost his job. It is not unreasonable to think that these coins could have been stolen, lifted by an employee who then ran, choosing an escape route where he'd be least likely to be intercepted. A rugged route that would take him away from all other travelers would also be a route with the greatest danger of injury for his horse. The area that Astor described was steep enough to sustain avalanches and rockslides. A horse could easily slip on such steep terrain and fall on his rider. Like a skier triggering the avalanche that buries him, the horse may have triggered the rockslide that buried him and his rider. And it took almost a century and a half for another slide to briefly unbury them."

"Where is Astor's coin now?"

Josie shook her head. "I don't know. Jamesie and I looked through Astor's things after Astor died, but we couldn't find it."

I watched her as she spoke, looking for any nervousness or discomfort or brazenness that might indicate prevarication. She seemed the same as before.

I looked over at Jamesie who stared at the floor as if he didn't even hear us. I had no idea of what kind of person he was, but I also had no trouble visualizing him finding the coin as the two of them searched for it, slipping it into his pocket and continuing on with the pretense of searching. He didn't seem to enjoy being a butler and I couldn't imagine him working at such a job for anything but a paycheck. In a year or so, after the fuss about it settled down, he could sell the coin and quit the daily demands of Josie.

"Josie, how much do you pay Jamesie?"

She jerked her head toward him, then looked back at me. "I believe that is private information."

"Room and board and eight hundred a week," Jamesie said.

"Seems generous," I said.

"We didn't start out that high," Josie said. "But Jamesie's done a good job and when I found out about his debts I..." She stopped and looked at Jamesie again. He glared at her.

"What debts, Jamesie?" I said.

"None of your business." His voice had angry gravel in it.

"It's easy to find out. If you don't tell me I'll know anyway by noon tomorrow."

Jamesie gave me the same look of hatred I'd seen him give Josie when I saw him peeking through the poolroom door. "My ex-wife never worked. While I taught school, she was off screwing any man who had money. She is younger than I and, while she's not beautiful, she has a dramatic body and a sultry demeanor, and a lot of men with means paid her attention. When I finally divorced her, the court said that she had taken care of the domestic side of our marriage and that was equal in worth to my earnings. They also said that half of my little pension belonged to her, too, and unless she got remarried to someone with greater financial resources than mine, I would have to keep paying her alimony even after I retired. I told them that I was due to retire in a couple years and that I wouldn't be able to live on half my pension. So they reduced the payment by half, but I had to give her the house in exchange. Five years later, I'm still paying her alimony, and she still has the house I bought before we were married. But for five years she has been living with a rich man. She stays at his houses in Tahoe and Palm Springs. He flies her back and forth in his private plane and he buys her a lavish lifestyle. I tried to get our settlement changed, but she denies her involvement with him, and because she hasn't married, the court won't make any change. She keeps her new Mercedes and clothes at his house. The car is in his name, and she still has her official address at my house. Her house. If I thought I could get away with it, I'd kill her."

"Do you have other debts besides the alimony?"

Jamesie took a deep breath. "I still owe the lawyer who helped me. And I have a high credit card debt from before the court settlement. The attorney told me what was likely to happen. That I'd have to fork over half of everything including my savings account. I couldn't stand that. So I went on a trip to France, determined to spend all my money so she wouldn't get any of it. I met an ex-pat South African who was living in Monte Carlo. He talked me into investing in a new gold mine. It was a vein that had been overlooked by the big guys. This man had a lot of impressive geological surveys and other scientific information demonstrating a high likelihood that an overlooked quartz vein to which he had rights was stained with gold. I fell for it, lost my head, and signed some papers saying I would invest seventy-five thousand in his operation. It sounded exciting because the payback was likely to be ten dollars back for every dollar invested."

"You had seventy-five thousand in savings?" I said.

"I was down to twenty. So I got cash advances on all six of my credit cards. The advances added up to fifty-five thousand dollars. I added that to the twenty, and it was gone as fast as that man could get on an airplane and disappear."

"How much debt is left from the fifty-five you borrowed on the credit cards?"

"I haven't been able to pay much more than the minimum payments. Five years later I still owe fifty thousand." Jamesie stood up. "I'm not feeling well. If you have no further questions?"

"I know where to find you," I said.

"Mrs. King?" Jamesie said.

"Yes, you may," she said.

Jamesie left.

FIFTY-NINE

"Why does he hate you?" I asked when Jamesie had gone upstairs.

Josie sighed. "You think so, too? I was hoping I was wrong in my thoughts. I think it's because I'm wealthy. Jamesie has a problem with anyone who has money. I believe it goes all the way back to his childhood. He was raised in Southern Cal by a very poor single mother. When he was a toddler she took him with her on her housecleaning jobs in Brentwood. He's been fixated about money ever since."

"And now we know he has a history of pursuing gold," I said.

"Yes. He..." She paused, listening. "My God." She hurried out of the room and down to the living room at the front of the house. Spot and I followed. She pulled the drape aside and looked out the window. "I thought he was going to bed. He's leaving. Jamesie is driving away in the pickup." She let go of the drape and turned to me. "I can't imagine what that is about. I thought he was just going to bed."

Spot stuck his nose at the edge of the drape where she'd been holding it. He thrust it aside and looked out the window.

"Is the truck his?"

"No. He has an old Nissan. But it doesn't have four-wheel-drive. He has permission to use the truck."

"Any idea where he might be going?"

"In the middle of the night? No. None at all."

"May I take a look at Jamesie's room?"

"Yes, of course. He has the third floor. You saw the stairs when you came in."

"Come, Spot." He left the window and came over.

Josie looked as if she were about to comment on whether it was appropriate that Spot come with me, but she didn't speak.

Spot and I climbed the outsized staircase up and around and up and around again. Jamesie's suite was comprised of multiple rooms, some with slanted ceilings here and there depending on the arrangement of gables on the roof. He had a bedroom and bath he used, two bedrooms he didn't use, a bath he didn't use, an office, a living room with a fireplace, a sunroom with a wall of windows, and a kitchenette with twice as much space and three times as many appliances as the kitchen nook in my cabin.

Spot explored and sniffed while I searched. As with my earlier search of the caretaker's cottage, there was no specific item I was looking for, although it would be fruitful if I spotted an 1870 CC Double Eagle.

Like the caretaker's cottage, it did not take a long time to determine that there was nothing significant lying out in plain sight or tucked in an obvious hiding place.

I went back down. Spot followed, detoured for a moment at the second floor, then later rejoined me on the main floor. Josie seemed to notice his delayed appearance, but didn't mention it.

"Jamesie's not back?" I said.

"No."

"I'd like to take another look at the cottage."

"I'll come and punch in the door lock code," Josie said.

"Don't bother. You're in your robe, and it's cold outside. I still remember the code from when I watched over Jamesie's shoulder when he let me in before. I can let myself in."

Josie raised her eyebrows. "Suit yourself."

"Another question about Jamesie."

"Yes?"

"Is he physically active? Is he in good shape?"

"Oh, yes. He's a serious skier. Downhill. Backcountry. He even does the amateur race circuit. Just two weeks ago he won a trophy for his age group."

I thanked her, and Spot and I left.

Spot and I performed a sniff-and-search in the caretaker's cottage. It was the same as my previous search except that it took me twice as long with only one good arm. Nothing appeared to have been moved or changed.

I picked up the map I'd seen on my last visit. It was a duplicate of the maps that March and Paul had. I sat down at the desk and flicked on the desk lamp. It still showed the same topographic depiction of the Tahoe Basin, but this time I was armed with new knowledge. The events of the last few days wouldn't change the map, but they might change what I made of it.

I took the time-honored approach of drawing an imaginary grid and then studied each column, careful to be thorough and not skip ahead. As with the room search, I had no idea what I was looking for.

In a few minutes, I had scanned all the imaginary columns and thus had scanned the entire map. Nothing came to my attention. But the trick is to also study the imaginary rows in the hope that a horizontal search might cough up tidbits that a vertical search would miss.

I hit paydirt on the penultimate row, near the bottom center of the map, just north of Hope Valley and up the shoulder of Freel Peak, where it said Armstrong Pass.

Armstrong.

It was the one name that April talked about that had nothing to do with the Civil War and everything to do with surreptitious looks between April and March.

Street and I had hiked Armstrong Pass. And in our hiking book we had read how it was a little used route over the Sierra during the 19th Century. Before the construction of what became Highway 50 over Spooner Summit, and Kingsbury Grade over Dagget Pass, most miners and pioneers heading toward California's Central Valley came from Carson Valley by way of a longer route. They rode their horses up the canyon to Hope Valley and then over Luther Pass into Tahoe, where it was an easy trek to

Echo Summit and down the American River Canyon to the Sierra foothills.

The odd traveler chose a steeper route from Hope Valley, climbing up over Armstrong Pass and then down to Tahoe's South Shore.

It was one of those horsemen who was caught in an unfortunate slide and lay buried until Claude's avalanche group uncovered his bones. And a bunch of 1870 CC Double Eagle gold pieces, the cumulative worth of which might be millions.

Seeing Armstrong Pass on the map gave me a sudden strong sensation that April was up on that mountain. I didn't have any specific evidence to support the thought, but it had a resonance. It felt inevitable. In Bill's presence, April had spoken of Armstrong in connection with the Carson City Mint. She and March had winked over the reference. Paul Riceman had gotten upset at her liberal use of Armstrong's name.

April had been out of communication, away from the news, unaware of Astor's and Paul's deaths. She was the last or one of the last surviving members of the avalanche class, a class where the Guru of the Sierra, Claude Sisuug, also taught them winter camping and survival skills.

We'd had a lull in weather the last few days. Bill had said his niece was strong-willed. April might try to do an excavation camping trip before the next major storm began, a storm that was due to hit Tahoe in little more than twelve hours. It seemed clear to me that April was trying to finish the business that had taken the lives of her brother and friends.

I hoped that my vision was a mirage, that I was wrong, and that she was safely in bed at the house-building charity's dorm in the Caribbean. But I wouldn't bet on it.

SIXTY

I folded the topo map and put it in my pocket.

I didn't stop to inform Josie King as Spot and I ran back to the Jeep, jumped in and drove away.

I steered with my knee and dialed Sergeant Bains as I raced back down Lakeshore Drive toward Highway 28. It was 2:30 a.m.

"Yeah," he said after I identified myself.

"I believe April Carrera is up on the shoulder of Freel Peak, somewhere near Armstrong Pass, trying to dig through snow and rock toward a bunch of gold coins that she and her avalanche classmates briefly saw during their class last November. After seeing the note with her name on it in Claude Sisuug's cabin, it's logical to assume that he is with her or nearby and won't let her get off the mountain alive. But it is also possible that any number of other people are the murderer, including Josie King's butler who has backcountry skills and money problems."

"Whoa, slow down, McKenna. I gotta wake up. Where's Armstrong Pass?"

"It's a hiking pass up from Hope Valley on the southern slope of Freel Peak."

"Oh, I've been up there. That's not too far from Hell Hole Canyon. Are you saying she's up there, now?"

"That's my guess," I said.

"There's a big storm coming in. The first wave is supposed to begin later this morning. Light snow is already starting here at my house. The main brunt of the system is supposed to hit in the early afternoon. Hundred-mile-per-hour gusts on the ridgetops.

Two to three feet of snow above seven thousand feet. How high is Armstrong Pass?"

"Around nine thousand feet," I said. "Hold on." I set the phone down and used my arm to make the turn onto the highway, then went back to steering with my knees. I picked the phone up. "I'm back," I said.

"So even without a murderer, we'd have a life-and-death situation up at that elevation if we don't get her off the mountain by late morning."

"Yeah."

"Where are you?"

"Heading south from Incline Village," I said.

"You got a plan?" Bains asked.

"Even if we could get a chopper, we couldn't land with the cloud cover that's currently racing through. So that leaves snowmobiles. But the snow might be too soft and deep for them. We'll have to bring skis as well. The problem is that the killer thinks that April is the only one left who knows about the coins."

"Meaning?"

"Meaning that if the killer hears us coming on noisy sleds, he'll probably kill her immediately and make his escape, thinking he can come back later and get the coins himself."

Bains thought about it. "So we get up the mountain on the machines, stop a good distance away and go in on skis."

"That's what I'm thinking."

"It's a lot of activity and department dollars based on your hunch," Bains said.

"I'm going whether you join me or not. But I'd like to have your help."

It was moment before Bains spoke. "You were right on your other hunches. I'll make some calls, see if I can shake loose some department snowmobiles. Oh, long as I've got you on the phone, I should let you know I tracked down some background on Sisuug, the mountain man."

"Yeah?" I was struggling to steer with my knee. I leaned forward with my elbow and sling to help. My biceps burned with fire.

"There was a restraining order on him back in Montana. He was obsessed with a woman he was dating, stalking her and such. She was seeing him and another guy, too. Sisuug beat up the other guy pretty bad. I'm here to tell ya, Sisuug is wicked with his fists. He pulverized the other guy's face. They emailed me the reports, pictures and all. I've never seen anything done with bare hands that was so vicious."

"He go to prison?"

"No. Turns out three witnesses said the other guy started it by pulling a knife on Sisuug. He tried to stab Sisuug but didn't have a chance. The DA had pursued this knife fighter twice before and won convictions both times. So he prosecuted again, and the jury convicted a third time. The guy is still in prison."

"What about Claude?"

"He left the state, came to California. Aren't you glad? Anyway, if Sisuug's our man and you get near him, watch out."

"Will do. Call me back when you find out about snowmobiles?"

Bains said he would and hung up.

I set the phone down on the passenger seat. As I came around a curve to the right, my headlights briefly pointed out toward the lake and illuminated a snow squall rushing toward the shore with such speed and power that I tightened my grip on the steering wheel, bracing for the impact of the wind.

SIXTY-ONE

I fought the buffeting snow that lashed the Jeep. I'd slowed down from 50 to 25 and still I could barely make out the road in the whiteout. Then the snow squall blew on past and I was back in clear weather. I dialed Uncle Bill. He mumbled a groggy hello into my ear.

"McKenna, here," I said.

"Hey," he said. "What time is it? I fell asleep. Where are you?" It sounded less like a question than a complaint about being awakened.

"I'm coming your way. I need your snowmobiles. Are they working? Do they have gas in them?"

"Sure they work. And I always keep them gassed up in the winter."

"Good. Get them ready, will you? Hook the trailer on your SUV. Collect some extra clothes, jackets, and such."

"I don't understand."

"I think April is up on the side of Freel Peak."

"What?"

"I think she's been in town for some time, working on the same project that March was working on, digging for treasure that her avalanche class found back in November. But there is a big storm coming through later today. We have to get her off the mountain before then."

"I could call her on her cell and let her know we're coming," Bill said. "She could dig a snow cave for shelter until we can get up there to rescue her."

"No, you can't do that."

"Give me a break, McKenna. I'll do whatever I want. She's my niece."

"We found the killer's list. She's the last one on it."

"What?"

"The killer is probably with her or nearby. If she gets a phone call and the killer thinks someone is coming up there, the killer may move up his plans and kill her immediately. If April has a companion helping her, that person would probably get killed, too."

"You know who the killer is?"

"Not for certain. But it's looking like the avalanche instructor, Claude Sisuug. He has a history of violence. Circumstantial evidence points to him."

"He will hear our snowmobiles coming," Bill said.

"We'll stop a good distance away and switch to skis."

"When will you be here?"

"I'm approaching Spooner Lake, but it's slow going. Maybe forty minutes."

"You want me to meet you someplace?"

"We'll be heading out over Luther Pass, so let's meet in the supermarket parking lot at the Y. Bring some food and water, too."

"I'll be there."

"Bill," I added, "choose the lightest-colored clothes you can. We want to blend into the snow."

I hung up, and went back to steering with my hand. My vision wavered. It was my second night without sleep. I struggled to concentrate. The snow was bad as I came down the steep grade toward Glenbrook. I pushed my speed, focusing on keeping the Jeep on the road. The traffic was almost nonexistent, just a long-haul truck up ahead and moving at a crawl through the blowing snow. I eased my way into the left lane. Snow and ice chunks sprayed off the big truck wheels and hit my windshield so hard I thought it might break. I kept floating to the left, but I was still too close to the truck as I pulled alongside of it. There was a heavy blanket of frozen slush at the center of the highway. The slush pulled hard on the Jeep, and I thought I was going to spin out and slide under the truck trailer.

I wrestled the wheel with only my right hand, tense as a pilot bringing a jet down toward an unseen runway in a blizzard. The wheel vibrated and shook as I tried to pass the big rig. The trucker veered my way, fighting the wind. Frozen slush shot out from the truck's wheels as if from a snow cannon, slamming the wind-shield, overwhelming the wipers. I drove blind as the wipers strug-gled on high speed to scrape away the crud.

Spot sensed my tension, sticking his nose over my shoulder, jowls next to my ear. He made a high whine.

And then I was past the truck. I eased back to the right, blast-ing down the steep highway, my wheels straddling the white line between the two lanes, nothing in front of me but an invisible road choked in snow.

At the bottom of the slope, I slowed around the curve by Glenbrook and then hit the gas on the straightaway and felt the Jeep fishtail as all four wheels spun in the thick, slick slush. I shot up to 40, then 50 before I backed off.

I grabbed the phone off the seat and dialed Street. She answered in two rings, sounding, as always, fully alert regardless of whether she'd been sleeping or not.

"It's late, hon. Anything wrong?"

"Sorry to wake you. But I wanted to let you know my plans. Bains and I are heading up to Armstrong Pass. I think April is up there, digging for treasure."

"That's what April meant when she talked about Arm-strong?"

"I think so, yeah." I gave Street an abbreviated rundown of what I'd learned from Josie King.

"I assume you don't want my help," she said.

"Thanks, but I'm worried enough confronting a killer."

"I don't like you going up on the mountain in this weather. You only have one arm. You haven't slept. So many things could go wrong."

"I don't like it, either," I said. "I'll be careful."

There was a long silence before Street spoke.

"I love you," she said.

"I love you."

I disconnected and set the phone down on the seat as I raced around the curves just north of the Cave Rock tunnel. In clear weather, the view across the lake would be the one they use on postcards, the mountains above Emerald Bay shimmering across the lake, a perfect view much the same now as it was before the Comstock Lode was discovered. Before they found the rich veins of silver and gold ore, before they cut down Tahoe's forests to prop up the mining tunnels, before they stamped those first few Double Eagles.

I charged into the Cave Rock tunnel. The sudden transition into air that wasn't filled with snow, air that I could see through, was jarring. In a moment I came to blowing snow at the end of the tunnel, a wall of white in my headlights, and I blasted back out into the wind.

I focused on trying to see through the blowing snow, divining with a sixth sense where the highway went. A mile south I went by a single car, chains rattling against its front fenders, chugging along at 15 miles per hour. For a moment, its headlights in front of me made it easier to see. Then I flew past it, back into the night, my headlights making a feeble attempt to pry open the darkness.

Eventually, the snow showers let up again, and I had clear driving through Stateline. The lonely lights of the hotels and casinos lit up the highway and reflected off the bottom of the clouds. For once I could see well enough to stop focusing on staying on the road and think for a moment about how to get to April.

There was no approach that seemed best. But I cobbled together a possible chain of events that put me and Bains's sheriff's deputies on skis in the night, approaching April's likely camp spot without giving ourselves away to the killer.

At the far end of town, I pulled into the parking lot at the Y intersection and saw Esteban's Escalade with the snowmobiles on the trailer. I parked next to him and let Spot out. I transferred my gear into the back of Bill's huge SUV, then let Spot in the back door. He jumped up on the plush seats, his nails digging into the soft leather. Bill may have noticed, but he didn't comment. Bill pulled out of the lot.

"Where are we going?" he said.

"Up and over Luther Pass. About halfway down to Hope Valley is an old Forest Service Road that goes off to the left. It won't be plowed, but I'm hoping that Caltrans has made a little place there where we can park. We're taking the sleds up that road. It runs about a half-mile below Armstrong Pass."

"What happened to your arm?"

"Another bomb at my cabin."

"Jesus, McKenna. I never realized what I was getting you into."

I got Bains on the phone as Bill drove.

"Any luck?" I said when he answered.

"Yeah. Deputy Rosten and I just finished loading a department machine in his pickup. We'll be leaving in a few minutes. We'll take Pioneer Trail out to Meyers. Where are you?"

"Heading out fifty past the airport. You bring skis?"

"In back with the sled," Bains said.

"We'll wait for you where eighty-nine turns off to Christmas Valley. By the way, what color are your jackets and pants?"

"I don't know, navy, I think."

"It'd be good if you could find stuff that's white. To blend into the snow."

"I'll see what we can rustle up."

Bill took it slow because he was pulling a trailer with over a thousand pounds of snowmobiles on it. He drove out through Meyers, turned left on 89 and pulled over to wait. My phone rang.

"We're here," Bains said as the pickup with Bains and Rosten appeared behind us. "I hope you got a plan and a real good sense of the territory, because I looked everywhere and couldn't find a topo map. I found a road map of Hope Valley that includes that area south of Freel Peak, but it's not like I could use it to find my way up the mountain in a storm."

Bill pulled out and drove down the highway.

"I've got a topo map and I've pretty much memorized it. We'll park just down the other side of Luther Pass. I'll show you where we're going on the map." I hung up. To Bill I said, "That's Sergeant Bains and one of the deputies behind us."

We headed out the deserted highway, through Christmas Valley, past darkened houses, whose residents were asleep in warm beds. At the end of the valley, we headed up the long grade to the top of Luther Pass, the snow getting even heavier as we gained elevation.

Bill had his wipers and the defrost both turned on high, but the slush was building up on the windshield, and we could barely see the white road through the snow squalls. The snow had built up four or five fluffy inches on top of another layer of heavy compacted snow mixed with slush. Bill's Escalade went through it pretty well, but a few more inches and we would be forced to stop and go the rest of the distance on the snowmobiles.

I hoped the SUV was heavy enough that the wheels could continue to crush through the freezing slush and find traction as we went higher and the snow got deeper. I could just make out the pickup behind Bill's trailer, its headlights dim and shining up at an angle because of the weight of the sled in its bed.

Several miles up the pass, the rear end of the Escalade broke loose on a curve. Bill backed off the gas and gently steered to correct the skid. But the trailer whipsawed around, pulling us sideways. Bains and Rosten backed off to keep space between us and give Bill plenty of room to maneuver.

Spot was standing in back, his legs spread wide for stability, preparing himself for something bad.

Bill counter-steered one way, then the other, and kept some power to the wheels so that he wasn't pulled to an incapacitating stop. Maybe his Escalade had computer control on all four wheels, or maybe he was the best snow driver that Texas has ever produced, but he got his rig and trailer straightened out, and he eased back on the gas to keep from bogging down in the deep snow at the top of the pass. But a half mile up the road, he hit a patch of ice, and the Escalade and trailer went sideways as a unit and slid off the highway into five or six feet of snow.

I watched out the snow-caked window as Bains and Rosten did the exact same thing. They skidded 90 degrees and came to a stop broadside at the rear of Bill's snowmobile trailer.

Bill was smart enough about snow to know that there was no point in spinning the wheels. We weren't going anywhere until a tow truck could pull us out.

We were leaning at an angle to the right, and when I tried opening the door, it was blocked by a wall of snow. Bill was able to push his door open, but I could see it was going to take him some time, so I rolled down my window and, my bad arm screaming, slithered out into the deep snow.

Rosten's pickup was immobilized and jammed tight enough against Bill's trailer that there was no hope of getting the sleds off the normal way.

Rosten was able to get out his driver's door, but because the passenger door was hard up against the trailer, Bains had to follow Rosten. Bains introduced us to Rosten, a serious man in his late twenties with a large Roman nose and a heavy brow topped with a single six-inch eyebrow.

While Bill watched, frustrated, and Spot ran around, Bains and Rosten, with a little help from me, muscled the sleds off the trailer sideways, lifting them over the trailer's edge rail and into the deep snow. Then we pulled the department's sled out of the pickup bed.

In my pack I carry a thin, custom windbreaker vest that Street made for Spot. I brushed the snow off his back, then put his front legs through the shorty sleeves and zipped it up so that it snuggled up from his deep chest back to his little show-girl waist. He went back to running around while the four of us did an equipment check. A snow shower moved in, so we tried to be fast.

Bains had a digital recorder in the event that April or Claude or anyone else got loose with their mouths and said something incriminating.

Bains produced pocket flashlights and strap-on headlights.

All of us but Bill had folding shovels strapped to our backpacks, including the new one I'd picked up after breaking my other one digging out Paul Riceman's body.

We had no transceivers, a stupid mistake, but one we'd have to live with.

Bains and Rosten each had ski goggles and, by a miracle, Bill had brought two pairs he had for snowmobiling.

Last, Bains and Rosten had their side arms, Glock nines. Bill and I had no armament but our wits and Spot's teeth.

I'd wondered during the drive about the appropriateness of bringing Bill along on the sleds. With his disability, he might make the situation more difficult instead of less. But I realized that he would make severe protest if I tried to prevent him, so I decided not to try.

Bill pulled snowshoes and custom crutches with huge ski-pole-type baskets out of the back of his vehicle. Bains and Rosten and I lashed our skis to the snowmobiles with bungy cords.

With a few pointers from Bill, I started the first sled and drove it out of the deep snow and onto the highway where Bill could easily get on. Then I started the machine that Spot and I would ride.

I'd debated about taking Spot. The downside was that he could get marooned in bottomless powder or get lost and suffer hypothermia. On the other hand, Spot had demonstrated his worthiness in difficult situations many times in the past. I decided to defer to past experience. When in doubt, have Spot on your side. I pulled a can of high-energy dog food out of my pack. I stomped an area of snow down, opened the can, and dumped it out for Spot. He inhaled it in about half a second. Having some fuel on board wouldn't prevent hypothermia in a dog, but just as with people, it would help.

While the machines warmed up, we assembled in a group a

little away so we could talk without shouting ourselves hoarse.

"Your plan, McKenna?" Bains said. His breaths were visible in the snowmobile headlights. "You know the map."

I squatted down and opened the map across my knees, angling it so one of the snowmobile headlights shined on it.

"We are here. We'll ride down the highway, then along this Forest Service road, which gradually climbs up to this meadow at eight thousand feet. Where the road curves here, we'll angle off to the northeast. We'll traverse up these shallower slopes, staying on the windward ridges where the snow won't be so deep. We'll follow the creek drainage off the south side of Freel Peak. Remember to stay off anything that is steep. If we must go on a steeper slope, we'll keep some distance between us. If one of us gets caught in a slide, the rest of us will still have a chance to dig the victim out.

"Up here is Armstrong Pass. Based on the map and what I learned from Josie King, April is probably over on one of these slopes that face northeast. But we can't know that for certain. And we can't afford to let the killer hear our sleds, so we'll go on up to this meadow and stop. Our sound will be blocked by this promontory. We'll be a quarter mile away from the pass, but we'll be at the same elevation. After we transfer to our skis, it shouldn't take too long to follow a level traverse around the promontory." I saw Bill's face gritted in the harsh light beam from the sled. "Bill will be able to follow our ski tracks on his snowshoes."

"When we get close," I continued, "our first priority is to stay low and out of sight. We are looking for at least two people. One of them may be the avalanche starter."

"You say 'may' be the avalanche starter," Bains said.

"Right. Claude. Or April, even. April may also be there with an innocent friend, just there to help her search for the coins. The friend could also be the murderer."

"If the killer isn't April and isn't with April, where do you guess he'd be?"

"Hiding. Waiting for April to find the coins. Just over a ridge, lying in the snow, wearing white, watching April from a distance, watching us approach, too."

SIXTY-TWO

Bains and Rosten got on their machine. Bains drove, and Rosten sat behind him, their right legs bowed over the bundle of their skis and poles.

Bill bungie-corded his snowshoes onto the back of his seat, got on his sled and revved the engine.

I had Spot sit on the back of my seat. He often sits on human chairs, his front feet on the floor. This was similar. I put his front feet on either side of the seat, down on the footrails. I sat in front of him, scrunched up next to the handle bars.

The machines had small windshields, but the snow blew hard from the side, so we all put on our goggles.

I started out, slow at first, struggling to handle the snowmobile with one arm. The others followed. As I gained familiarity with the machine, I sped up.

We went down the highway, following our bouncing headlight beams, and then turned and followed the Forest Service road. The snow was deep, and the machines wallowed in it, spinning their tracks, barely able to stay afloat. Eventually, I angled onto a windward slope that faced west. The snow was more windblown and it supported the sleds better. We climbed up toward Freel Peak, which, at just under 11,000 feet, is the highest mountain in Tahoe.

For a time the snow continued without relenting, plastering my face with snow so thick I had to continuously wipe off my goggles. I hoped that Spot got some shelter behind my back. I could feel his head against me, pushing this way and that as we followed the curving undulations of the ground.

Snowmobiles make a lot of noise, but our three sleds seemed strangely quiet, the snow in the air muffling and absorbing the engine noise. Despite my tension and worry, I struggled with fatigue, my eyes closing. I managed to lead the men for half an hour until the snow got so deep in a meadow that our machines bogged down.

We turned off the sleds and waited for our eyes to adjust to the darkness without the snowmobile headlights. At first it seemed totally black. Gradually, the blowing snow became permeated with a dull gray light, very dark, but sufficient to give depth to the night. We put on our skis and snowshoes. The snow in the meadow was so deep that Spot was hobbled by it. He made leaping motions to move, and I feared I'd made a terrible mistake in bringing him. But it was too late to turn back. He'd have to follow in our tracks as we broke trail. The compressed snow from our skis would give him some support.

I went first, with Bains and Rosten following on skis and Bill on his snowshoes. Spot tried running ahead into the deep snow, but quickly gave up and followed in our tracks.

I was aware that our pace would leave Bill behind, and if he got confused and lost it could be life-threatening. But April's life was probably in danger and Bill's life was only potentially threatened, so I charged ahead. I also knew that Bill would have it no other way. He would probably be able to follow our tracks even as the wind and snow tried to obliterate them.

We traversed along a medium slope, possibly steep enough to slide, but there was no other way to the pass. We spread out to minimize the chance that more than one of us would be caught in a slide. The early storm clouds attacked us in waves and sudden gusts. It was the kind of wind that killed winter campers. Even if their tents withstood the assault, the drifting snow sometimes buried the tents and eventually suffocated those inside.

I couldn't see far enough in the blinding snow to identify any landmarks. They were all just concepts in a blizzard. But I did have the compass and my sense of up and down. With those two information sources, I could match the slopes to the ones I'd memorized on the map.

I worked the slope from map memory, following imaginary topo lines, navigating by finding a level traverse across the face of the slope. I came to a much steeper section and hoped it was the base of the promontory. Once we got around it, we'd likely be in a sightline to April, but for the blowing snow that made it impossible to see more than about forty feet ahead.

I stopped and let Bains, Rosten and Spot catch up. Bill was nowhere in sight.

"We're in a straight shot to our target," I said in a loud whisper. "The snow is too dense to see that far. Sound carries better than light in this stuff. It's five in the morning. If anyone is up here, they're probably asleep in their tent, but we can't count on it. They may have heard the weather forecast and got up early to try to finish their project before the storm comes. So stay quiet and listen carefully. Even when we get close, we may hear them before we see them."

They nodded and I turned back to lead them forward into the dark wind. I hadn't taken more than two steps forward on my skis when we heard a woman talking, her voice carried on a freak confluence of wind currents.

SIXTY-THREE

The voice came from the same direction as the wind. I climbed uphill and upwind, straining to see anything through the dark forest. The snow was so deep that I couldn't stride on my skis. I could only step up and forward, pushing the soft snow down and compressing it in one motion. It was like jogging through molasses while half asleep.

The wind pulled at my cap. Blowing snow pelted my goggles. The cloud cover got thicker, a furious gray fog that fatigued my brain. I could see nothing but a vague sense of dull gray, like the mist in the Chinese landscapes, obscuring all detail and hiding the destination at the end of our path.

The world turned. I tried to ski straight, tried to keep the wind directly into my face. But the wind kept changing. Or my perceptions kept changing. I thought we were skiing up the slope. But now I was skiing down the slope. Going down required more effort than going up. Gravity itself seemed to shift directions. Like a pilot with vertigo, I struggled with confusion. Voices seemed to whisper from the snow, taunting me with promises of revelation, secrets to be exposed. But each arduous step seemed to push the secrets down into the powder snow shroud while the wind sang a fright song that drowned the whispers out. Events of the previous days became jumbled. I tried to revisit them, place them back in order as I skied through the dark.

I focused on the suspects. Nearly anyone could have had contact with someone in the avalanche class, learned of the Double Eagle gold coins and, as a result, had motive to kill. Numerous people could have had an opportunity to acquire explosives and send Lori Simon to purchase detonators.

It was when I reconsidered my visits to Lori Simon's parents that I stopped skiing for a moment.

Clarice and Samuel Simon were so self-focused that they didn't even know what Lori's major was in college. But as soon as I thought about it, I realized that the one thing they did say about their daughter's college was the thing I missed. That realization brought me to the killer.

I resumed skiing as I considered the implications. I kept the wind in my face, and I kept breaking trail. In a moment the blowing snow and clouds opened up and then raced off to the east, big billowing puffs of white against the black night. We were suddenly in the vast dark universe with a gibbous moon above and uncountable stars filling the sky. The dark shape of Tahoe stretched out 3000 feet below.

I studied the lay of the land, memorizing the rise and fall of the slopes, the twisting ravine that gouged into the mountain down to the left, the broad swath of a white snow-draped meadow that meandered through the forest. Then came more clouds, rushing toward us like huge nightmare cotton balls, and we plunged back into the world of a night-gray foggy gale, dark as a cave. I kept my direction by always facing into the wind.

Soon, the slope rotated from high on the right to high on the left, and I realized we had come at an angle through the pass and were now trudging down the other side. We continued ahead, coming upon dark trees in the darker night, walking straight into their boughs, ducking as the needles grabbed at our hats.

I stopped, got out my compass and studied the glow-in-the-dark face. The slope faced northeast. Based on my memory of the map, we were getting close. I pushed on, then stopped fast as the clouds opened up and I saw a light in the distance. The clouds came back, shutting us inside their clammy grip like a giant clam closing on a wayward visitor stupid enough to come close.

The other men came up behind me. I pulled my penlight out of my glove, pointed it at my chest and turned it on. I held my finger up in front of my face, moving it to catch their attention. Spot came past both men and stuck his snow-caked head toward me.

"Light ahead," I whispered loudly.

Through the thickness of cloud, carried downwind with the snow flurries, came voices. Spot jerked his head toward the sound and began a low growl. I tapped my finger across his nose, the signal for silence. We couldn't make out the words, but the voices were both female.

"Two people," I whispered. "But someone else may be hiding. My guess would be that the killer is up above them. Spot and I will circle around that way. Bains, I think you should go straight toward the glow, very slow, and get down in the snow to watch so they don't see you. Rosten, you approach them from below. Be aware of the potential for a slide. The slope is steep and it faces northeast, the most dangerous combination. If you sense movement under your feet, skiing sideways to the mountain is the best way out.

"If the clouds part, squat down fast and don't move. Even if they can see your shape against the snow, if you're motionless, they might think you're a rock or tree trunk.

"I'll climb up above, searching for anyone who's hiding. If I don't find anyone, I'll come down to where the voices are coming from. If I do find someone, I'll try to disarm them and then come down. Bains, you should come forward as soon as I make my appearance or start talking. Rosten, you should stay hidden the entire time. There could be someone else out here who I can't find. In which case, you will be our backup. We want any unseen person to think there's only Bains and me. Don't make any move until we call you."

Both Bains and Rosten nodded.

"I'm off," I said. "Come on, Spot." I again put my finger across his nose for silence. He followed, stepping in my tracks, sometimes stepping on the tails of my skis.

I climbed a rising arc around the lightness in the cloud below. I kept a good distance above the women, staying in the dark, looking for another person, an amorphous shape in the snow or behind a tree or a rocky outcropping.

The light dimmed, then flashed bright as the clouds cracked open. I saw two figures down below, digging with avalanche shovels. There was a lantern stuck in the snow nearby and another perched in a nook in a rock face that rose up to the west of the people. Next to a jog in the rock face was a tent. It was low and rounded, designed to handle high wind. The placement was smart. If the slope above them slid, the jog in the rock face would tend to protect the tent and force the snow to the side. A supply toboggan was propped up between some rocks. A line went from the rock to the toboggan. Stretched from the line to the snow, like a sheet on a clothesline, was a tarp pulled tight by the breeze but protected from the worst of the wind by the rock wall. The tarp provided some shelter for the people digging.

The cloud swirled around us, and for a moment it was darker than ever. I waited while my eyes readjusted.

I made a circuit far above the light-glow and the people digging, then another circuit down closer. I saw no person or any sign of recent tracks.

Spot stayed directly behind me, and we descended closer to the light, moving very slowly. I stopped skiing forward when I was directly above them, about a hundred feet up the slope. I could hear the voices, but I still couldn't understand the words.

I took a sidestep down, and then another.

They were both breathing hard. Their words were faint, but by cupping my ears and listening carefully, I could now understand most of them. Both voices sounded vaguely familiar to me, but I couldn't identify more than that.

"The last radio report said the storm will hit by early afternoon, so this is our best opportunity."

"I didn't realize that you know Claude Sisuug, our avalanche class teacher? How did you meet him?"

"Through Paul before Paul died. We saw him in a bar in Tahoe City. He creeped me out. It was dark, but I could see that he had one brown eye and one blue eye. Like on a Husky dog. And Paul told me he had a record. I'll be honest, Claude really scared me."

"Did Paul say what he did wrong to get in trouble with the law?"

"He said it was some kind of an assault charge. I guess he beat a guy to a pulp. And some woman got a restraining order on Claude because he smacked her around. I wouldn't be surprised if he reacted violently if he found out we were up here."

"So we won't tell him. No one knows we're here. The secret is safe."

There was a pause.

"Yeah. We'll split the money and never say a word."

"How well did you know Paul?"

"Like I said, we were close."

"You were in a relationship?"

"More or less."

"What does more or less mean?"

"We had sex, we confided some things, but no way would I ever have married him. It was just a date thing."

"I thought you seemed pretty nonchalant when Paul died."

"I thought you were nonchalant when March died."

"I was devastated! But what was I going to do? Feel sorry for myself? Go crawling back to my suffocating uncle? Or come back here and finish March's plan? This was his passion! This was what got him excited. He went from not caring about anything but skiing to having a focus."

They had turned and I missed more words in the howling wind. I reached down with my right hand and wadded up snow against my legs, packing it so it was shaped like a large roll of paper towels. I aimed it carefully and gave it a push toward the bright fog below me. It slid a few inches, then rolled over. It rolled again and, picking up speed, it gathered more snow into a bigger ball and rolled faster directly down toward the light in the cloud.

As it disappeared into the foggy whiteout, it was the size of a basketball and moving fast. A moment later I heard a woman say, "Shsss!" Then one light went out followed by the other.

SIXTY-FOUR

"April, this is Owen McKenna," I yelled out through the dark wind. "Get away from Carmen. Move quickly while the cloud is here and the lights are off. Her plan is to kill you as soon as you dig up the gold."

There was a pause.

"Mr. McKenna," Carmen called out of the darkness, her voice high and sweet. "What are you talking about? I would never kill anybody."

"Keep moving April. Don't speak."

"Don't listen to him, April. He's confused."

"I should have known a long time ago, Carmen," I said. "Lori Simon went to Humboldt State in Arcata, right next to Eureka where you're from. Such little twin towns, it makes sense that you could have known her. You said you don't ski, but there are downhill skis sitting outside your apartment door. And here you are up on the mountain, a trek that requires significant ski experience. Your neighbor lady also told me that you were up in Eureka to drive your father to Redding for his medicine."

"The coins belong to us, April," Carmen said. "You found them. Now I'm helping you find them a second time. We're going to split it just like we talked about. You know you can trust me. It's McKenna you can't trust."

"April, I can prove that Paul killed March and Lori and Astor. Then Carmen killed Paul."

"That's ridiculous. He's trying to take the coins for himself."

The clouds opened just for a moment, but without lights, I

couldn't see anything other than the vague white slope leading down and the rock wall to the side. I sensed movement to one side, but then the clouds were back.

"It was a good setup," I yelled, trying to keep Carmen engaged so that April could move farther away. "You put the note in Claude Sisuug's cabin to make it look like he was the killer. Where'd you bury him? In some slide by his cabin?"

"Don't listen to him, April!" Carmen hissed in the dark. "The others died in avalanches!" Carmen shouted. "They were accidents! You can't just kill people with avalanches."

"Carmen, we have remnants of the explosives used to start the slides as well as pieces of the bombs you and Paul set off at my cabin. In the spring we'll have remnants of the detonators."

"You can't honestly believe that." Carmen's voice was shrill. "Push a button on a remote or something and start an avalanche?"

"I just talked to your father a few hours ago, Carmen. He said you'd just called. You told him you were in Redding and would be in Eureka in a few hours. You wouldn't lie to him, Carmen, unless you were trying to misdirect me and the cops."

"April, tell him he's wrong." Carmen sounded sad and frustrated. It was good acting. There wasn't any hint of calculation.

April still hadn't said anything.

"April," I called out through the dark. "Lori didn't die in the avalanche. Paul smothered her with snow at Ada's vineyard and brought her body up to Tahoe in the back of his truck."

"You know that's not true," Carmen said. "She died in the avalanche. It was in the paper."

"The dirt in the vineyard had unusual bugs in it. The coroner found one of those bugs in Lori's lungs."

A light switched on down below, sending a glow up through the fog. A break came in the cloud. A small figure was holding the lantern. She was off to the side of the campsite, away from the compressed snow where they'd been working. She was waist-deep in soft snow, stranded, unable to go farther without skis or snowshoes. She held the lamp up as if trying to look around.

Over at the rock wall stood a stockier figure. Carmen held

her arms out in front of her. There were small dark objects in her hands. She was looking at them.

A bright flash of light lit the clouds above like a camera flashbulb. I couldn't tell where the flash came from. A fraction of a second later came another flash. Two deep muffled booms came from up the slope behind me. The time delay from flash to boom was about a second. Sound travels about one thousand feet per second, which meant the avalanche was beginning a quarter mile or less up the slope. We only had a few moments.

"APRIL, RUN!" I shouted. "BAINS AND ROSTEN MOVE! CARMEN SET OFF A SLIDE!"

I saw April try to move, lifting one boot out of the deep powder, struggling to take a small step forward.

I turned back toward Spot. "Come, boy!"

I skied forward across the slope as fast as I could, lifting my skis and stepping up, breaking trail through the deep powder. I tried to push back with my single pole, but it was like pushing at air. I angled down a little, thinking that I could develop a bit of forward momentum. But the snow was too deep and my skis would not slide forward. I turned so I was pointed more down the slope. Gravity started to help, but I still was barely moving forward.

From up above me came a deep rumble. I turned to a 45-degree angle and high-stepped down through the deep stuff, doing a kind of run, trying not to lose my balance. I got up a little momentum. I tried to push it faster, but the soft snow provided too much resistance.

I worried about Spot, but my thoughts went to the growing roar like rolling thunder and the heavy wind that pushed down the mountain from above. The wind seemed to explode and it lifted me into the air. I had a sudden thought about a town in Texas where the people saw black clouds coming and shouted 'Muerte Cielo'...

SIXTY-FIVE

The snow hit me like it was a solid object. The surging white wave knocked me off my feet and onto my side. I remembered the mantra. Try to swim as it moves, try to stay afloat. If you are buried, try to make a space in front of your face for air before the slide comes to a stop.

But swimming with my skis on, my left arm in a sling, and my right arm holding a ski pole, felt like trying to swim with no limbs at all. The snow flowed up around me, and I quickly sunk. Rushing snow closed in around my head. I tried to take a breath at the last moment, but I was too late and I inhaled a mouthful of snow that choked me.

I coughed violently. But it felt like my mouth was filled with cement. In a mere second my brain was already suffering from oxygen deficit. I had a sudden understanding that I was going to die. In my last moment of consciousness, I had none of those final thoughts we hear about, no flashbacks about my life, no regrets, no tunnel of light. Only severe frustration that I hadn't succeeded at what I came up on the mountain to do. I was mad as hell.

Then a quirk of snow currents spit me sideways in the river of snow, and I popped up and out to the side of the flow. I came to a stop with my upper body projecting out of the snow as the rest of the slide blasted on down the mountain.

I coughed out a mouthful of snow and bent over, right hand on the snow in front of me, gasping and choking, trying to get some air into my lungs. I spit and hacked, and snow still went into my lungs. My ears and eyes were caked with snow. My hat and head lamp were gone. I was okay, but my legs were buried.

I wiped snow from my eyes and turned to look down through an opening in the fog.

Bains was down below me, on the other side of the slide, out of the avalanche path. He held his flashlight out, pointing it toward Carmen, who was climbing the rock wall, flashlight in hand, safely above the avalanche that raged beneath her.

Then Carmen slipped, her right boot scrabbling at the rock. She shifted her other hand, trying for better position. Her left boot shifted, then slipped, and her hands lost their purchase. She slid down the rock, flashlight jerking.

The avalanche hit Carmen the way a racket hits a tennis ball. She was bounced down below the rock wall and buried in a couple of seconds.

In a moment it was over. As the snow in the air began to settle, I saw Bains playing his light back and forth over the slide residue. There was nothing to see. No tent, no toboggan, no tarp, no women.

If we got to them soon enough, we could still save them. I tried to move, but it was futile. I was buried at an angle up to my thighs.

I looked across the slope, scanning for Spot.

"Spot! Are you there?"

He made a frustrated woof. I turned toward the sound. There was movement down below me. Spot was struggling. "Are you okay, boy?" I stared at him, trying to make a pattern in the darkness. He appeared to be on his side, his right front leg free and his left front leg partly trapped. His rear half was buried. He jerked and pulled, turned and bit at the snow.

"Come on, Spot!" I yelled. "You can do it!" My hope was that because he didn't have big feet like people and because his legs were tapered, he'd be able to pull himself out. But cement-like snow would hold a dog nearly as well as a person.

"Spot, come!" I shouted.

He twisted and turned, popped out his left front leg, then his right rear leg. He bucked and pulled and I worried that he would tear the ligaments and tendons of his left rear leg.

From down below came the sweep of Bains's flashlight beam.

I yelled out. "ROSTEN! ARE YOU THERE?"

"I'M HERE!" shouted Rosten.

"The girls are buried," Bains shouted up at me, unaware that I'd seen Carmen fall into the slide. "I saw April go down, too, but I have no clue where to dig. The slide could have carried them a long way. We'd need a full team with avalanche probes."

"If we can get Spot and me out, I can get him to search."

Bains bent down and took off his skis. "I'll help get you out," he shouted and started running up the compressed slide residue.

The clouds came back and I was surrounded by a gray mist.

In a minute he appeared in the fog.

"You okay?" he said when he saw me.

"Yeah. Help me get out of here, then we'll dig Spot out. Maybe he can find them."

Bains threw off his pack and unstrapped his shovel.

He started digging in front of me.

"My feet go back at an angle," I said. "Move behind me. Yeah. A little farther. Good. I'd guess my feet are about three feet below you."

I saw a light in the cloud. Rosten came sidestepping up the compacted slide at a fast pace. He had his headlight on. He jerked off his pack, grabbed his shovel and joined Bains. They worked like machines.

"Try not to chop off any of my body parts," I said, dead serious.

They got down to my skis, unhooked the bindings and, leaving the skis buried, had me free in a few minutes.

I grabbed my own shovel and scrambled down to Spot who was still trying to free his left rear leg. I stepped the shovel in carefully. It would be easy to cut a dog's leg. I levered snow out of the area, moving gently but as fast as possible.

The snow must have loosened, for Spot jerked his leg out in a minute. He walked away, limping on his left rear leg.

"Come here, boy," I said. He came to me and I ran my hands over his leg, feeling for broken bones or bad swelling. Everything felt fine and he didn't cry out, so I hoped that he was just sore, or that he had pinpricks from a pinched nerve. He moved around, walking better with each step.

"Okay, Spot. Come with me."

I ran down the hard-packed surface of the avalanche path. The wind was coming down the mountain and I wanted to get Spot below where April and Carmen had been so that he would be downwind of any scent.

"You think he can smell them?" Bains shouted, as he and Rosten ran next to me.

"Maybe. Maybe not. The wind is so strong that any scent coming out of the snow is likely to be immediately dispersed."

We got to an area well below and downwind of where I'd last seen April and Carmen.

Bains shined his flashlight on the mountainside. "April was to this side, so I'd guess that she is somewhere along a line below that point." Bains turned and shined his light toward the far side of the slide. "And Carmen is likely under that area."

From the length of the slide residue it looked like the snow could have carried the women a long distance. I ran farther down the mountain, stopped and turned to Spot. I grabbed him on his chest and back. "Find the victim, Spot!"

He looked at me, almost puzzled, as if he didn't understand why this was something we were doing so frequently.

I held him again and gave him a strong vibration. "Find the victim, Spot!"

I gave him a little smack, and he loped up the slide, nose in the air. He went up at an angle to the left and turned around and came partway back down. He stopped and sniffed at the snow and walked over to the right a few feet. He seemed to look off to the side, and then started walking back up the slide.

Bains and Rosten kept their lights on him as Spot faded into the storm, but I could sense where he was.

When Spot had gone up farther than the women had originally been, I knew there was no chance they could be up there. He was upwind of them, so he couldn't smell them, either.

"Spot, come. Come on back down." I called him back.

He trotted down, his limp mostly gone.

I went through the staging again, the hold, the vibration, the command.

He did the same as before, trotting back and forth. It wasn't the organized search of Honey G. It was haphazard and random. Then he alerted.

He was under the area where Bains had predicted that Carmen would be buried. Spot sniffed at the air, turned and ran a short distance, then sniffed at the snow. He moved around in a lopsided circle. Then he stopped, pawed at the snow, stuck his nose on the snow and began digging.

"That's got to be Carmen," Bains yelled.

Bains yelled to Rosten. "Come help dig. Owen can get Spot to search again for April."

We ran toward Spot. I praised him, petted him, told him he was the best, then pulled him away as Rosten began digging furiously.

I brought Spot a good distance down the slope, far enough to be downwind of any percolating scent, and again gave him the command to find the victim.

Spot ran directly back up the slope to where Rosten was digging.

I followed, frustrated, not knowing what to do. Any approach I could think of, positive or negative, would seem to give him the wrong message. If I told him he was good, he would keep going back to Carmen. If I told him he was doing it wrong, he might think he wasn't supposed to find a person, but maybe something else.

I took his collar. "Good boy, Spot. But there's another victim. Over here." I turned him to face down the mountain, toward the other side of the slide. I made a hand motion, pointing toward where I thought April might be buried. "Find the victim, Spot. Find!"

He trotted a few steps down the slope, then stopped and looked back at me, his confusion clear in the furrows of his brow.

"Go on, boy." I gestured downslope. "There's another victim. Find the victim."

It felt hopeless. I was trying to communicate as if he were human. I was pointing him away from Carmen, but he probably wasn't downwind of April, so he couldn't pick up her scent. But if I took him downwind again and sent him on a search back up the slope, he'd focus on Carmen's scent.

Spot went another few yards, sniffed at the air and stopped, his misunderstanding obvious.

I trotted down the slide. Spot came with me. "Find the victim, Spot," I said, over and over, trying to get him to consider the area where I was taking him.

We got well down the slope and came to the bottom of the slide. Spot still showed no sign of any other scent. We were now downwind. I turned him around and pointed him back up the slope. I gave him the command again.

He trotted up the slope, stopped, and gazed toward where Rosten and Bains were digging.

"Not there, Spot. Another victim," I said, thinking my attempt at communication was futile. "Find," I shouted, trying, but failing, to put enthusiasm into my voice.

I tried not to think about the minutes ticking away. But I couldn't help realizing that if fifteen minutes was the average survival rate, then we were down to maybe five minutes before all hope of finding anyone alive was gone.

I wanted to run up and grab Spot and demand that he be more efficient! Why couldn't he do like Honey G and follow a grid? Why couldn't he go left across the slide, move up just a little and go back to the right?! Honey G methodically searched the whole damn mountain, and my dog was ambling around as if he were at a picnic. It looked like he might still be sniffing the air, but he was so casual. It was infuriating to realize that if only I'd done a better job of preparing him, teaching him, he would do a better job of searching.

I wondered if I should call him back down and start him over. I wondered if April and Carmen were already dead, their warm breaths having glazed the snow around their mouths, cutting off the oxygen and suffocating them.

I turned a full circle in the snow, ready to explode at my inability to do anything. I dropped to my knees in the snow, wondering if I was missing something, wondering if I should just start digging where I guessed April had been carried by the slide. Anything was better than nothing. But it would be pointless. When you're up on the mountain with a major storm coming, any activity you do just for the sake of making you feel like you're doing something is stupid. It wears you out, makes you sweat, and ultimately puts you at greater risk for hypothermia when the sweat starts evaporating. The only thing worse than losing people to an avalanche, is to lose more people because of stupidity after the avalanche.

The simple reality was that our only chance was my dog, and I hadn't given him enough training.

I looked up again, ready to call him back, when he alerted.

SIXTY-SIX

Spot stuck his nose in the air and spun around in a circle. He stopped, then ran straight up the mountain, into the wind. He somehow understood that the scent came out of the wind, not out of the snow at his feet.

I started running up the slope, carrying my shovel in my good hand.

Spot jerked to a stop, sniffed at the snow, moved several paces back down the mountain. His movements were frantic, almost as if he were panicked with fear.

He swiped at the snow with his paw, then stuck his nose in the depression. He moved to another place, dug and sniffed.

He made a barking cry and began digging. His foot-strokes were furious, his hind legs spread for stability, his front legs throwing the snow out between his rear legs.

I heard Bains shout, and saw Rosten leave where they were digging for Carmen and run toward Spot. Rosten slipped and fell. He slid down the compacted snow. His shovel flew out of his hands, and it rocketed down like a sled.

I angled sideways, tried to grab it and missed. It flew on by. I turned to watch it in the faint hope that it might hit a rock or snowy obstruction and stop. But there was nothing. I was turning back when I saw a movement below.

Out of the shadows came Bill, leaping sideways like the football player he was thirty years ago. He plucked the shovel out of the air, hit the ground and slid to a stop.

I started back up the mountain, aware that even though Bill

had caught the shovel, he wouldn't be able to hobble up the mountain fast enough to help us in time.

I got to Spot. I held the end of the shovel with my left hand, which was still in the sling. With my wounded arm screaming, I shoveled like a backhoe, churning through the snow, hurling it off to the side.

Spot was already down two feet, his long front legs perfectly suited to digging deep holes.

When Rosten got to me, I handed him the shovel. When he'd made good progress in one direction, he shifted around to widen the hole in the other direction. I kneeled down and dug with my right hand. More movement caught my attention. I looked downslope.

Bill had shucked out of his snowshoes and tossed aside his crutch poles. He was down on the snow, churning up toward us at an astonishing pace. He wasn't belly-crawling, and he wasn't up on his hands and knees. It was a kind of crab run, employing hands and feet and elbows and knees. Like a sand crab sprinting across a beach, Bill was a snow crab on overdrive. He moved up the slide as fast as I'd run up it, and he got to us in less than a minute.

"I heard you talking," Bill shouted between gasping breaths. "Carmen is the killer?"

"Yeah," I said, as I scooped snow.

"Which one is Carmen?" he shouted.

I pointed. "Over there, where Bains is digging," I said. I gestured at the hole next to us where Rosten was digging. "I think April is under here."

Bill looked toward Bains who was digging down toward Carmen. In flashes of Rosten's headlight, Bill's leathery forehead was as wrinkled as rhinoceros skin. His eyes were pinched together, anxiety concentrated at the bridge of his nose.

Several times over the years, I'd seen people make tough decisions, triage imbued with moral ambiguity. But it wasn't like that with Bill. He made a little nod to himself as if he'd suddenly found a clear resolve.

Bill splayed his legs out at an angle and jammed his boots into the snow, the metal braces digging in like crampons. He began shoveling just below Spot.

Although Rosten was younger and fitter and stronger than Bill, Bill moved more snow in the next two minutes than Rosten and I had in total.

Spot cried out, and I knew he'd gotten to April.

"Good Boy!" I said as I moved him aside so I could see. Spot had gone directly to the top of her head. I took off my right glove and pulled off her knit cap so that I could get my fingers down next to her temples. Bill handed me a flashlight, and I shined it into the hole. I scooped snow out from around the sides of her head, digging my fingernails into the cement-like snow. I found her face and worked to clear the snow away so that she would have air if she was still breathing. My fingers caught on something near her mouth. It was the woven Washoe Star.

"Her body goes this way," I said, pointing. "Bill, if you dig over to the side and down. I think you'll be over her hips."

Rosten was shifting, trying to shovel at the best angle.

"You're sure this is April?" Bill asked, his lungs huffing like bellows.

I had cleared more snow from around her face. "Yes. And she's still breathing."

EPILOGUE

We were at Heavenly, up above the top station of the gondola. It was the beginning of May, a day for the mountain gods, windless and 50 degrees, the cloudless sky like sapphires dissolved in the heavens, and the lake, 3000 feet below, glowing a deep, rich blue.

Street and Bains and Rosten were trying to talk over the blast of the announcer on the loudspeaker. Diamond and Spot were smart enough not to compete with the surrounding noise. Diamond lay back on the blanket, sipping his Tecate, watching the racers. Spot lay next to him, his head on Diamond's lap, his rhinestone ear stud glinting in the high altitude sun.

Glennie was pummeling me with questions.

"You promised you'd give me an exclusive."

"Ask away."

"Is it true what Rosten told me, that Bains kept digging for Carmen while you and Rosten and Bill dug for April?"

"Yeah."

"So Carmen didn't die for neglect? Bains just didn't get to her in time?"

"Yeah."

"Then you all went back up the mountain two weeks ago to camp and dig in the snow?" Glennie asked.

"Not Bill. He had to go to Houston and take care of some business. I went up with April and Street and George Clooney meets Pierce Brosnan."

Glennie turned and slugged Bains on the shoulder. "But he

won't even tell me where you were digging."

"No. We have an agreement."

"And the big snowfall the day after you came back covered your tracks," she said. "Your secret is safe. But you found the coins under all the rubble from the avalanche? That's incredible."

"Just four of them. We wouldn't have even gotten those, but with this incredible spell of warm weather, the snowpack was reduced. Even so, we dug for hours, three days in a row. Bill also got us a very techy long-range metal detector. The four coins we found were scattered. There might be more, but they're probably buried for good. The avalanche kicked loose a lot of rock."

"And the sixty-four thousand dollar question?" Glennie said.

"Actually, that's pretty close. The coin broker said that adding four eighteen-seventy CC Double Eagles to the tiny stock that's out there reduces the value of all of them. They weren't in excellent condition, but their existence still creates a worry that more will be found, which reduces demand further. If there'd been just one, it would have been worth over a hundred grand. But we were very glad that the broker found a buyer willing to pay seventy-five thousand each for the four. Three hundred, total. And the price will go down further if we find more of them."

"Bains said that you're giving it away."

"We left that decision to April. She's the only person left alive who was in that class. She decided to donate it, half to a sports charity for physically-challenged athletes, and half to a nonprofit that builds houses in the Dominican Republic."

Glennie smiled and nodded. "And if you find more coins when the snow melts this summer?"

"Same agreement."

"What about the mountain man avalanche instructor?"

"Claude Sisuug? My guess is that Paul Riceman or Carmen killed him. With both of them dead, we'll never know. Maybe Sisuug's body is up on a mountain someplace, killed in an avalanche. Or maybe he walks out of the wilderness a year from now."

"How is it that Carmen got Paul in the avalanche off his own roof?"

"We'll never know that for sure, either. Maybe she tossed a coin under the eave to entice him to walk under the roof. Then she pulled on the rope she'd strung from the upper deck and broke the cornice off."

"Either way," Glennie said, "a multiple murderer dies, not too many complain. And with Carmen dead, as long as none of you tells, the location will be secret forever."

"Right."

"The people in the avalanche class also had an agreement not to tell the location," Glennie said.

"So?"

"At least two of them told other people. Isn't that a possibility with this new group?"

"No."

"You sound so sure."

"A detective has to be a good judge of character."

Glennie pushed my shoulder, and we focused again on the event that was going on around us.

The loudspeakers barked from up in the trees and over by the barbecue tent.

"Okay folks, that was Olaf Olson, from Trondheim, Norway, kicking butt with twenty-four seconds at the finish gate! That's good enough to move Olaf into second place in the Tahoe Challenge!"

For the fourth or fifth time, a vigorous cheer went up from three women sitting on a blanket near us.

"Go Olaf,
Go Olaf,
Go, go Olaf!"

The women were all blonde, blue-eyed, and in their twenties. Their accent was clear, even with their limited cheer vocabulary.

"Must be the Norwegian contingent," Street said.

"Are they eating lutefisk?" Diamond asked.

"No, they're eating Big Macs," I said.

"But if they are from Trondheim," Diamond said, "I can see some young men around here who are going to sign up to take

Norwegian classes and then book travel to Norway."

The man they'd been cheering came around the curve at the bottom of the run. He used his powerful arms to pull at the snow and keep his ski sled coasting toward the crowd that was spread out across the snow, sitting on blankets and fold-up chairs, eating hotdogs and drinking beer from big plastic cups. Olaf worked it so that he slowed to a stop when he got to the girls on the blanket. He tipped the ski sled over on its side, timing the move so that he literally fell out of the sled and into their laps. They shrieked with excitement. As the women hugged him, I couldn't help thinking that a picture of his huge grin would change the heart and mind of any handicapped person who had similarly withered legs and thought that they were an insurmountable obstacle to a joyful life.

The announcer continued, "Hey, all you beach babes, next up in the starting gate, hailing from all the way over in the Tahoe Keys, is a new contestant on the Tahoe Challenge circuit, William Esteban!"

The announcer kept talking over the giant speakers, but he was drowned out by a new cheer that rose up from a group of dozens of people, mostly young, including Packer and Will and Ada, the girl who decided not to go to France with her parents. They were all led by April who was standing in front of them, her back to the mountain. She had her arms up, a bare hotdog for a baton, and she directed with the energy of Leonard Bernstein.

"Hey, Bill!
Show us, Bill!
How fast do you go, Bill?
Who's the best,
On his sled?
It's obviously Bill!"

The announcer's voice was once again audible as the cheer paused. "...on the upper course, and he's really pushing that custom blue sled into the turns. Annnnnd Esteban is unscathed through the double gates seven and eight! Now he's carrying that speed into the royal flush. This is the trickiest part of the course, folks! He's got to graze those gates... Watch himmmmmm... and he made it! Esteban is running like a true veteran! He's coming up to the big turns beginning at gate fifteen. He's pushing it hard, folks, with more speed on board than any other contestant, and he'sssssss, he's down!"

We watched as Bill's sled went down on its side, spinning in circles, taking out several gates. He tried to pop it back up on the ski like a kayaker righting his vessel. The sled wavered and went down on the other side. Bill dragged his outrigger crutches to slow down. When he finally came to a stop, he levered his crutches into the snow and got the sled back up on its ski. He worked his outriggers on each side of the sled, maintaining a precarious balance until he picked up a little momentum.

Bill angled back across the course, going very slowly, then coasted, wobbling, directly toward us. He made an awkward stop, pulled himself out of the sled and crab-walked over to us. He sat on the snow, his nerves making his metal knee braces clatter like castanets. April waved at him and he made a little self-conscious nod.

I watched her as she shifted, and it was obvious that she was about to stand up, about to come over and begin anew with Bill. But she stopped, hesitant, and I thought about the frozen mass of snow we dug through to pull her out, alive, but just barely. Even though she was unconscious, Bill was slow to reach out and touch her. But he eventually did, and she would eventually connect with him as well. Their relations would thaw and some day generate warmth, but it would be like watching mountain snow melt in the summer. It would happen, but it would take a long time.

Bill pulled off his Washoe Star and handed it to me. His hands shook. "Maybe I don't need this anymore. I want you to have it."

I took the Washoe Star and put it around my neck. I handed him an iced tea, and he thrust it, shaking, to the sky. April beamed more brightly than all three Norwegian girls put together, and Bill's sudden grin in that rusted-fender face was like the sun itself.

About the Author

Todd Borg lives with his wife in Lake Tahoe. To contact Todd or learn more about the Owen McKenna books, please visit toddborg.com